The Garden Club Murders

JONATHAN WHITELAW

Harper North

HarperNorth
Windmill Green
24 Mount Street
Manchester M2 3NX

A division of
HarperCollins*Publishers*
1 London Bridge Street
London SE1 9GF

www.harpercollins.co.uk

HarperCollins*Publishers*
Macken House, 39/40 Mayor Street Upper
Dublin 1, D01 C9W8, Ireland

First published by HarperNorth in 2025

1 3 5 7 9 10 8 6 4 2

Copyright © Jonathan Whitelaw 2025

Jonathan Whitelaw asserts the moral right to
be identified as the author of this work.

A catalogue record for this book
is available from the British Library.

PB ISBN: 978-0-00-862645-7
TPB ISBN: 978-0-00-862646-4

Printed and bound in the UK using 100% renewable electricity
at CPI Group (UK) Ltd, Croydon

This novel is entirely a work of fiction. The names, characters and
incidents portrayed in it are the work of the author's imagination.
Any resemblance to actual persons, living or dead, events or
localities is entirely coincidental.

All rights reserved. No part of this publication may be
reproduced, stored in a retrieval system, or transmitted,
in any form or by any means, electronic, mechanical,
photocopying, recording or otherwise, without the prior
permission of the publishers.

This book contains FSC™ certified paper and other controlled
sources to ensure responsible forest management.

For more information visit: www.harpercollins.co.uk/green

For Cumbria and the Lake District, 'the loveliest spot that man hath ever found'

Chapter 1

FOENICULUM VULGARE

Jason sat bolt upright. Going from sleeping soundly to wide awake in a matter of microseconds was bad. It always had been. Christmas mornings as a child had been the worst. When he'd finally been able to get some shut-eye, usually several hours after being sent to bed on Christmas Eve, he'd wake up in something more akin to panic rather than excitement. The sudden change in state brought on by the realisation that it was *finally* Christmas morning always got the adrenaline flowing. And as Amita, his mother-in-law, liked to remind him, he was still a big kid at heart, despite supposedly being older and wiser.

Tonight, however, it was different. No sleigh bells, no 'Ho-ho-hos' to wake him up. This time it was something else, something sinister that had roused him. He knew from the cold chill that pricked his skin.

Jason looked around the bedroom. It was dark, yes, but unsettlingly so. The new blackout curtains he had bought were working, a little too well in fact. The blazing, sulphurous glow of the streetlight outside had ruined his sleep for decades. He had finally taken action last month. Now, in an unexpected turn, he had given himself a new problem, namely the pitch-black obstacle course of the bedroom if he ever wanted to get up during the night.

His shins were black and blue from bumping into things. And he'd sent a lamp and a glass of water flying in the past week alone. The simple solution would be to take down the curtains, but that would be a sign of defeat. They were staying forever, Jason was adamant about that. Even if he ended up maimed and broken by the bedroom suite.

He let his eyes adjust to the darkness. Slowly, the shapes and layout came back to him. He shook off the grogginess of sleep and listened carefully. There was nothing. Only silence.

It was after midnight. The whole house was still now, peaceful even. Almost as if it was holding its breath. The children were likely sound asleep down the hall – no small person stood in the doorway asking for a drink or proclaiming a headache. And Radha was beside him, back turned to him, deep in slumber.

So, what had woken him? He'd been dead to the world, but through his sleep he knew he had heard possibly a thump, maybe even a crash? Had it come from outside? Were the neighbours making a late-night dash to the hospital for some awful emergency? Or was this them just getting home?

Sunday morning before sunrise really wasn't the Bidmeads' style. In the fourteen years that Jason had known them, he'd never seen his neighbour, Patrick, without a shirt and tie on. Even when he cut the grass. Which he did with military precision once the season started. It put their own straggling front lawn to shame.

No, this was something altogether different. It was something suspicious. Jason flung the duvet back. He half-hoped the movement might stir his wife. Two heads were better than one, after all. Radha didn't budge. Jason cursed a little. He envied his wife's ability to sleep soundly through almost any noise from outdoors. And yet she was up like a coiled spring as soon as one of the kids coughed, sneezed or even hiccupped in the night.

Jason slipped out of bed. Carefully making his way to the door, he crept out into the hallway. It was just as dark out there. All the bedroom doors were closed. He lingered for a moment, standing in the silence like an unearthed Roman statue. He was beginning to think his imagination was playing tricks on him, that there had been no sound at all. Then he heard it again. A bump, dull and quick, but definitely there.

'Bloody hell,' he muttered, feeling a creeping dread come over him.

Another bump just heightened the sensation. It was coming from downstairs, directly below him, in the kitchen. Jason panicked, as he tended to do. He couldn't remember if he'd locked the back door before going to bed. Not that it mattered, he supposed. Any self-respecting burglar would be able to bust the rusty Yale lock and dodgy hinges.

A good gust of wind from the garden would be able to open that thing, he admitted.

He looked about the hall for some kind of weapon. Of all the nights, the intruder had picked the one when the house was remarkably tidy. There were no Lego bricks to stand on, no Barbie Dream House to get entangled in and twist an ankle. There weren't even any teddy bears to use as an improvised, very cuddly mace. It was times like these that he wished he golfed. A nine iron would be handy right now. The regret was fleeting. Jason loathed golf.

The inevitable was growing *more* inevitable. Jason was going to have to go downstairs. Maybe he would get lucky. Maybe the intruder would be frightened off by the sound of his footsteps trudging down the stairs. He did his best to stomp as hard as he could with every step. Intimidation had never been Jason Brazel's strong point. And both of the two fights he'd ever been involved in he had lost fairly substantially. Hardly a glowing record.

He reached the bottom of the stairs. The noise was still coming from the kitchen. As he passed the front door, Jason spied an umbrella leaning against the wall. Grabbing it, he eased his way up to the kitchen door. A chink of light was shining out across the carpet from the bottom. A shadow was passing back and forth. Not the wind, then.

He reached the door and raised the umbrella up high, ready to strike. With a last breath and silent prayer, he barged his way into the kitchen. 'Get out of here!' he screamed, eyes firmly closed.

There was a gasp before something dropped and hit the floor with a smash. Jason waited another microsecond. Once he realised that he hadn't been bottled or punched in the face, Jason knew something was off. This wasn't how home invasions were supposed to go. He would know, he'd seen enough episodes of *Crimewatch* over the years. 'Don't have nightmares,' his backside.

Slowly, he opened one eye. What was waiting for him was enough to open the other? 'Amita?' he asked, more in disbelief than anything else.

His mother-in-law was standing on the other side of the kitchen table. A small pile of broken crockery littered the floor around her feet. Her eyes were as wide as saucers. He lowered his umbrella/club.

'Jason,' she said disapprovingly. 'Do you know what you've just made me do?'

He didn't want to answer that one. Thankfully she didn't let him.

'I've just dropped and smashed my teapot,' she said. 'I just dropped and smashed the Le Creuset I bought in 1976. It's survived three children, two grandchildren, dozens of Prime Ministers, countless flittings, my daughter's marriage to you and the Falklands War. But now look at it!'

She spread her arms, gesturing to the destruction. Jason felt more than a pang of guilt. He wasn't one for wanton vandalism, but he thought he had been about to confront a burglar. He had been protecting his family.

'You're lucky I didn't bash you over the head with this!' he said.

'Bash me over the head?' Amita wrinkled her nose. 'With what?'

'With this!'

He shook the umbrella about. Only now, in the light of the kitchen, did he realise why Amita wasn't impressed. The small, pink, Hello Kitty umbrella wasn't the most intimidating of makeshift sabres. In fact, it was about the *least* intimidating weapon in the history of conflict.

'Oh,' he said, feeling foolish. 'Probably for the best I didn't lamp you. It would more than likely have broken this bloody thing.'

'And then Clara would kill you for breaking her umbrella. Then Radha would kill you. Then I would kill you. Then Clara would kill you again. She loves that thing, and you would have snapped it in two by whacking it across the back of her gran's skull!'

Jason was defeated. He carefully, delicately, placed the umbrella on the kitchen table and backed away. With everything safe, he turned his attention to Amita. As the adrenaline began to wear off, he noticed something about her. Something unusual.

She was swaying. Not too much, just enough, from side to side. Given how panicked he'd been as he raced into the kitchen, it had been easy to miss. Now that he was thinking straight, he could see that his venerable mother-in-law was not her usual poised self.

'Amita,' he said, unable to hide the wry smile creeping across his face. 'Are you . . . drunk?'

'Certainly not,' she replied curtly. 'I was in Manchester, for the night. You know this, Jason.'

'Oh yes, of course,' he said. 'Only, it's just, well, we're well past midnight, you're only just getting home and . . .'

He sniffed the air between them. Amita remained tight-lipped.

'Is that . . . white wine I can smell coming off you?'

Amita's face dropped immediately.

'I beg your pardon,' she said. 'I'm not some teenager that's been caught pilfering booze from their parents' drinks cabinet.'

'Naturally,' he said, folding his arms. 'You're just reeking like a winery, that's all.'

Amita blinked, one eye followed by the other. She sniffed a little of herself and scowled. 'I've got no idea what you're talking about,' she said adamantly.

'Am I to assume you and the rest of the bingo club had a good time in Manchester?' he asked. 'What was it you were at again? An all-night rave in the Haçienda?'

'A rave?' Amita's voice reached a new pitch. 'I beg your pardon, Jason.'

'That's twice you've begged for my pardon,' he laughed. 'Must be a new record. It's almost one in the morning, Amita. Don't these mega bingo games finish up around nine?'

'They do,' she said, pawing for the kitchen worktop to steady herself. 'And it did. But one or two of the club won some money and they wanted to celebrate in town.'

'Georgie Littlejohn?'

'No, thank goodness,' she said. 'Can you imagine if she won big? We'd never hear the end of it. She's bad enough if she scoops the rollover here.'

'Who won?' asked Jason, rubbing his eyes.

'Margaret Cullen,' she said.

'How much?'

'Five thousand pounds.'

'Five grand!' Jason yelped. 'Five grand? At bingo? You've got to be kidding me.'

'It's big money in these places.'

'But . . . but five grand, Amita. That's a small fortune for what is effectively total luck and chance.'

'We've been through this before, Jason, it takes skill and acumen to win at the numbers. You need eyes like a hawk, the hearing of a bat, the reaction times of a cheetah . . .'

'But . . . it's bingo, not feeding time on the Serengeti.'

'Well, Jason,' she said. 'The big beasts of the bingo world would disagree. Anyway, Margaret wanted to celebrate, and we couldn't very well say no, could we? We went into the city centre.'

'Manchester, on a Saturday night, marched on by the Penrith Bingo Club,' he whistled. 'I wish I'd been there to see that.'

'See what?'

'You lot, with your hair nets and your Zimmer frames. Out on the town with all the young folk. You must have been like a geriatric version of that show, what's it called again?'

'*Love Island*?'

'That's the one,' he snapped his fingers.

'That's offensive,' said Amita. 'None of us had a mobility walker and we certainly wouldn't ruin a good shampoo and set with a hairnet. Plus, we were immaculately behaved, not falling around in the street, drunk as mules.'

'Judy Moskowitz's steel hip wouldn't let you, eh?' he smirked.

'We had a couple of celebratory drinks, yes,' she said. 'And then we came home. Very demure and *very* dignified.'

'I see,' he suppressed a snigger. 'So why are you still up at this hour? Tinnitus from the nightclub speakers?'

Amita Khatri wasn't easily embarrassed. She was too used to being on the lookout for trouble to allow circumstances to sneak up on her and catch her unawares. She wasn't called the Sheriff of Penrith for nothing. That's why Jason felt another little twang of guilt when he saw her face drop.

'Amita,' he said. 'Everything alright?'

'Yes,' she said. 'Only, it would seem that in all of the hubbub, noise, commotion and something called 'shots', I seem to have lost my phone.'

She let her hands flop down to her sides. Jason felt a stab of fellow-feeling. Suddenly he was back to his days as a much younger man, partying until four in the morning and then in work on an early shift at the paper covering giant marrows and ugly dog contests before nine. Phone, keys, wallet, cards, money, everything had been misplaced at some point over the years. And knowing how closely Amita guarded her belongings, he now knew exactly how embarrassed she was.

'Oh Amita,' he said. 'Welcome, at last, to the world of the 24-hour party people.'

'The what?'

He walked over and put his arm around her shoulders. He squeezed her tightly into him. 'You're a woman of the world now. This is the price you pay for the high-life,' he said. 'Nights out, partying, big-money jackpots. Who needs Vegas?'

'Stop it, Jason,' she said. 'It's mortifying. Imagine me, a woman of my age, with the reputation I enjoy around town, losing her phone on a tipsy night out. What will people say?'

'It happens to the best of us,' he said. 'But it's not the end of the world. A phone can be replaced. My already depleted energy, however, cannot. So, I'm going to bed before I lose any more of my beauty sleep.'

He squeezed her again then sauntered over to the door. As he was leaving, something pinged in the back of his mind. He poked his head back into the kitchen and looked over at her.

'Shots?' he asked. 'Did you say shots?'

Amita didn't answer him. She just shrugged.

'24-hour party people,' she said.

Chapter 2

SOLANUM TUBEROSUM

Amita kept her head down. She wasn't quite sure why. It wasn't like she was a wanted criminal or anything. There were no government secrets stashed in the pockets of her shell suit. And nobody had tapped her phone. That was the problem, of course. She didn't even have a phone to tap. The pounding headache she'd had since she woke up might have been contributing, too. A hangover, at her age. She'd never live it down if the news was ever made public. A very painful breakfast, wincing at the whoops and yells of her grandchildren, had been endured before she could make her way out of the house. The fresh air was helping, but only a little. A lost phone and a hangover. She was mortified.

The thought made her bury her chin a little deeper into her chest. She could swear that the public could tell. Everyone was a mind reader these days.

'You're being ridiculous. You know that, don't you,' she mumbled to herself.

The young couple sitting dangerously close to each other at the bus stop looked up at her as she walked by. Amita gave a little forced grin and continued.

'Talking to yourself now, that's a new low,' she said.

The couple didn't hear her. Amita pressed on up the street. Every moment she spent without a phone felt like an age, an eon. Nobody was more surprised by this fact than her. She had dismissed them as gadgets and novelties when her family had first suggested she get a mobile, scoffed at how addicted everyone appeared to their little techno-bricks. But it had crept up on her. As a staunch advocate for an easy life, Amita Khatri, it seemed, had unwittingly become totally dependent on being connected to the digital age. Normally, she'd check the weather when she woke up, then go through her recent WhatsApp messages with coffee, the news headlines with breakfast, then she'd sit and attend to her e-correspondence before she left the house every morning. From the latest goings on at the bingo club to the planning of the W.I.'s spring coffee morning, she was missing out on everything. By this time of the day, she'd have had a slew of alerts – an appeal to find a missing wheelie bin, reports of someone's begonias being blown over by the wind, or wild rumours that Sean Bean had been seen in the Co-op.

How could she have been so clumsy, so reckless, to lose her phone. What had she been thinking? The truth was, she couldn't remember. The club's rip-roaring trip to Manchester was nothing more than a blur. In the hours since she'd come back, there had been flashes of memories here and there. A lot of colourful lights, loud music and happy faces. Amita didn't know exactly where they'd been, and she didn't want to know. She couldn't face the thought of admitting what had happened to her friends, or calling round the hostelries of Manchester to ask if her phone had been handed in. After all, it had probably been half-inched immediately. Best to leave it all to history. And the first step towards moving on was getting a new phone.

Penrith was busy for a Monday afternoon. The spring sunshine was giving everything a renewed sense of vigour after what had been a long and dismal winter. The streets were dry for a change. There was a freshness to the air, something Amita usually appreciated. Not today, though. She was on a mission.

She made her way through the town centre. Even the Musgrave Monument, that stalwart beacon for most of her adult life, seemed judgemental today. Its huge clock faces looked down on her with scorn. She couldn't blame it. A woman of her age losing her phone in a drunken escapade. What was the world coming to?

Ducking down into the back streets, she made sure to avoid even a glimpse of the church hall where bingo would be played as usual on Wednesday. That was all still a little too fresh. Amita picked up the pace as the shops and flats retreated, replaced by a row of modest terraced houses. She was close now, almost there. If she could just last another ten minutes, this ordeal would be over.

The allotments of the appropriately titled Folly Lane stretched out in front of her. The keen green-fingered community was out in force today. Just her luck. She didn't need this many prying eyes spotting her here.

'Blast,' she quietly cursed to herself. 'No going back now, I suppose.'

Taking a deep breath, Amita stepped down from the street and followed the rough path through the plots. While the delights of home-grown beets, radishes and courgettes would normally spark at least some semblance of interest, today was a different matter. This was business. And the sooner it was over, the better.

'Morning,' came a voice from ahead, knocking her off her train of thought.

'Oh yes, is it?'

She silently cursed herself this time. What was wrong with her? Had she forgotten how to behave like a normal human being. A man in an old wax jacket, dirty jeans and wellies was looking perplexed at her.

'Last I checked,' he laughed. 'Good weather we're having, eh?'

'Weather? Ah yes, the weather. Yes, lovely day. Nice and brisk.' That sounded better, she thought.

'You new around here? Fancy joining our club?' He tipped back his baseball cap and leaned on the handle of his shovel. 'Haven't seen you before.'

'I've lived here most of my life,' said Amita.

'In the allotment?'

'What? No, don't be ridiculous. Penrith.'

'It was a joke,' he said.

Amita bit her tongue. This was a disaster. She had to get moving. Polite chit-chat was normally her forte. She prided herself on being able to speak to anyone and everyone. But she had a job to do. Then, as if the wind had decided to blow in her favour, she spotted who she was after a little further into the allotments.

'Excuse me,' she said. 'I hate to be rude, but I think I've found what I'm looking for.'

Amita dashed a little to get away from the kindly gardener. She was already a hundred yards from him when he nodded at her and returned to shovelling the earth at his feet.

Amita skipped over the grass, trying desperately not to trample on anything living. The absolute last thing she needed was to offend the other allotmenteers. A vegetable uprising was *not* on her agenda for today.

Her target was getting closer. She wanted to call out to them, to get their attention, but she didn't dare. This was all supposed to be covert, secret service stuff. Shouting and bawling across wide open spaces was absolutely *not* that.

Almost there. A few more steps and she'd catch them before they disappeared into one of the sheds. If she could just get there quicker. A rather pesky row of tall leeks stood in her way. Sidling around would take too much time. There was nothing for it. She'd have to jump.

And jump she did. Amita Khatri had been something of an amateur athlete in her day – Chaucer Comprehensive 200m Hurdles Champion, 1970, in fact. While she'd maintained her relative fitness, it didn't take long for her to realise this had been a bad idea. As she less than gracefully sailed over the row of burgeoning leeks, Amita braced for impact. When it arrived, she vowed never to do something as stupid like this ever again.

'Bloody hell, Mrs K!' Malcolm Brunger yelped.

Amita skidded to a halt beside him. She just about kept her balance, amazed she was still in one piece.

'I thought Nijinsky had landed in Penrith,' he said.

'That's very kind of you, Mr Brunger,' said Amita, catching her breath. 'But I'm hardly balletic.'

'I meant the horse!'

Amita steadied herself, recovering from the impact of her less than soft landing. Brunger put down the large cardboard box he was holding and took her arm.

'Do you want to have a sit down, Mrs K?' he said.

'Yes, please,' she said. 'It was you I came to see actually.'

'C'mon then, step into my office.'

Brunger led Amita to the door of a large shed, the largest of the sheds in the whole allotment. He opened it up to reveal a veritable treasure trove within. Even in her distressed state, Amita couldn't help but gawk. Instead of the tools and sacks of compost you'd expect, the shelves were brimming with stranger contents.

'Oh my,' she said.

From ceiling to floor the shed was stuffed with Malcolm Brunger's eclectic stock. Here was a man who prided himself on being able to get you anything you wanted – as long as you didn't ask where it came from. There were boxes with writing from every corner of the globe scrawled across them, some of which Amita was sure said 'reject' or 'not for export'. From electric razors, televisions and shower gel to tins of baked beans, ski trousers and bottles of whisky, by way of children's toys and even a bicycle, there was quite literally something for everyone inside.

Brunger helped Amita sit down on a small wooden chair by a calor gas stove. As she sat and composed herself, she thought that this chair was probably for sale too, if she asked. Malcolm Brunger would sell you the steam from his tea if you looked at it twice. Brunger fetched the box he'd left outside, taking a quick shufty about to make sure nobody was watching, then clapped his hands.

'Nice cuppa, Mrs K?' he asked. 'I've got Earl Grey, Darjeeling or something a little more organic, if you fancy it.'

'Breakfast tea would be smashing. Thank you, Mr Brunger,' she said.

'Coming right up.'

He manoeuvred his way around her with expert ease. Brunger was something of a legendary figure to the Penrith Bingo Club. In a fluctuating economy, he was the go-to man for a bargain. And while Father Ford didn't quite like him operating on church grounds, Amita and the others were just glad to get a bargain once in a while. Since he'd started accepting visitors to his allotment, rather than plying his trade from the boot of his car, business seemed to have boomed, although she'd never visited the shed before. She couldn't help but stare at the cornucopia of goods stacked floor to ceiling.

'Spot anything you like, Mrs K, let me know. Always the best price for you, you know. I've, what you might call, diversified since I took on these premises. Lovely little spot here, none of those nosey parkers from Trading Standards in the middle of an allotment. About the only place in Penrith where you've not got CCTV watching your every move. Or where I get my stock from, if you know what I mean. Discretion is the name of the game when it comes to getting hold of the kind of bargains and low, low prices I can offer. Friendly bunch, the Garden Club, too. I gave them a job lot of trowels and they've been as good as customers as you and your bingo pals. Which reminds me,' said Brunger, clambering back around, kettle brewing in the background. 'How was your trip to Manchester?'

'Manchester!' Amita blurted. 'How do you know about Manchester?'

Brunger flashed a rakish smile to reveal his gold tooth. He tapped the side of his nose and laughed. 'I've got moles everywhere, you know that,' he said. 'Don't worry, your secrets are safe with me. You know my motto, Mrs K. What happens in Manchester stays in Manchester. Am I right?'

'I'd rather not talk about it, if you don't mind,' she said. 'The embarrassment is hanging over me like a cloud, Mr Brunger.'

'Oh, don't be so silly. You're allowed to let your hair down once in a while.' He poured Amita a cup of tea.

'The lost weekend, that's what Jason is calling it.' Amita sipped at her tea. She was starting to feel a little more normal.

'Am I to take it that you're not here to fill me in with all the gory details, then?' he asked.

'No, I'm afraid not,' she said. 'Although even if I could remember what those gory details were, I probably still wouldn't say.'

'Fair enough,' he shrugged. 'What can I do you for then?'

'A phone, please, Mr Brunger. If you have any?'

'If I have any? Good one, Mrs K,' Brunger chuckled. 'I've got more phones than Penrith switchboard.'

While the contents of the shed appeared to be in no order at all, it took him a matter of seconds to find not one but three different handsets for Amita. He pulled the boxes open and laid everything out in front of her.

'There you go my lovely,' he said. 'Two of the latest models and one that's not out until later in the year. Actually, you might want to avoid that one for now, best not to raise questions.' He pushed the offending handset out of the way.

'Mr Brunger, as you can probably tell, I'm not wholly up to date on all things technological,' she said. 'I had my old number for over twenty years and the handset did everything I needed – one like that would be ideal.'

'Understood,' he said. 'Probably best going for this one, then, if you don't want all the bells and whistles. I've got a lovely selection of what I like to call 'pre-loved' and 'new to you'. Perfect for the connoisseur of vintage phones.'

He reached into a plastic tub and passed a different one to Amita. She took the handset, clearly relieved by its familiarity and decided that it would do. Already she was feeling much better, knowing she was close to normality again.

'What do I do about my number?' she asked.

Brunger made a hiss that sounded like air escaping from a tyre.

'That's a tricky one, Mrs K,' he said. 'I've got SIM cards coming out of my ears. But getting your old number back, that might be a bit tricky.'

'Even for you?'

'I won't lie to you, Mrs K. It's mostly *because* of me. I can let you have all of this for a song, that's presumably why you didn't go to our high-street friends down the road. But with the top-flight levels of service and charm that you receive by shopping with Malcolm Brunger Enterprises, there comes a few little niggles here and there.'

'You're telling me I'll have to get a new number,' she said.

'Not necessarily, Mrs K,' he said. 'A few calls to your provider and they'll sort you out, but it will take a few days. I don't like to get involved in that side of things – a few too many questions asked for my liking. But you know how things are these days, all your data and pictures are stored in the cloud somewhere. Whatever that means. You'll be up and running in no time, but you'll have to use a temporary number until then – and I can help you out with that.' He smiled over at Amita. 'This device you've chosen actually comes with a SIM already in it, a temporary number that should tide you over until you get your old one back.'

'I knew there would all sorts of admin,' she sighed. 'Serves me right for my own stupid fault. Foolishness, Mr Brunger – it seems it's not just a preserve of youth.'

'I always said you were young at heart,' he winked.

'Oh, stop it,' she patted him away.

He took the phone back from her and started up the device. Clicking a few buttons, he handed it over.

'How much do I owe you?' she asked.

'Don't worry about that just now,' he said. 'You can pay me when I'm at bingo on Wednesday. Just don't tell the padre I'm coming, would you? You know what the old man is like. But if I tell him I'm there to see you he can't send me packing.'

Amita laughed and finished her tea. Brunger opened the shed door and let her step back out into the sunlight. The man with the shovel saw them and waved. Brunger nudged Amita in the ribs.

'I think you've got an admirer there, Mrs K,' he said.

'Now, now,' she said. 'I've got to go and make some apologies to that man for behaving like a complete imbecile earlier.'

'Ah, young love,' Brunger fluttered his eyelashes.

Amita gave him a friendly pat on the arm, slid her phone into her pocket and started off towards the man with the shovel. The road to recovery had been started in earnest. She'd be back online and back in the know before the day was out.

Chapter 3

KOLKWITZIA AMABILIS

There was a distinctly muted silence about the Penrith Bingo Club this Wednesday night. When she'd arrived at the church hall earlier, Amita had hoped it wasn't to rapturous applause and laughter. But nobody at her table wanted to be the one who spoke, let alone mention the trip. Speech could lead to memories. And memories of the collective madness in Manchester were absolutely forbidden. Best just to get this first session after the trip out of the way. Then they could all move on with their lives.

Keeping quiet was usually an almost impossible task for Amita's comrades. She was amazed that, nearly an hour into tonight's games, nobody had said a word beyond the customary 'house' when the numbers went their way. Telepathy appeared to be the order of the day at halftime. Everyone just accepted they wanted tea and biscuits and they were fetched without question. No gossip, no whispers, no speculation and no hubbub about local goings on. Amita quite liked it all in a way. No reason to give her jitters.

Even Georgie Littlejohn had somehow put a cork in it. The selfanointed doyenne of the club was tight lipped and businesslike. She was here for the numbers and that was all. Get in, win, get home again. Everything would be better next week.

'Duck and dive, twenty-five,' said Father Ford.

The meek vicar was dutifully manning the bingo machine as usual. He had sensibly managed to avoid the trip. Being the official, if reluctant, number-caller for the Penrith Bingo Club rather than a participant, he would have been redundant at the bigger Manchester halls. And while he normally shed his bodyweight in sweat on Wednesday nights, uncomfortable as he was with a man of the cloth being seen to encourage gambling, he seemed strangely at ease this evening. Perhaps the lack of chatter and berating from the players was quite good for him. Amita made a note to try and congratulate him at the end of the evening. He would like that.

Amita thought the unspoken vow of not mentioning Manchester might have been broken when Sandy came in. Unusually late, he had sat down and looked around at everyone at the table. There had been a few minor gasps at the black eye he was sporting. But nobody said a word, even though the air almost crackled with the tension of people desperate to ask. But 'cast the first stone' thought Amita – ask anyone else about their misdemeanours and your own would be fair game. Amita couldn't remember how Sandy had got the shiner, but she was convinced it must have been on their night of iniquity. Her lost phone seemed to pale in comparison.

'All the eights, eighty-eight,' said Father Ford.

In the group's defence, she thought, none of the other tables appeared to be very chatty. The club's foray into the bright lights of the big city seemed to have affected everyone. Best to let sleeping dogs lie was the order of the day. And Amita wasn't going to upset the applecart.

'Three-score and ten, number seventy,' he said.

Amita lazily marked off the number. She was certain she would have won this game at least three times by now if only she'd paid attention. Her head wasn't in it. Nobody's was. They would all just slog through until the end and go home. Best for everyone.

'Oh,' said Father Ford.

The break in the rhythm seemed to send a jolt of life throughout the hall. Everyone looked up from their bingo cards. Sweat started to form on the vicar's forehead.

'It would appear that we've run out of numbers?'

A small ripple of mutiny began to spread from table to table. Father Ford scratched the back of his head and looked about the hall.

'In my time as your official bingo caller, I don't think this has ever happened before,' he said. 'Is it possible that somebody has missed a few numbers and is sitting with a winning book?'

That drew a few groans. Chairs screeched as they were pushed back, old aching bones stretching.

'Anyone, no?' asked the vicar. 'I think we'll probably have to go through the list of numbers drawn again to make sure we have a winner. I wouldn't want anyone to miss out.'

More groans. The impending audit was finally enough to break the silence of Amita's table.

'Give me strength.' Judy Moskowitz rolled her eyes. 'I'm barely keeping my eyes open as it is. What the hell is wrong with people? Can't they keep track of the bloomin' numbers?'

'I don't think our hearts are in it tonight, Judy,' said Amita, rolling her neck and shoulders. 'Distracted minds.'

'You can say that again.'

'I was keeping track of everything,' sniffed Georgie. 'It's just luck that's my problem tonight. Absolutely none of it.'

'Makes a change,' murmured Judy.

'Yes, it does, doesn't it, Judy,' she snipped. 'Although I'm certain I saw you miss a couple of numbers during that game just there.'

'And what exactly were you doing looking at my book?'

'Just keeping everything in order, that's all.'

'Nosey parker more like,' Judy snapped back.

'I beg your pardon.'

'You heard me, Littlejohn.'

'I most certainly did *not*.' Georgie looked like a cat about to hiss.

'Ladies, please,' said Sandy, rubbing his flat, cliff-like forehead with rough fingers. 'Not tonight, okay? We've all been through the mill with that bloody jolly to Manchester. Can we just get through this evening without an argument.'

'That's rich coming from you, Sandy Prentice,' said Georgie, spitefully.

'What's that?'

'Take a look in the mirror,' she nodded at him. 'You look like you've been in the wars with that eye.'

'Yes, thank you for that, Georgie. I had noticed. Thanks for asking if I'm alright. Your concern is always greatly appreciated.'

That seemed to shut Georgie up. Amita smiled to herself. Trust Sandy to be the voice of reason. The others took the less than subtle hint and remained quiet. Ethel, the oldest of the group, sat at the end of the table in her wheelchair, gently dozing. Amita wondered what she thought of the whole affair. On too many occasions had the old dear been dismissed as something of a coot. But she had a memory like an elephant. Perhaps it was best that she was asleep for tonight's gathering.

Amita checked her watch. Time was ticking on, and Father Ford had recruited some help up at the main stage. They were going to be late out tonight, she could feel it. Only good manners were keeping her in her seat.

'Are you alright, Sandy?' she asked.

The big man across from her shrugged and gave her a warm smile.

'You should see the other fella,' he said with a chuckle.

'Yes, quite,' she said. 'So long as it doesn't hurt too much.'

'Not at all,' he shrugged it off. 'I've had worse shiners than this in my time, Amita. I'll tell you about them sometime when the audience is a little more amenable.'

He darted a look at Georgie who was busy pretending to pick at a loose thread on her blouse.

'So long as there's no lasting damage,' said Amita.

'Just my pride. I wish I could say I'd got it defending someone's honour rather than missing my chair when sitting back down after one too many trips to the bar. Although looking about here tonight, I don't think I'm the only one who had a few too many when we were in Manchester,' he said. 'Margaret Cullen is nowhere to be seen.'

'I did notice that,' she said. 'Still, all in the past now, as they say. Where it belongs.'

'Indeed.'

The mood lightened a little. Amita sat back in her chair. She looked about the club, there was a safety here, despite everything that had gone on over the weekend. The last few years had been a rollercoaster. She'd imagined her golden years would be the calmest of her life – not seeing her dash across the county solving crimes. And while she could throttle Georgie Littlejohn with her bare hands at times, she was still glad to be in her company. Everyone's company, at that. The members of the Penrith Bingo Club had been instrumental in uncovering a few secrets over the years – now she was sure they'd be able to keep this one and not share their indiscretions.

'I think we're getting somewhere,' announced Father Ford. 'Just a moment, ladies and gentlemen, then we can start again.'

The pastor's announcement drew everyone back to their seats at the tables. While the mood of the hall hadn't been as buoyant as usual, everyone still respected the game. Amita more than most. She cracked her knuckles, centred her bingo book and took up her blotter, ready for the audit.

Sandy did the same, as did Judy and Georgie beside her. The other regulars were all poised, too. Ethel remained blissfully asleep down the end, a little knowing smile tugging at the wrinkles around her mouth.

'So, ladies and gentlemen, if you're ready,' said Father Ford. 'The first number that came out was . . .'

The unmistakable effervescent sweeping piano of the opening bars of ABBA's *Dancing Queen* rang out across the church hall at a blaring volume. Rarely in the song's illustrious history had it been less welcomed. Father Ford flinched in shock and bumped into the bingo machine, making it shudder with an unhealthy wheeze.

All eyes turned in unison to Amita Khatri – the source of the sudden, loud Europop distraction. She was panicking, as she fumbled around with the zip of her shell suit jacket pocket. The beat went on, the angelic Swedish vocals driving Amita's blood pressure through the roof. By the time she had recovered her phone, Friday night had arrived, and the lights were, naturally, low.

She didn't know what button to press. Only that stabbing at the screen with as many fingers as she could muster would, should, turn off the music. Mercifully, after what felt like eternity, the music stopped.

'Sorry,' was all she could say. 'Sorry everybody. It's . . . it's a new phone. I haven't quite worked out what all the things on it do yet. Or where the volume is.'

'Clearly not.' Georgie cocked an eyebrow.

Amita could feel the blood rushing to her head. Wasn't she due to be swallowed by the ground by now?

Father Ford helplessly fiddled and tinkered with his bingo machine, but everyone knew that the jig was up.

'Err . . .' he said sadly. 'I think we may have to end it there for the evening, ladies and gentlemen. I appear to have completely broken the device.'

His apology was a starting gun, the one the whole club had been waiting for since the first game of the evening. The geriatrics all moved with deceptive speed, gathering their cardigans, coats, hats and other paraphernalia and heading for the door. Amita's table was no exception.

'Thank you for that, Amita,' said Georgie, making a lavish display of getting to her feet. 'I normally hate my evening to end too early, but you knocking Father Ford off his stride has probably saved someone else claiming the prize pot. I think I was the only one paying any attention this evening.'

'Sorry about the ringtone,' Amita said.

'Yes, well, I'll speak to you tomorrow about the Brownies' summer show.'

'I bet you can't wait for that,' said Judy quietly.

Georgie shot Judy a suspicious look as they both started for the door. Sandy was laughing as he went to collect Ethel from the end of the table.

'I never had you down as an ABBA fan, Amita,' he said, popping his flat cap on his head.

'I'm not!' Amita protested. 'It's this blooming phone I got from Brunger. I've spent the last two days trying to get everything working the way I want, and it keeps going off whenever something comes through. He said he'd be here tonight, and I was going to give him a piece of my mind. But he's not turned up and I'm left stuck with this infernal device!'

'That's Brunger for you,' said Sandy, wheeling Ethel around. 'You always get more than you bargained for with that rascal.'

'Don't remind me,' she said. 'I've had emails from the Middle East, a voicemail telling me I'm eligible for compensation for a loan I've never taken, phone calls asking about a phantom car crash and text messages urging me to return to a clinic in Ankara for something called intracoronal bleaching. I've never even *been* to Turkey, let alone had whatever *that* is.'

'Sounds painful,' said Sandy. 'Anyway. I'm sure you'll get it sorted. I know what a wizard you are on WhatsApp. Right, best be off. Take care of yourself, Amita. Don't do anything I wouldn't do. And if you do, don't get caught, eh?'

He winked and pushed Ethel towards the throng making its way out of the door. Amita watched them go. She shook her head. A few of the other members of the club whispered and gossiped as they left, glancing in her direction. The sooner she was home, the better.

Amita gathered up her things. She tucked her dabbers into her handbag. Making sure her glasses were still firmly on her head, she stood up. The offending phone was lying on the table, staring back at her like a cursed relic.

'I don't know what you're looking at,' she said to it. 'This is all your fault. Just wait until I get my hands on that Brunger.'

As she lifted the phone, the screen lit up. An unopened message was waiting for her. Was it the source of the sudden ABBA outburst? She unlocked the screen and opened it up. The number was strange, unknown to her or the device. Expecting some sort of spam or gibberish, Amita froze when she read the words on the screen. A chill ran through her as she stared down at the phone in her hands.

'I KNOW YOU'VE KILLED HIM'

Chapter 4
ACTAEA PACHYPODA

'You're letting your imagination get the better of you. As usual, I may add,' said Jason.

'How on earth could this be my imagination, Jason? Look at it!' Amita protested. 'It's there, in black and white, on the screen. "I know you've killed him." There's very little to be *left* to the imagination!'

Jason shook his head. He was down on the floor beside the front door, helplessly trying to pull on his dirty old trainers. A whiff of dust and motor oil met him as he struggled to pull them on. The first grass cut of the year was imminent and these were his official mowing footwear. He was looking forward to giving these tatty old things a good airing.

'It could mean anything,' he said between grunts.

'Anything? Don't be ridiculous, Jason. How can "I know you've killed him" mean anything?'

'It's seven words, Amita, with no context. You've told me you've had all sorts of scam callers and phishing emails since you changed phones. That's how it can mean anything. Just delete it and carry on with your day.'

'And since when did something as explicit as this become the kind of thing you and I ignore? We've got form with things like this.'

'That's my point,' he said. 'You're letting your imagination run wild, as it always does. This is nothing, Amita, believe me. If it's not a hoax, it's probably just a private joke intended for whoever had the number before you.'

Jason pulled himself up.

'But speaking of our past, don't you think it merits investigation?' Amita said, following him out into the front garden.

'Oh please,' he said. 'Can't we go a day without suspecting there is murder and mayhem unfolding on our front step.'

'You've said that before and look where it's gotten us!'

Jason didn't answer that. He scurried around the house to fetch the lawnmower. Amita, however, was not in the kind of mood where she wanted to be ignored.

'Jason! Are you listening to me?' she asked.

'I am listening to you, Amita. I've been listening to you all morning. And last night when you came home from bingo. Rarely a day goes by when I *don't* listen to you, whether I'd like to or not.'

'Then why aren't you as worried as I am?'

Jason dragged the lawnmower along the gravel path and dumped it on the overgrown lawn. The smell of petrol wafted up from the old, rickety engine and he suspected it was leaking. But the promise of enough noise to drown out his mother-in-law was too alluring. To hell with safety protocols.

'I just think you're jumping to conclusions, that's all,' he said.

He tugged at the starter cord. The engine sputtered and coughed. He tried again. Same result.

'Well look at it this way,' said Amita. 'What if something awful has happened and we can do something about it? We have a moral duty, Jason, to at least do *something*!'

The lawnmower was being deliberately difficult, Jason was convinced. He kneeled down on the grass and began looking over the engine. He had absolutely no idea what he was looking for. He only hoped the appearance of being busy might give Amita cause to leave him alone. It didn't.

'Jason!' she said, tugging at his shoulder.

'Amita!' he barked. 'What do you want me to say? Tell me what you want me to say, and I'll say it!'

'I want your advice is what I want,' she said. 'I'm standing here with a message on my new phone that's talking about a killing. That doesn't seem at all iffy to you?'

He sighed loudly.

'If you're absolutely determined to blow this whole thing out of proportion, then I suggest you go the police,' he said. 'If that's what you really want.'

'The police!' Amita wrinkled her nose. 'I can't go to the police. Have you lost your mind?'

'Why not?'

'What am I supposed to say to the police, Jason? Excuse me, constable, but I appear to have some sort of incriminating message on a phone that I bought off the back of a lorry. What if I'm unknowingly handling stolen goods. Can you imagine the scandal?'

'Scandal seems to be following you around like a bad smell at the moment, Amita,' he said.

'Jason, please keep your voice down.'

She looked up and down the empty street beyond the front garden.

'No, no, I can't go to the police with this. We don't know what we're dealing with.'

'*We* aren't dealing with anything,' he said, standing up with a creak. 'It's probably just a laugh between mates or some ill-judged promotional stunt from someone trying to sell you something. Not everything turns into bloody murder, Amita. As hard as that is for us to imagine.'

Amita considered this for a moment. She looked down at her phone and pulled up the message again. The words were there, screaming in her own head. This didn't feel right. Everything about this whole scenario was making her teeth itch.

Jason pulled the starter cord again. The engine thought about turning over, then thought better of it. He gave the lawnmower a kick then tried again. That seemed to do the trick. With a splutter and spew of black smoke, the frame began to rattle as the engine chugged into life. Jason was about to congratulate himself when Amita switched the motor off.

'Amita!' he found he was shouting. 'I just got the bloomin' thing going and you've switched it off!'

'Jason,' she said quietly.

She rested her hand on his arm. Immediately his frustration was gone. He could tell from the grave expression on her face that this was more than one of her wild theories.

'I don't know what it is,' she said, equally softly. 'But I've got one of those feelings about this.'

'What feelings?'

He looked at her, confused. Amita stared back. There was a moment of silence, when the cogs and wheels ticked around in their minds. Slowly, Jason realised what his mother-in-law was on about.

'Oh, right,' he said. 'One of *those* feelings.'

'Yes, Jason. One of *those* feelings,' she said.

'Are you sure?' he asked. 'Are you sure it just isn't a bit of gas from something you ate last night? You were quite late getting in, and I noticed a big scoop of my chilli was missing from the pot.'

'Jason, could you be serious, just for a moment?'

He laughed and took up the starter cord of the lawnmower again. 'Oh, come on, Amita. Lighten up,' he said. 'I'm only joshing you.'

'This is a serious matter, Jason. We could have another murderer on our hands,' she said. 'And all you're interested in is making fun of my indigestion.'

'I certainly wouldn't dream of making fun of something as serious as that, Amita. Remember we share a bathroom.'

'Oh, Jason, you're appalling!' Amita looked aghast. 'You can't honestly stand there and think that this kind of message is perfectly normal, can you?' she said, ignoring him.

'No, I can't,' he said. 'But again, I don't know the context. Yes, it does seem to be a very strange thing for anyone to send. Without some frame of reference, I'm failing to see the reason.'

She was about to pounce. Jason held up a finger.

'However,' he said. 'And this is a big one. One I'm sure you've not even considered. How many of *your* texts could convey something completely different if a stranger was to receive them? What are your messages to the W.I. like when you're organising a raffle or a fete. I'm sure they would seem just as daft or odd, if not sinister, if read by the wrong person. After all, when I picked you up from bingo after ABBA-gate, you told me you were going to kill Malcolm Brunger for the shame he'd caused you. Imagine if you'd texted me that. To a stranger, that's a murder threat.'

Jason was right. Amita hadn't considered this. Not that she was about to let him know it. Some things between a mother-in-law and her smart alecky son-in-law could remain undisclosed.

'Hmm,' was all she mustered. 'I suppose that *could* be the case.'

'Exactly,' he said, pulling the cord. 'Mountain out of a molehill.'

'Brunger had loads of phones and bits of kit. Maybe I should go and get a new one of those SIM card things off him, instead of this old one . . .' Anita pondered.

The lawnmower roared back into life. This time Amita didn't interfere. Jason pushed it forward, the unmistakable smell of freshly cut grass wafting up his nostrils. He trudged on in a wobbly line, scything through the overgrown lawn, feeling rather good about himself. A crisis averted.

Amita lingered for a moment on the path, watching him go. Her head was spinning, as it usually did when these sorts of situations came up. A scarily frequent occurrence these past few years. She looked at the message again. Could it really just be a joke? Was she jumping to conclusions far too easily? The message could mean a whole pile of things after all. A pet fish not fed while the owner was on holiday. It didn't necessarily have to refer to a corpse. Or even a murder victim at that.

She sighed and clicked a button so the phone screen went blank. Amita wasn't sure if she should feel disappointed or relieved. The danger and responsibility that came with murder investigations was not something she ever jumped into lightly. Quite the opposite in fact. But she couldn't deny the satisfaction it had brought her since she and Jason had teamed up to get to the bottom of some unfortunate Cumbrian crimes.

So here she was, trudging back towards the house with something gnawing away in the pit of her stomach. Was it sadness that this wasn't another maniacal murderer on the loose? Or was she just off colour, as Jason had suggested.

She was almost at the front door when the gargling racket of the lawnmower stopped dead. Amita was about to head back into the house when Jason called to her from the lawn.

'Brunger?' he asked.

Amita turned around to face her son-in-law. 'Yes, Mr Brunger. What about him?'

'You got that phone from Brunger, and you said he had lots of them?' Jason walked slowly towards her.

'That's right, yes,' she said. 'What of it?'

'Amita, Malcolm Brunger is as dodgy as they come.'

'But he offers some really quite good bargains. I haven't even paid him for this thing yet,' she waved the phone at him.

Jason's face had turned a shade of grey. Amita could feel the gnawing getting stronger.

'What's wrong, Jason,' she said. 'You look like a boiled flannel.'

'Let me see that message,' he said.

She handed the phone over. Jason read the message, then read it again. He swallowed, his throat suddenly quite dry.

'I think we might be in a spot of bother, Amita,' he said.

'Why?' she asked.

'I think we might have another murder on our hands.'

Chapter 5

SACCHARUM CRYSTALLINUM

'Okay, we have to get our story straight here, before we do anything else,' said Jason. 'What *is* our story again?'

Amita watched him pace back and forth across the front room, her phone still in his hand. If he wasn't careful, he was going to wear a hole in the rug. She decided to tell him as such.

'Please sit down, Jason. You're making me feel seasick,' she said.

Jason stopped in the centre of the room. He was deep in thought, the tendons in his temples flexing in that slightly odd way of his. Amita was regretting telling him anything now. Since his sudden change of heart over her suspicions, he'd become a jittery wreck. The curtains were drawn, the front door locked. He'd even checked that the windows upstairs were closed so nobody could hear them conspiring.

'What's our story then?' he asked again.

'If you would sit down for a second, I'll tell you,' she tutted. 'Jason, honestly, you need to calm down.'

'Calm down? Calm down? You're the one who could be texting a murderer.'

'That's not what you thought ten minutes ago!'

'That's before you told me that Malcolm Brunger was likely dealing in old phones, with other people's data still in them,' he snapped. 'The man is a walking, talking fly-by-night. If you'd had a shiny new SIM card in it then I could chalk this up as a scam, but if Brunger's given you this whole thing – conveniently realising you didn't want a fancy new phone – there's something fishy. Seriously, Amita, that message could be coming from anywhere in the world. About anything. Russian gangsters, Italian Mafia, Hells Angels, you name them – but it was intended for someone!'

'And what about it being a prank between friends?' she asked. 'What about there being no context and no frame of reference. That's what you said, wasn't it?'

'I did say that.' He sat down on the sofa. 'But that's before I thought it through. Honestly, Amita, this handset and SIM could have come from any of the four corners of the planet, but I don't think Malcolm is running an international crime ring. He's much more likely to have got this from someone local. Which means we could not only have trouble on our hands . . . We could have trouble on our doorstep.'

'You're exaggerating, as usual, Jason.'

'Am I?' he chirped.

'Yes, you are,' she said. 'Yes, I acknowledge that Mr Brunger's methods of trading aren't quite up to code. But he's hardly a godfather of the underworld, is he? His stockroom is a shed in the Folly Lane allotments for goodness sake!'

Jason's tendons went into overdrive. Amita took her phone from him and looked at the dreadful message again.

'I KNOW YOU'VE KILLED HIM'

'And as for your plan to tell the police, I can't say I'm hugely enamoured,' she said. That seemed to snap her son-in-law out of his panicky trance.

'Then what do you suggest?'

'I'm not sure,' she said. 'But supposing this *is* something altogether sinister. Do you really think the police will investigate thoroughly?'

'I think it's about as good an option as we're likely to have,' he said. 'But you are right – it won't do us any good if it is all a stunt. I don't really fancy presenting Detective Inspector Arendonk with what turns out to be a couple of teenagers having a prank at our expense.'

'True,' she agreed. 'The detective inspector has been very patient with us. Seeing us marching into Penrith Police Station would probably give her palpitations. No, I think we can handle this ourselves, as long as we get our story straight from the off. We can text a reply. See what comes back, if anything, and we can take it from there.'

Jason looked paler still. 'When I said we should investigate I meant we should track Brunger's sources – not text a murderer! What about tracking, or tracing, or whatnot? What if they can tell where we are?'

'Nonsense!' said Amita. 'They probably won't bite, but it's worth a try. It's not like I'm going to send them our address. We just need a cover story. So, what's our story?'

Jason looked blankly at her. 'That was what I asked you!'

'No ideas?' she asked. 'I thought you were a journalist.'

'I *am* a journalist,' he said.

'Then aren't stories meant to be your forte, your professional calling?'

'Not made-up ones, Amita.'

'But I . . .'

'And before you say it,' he interrupted her. 'I never once embellished the truth in a story that I covered. It was the truth, the whole truth and nothing but the truth.'

'So help me god.'

'Yes, something like that,' he said.

Amita was only joking. She knew how highly Jason held his journalistic principles and scruples. But she couldn't resist. What kind of mother-in-law would she be if she didn't keep him on his toes.

'I don't see the problem with just messaging back and asking what's going on,' she said. 'We don't have to say who we are. We could be anyone.'

'Hmm.' Jason didn't seem too convinced. 'And what happens if whoever is on the other end doesn't like anyone knowing their business?'

'Well, that's up to them, then, isn't it. All that matters is that we're in agreement that we should at least reply to this rather cryptic message.'

Jason thought for a moment. Then he nodded. Amita flexed her fingers and stared at the screen. Suddenly her mind was blank.

'What's the matter?' he asked her.

'I can't think of anything to say.'

'I don't believe that for a second,' he said.

'No, seriously, Jason. I can't think of something to text back.'

'You're trying to tell me that the Sheriff of Penrith is lost for words? Pull the other one, Amita.'

'Alright, you do it then.'

She went to give him the phone. Amita had rarely seen Jason back away so fast. He raised his hands above his head and slithered off the end of the sofa.

'Oh no, not me,' he said. 'If whoever is on the other end of that line likes to put horse's heads on pillows, I'm making sure it's not mine.'

'I don't have the faintest idea of what you're talking about,' said Amita, rolling up her sleeves. 'Once again, cometh the hour, cometh the woman.'

She hesitated again, looking down at her phone. Then she smiled as she typed out a message. A little whistle sounded from the phone to say it had been sent.

'There,' she said.

'There what?' asked Jason.

'It's gone.'

'It's gone?'

'That's what I just said.'

'Aren't you going to let me read it before you send it?'

'You've hardly been a font of help so far, Jason. What difference would it make?'

'But . . . but you could be texting a crazed killer, Amita! That could be some blood-thirsty maniac on the other end of that message ready to strike again. Don't you think another pair of eyes would have been of some use?'

'No, not particularly, when they're *your* eyes,' she said bluntly.

'Well, what did you say then?'

'Nothing really,' she shrugged.

Jason rolled his eyes.

'This is like pulling teeth,' he groaned. 'Look, you must have said *something*. What did you reply?'

'I just said hello there, lovely to hear from you and no, I haven't killed anyone. Would you like to explain further?'

Jason clapped his hand to his forehead.

'Unbelievable, Amita. You are truly unbelievable.'

'What? I don't see what's wrong with that. It's polite, it's courteous, it's to the point.'

'We could be dealing with some very dangerous people, it doesn't matter how polite you are,' he said.

'Manners cost nothing, Jason. You of all people should know that,' she said, flattening some creases in her shell suit jacket. 'I hope you're teaching my grandchildren how to be good little citizens. And another thing . . .'

ABBA's *Dancing Queen* rang out from the phone. Jason and Amita both jumped a little, the song blaring from the handset. She quickly silenced it and looked at the screen.

'They've replied,' she said, swallowing hard.

'Oh lord,' said Jason. 'What have they said?'

'*Who is this?*' read Amita.

'Is that it?'

'Yes.'

'Not a lot to go on, is it?' he asked.

'Nothing, Jason. Absolutely nothing.'

Jason scratched at the stubble on his chin. Before either of them could react, the phone went off again.

'It's another message,' said Amita.

'And?'

Amita adjusted her spectacles.

'It says, "I'm going to the police. Where is he?"'

'The police?' he said. 'That's more than a little spat or a joke.'

'What are you talking about?' she said, typing in the words. She hit send.

Jason was biting his nails now. He wasn't used to this kind of drama so early in the day. He wished he'd stayed outside cutting the grass. The front lawn could have been done by now and a start made on the back garden. Radha would have been glad to see he had something to show for today while she was at work and the kids were at school. And he could lord it over Patrick Bidmead next door. He hadn't even started the spring cut yet. Everything was a competition.

Agnetha and Anni-Frid belted out their famous hit once more. Jason bent down to see the screen beside Amita.

'"What have you done with Fran?"' she read out.

'Who's Fran?' asked Jason.

'I have no idea. I don't think I know anyone called Fran, not in my circle anyway. What about you?'

'Amita, please. If *you*, the most connected septuagenarian in Cumbria, doesn't know who Fran is, I'm hardly going to stand a chance, am I?'

'Point well made,' she said.

The phone buzzed in her hand as raft of messages all came through at once, each a little more frantic than the last.

'"Where are you? Where is Fran? What have you done with Fran? I need to know ASAP."'

Jason felt his stomach flip. He didn't like this.

'This is getting a bit serious,' he said. 'I think we should let the police know.'

'So, you do think we could have a killer on our hands?' asked Amita.

'It's hardly time for I told you so's, Amita. Come on, let's get down the station.'

'No, we can't, Jason. It's not just me and my dodgy phone I'm thinking about. We can't risk whoever this is going underground if they find out we've gone to the authorities.'

'How would they know that?'

'If we stop messaging suddenly,' she said. 'Think about it. Whoever is on the other end of the line is clearly panicking, look how quickly they are texting now. If we suddenly go silent then they'll know something's the matter. And we might never find out who this Fran is or what's happened to them.'

There was a kind of logic to Amita's reasoning. Even if it was the kind of logic that could again see him and his mother-in-law risking everything to unpick a murder.

'So, what do we do?' he asked.

Amita bent over the phone. Her thumbs tapped away at the keypad before she sent a reply.

'What did you say?' he asked.

'I've asked to meet them,' she said.

'You've done *what*?'

Jason's voice was both earsplittingly loud and surprisingly high-pitched. He began to pace again, tendons in overdrive.

'Amita, are you insane?! You've done some incredibly foolhardy things since we started this investigation business, but this might take the biscuit!'

'Calm down,' she said. 'You're going to give yourself a heart attack.'

'Heart attack?! That'll be if we're lucky! You've likely just invited the Russian mob to our front door! We'll be chopped up and made into pâté before *University Challenge* starts. Poison on door handles, razor blades in our Battenberg . . .'

'Jason, would you please give me *some* credit,' she said, the phone buzzing in her hand. 'I'm not completely dimwitted, you know. I have played this game before.'

Jason could feel his heart beating so hard, it was starting to climb up into his throat. He had to sit down before he fell down. 'That's the thing with you, Amita. I think you love the game – even when it's life and death.' He was about to continue when ABBA pealed out once more.

'There,' she said, reading the prompt reply. 'Lowther Castle at eleven tonight.'

'I feel ill,' he said.

'No time to feel ill. We've got to drop in to see somebody first, if we're going to keep this appointment later.'

She stood up and pulled the curtains open. Jason winced as the streaming sunlight of the beautiful spring day flooded into the living room. Amita buzzed around him and clapped him on the shoulder.

'Come on, get changed out of those smelly old trainers and put a pair of trousers on,' she said. 'You don't want to give him any ammunition. Your legs are white enough to glow in the dark.'

Jason rubbed his eyes. Suddenly he felt very old and very haggard. Then what his mother-in-law had just said slowly dawned on him.

'Give *who* any ammunition?' he asked.

Amita didn't hear him. She was already climbing the stairs, a renewed energy about her. She was always the same when she was on the trail of a murderer. It seemed to bring out the very best in her.

Chapter 6

VACCINIUM MACROCARPON

Amita had remained almost silent throughout the drive. The only time she spoke was to direct Jason along the backroads. Left here, right at the next lights, whatever the map on her phone told her. They had very quickly left Penrith behind, heading west towards Ullswater and the Northern Lakes. Winding and weaving through the countryside, the hedges in bud, with every twist and turn, Jason grew more suspicious.

'Could you at least give me a clue as to who we're going to see? It's hard enough knowing we've got a date with a criminal later without adding in your mystery stop-off too,' he huffed.

'Just carry on down this road,' said Amita, glued to the screen of her phone.

'It's not very fair, Amita. I had plans today. None of them involved risking my skin facing up to a bloodthirsty maniac, I might add.'

'All will be revealed soon enough.'

'That's what I'm afraid of.'

Dappled sunlight spread out across the narrow road in front of them. While the trees hadn't started to bloom yet, their spindly arms and branches created a magical lattice above. The bright spring sunshine was doing its best to break through, but the trees stood firm as if the harsh winds and cold of winter had hardened their spirits.

Jason pressed on. It was clear now that he was getting no more info from his mother-in-law.

The forest that had enveloped the road cleared and the rolling, imposing hills of the Cumbrian countryside opened up in front of them. The Lake District in all of its glory. That was the thing about the Lakes.

It didn't need Wordsworth's daffs to be beautiful – there was majesty all year round. He appreciated it even more as he wondered whether he'd still be around to see summer if he kept following Amita and her wild hunches.

The road wound and twisted its way down the side of a hill and, at the bottom, a small village, nestled at the base of the valley, sat waiting.

'Try to find a place to park,' said Amita, putting her phone back into her pocket. 'Anywhere near the start of this little village.'

'Here?' asked Jason. 'This is the middle of nowhere, Amita. You've brought us here?'

'That's right.'

'Who could possibly live out here that we know?'

'Oh, ye of little faith, Jason. Park us up and all will be revealed. Trust me.'

A shiver went down his spine. He didn't like it when Amita told him to trust her. Usually, that meant they were seconds away from disaster.

He parked the car and they both got out. The village was little more than a dozen houses, scattered evenly on either side of the narrow road that had brought them down the hillside. There was no shop, no bus stop, not even a post box. Jason knew that the Lake District, and the county for that matter, was full of these places. Little pockets of picture-postcard civilisation hidden away among the brambles and oak trees, dwarfed by the hills, tucked into the valleys. Even though he had lived here for years, he could still be surprised by a road he'd never travelled, a turn-off not yet taken. Normally he liked discovering these places. He just wished he knew what they were doing in this one now.

Amita strode purposefully up the road. She was counting the house numbers as Jason walked behind her. How anyone who lived in this part of the world was going to be able to help them with their rendezvous later was beyond Jason. He had half-hoped that they were going to get Sandy, or someone else who knew how to handle themselves, but none of Amita's bingo chums lived this far out of Penrith.

'Ah, here we are,' said Amita.

She stopped at a modest-looking house close to a break in the row. The garden sloped upwards towards the entrance, a rickety handrail to help anyone trying to make the hike up to the front door.

'Come along,' she said.

Jason couldn't place how he was feeling. Maybe it was instinct, a fight-or-flight response triggered by not knowing what he was walking into. Now that he was here, something was telling him that this wasn't going to be pleasant.

'Amita,' he said, climbing the narrow path towards the door, half wishing he had some of his mother-in-law's fearlessness, the other half wishing she had some of his caution. '*Now* will you tell me who we're here to see?'

She didn't answer him. Instead, she marched right up to the door. A note was stuck to the knocker. She pointed at it.

'"Deliveries around the back,"' she said.

'So, they're not expecting us then?' asked Jason.

'Around the back. Come on.'

Amita followed a narrow gravel path that led around the little house. With every crunch, Jason's stomach did another flip. They passed through a high gate and a huge, sprawling garden appeared on the other side. Jason was quietly impressed. The lawn was lush and green, perfectly cut into alternating dark and light stripes. Better than his attempt back at home.

'I should have brought my football boots,' he said as they walked a little further into the garden. 'This is like Wembley.'

'I'll have to take your word on that,' said Amita.

The lawn seemed to stretch on forever. How such a modest house could have so much land behind it was a mystery to Jason. Towards the rear of the garden, the woodland at the base of one of the huge hills had bunched up. More of the bare tree branches hung down over a wooden pergola, like water cascading off a cliff. Beneath the elegant frame was a little deck, a small figure sitting in the centre surrounded by cushions.

Amita walked on ahead as Jason lingered behind. His eyesight wasn't as good as it used to be, so he couldn't make out who was sitting there. Cautiously, he followed his mother-in-law across the lawn. The figure didn't move, almost as if they hadn't seen the pair approaching. Or that they didn't care. That made Jason even more nervous.

Amita was the first to reach the pergola. Still the figure didn't move. Jason's feet felt as though they were made of concrete. The closer he got to the end of the garden, the more he felt like he was walking into a spider's web. And it was feeding time.

Then he saw who it was. There, sitting with his legs crossed, hands resting on his knees, a look of tranquil bliss on his face, was former Detective Inspector Frank Alby.

'No,' said Jason. 'No. You've got to be kidding me, Amita!'

That was enough for Alby to open one beady eye. He looked about, spying Amita standing over him. Then he clocked Jason. All tranquillity vanished in an instant. Alby's round face went from red to scarlet and bordering on purple within seconds. The ex-policeman, who had loathed Jason since they first met, looked ready to burst.

Only he didn't. There was no outburst, no sweary ebullition, not even so much as a grunt from Alby. Instead, he closed his eye again, took a long, deep breath through his nose and let it out through his mouth, tobacco-stained moustache twitching as he did so.

'Are you two delivering my missus' slow cooker, then?' he asked. 'I left a note on the front door. Don't want to miss it, you see. That's the only delivery I want today. She makes a delicious Irish stew.'

'Detective Inspector Alby, I . . .'

'DI Alby, *retired*,' he said, still with his eyes firmly closed. 'I'm retired, Amita. If you've got a crime to report, you should call nine-nine-nine and ask to speak to the police. They will be able to help you from there.'

'There, he told us what to do,' said Jason, tugging at Amita's arm. 'Let's go and do that and not disturb his retirement any further.'

'Jason,' she quietened him down. 'Detective Inspector . . . Frank . . . We were wondering if I, we, could speak with you for a moment.'

A soft wind made the branches above the pergola tremble. That was enough for Alby to open his eyes. He sniffed, hands still resting on his knees. For a man in his late sixties, with a pot belly and, Jason suspected, a liver ready to give up the ghost, he was remarkably spry. Jason doubted he'd be able to sit for as long with his legs crossed. Could it be that Frank Alby had given up his old-fashioned ways? Could retirement have created a new man where a dinosaur once roamed the streets of Penrith and beyond? He hadn't seemed the type to dedicate his retirement to yoga when he'd been on the job – he'd been a policeman's policeman. Shoe-leather, shouting and a pint or ten at the end of each case. Hardly one for mantras and meditation.

'You two are an almighty pain in the arse, do you know that?' grunted the former DI.

There was Jason's answer. He refrained from telling Amita that he knew better. She still seemed keen to speak with the former policeman.

'Can't a man enjoy his hour of mindfulness in his *own* garden, by the way, without being disturbed by a couple of do-gooders?'

Alby climbed to his feet. The robe he was wearing didn't quite cover everything as he moved. Jason winced as he caught an eyeful of the older man's bright pink boxer shorts.

'Frank, we'd like to talk to you about a rather serious matter,' said Amita.

Alby ignored her. He marched right past Amita and onto the lawn. Jason watched him approach, half expecting a punch on the nose. All he got was a feigned smile instead.

'Sorry, let me correct myself,' he said. 'One do-gooder, you, Mrs Khatri. And one complete and utter waste of space in your son-in-law here.'

He walked past Jason and headed across the lawn.

'I see you've lost none of your charm in retirement, Frank,' said Jason. He was unable to hold his tongue.

'That's still Detective Inspector to you, sunshine!' Alby spun around and pointed a mean finger at him.

'How come she's allowed to call you Frank, then?' protested Jason.

'Because *she* is a lady, Brazel, that's why. *You* are the answer to a question that nobody asked in the first place. Got that?'

'Ouch.'

Amita hurried past him, chasing after Alby.

'Frank, please. I'm sorry to come to you like this, unannounced,' she said. 'But we need your advice. Well, more than that, guidance actually. You see, Jason and I have found ourselves in a bit of a pickle and, well, a man with your experience, it really could come in quite useful.'

Alby wasn't having any of it. He stalked across the pristine lawn, heading for the patio and back door of his house. Jason watched Amita try to grab his attention, but he could tell already that Alby was in no mood to entertain. He also understood now why she had kept him in the dark all morning. One mention of the former detective inspector and he never would have started the car. Or even left the safety of their living room. Jason had to hand it to his mother-in-law, she could be as devious as the best of them when it came to getting what she wanted. A real man manager, a mind like a steel trap.

'Not interested, Amita. Not interested in the slightest,' Alby held up a hand. 'There's a perfectly fit, young and able new DI serving His Majesty at your local station. I'm sure they'll be able to help you out with any guidance or assistance you need. I am officially retired.'

'No, you don't understand,' she pleaded with him now. 'It's you we need to speak with. You specifically, Frank.'

He reached the back door and opened it. Stepping up, he was at last taller than Amita. A smug smile was stretching his pockmarked face, making him look like an overinflated football.

'Sorry, I can't help you out,' he said sarcastically. 'But I'm late for *This Morning* and the dishes aren't going to do themselves now, are they? Goodbye.'

Alby was about to close the door in Amita's face. Jason cursed himself. He knew he should just let the ex-copper do it and they'd be on their way. They could be home by lunchtime, a plan formulated before dinner and then on to meet their mysterious texter. They wouldn't have to give Frank Alby a second thought. They had, after all, been successful on their own in the past. Why should this be any different?

But Jason knew it wasn't that simple. He knew that if Amita had gone to the trouble of finding out where Alby was living these days, and the effort that would have taken, she clearly needed to speak with him. Even if it meant giving the cantankerous old detective airtime and eating some humble pie, Jason knew he had to do it. For Amita.

It was his turn to sigh. He shook his head and started off towards the house.

'Hang on a second, Alby,' he shouted.

Alby had almost closed the door. Foolishly, he left it open, just a crack. Jason had gambled that his old adversary couldn't resist another chance to berate and ridicule him. And he had been right.

'This should be good,' said Frank. 'What is it, Brazel?'

Jason eased past Amita. She had that worried look on her face, the one she wore when she didn't know what he was going to do or say next. She liked to be in control, he knew that. Especially if they needed something.

'As usual, my mother-in-law is being too modest,' he said. 'You see, we're in desperate need of your insight and experience, given you were one of Cumbria's best coppers in your time. Isn't that right?'

Alby's face took on the scarlet hue from earlier. Jason couldn't resist a little wry smirk. Again, the ex-policeman was able to contain himself. Whatever new-age medication he was indulging in was clearly working. Although Jason was certain he was pushing it to the limit.

'Is that so?' asked Alby. 'And since when did you think I was Cumbria's best copper?'

'I said *one* of, Alby. Don't get ahead of yourself.'

'Jason!' Amita tried to reel him in.

'Look, we're in a bind and we need your help,' Jason went on. 'We need somebody who knows how to handle himself if things get a bit rough and ready. Not to mention, somebody who has the backing of the law on his side if it gets ugly.'

Alby remained stoic, but he looked intrigued. Jason had him.

'And there's nothing wrong with a bit of good, old-fashioned experience when it comes to that kind of thing, is there?' he asked. 'You know the stuff, salt of the earth, true grit, Gary Cooper in *Rio Bravo*, am I right?'

Jason smiled at Alby, who was still barring the way to the house, robe fluttering disconcertingly in the spring breeze. Amita fidgeted nervously beside him. Alby pursed his lips, then he cocked a sandy eyebrow and stepped to one side.

'You better come in then,' he said. 'If it's that serious.'

Amita breathed a sigh of relief. Jason needed a moment longer to hide his own response. He let her step into the house first and then followed. No sooner had the door closed behind him than Alby bit back.

'It was John Wayne who was in *Rio Bravo*,' he said with a nasty smile. 'Nice to see you're still as competent as ever, eh, Brazel.'

Chapter 7
CARAGANA ARBORESCENS PENDULA

If Jason had been asked the night before to describe what Frank Alby's front room looked like, he was almost certain this is what he would have come up with. It felt like something from a bygone era, certainly the last century. A line of horse brasses and tankards were hung across the low ceilings, adding to the air of 1970s' country pub. From the outdated swirly shagpile carpet and matching curtains to the big lump of a television that still had a Cathode-ray tube, sociology students would no doubt have a field day in here. Just looking at that huge, cumbersome television set in the far corner was giving Jason a hernia.

Pride of place on the mantelpiece above the fireplace was a trophy. As he sat down, Jason had spied the nameplate made out to 'Frank Alby – Cumbria Police District Darts Champion, 1996'. He was sure there would be others elsewhere in the house, dotted around to remind everyone of Alby's prowess at the oche.

He shook his head in disbelief. 'Remind me never to let you have any bright ideas in the future,' he said quietly to Amita.

'Remind me to give you a clip around the ear when we get out of here for speaking to me like that, Jason,' she fired back. 'I don't need you to let me do *anything*.'

'You know what I mean,' he said. 'Frank Alby. Seriously, Amita? There's nobody else we could turn to?'

'Can you think of anyone better?'

'I'd like to think there's *somebody*. How could there *not* be?'

'Mr Alby is an experienced detective,' she whispered. 'He knows the law inside and out. He's also probably skilled in unarmed combat and self-defence, should things turn nasty.'

'Alby? Are you serious? Have you seen the state of his knees?' he whispered back. 'The only combat Alby is used to these days is the fight to get his slacks fastened. He's an old man, Amita. What's he going to do to fend off murderers, if that's who's waiting for us tonight?'

'He's younger than me,' she said.

'Yes, I know, but you're trim and fit. You could power-walk your way past most people half your age,' he said. 'Alby's been behind a desk for thirty years. The last time he collared a crook, the Romans had just invaded Syracuse.'

Jason was proud of that one. He had the calendar Radha had bought him for Christmas. A daily historical fact printed beneath each date.

'Just bite your tongue, Jason, and trust me,' she said. 'If he agrees to accompany us to Lowther Castle then you'll be grateful he's there.'

'I don't think I'll ever be grateful for Frank Alby's company,' he huffed.

The door of the front room opened. Alby came walking in with two mugs, both with the Brunswick star decal of Cumbria Police on them. He handed one to Amita and then sat down on the large chair across from them, cradling the other mug.

'Seriously?' asked Jason.

Alby sipped from his mug. He groaned with great satisfaction as he reclined in his chair. Jason had to give it to the old copper. He knew how to hold a grudge.

'Start at the beginning,' said Alby. 'Don't skip any details. Don't mess me around. There's golf on at midday and I'd like to see it from the start, if you don't mind.'

'Not the darts?' asked Jason.

Alby gave him a feigned smile.

'That doesn't start until seven, Brazel, you ignoramus.'

'Gotcha,' he winked.

'Frank,' said Amita, playing referee. 'I can call you Frank, can't I?'

'You may,' said Alby, draining his mug already.

'Can I?' asked Jason.

'You'll be speaking through a mouth full of broken teeth if you keep up the lip, son.'

'Frank,' said Amita, nipping it in the bud. 'Thank you for seeing us. I'm certain we weren't the people you were expecting this morning. Or any other morning for that matter.'

'No, you weren't,' said the former detective. 'But you're here now. So out with it.'

'Yes, well, it's a bit complicated.'

'Always is with you two.'

'It all started because I needed a new phone and promptly got one,' said Amita. 'Only, it seems that the number I've now inherited was, up until recently I presume, still being used by someone else. And for the last few days I've been getting messages.'

'Messages?' asked Alby, taking it all in.

'Yes, messages. Text messages to be precise,' she went on. 'I wouldn't have bothered, only these messages are somewhat . . . sinister in nature.'

Alby leaned forward, the old, battered leather of his chair creaking beneath him.

'Sinister in what way?' he asked.

Amita took a deep breath. She looked at Jason for some inspiration, but he was simply bored.

'Well, they allude to the possibility of a body being hidden,' she said. 'Which sounds like preventing lawful burial at best and, well, at worst . . . murder.'

Alby leaned in. He steepled his fingers, his brow wrinkling beneath his bad combover.

'Murder, you say?' he said.

There was a seriousness to his tone that made Jason sit up a little stiffer. Maybe he'd been too quick to dismiss the old policeman. Was Amita right all along in bringing Alby in on this?

'That's our theory anyway,' said Amita, her voice low.

'You've seen no evidence? No images of bodies, names or anything?' asked Alby.

'No, nothing,' she said. 'Just desperation from whoever is on the other end of the line. They seem adamant to know what we've done with the body, as they call it. It's quite unsettling, Frank, I don't mind telling you.'

'And you think they're . . . a killer?' he asked.

'Well,' said Jason, butting in. 'We think someone is. Whether it's our texter or whether they think they're messaging the murderer, it sounds like someone's come to a sticky end.'

They were all quiet now, speaking in hushed tones as if the person on the end of Amita's text messages could somehow hear them. Jason's pulse had picked up and Amita looked more troubled than usual. Alby slowly nodded.

'Alright,' he said. 'You two were correct to come to me about this. It's not a matter for amateurs.'

He stood up. Tucking his hands behind his back, he walked over to the mantelpiece. Leaning on it, he let out a heavy sigh and rubbed his face. Jason and Amita were gawking, waiting for his response.

'You've done the right thing coming here,' he said again.'

'We have?' asked Amita.

'Yes,' said Alby, looking around to face her. 'Because otherwise, I wouldn't be able to tell you both, in person, just how . . . bloody stupid you really are!'

He let out an awful cackle, his head thrown back, pot belly jiggling beneath his robe. Jason instantly felt like a fool. Amita, too. Alby continued to guffaw at them, bending over and slapping his bare knees. Still laughing, he staggered a little and steadied himself on the mantle.

'Alright. That's enough, Alby,' said Jason, sensing Amita's discomfort. 'Pack it in.'

Alby didn't relent. He was having too good a time of it all. Eventually his hilarity began to ease. He wiped tears from his cheeks and continued to snigger a little.

'Honestly,' he said. 'You two crack me up, you really do.'

'We're not here to be laughed at, Detective Inspector,' said Amita. 'If I wanted to be the butt end of the joke, I would have turned Jason loose on you.'

'Hey,' said Jason, offended.

'Oh, give over, Amita,' said Alby. 'Text messages, bodies, murderers. You know your problem, don't you? You've been spending too much time with Brazel. All his journalistic lies and editorial liberties have fuelled your imagination.'

'Hey, again,' said Jason. 'What is this? Punch Jason in the metaphorical gut day?'

'Nothing metaphorical about the punch I'm about to give you if you don't sling your hook,' said the ex-copper. 'Although I'll give it to you. You had me going there for about ten seconds. I thought you were serious.'

'We *are* serious,' said Amita, shooting to her feet. 'We wouldn't be here wasting your time and ours if we weren't.'

Alby cleared his throat. He adjusted his gown and dried the last of his tears on his sleeve. He sniffed as he fetched up his own mug.

'We came here today because we thought you might be able to help us,' said Amita. 'We're due to meet whoever it is who's been messaging us at eleven tonight and we thought, perhaps foolishly, that you might be able to come with us and provide some support.'

'Very good,' he said. 'And just what exactly would you want me to do during this sting operation you've both got planned? Armed support? Call in the Flying Squad to collar the blaggers? You're living in a fantasy world, both of you.'

Jason could take the insults. He'd been a journalist his whole adult working life. A thick skin to deal with some of the editors he had known was only natural. As Alby stood over them both, it was Amita he felt for. He knew she wasn't going to take this at all well.

'How dare you,' said his mother-in-law.

Both Jason and Alby were shocked into silence. Amita was commanding the room now. Everything was drawn to her, like a black hole in sequinned leisure wear. She was angry, Jason could see that, but more than that, there was a determination in her eyes that he knew only too well.

'How absolutely dare you, Mr Alby,' she said. 'Speaking to us like we're a pair of silly schoolchildren. In fact, that's insulting to the children. I wouldn't dream of speaking to mine like that. Let alone my grandchildren.'

'Amita, hold on a minute here—'

'No, *you* hold on a minute.' She cut him off with a rigid finger.

She stalked towards Alby, who flinched a little. He kept his chin up as high as it would go, but he was clearly nervous. Jason could see the sweat forming along his hairline.

'We've come here for your help,' Amita continued. 'Out of all the people we know – and believe me, former Detective Inspector, that's a lot of people – we chose you. Now we're not saying what we have on our hands is definite, we don't *know* exactly what we have on our hands. That's the problem. And that's why we're here, now, at your home, appealing to your good nature and experience to help us. Whether you do or not is your business, of course it is. But I want you to remember something, and it's very important.' She paused for breath, making a point of letting Alby sweat a little more.

'We're here for *your* help, not your insults. Jason and I are perfectly capable of handling ourselves, whether you choose to believe that or not. And the only foolish thing I've done is thinking that someone like you would appreciate not been overlooked for some young whipper-snapper. So please don't insult my intelligence, or that of my son-in-law, by thinking you're some great hero we can't do without. Like I said before, we find ourselves in a predicament that I truly believe would benefit from your extensive knowledge and history within the police service, and dare I say it, someone who might have the discretion not to go to your still-serving colleagues until we have some evidence. So, I'll ask you straight, former Detective Inspector Alby. Will you help us?'

Jason was astounded. When it came to the great speech makers and orators, none of them could hold a candle to Amita Khatri when she was in the mood. Alby, it seemed, was just as flabbergasted.

'I . . . I don't know what to say,' was all he could manage.

'You can say either yes or no,' Amita twisted the knife. 'We have rather a lot to be getting on with, so a prompt answer would be appreciated. I have spent my golden years being overlooked as a pensioner, best put out to pasture, and perhaps naively, I'd thought you would like the opportunity to show people that you don't hang up your brain cells when you hang up your badge.'

She crossed her arms and stood glaring at him. Alby fumbled with the cord of his robe.

'Well . . . I . . . That is to say . . .' he mumbled.

'Speak up, man,' she snapped. 'Enunciate.'

'Yes, yes, alright then,' he said. 'Yes, I'll come with you.'

Jason wanted to leap up from the sofa and applaud. This had been a lesson from Amita, a complete and utter demonstration in leadership and taking the situation by the scruff of the neck. He didn't spring up, though. It would have ruined the moment.

'There, that wasn't so hard, was it?' she asked. 'To be civil and sensible. Thank you, Frank. We can pick you up from here around ten, if that suits.'

'Yes, yes, that's fine Mrs Khatri.' Alby swallowed a dry gulp. 'Yes, that's completely fine. Yup.'

'Thank you.'

She bowed a little before giving Jason a nod. He hopped up like a well-trained dog and they headed for the back door, Alby trailing behind.

He saw them out and they rounded the house, making for the main road that ran through the little village. As they made their way towards the car, Jason couldn't contain his excitement any longer.

'Bloody hell, Amita.' He was laughing. 'You certainly gave that old trout what for! I'm very proud of you.'

'Come on, Jason, we've got things to do,' she said, climbing in the passenger seat.

'I tell you what, though,' he said, starting the engine. 'The Sheriff of Penrith is quite a force when she gets going.'

'You know I don't like that nickname, Jason. It makes me sound like Gary Cooper.'

'Blimey,' he said, turning and starting back up the road. 'Two Gary Cooper references in one morning. We'll be hearing *Distant Drums* soon enough.'

Amita looked at him blankly.

'*Distant Drums*,' he said. 'The film. Gary Cooper's finest in my humble . . .'

'We're not here to talk about your dubious taste in cinema, Jason,' tutted Amita.

'Honestly,' he said as he climbed into his battered car. 'Some people have no taste.'

Chapter 8

DAUCUS CAROTA

There was a strange mood at dinner that evening. Even Josh and Clara, Jason and Radha's children, seemed to sense that not everything was jovial and boisterous as usual. For the most part, everyone gobbled down their sausages, mash and gravy with a calculated, respectful efficiency.

The children disappeared upstairs not long after they'd all finished. Jason had volunteered to do the washing up, the first sign in Radha's mind that all was not well. She had retired to the sofa, pretending to watch the early evening news, but instead keeping a close eye on her mother. Amita sat as if in a trance, staring blankly at the television screen. The only move she made was to check her phone or the clock in the kitchen. Radha had bitten her tongue long enough. She decided to put her concerns and theories to the test.

'Honestly, it was a madhouse at the office today,' she began.

Amita didn't acknowledge her. Jason was still in the relative safety of the kitchen, clanking away with the pots, pans and seemingly doing his best to break the new plates she'd bought.

'Yeah, I mean, for a lawyers' office, you don't ever really expect to see a strippergram in reception. Not these days anyway,' she said, still watching her mother closely. 'I thought in this new enlightened age, that sort of thing had been done away with. Funny, I always imagine there's a long line of handsome young men with spray tans, tight abs and rock-hard backsides queuing outside a Job Centre somewhere, now the industry is shot.'

Still no reaction from Amita.

'And what's more, old Dolly who does our accounts, she was understandably affronted when this stud hopped up onto her desk and began to gyrate to the beat,' Radha went on. 'I thought she was going to swallow her molars with the shock.'

The first sign of life from Amita was conclusive proof to Radha that her mother was preoccupied with something other than the usual Westminster machinations filling the news.

'Sounds nice, love,' she said, still staring at the television.

'What's nice?' asked Jason.

He sank down on the sofa beside Radha, dish towel thrown over his shoulder.

'Oh, nothing,' she said. 'I was just telling Mum about the strippergram we had in the office this afternoon. He was gorgeous. Chiselled jaw, shoulders that stretched from here to Land's End, and a full head of luscious locks that would put Samson to shame.'

'Ah,' said Jason, now locked on the television, too.

'And I was saying to Mum, that Dolly from accounts almost had a coronary when he mounted her desk and began to dance to the sound of Right Said Fred's *I'm Too Sexy*. You remember that song, don't you Jason?'

'Mmm-hmm,' he nodded. 'Great.'

That was the final straw. Radha threw her arms up in the air. It still wasn't enough to snap her husband and mother out of their trance. She decided to take drastic action. Fetching the remote, she turned off the television.

No sooner had the screen gone blank than Amita and Jason seemed to reawaken.

'Oi!' he protested.

'I was watching that, Radha,' Amita joined the furore.

'You absolutely were *not* watching *anything*! Either of you!' said Radha. 'And more importantly, I'm not turning the bloomin' thing back on until you tell me what's got you both in such a funk.'

'I don't know what a "funk" is,' said Amita.

'It's when you can't stop yourself from dancing, Amita,' said Jason.

'What?'

'Jason, stop it.' Radha threatened him with a cushion.

'Sorry,' he smirked. 'Couldn't resist.'

'I'm struggling to resist the temptation to make you sleep on this couch tonight. How does that sound?'

'Not very appealing.'

'Then you better start talking, Brazel. I'll get nothing out of the Sheriff over there, so there's no point in even trying.'

Amita sat up a little straighter after that jibe. Importantly, she didn't argue. Radha was right. She frequently was. Her mother's daughter, as Jason liked to say.

'Alright,' he said, sighing. 'Firstly, I'd like to apologise if we seem a little distracted this evening. It's nothing you've done, believe me.'

'If there's a first part, usually there's a second, too.' Radha cocked her eyebrow.

'Yes,' he said. 'Secondly, it's all your mother's fault, so I'm going to let her explain.'

He sat back and crossed his arms. Amita was seething. She had a select few looks that she reserved for Jason when he was misbehaving. They were *all* being rolled out now.

'Thank you for that introduction, Jason,' she said through gritted teeth. 'Very selfless of you.'

'Would one of you, either of you, just get on with it please,' said Radha. 'I'm not getting any younger or more patient here.'

'Yes, of course,' Amita cleared her throat. 'I won't lie to you, Radha. We're not in good spirits for a number of reasons. Chiefly amongst them, in about four hours' time we're going to meet a potential murderer in the car park of Lowther Castle.'

After that bombshell she remained silent, awaiting judgement. Radha was confused. She looked between her mother and then to Jason.

'That's it then?' she asked. 'That's all I'm getting?'

'That's all there is,' he shrugged.

'You're going to meet a potential murderer, at eleven o'clock at night, in a car park, out of hours at a tourist attraction, in the middle of nowhere.'

'That's correct, yes,' said Amita.

'And you don't think that warrants some sort of further explanation?' she asked. 'I mean, am I just supposed to sit here and assume you both know what you're doing.'

'Don't look at me, I'm not the brains behind this operation,' said Jason. 'I'm just as flummoxed as you are and I'm part of the bloody scheme.'

'Mum?' Amita turned to her mother. 'Nothing else to say?'

'Nothing other than we'll be picking up former Detective inspector Frank Alby on the way.'

'Alby?!'

That name was enough to lift Radha off the sofa.

'Alby?! That nincompoop who thought Jason was a thief?'

'That's him,' Amita nodded solemnly. 'He's very generously agreed to accompany us should there be any nastiness.'

'Nastiness?'

'There hopefully won't be any time for that sort of thing,' she added.

'Although what use Frank Alby is in a scrap is quite beyond me,' Jason said.

'We've been through this before, Jason. Frank is an experienced policeman and . . .'

'Yes, yes, I know, I know. He can help with judgement and what to do next. I got that memo.'

'I don't believe I'm hearing this,' said Radha. 'I think I've had a bonk on the head, and this is all a bad dream cooked up by my imagination. I'm going to wake up in a minute in the office, Dolly holding a damp cloth on my forehead, still humming Right Said Fred.'

Jason felt guilty. It did sound preposterous when you said it out loud. While most of their investigations wouldn't win any prizes for health and safety, he had to admit this one sounded even more inadvisable than most.

'Look, I'm sure it's not going to be anything serious or dangerous,' he said, trying to bring some sense back into the room. 'Your mother has been getting some odd messages on her new phone and we're just making sure there's nothing sinister going on, that's all.'

'Iffy? How iffy?' asked Radha.

'Oh, nothing really *that* bad,' said Amita. 'Just things about somebody called Fran and what's happened to their body.'

'That's all, is it?'

'Yes.'

Radha looked at them both in disbelief. While either could have come under fire from her frustrations, she decided that Jason was the best target.

'And you're alright with this?' she asked.

'I'm alright with the idea of it,' he said.

'Whatever happened to Mr Sceptical? Where's the man I know and love who will argue black is white if given half the chance. More so if it involves my mother?'

'I tried,' he shrugged. 'But she has her heart set on this. And you and I both know that without her weather eye, there would be criminals still free to walk the streets of Cumbria who are now doing time thanks to her. What do you want me to do?'

'I'd appreciate it if you didn't speak like I wasn't in the room,' said Amita. 'I'm right here, you know.'

Radha furrowed her forehead.

'I've heard some corkers from you two over the years, but this one takes the biscuit,' she said. 'You're telling me that you're going to collect a retired detective, one who hates the sight of both of you and from memory seems to be handier with a pack of pork scratchings than with his fists, to then go and meet goodness knows who in the car park of an old castle.'

'In the dead of night,' said Jason for good measure.

'Yes, sorry. How forgetful of me, in the dead of night,' Radha went on. 'And you expect me to be alright with this?'

'I don't think we expected you to be anything other than incredibly concerned,' said Amita. 'Which is why we didn't want to worry you with it. I can see that from some angles, it does seem slightly bonkers.'

'Bonkers!' Radha let out half a laugh. 'Bonkers! You're bloody right, it sounds bonkers. Mum, have you lost all leave of your senses? This is madness, complete and utter madness. You've got no idea what you're walking into.'

Jason was beginning to regret being so blasé about the whole thing. While he and Amita had been running around Cumbria trying to catch villains, Radha had often remained the sober voice of reason throughout. He liked to think of himself as the sensible one out of the pair. But even he could get caught up in the excitement and danger of a live case from time to time. That was the problem – despite the difference in age, interests and style, he had to admit they both loved a mystery.

'Radha, please,' said Amita. 'Don't worry about us. We'll be fine. It's not like we're going alone. There will be three of us there.'

'What if whoever is on the end of your phone brings thirty people? What will you do then?' she asked back. 'And another thing, have you let the police know about this?'

'I suggested it,' said Jason. 'But as your mother very rightly pointed out, she got her new phone from Malcolm Brunger and a) she doesn't want to advertise that fact and b) we've got in enough trouble for wasting police time in the past, so until we've got some evidence, we thought a bit of fact-finding might be wise.'

'Oh Mum,' Radha sighed.

'I know, I know,' said Amita. 'I've brought this all on my own head by going to Brunger for a phone. It's the last time I'll be so stupid.'

'Can I have that in writing,' snipped Jason. 'The next time he's down at bingo offering cut-price electric blankets, I know you'll be first in the queue.'

'Jason!' Both Amita and Radha hushed him down.

He kept quiet. As did Amita. Their actions and words had gotten them into enough trouble as it was. And they hadn't even left the house yet. Radha shook her head, arguing with herself.

'You know what, fine.' She clapped her hands. 'Neither of you has shown any willingness to even consider what you're going to do tonight as being the wrong thing. Let alone decide against going through with it altogether. So, on your heads be it. You're both adults. You're both old enough and ugly enough to make your own mistakes.'

'Which is which?' asked Jason.

'What?'

'Who's old and who's ugly?'

'Jason,' Amita hissed.

Radha let a wry smile tug at her cheeks. Jason knew that smile. It was the one that let him know that he was skating on very, very thin ice. So thin that he could see the freezing cold water flowing beneath his feet.

'Don't push my buttons, Jason,' she said, heading for the door. 'Don't even *think* about it.'

She pulled the living room door open as hard as she could. Amita went to go after her, but she wasn't quick enough. Radha slammed the door behind her forcefully enough to shake the big light in its fixture above them.

'Well,' said Jason, fetching the television remote. 'That went about as well as could be expected.'

'Well? She's furious with us, both of us,' said Amita.

'I was being sarcastic, Amita,' he said. 'It's probably just as well that we're going out later. I think I will be sleeping on the sofa when we get home. Assuming we make it home.'

The clock on the wall seemed to be running slow. There were still hours to go. Plenty of time for Amita to wrestle with her conscience. She knew that they were running a terrible risk. It wasn't hard to see that. But it was the only way they were going to get answers, real answers, before the authorities took over.

Chapter 9

PRUNUS LAUROCERASUS

The car park of Lowther Castle was dark and louring. Anywhere could look sinister at night, but the grand ruin of Lowther, with its abandoned turrets and crenelations, felt uncomfortably like a reminder of how the mighty could fall. The thick forest surrounding the car park seemed to loom in around their car. Even the night sky felt like it was somehow both too far and yet oppressively too near.

Amita, Jason and Frank Alby had been sitting for forty minutes, staring at that blackness. The dark skies of Cumbria let a swathe of stars shine down on them that made the blackness around them all the deeper. The radio was firmly off, as was the engine and the headlights. The silence had occasionally been broken by a cough or a clearing of a tickly throat. Amita had made tea and brought it in an old Thermos flask, the tartan pattern almost completely worn off. Jason had declined every offer. He always thought it tasted like plastic out of that thing.

Alby had opened a packet of crisps in the back seat not long after they'd parked up and hadn't offered any to Jason. Not that he would have taken any – he loathed salt and vinegar.

The digital clock on the dashboard was slowly moving towards eleven o'clock. And the closer those little numbers climbed, the more nervous Amita was starting to feel.

'Have you ever been to Lowther Castle?' asked Jason.

His voice sounded strangely out of place here. Amita shifted a little uncomfortably in her seat in the front. '*And silent years unharming shall go by . . .*'

'What are you on about, Amita?' Jason asked.

'It's a famous poem about this place. Don't you know anything? We got a coach trip here when they were doing a pensioner's special. Heard all the history. You must have been here. Didn't you take the children one summer?' she asked him.

'I think so,' he replied. 'Although I can't be sure. All of these old estates begin to merge into one after a while. A walk around the gardens, an overly expensive ice cream and then off home. Tale as old as time.'

'Really, Jason?' she said.

'What?' he asked.

'A little bit of appreciation of your local history wouldn't go amiss. You never know what you might find out.'

'Is that why,' he turned to look at her, 'you're always incredibly enthusiastic when we're going on these family days out.'

'Well, partly that, and partly the fact that I'm usually in line for a cream tea and a sit down while you and Radha watch the kids run around. There's no crime against that, is there?'

'Oh my god. Would you both just shut your cakeholes for five minutes?' snapped Alby in the back.

Jason looked at him in the rearview mirror. He was massaging his temples.

'Being stuck in this tin can with you two is like having my head forced into a washing machine on full spin. Around and around and around. Just drop it, would you?'

Jason drummed his fingers on the steering wheel and left Alby to his misery. Another painfully slow five minutes went by. The boredom was starting to take its toll. He couldn't sit still, and everything was distracting him. From the speck of dirt on his nearside window to the collection of sweet wrappers in the ashtray beside the gear stick. He decided to try a different tactic.

'Have either of you ever worked in retail?' he asked.

Amita and Alby were stunned into silence.

'No?' he asked them again.

'What?' asked the former policeman.

'Retail? You know, selling things. Working in a shop?'

'You know I haven't, Jason,' said Amita.

'I joined the force when I was sixteen, Brazel,' said Alby. 'Man and boy in front of the mast.'

'I did, very briefly,' said Jason. 'When I first moved to Manchester and needed the cash at uni. I got a job in a gentleman's outfitters, Dawson's Wardrobe it was called, tucked away in Saint Ann's Place. It was very swanky actually. Lord knows why they ever gave me the gig.'

'I didn't know that,' said Amita. 'How long did you do that for?'

'Oh, let me see.' He counted the fingers on his right hand. 'About five and a half hours. Plus lunch.'

'Five hours?' Alby blurted. 'Five hours? That's not work, Brazel! There'll be customers who spent more time in that shop than you did.'

'Funny story actually,' said Jason. 'I'd been shown the ropes, given my own tape measure and everything, then turned loose on my first customer. He wanted to return a jacket that needed mending. He'd torn it, you see. Do you see where this is going?'

'Give me strength,' Alby groaned.

'I thought I'd try and lighten the situation a little with a joke,' he went on. 'So, I said to him, "I think we can fix this, sew its seams? Sew its seams, get it?" Well, it turned out that my injection of humour rubbed this customer up the completely wrong way. I was taken aside by the manager not long after the man left. Apparently, he was a regular and was incredibly sensitive about the tendency of his prodigious girth to wear out his suits. I was dismissed there and then, on the spot, for insubordination. I even had to give back my tape measure.' He looked at Amita and Alby for a reaction. None was forthcoming.

'Is that it?' she asked.

'That's it,' he replied.

'Give me strength,' said Alby, puffing out his cheeks. 'Remind me again why I agreed to come along with you two? Let me give you amateurs a little advice,' said the ex-cop. 'When you're staking out a crime scene, you don't have to fill every moment with aimless chitchat.'

Jason took offence to that.

'My story wasn't aimless,' he said. 'I was about to say . . .'

'Stakeouts are meant to be boring,' said Alby. 'Contrary to what most people think, most police work is.'

Alby leaned forward. Jason could smell his cheap cologne and a whiff of salt and vinegar on his breath. He resisted cracking the window.

'Observation and patience, that's what my first sergeant told me when I started,' said Alby. 'The bloody telly and people like you, Brazel, you're to blame for the dropouts of new recruits all over the country.'

'Go on,' he said.

'You read in the papers and magazines that police investigations are glamorous, high-octane affairs, but they aren't,' said Alby. 'The best detectives are the ones who keep their cool and hold a level head. Not like on the telly and at the pictures, all bang-bang, kicking down doors and fighting with crooks. Good police, great police, are grinders. They keep going and going and never stop until they get their man.'

'Or woman,' said Amita.

'Or woman,' he agreed.

'Let me guess, you were a grinder, Alby. Is that right?' asked Jason.

'Naturally.' Alby's moustache bristled. 'I was one of the best. More nicks than you've had hot dinners, and that's not an exaggeration, Brazel. You can trust me on that one. And you know why? Because I had the temperament, the foresight, to know that I wasn't going to make a big splash right away. No, instead I stuck to my guns, trusted my instincts and went about my business as a policeman with a ruthless, dogged determination. Shoe leather and late nights solve more crimes than raids and car chases. Kids these days, they see shows like *Line of Duty* and . . . What's that other one? The something?'

'*The Locus*,' said Amita.

She threw a quick glance at Jason who met her eye. Then Alby moved on.

'Aye, that's it,' he said. 'It's all smoke and mirrors, all trussed up for the cameras. You can't tell me that bit of skirt who replaced me as Detective Inspector is going about knocking down doors and running over bad guys day in and day out. No, she's behind the desk, up to her earrings in paperwork, as we all are on the frontline.'

Jason didn't know where to begin.

'Firstly, her name is Sally Arendonk,' he said. 'And she's a detective inspector, not a "bit of skirt". Secondly, she'd probably knock your teeth out if she heard you calling her that. Thirdly, she's a very good police officer.'

'She is, Frank. I can't argue with that,' Amita nodded.

'Whatever.' He sat back. 'Don't forget, you two came to me for advice. I'm only here because *you* wanted *me*. If she's such a good copper, how come she's not sitting here, covered in crisp crumbs, watching outtakes from *Are You Being Served?*'

Jason was going to explain, but a flash of light distracted them all. Two headlights appeared through the gloom, broken by a row of trees.

Everyone sat up a little stiffer as they watched a car make its way through the woods and pull into the car park.

'Here we go,' said Alby, checking his watch. 'They're early.'

'What does that mean?' asked Jason, his throat suddenly dry.

'Could mean anything,' replied the former detective inspector. 'That they're keen.'

'Or they want this all done and dusted quickly,' whispered Amita. 'Whatever *this* is.'

They watched in silence as the headlights from the car passed over them. The other motor slowed right down, making sure it was as far away from them as possible. Jason tightened his grip on the wheel. He was suddenly very aware of the fact that the exit of the car park was beyond the other vehicle. If they were going to make a quick break for it, they'd have to go past their visitor first.

'What do we do?' asked Amita.

'Nothing,' said Alby, leaning forward, beady little eyes watching like a hawk. 'We let them make the first move. See how many of them there are, see what we're dealing with.'

'What if we don't like what we're dealing with?' asked Jason.

'Then you put your foot down and get us out of here sharpish, Brazel. Got that?'

He nodded. He did get it. He got it all too clearly. They all sat staring out at the other car. It had parked up close to the entrance of the castle car park. Their headlights were still on, engine running. For a brief, tense moment, nobody did anything. A silent, still, empty stand-off between the two vehicles. Then the other driver flashed their car headlights once, twice, three times. Jason and Amita both turned to Alby in unison. The former detective inspector was thinking.

'Give it a minute,' he said.

'Give it a minute for what?' asked Jason.

'Let them think.'

'Think about what?'

'They could be sitting in their car asking the same questions as us,' said Amita. 'Maybe they're waiting to see if I've turned up alone or . . .'

'Or brought a posse.'

Amita let the Sheriff of Penrith jibe slide this time. They all stared out at the other vehicle. The headlights flashed again three times.

'Alright,' said Alby. 'Amita, have you got your phone there? Send them a message. Let's test them.'

'Test them? Is that a good idea?' asked Jason.

'What's the matter, Brazel? Lost your bottle? Text them, Amita. Let's make sure that it's them over there in that car and not some bloody randomers. I'm not going to speculate on what else people might be doing in a car park in the dead of night.'

Amita grimaced but did as she was told. She opened up the message thread and waited for instructions.

'Ask them to get out of their car,' said Alby. 'Tell them to go first and then we'll join them.'

'What if they don't take the bait?' she asked.

'Let's deal with that when we come to it. Come on, get typing.'

Amita sent the message. A few seconds later, there was an ABBA-heralded reply.

'Okay, it says . . .'

They all looked at the car opposite. The headlights went out and then the driver's side door opened. A head appeared, hooded, face obscured by the darkness. Even straining, none of them could make out any details. The person held their hands up and walked around the front of their car. They stood there, arms in the air, waiting.

'Just one of them,' whispered Jason.

'That we can see,' said Alby. 'There could be another three stowed in their motor and they're waiting for us to show our hand.'

'Well, we have to do something,' said Amita. 'They know we're here.'

'You two go,' said Alby. 'I'll wait here and if there's any bother, I'll come and help.'

'Cumbria's finest, indeed,' Jason rolled his eyes.

They climbed out of the car, slowly. Jason headed around to be beside his mother-in-law and they stood there, looking at the person across the car park.

'What do we do now?' whispered Jason.

'I suppose we do what we always do with strangers,' she said. 'We introduce ourselves.'

Amita took a step forward. The figure at the car across from them didn't budge. She held up her own hands and tried to appear as unthreatening as possible.

'Hello there!' she shouted. 'Nice to meet you. I'm Amita Khatri, you've been messaging me on my new phone.'

Jason was sure that if this was some sinister situation, it was possibly the worst and fluffiest introduction they could have made. They'd shown all their cards and sounded more like they were saying hello at a bring-and-buy sale rather than interrogating a potential gangland kingpin. He remained close beside his mother-in-law and hoped that Alby hadn't dozed off in the car.

'Where's Fran?' came a woman's voice. 'What have you done with him?'

'Him?' asked Jason.

'We don't know who Fran is,' said Amita. 'And we certainly don't know where he is. More to the point, who are you?'

The woman stood perfectly still for a moment. She pulled the hood of her coat down, revealing her face for the first time. She was crying, her shoulders bobbing up and down as a flood of emotion engulfed her. She fell backwards against her car and slumped down to her knees, sobbing uncontrollably.

Amita was off like a shot, too quick for Jason to protest. She ran across the car park and helped the stranger up, holding her close to her chest.

'Jason!' she shouted over to him. 'Fetch some of that tea in the flask. This woman is distraught.'

Jason went into autopilot mode. When that happened, he followed orders blindly. Turning back to his car, he was met with Alby's bloated face scowling at him.

'What the hell is going on?' snarled the former policeman.

'Tea,' he said. 'The woman's distraught.'

'What is this? Afternoon tea at The Ritz?'

Jason ignored him. He was getting quite used to doing that. And he loved every minute.

Chapter 10

URTICA FEROX

Amita knew the tea was awful. She regretted not packing more drinks and snacks for the stakeout. She'd be on to the emergency Murray Mints in her handbag at this rate.

The woman who had met them was sitting in the back of Jason's car with Amita comforting her. The doors were open, and Alby was standing guard, more in name's sake than anything. He claimed to just be having a cigarette, but Amita knew better. Once a sentry, always a sentry. Jason was in the driver's seat in front of them. He was drumming his fingers on the steering wheel in that nervy, jittery way he always did when he was on edge. She would have to let him be nervous. There was a more pressing issue. Namely the mysterious woman beside her.

'Would you like some more tea?' she asked, feeling more than a pang of guilt.

'No, thank you,' said the woman.

Amita couldn't place her accent. It wasn't local, certainly not from Cumbria. There were little hints of Geordie in there. Although it could have been Scottish, too.

'Are you feeling any better?' she asked her.

'Not really,' the woman sniffed. 'It's been a bit of a nightmare these past few days. Not knowing what's going on. I think the weight of everything, the emotion, it just got to me. I'm sorry.'

'You don't have anything to be sorry about,' said Amita. 'We're here to help, if that's what you'd like.'

The woman choked back more tears. She handed the flask cup back to Amita.

'I really should be going, I'm sorry for wasting your time like this,' she said, reaching for the door. 'This was a terrible, terrible idea. I've made a mistake. I'm sorry.'

'You don't have to be sorry, not with us,' said Amita, trying to calm her down. 'We've got no ill intent, believe me, we just wanted to find out what was going on.'

The woman hesitated at the door. Alby was lurking about somewhere outside. Amita could smell the tobacco drifting into the car. She was tempted to ask him for one but knew she never could. Not in front of Jason, anyway.

'Please, just sit for a minute. You're in no state to go driving on these country roads at this time of night, anyway,' she said. 'Please, tell us why you're so upset. A problem shared and all that.'

The woman stared at her, glassy-eyed. She settled back into her seat. Her hands were shaking, and she held them, trying to stop. She sniffed again.

'Thank you,' she said.

'What for?' asked Amita.

'I don't know,' she shrugged. 'Just thank you. Thank you for being here. Thank you for not being some nutter who's killed my husband. Just thank you, I guess.'

Amita squeezed the woman's shoulder.

'You know, my son-in-law and I have some history when it comes to missing people,' she said. 'Maybe we could help you?'

'Oh no, I couldn't ask that of you,' she said. 'No, no, no. This is much too dangerous and complicated. I don't even know you.'

'Well, let's put that to bed immediately,' she offered a hand. 'My name is Amita Khatri, and this is Jason Brazel. Like I said, he's my son-in-law.'

'How do you do . . .?' said Jason, twisting around in his seat.

'Delice,' said the woman, taking Amita's hand. 'Delice Weaver.'

'Please to meet you, Delice,' she said. 'And the man smoking like a chimney outside is Frank Alby, he's a retired detective.'

'A policeman?'

There was a sudden nervousness in her voice.

'Yes,' said Amita. 'You'll have to forgive us, we weren't exactly sure what we were walking into tonight. Don't read anything into it, Delice. We were just being sensible. But it sounds to me like you might need to speak to the police at some point if your husband's missing.'

'Right.' Delice sounded unconvinced as she looked about trying to find Alby, but he had wandered off across the car park, only visible in the dark by the glowing ember of his cigarette.

'Do you mind telling us what's happened to your husband?' asked Amita. 'We're very discreet and we never like to see anybody come to harm. Isn't that right, Jason?'

'You could say that,' he said realising this wasn't the moment to share their tendency to stumble across bodies.

'Jason is a journalist, Delice. You'll have to forgive him if he sometimes sounds a bit glib or asks one question too many. But he's got a great nose for a story. He's had more scoops than an ice-cream shop.'

Jason was surprised at Amita saying something nice about him in public. But Delice didn't seem to get the joke. She looked too frightened, too vulnerable for humour right now.

'Fran, that's my husband, he's been missing for two weeks now. I haven't had sight nor sound of him,' she said. 'He just got up one morning to go to work, kissed me on my forehead and left. It's not like him, not like him at all, Amita. I think something terrible has happened to him and . . . And I . . .'

She was struggling to catch her breath. Amita tried to calm her down, rubbing her back through her thick coat.

'It's alright my dear, it's okay,' she said. 'Just take deep, long breaths in through your nose and out through your mouth. When you're ready, tell us everything you can.'

Delice nodded slowly. Amita kept rubbing her back. How many times had she been in this position, comforting someone in great distress. Whether it was down to motherly instincts or a need for the truth, she couldn't ever be sure. But lately she'd been called upon like this more and more. And every time it had been important.

'My husband, Fran, he wouldn't hurt a fly,' she said. 'This is so unusual, so strange. He's never done anything like this before in all the years I've known him.'

'What does he do?' asked Jason from the front.

'He's a researcher, a university fellow,' she said.

'I see.'

'Is that important?'

'It could be,' he said. 'If you'd told me he was a rock star or a professional footballer – you know, a party animal – I might have been a little less concerned that he's been gone for so long.'

'Jason!' Amita snapped. 'What kind of thing is that to say?'

'I'm just pointing out that university fellows and researchers aren't usually wild playboys, are they? When was the last time you read of boffins falling out of nightclubs at three in the morning in the tabloids or scandal columns?'

'I'm sorry, Delice,' she said. 'I told you, he's a journalist. They don't think like normal people.'

'Oi,' he protested.

'It's alright,' said Delice. 'I understand what you're saying. Fran is a good, honest man who loves his work. He would never do something like this on a whim. I think something's happened to him. I think somebody has done something to him, something awful.'

'Why?' asked Amita.

'Pardon?' Delice said through more tears.

'Why do you think something's happened to him?' she asked. 'Why don't you think it's a midlife crisis and he's just vanished or, pardon my insensitivity, he's left you.'

Denice shook her head furiously. 'He'd never leave me. We've been married for twenty years, Amita!' she said. 'He's not the type. Believe me, he's not. We're as much in love as we were when we first met. If something like that was wrong, he would have told me. We would have talked about it. That's why, I think . . . I think he might have been hurt.'

Amita glanced over at Jason. He shot her back a look of equal concern.

'Could he have had an accident?' Jason ventured. 'I don't mean to trouble you, but there's a reason the local Mountain Search and Rescue is kept busy round here.'

Delice shook her head. 'He wasn't a hiker. And he wasn't a risk taker. He was too careful a man, too precise . . .' She trailed off as the tears welled in her eyes again.

'Delice, please,' she said. 'If you think he's come to harm then you must have an idea of who has hurt Fran.'

Delice nodded.

'You can tell us, Delice,' said Jason. 'We can help.'

'It's a long story,' she said. 'You don't want to know the ins and outs right now. But I think Fran's business partner is involved.'

'Business partner?' he asked. 'I thought he was an academic.'

'He is,' she said. 'This is something he's worked on for years on the side, a little pet project.'

'What is it?' asked Amita.

'I don't know all the details,' she said. 'It's all over my head, all the technicalities of the work he does at the uni. He's Professor of Computer Engineering, even saying that aloud confuses me. Something to do with security systems, state-of-the art imaging that can help banks and private business, something like that.'

'Tech?' asked Jason.

'Yes,' said Delice. 'Fran is an IT engineer. Or he was, when he first graduated. He got into the tech boom at the right time. He's always loved technology, all the little bits and bobs that go into how things work. When we first met, he was forever taking things apart, radios, televisions, you name it. His old flat was awash with circuit boards and wires. I used to joke with him that if he ever got a cleaner, she'd think he was building a Terminator.'

She laughed, but the happiness quickly evaporated. She rubbed her forehead. 'I just miss him so much,' she said. 'I've been lost these few weeks without him. He's my soulmate.'

'You're very brave,' said Amita. 'Tell us though, Delice, who is his business partner?'

Delice composed herself.

'Grahame Sutcliffe,' she said. A darkness came over her at the mention of his name. Anger sparked in her eyes like a naked flame. 'He's bad news, always has been,' she said. 'He's a nothing more than a mouthpiece, a con man. Fran knew him from his undergraduate days, and he's bounced around jobs his whole life. Failed company after failed company, up to his ears in debt. You know the type, I'm sure.'

'Oh yes,' said Jason. 'Rogue traders, eh?' It was his turn to give Amita a dirty look. She ignored him as usual.

'Why would he harm Fran if they're partners?' asked Amita.

'I have no idea,' said Delice. 'I've got no proof, nothing. That number, your number, I thought that was Sutcliffe. I mean, it *was* Sutcliffe until about two weeks ago, since before I started texting you.'

'Why did you think he'd killed Fran?' asked Jason.

'I . . . I wasn't thinking straight,' she said. 'I can't think at all, I'm sick with worry. I just . . . I just thought that if something had happened to Fran then Sutcliffe would be involved somehow. And if I could catch him out, get him to tell me what had happened, I thought I might find out where Fran is and this whole nightmare would come to an end. Fran wouldn't leave me, he just wouldn't . . .'

Her voice cracked and she sunk her face into her hands. Amita knew then that no amount of back rubbing and consoling was going to help. Delice was a broken woman, devastated, wrapped up in something that definitely appeared nefarious.

'It's okay,' she said, hugging Delice. 'It's going to be okay.'

Jason looked concerned. Amita silently nodded her head a little, just enough to tell him to call off his dogs. For the time being anyway. They all sat like that for a moment until Frank Alby rapped his knuckles on the bonnet.

'It's after midnight,' he said, sticking his head through the open passenger door. 'If you want me any longer, it'll cost you.'

'Frank, please,' said Amita. 'Can you give us a minute. This lady has been put through the wringer. She doesn't need your crassness just now, okay?'

Alby took a step back, muttering something unsavoury under his breath. Delice took a deep breath. She wiped her face.

'I'm okay, honestly, I am,' she said. 'Now I've told someone. I think I just need to sleep. I haven't had a wink for weeks, not knowing what's been happening.'

'You should go to the police,' said Jason. 'Missing persons and all that.'

'Persons?' asked Amita.

'Fran and this Sutcliffe character,' he said. 'If you've got Sutcliffe's number then he's clearly not paying his bills, or has changed phones, or something has happened to him, too. And Fran is gone, that's two people who are unaccounted for.'

'I don't know,' said Delice. 'Maybe I'm wrong. Maybe Fran *has* left me. Maybe I'm just clinging onto hope that it's not as obvious as that. We've been together a long time. I don't *want* to think he's run off with somebody else. That's why I couldn't face telling the police until I'd heard back from Sutcliffe. I couldn't bear them telling me he'd run off with someone else.'

'Now isn't the time for worrying about that,' said Amita. 'I think you need some rest and recuperation. If you like, Jason and I can look into this for you, do a little digging around. We have some very good connections around these parts.'

'Nothing gets past us,' he said. 'Well, Amita anyway. I'm just the eye candy.'

Delice laughed a little. Jason was happy to be the brief moment of respite for her.

'I don't know,' she said. 'I probably should just go to the police. They could probably sort it all out in a jiffy. It's what they do.'

'It is,' said Amita. 'We know a very good detective inspector.'

'It's not that man out there, is it?' she asked.

'I heard that!' Alby shouted back.

'No, it's not,' said Amita. 'Why don't you sleep on it and let me know how you want to proceed in the morning. You've got my number, obviously. The police should really be informed if there are missing people. It's best to keep things official. Jason and I, however, we don't have to deal with all the red tape that detectives are burdened by. We can ask about, keep our ears to the ground. Like he said, we know everyone, more or less. But I want you to know, Delice, you're absolutely not alone in any of this. We're here to help, happy to in fact, if that's what you want.'

Delice brightened a little. She gently eased herself out of the car, Amita following her.

'Are you okay to drive?' she asked.

'Yes, I'll be fine,' she replied. 'We live . . . I live in Kendal, so it's not far. Thank you, Amita.'

'For what? We haven't done anything. Not yet.'

'You've been here for me, tonight,' she said. 'I've felt so alone, so isolated these past few weeks. I keep catching myself looking at the front door waiting for it to open and Fran to walk in. It doesn't happen and I cry and cry into the night. Then the next thing I know it's a new day and more pain, agony even, of not knowing what's happened. You're the first person I've told, and you didn't dismiss me, you showed real heart. And to think, I came here tonight worrying you were Sutcliffe, and you were going to kill me or something.'

'I may be many things,' she said. 'But I'm not a murderer. And don't mind Jason, he has his funny ways but he's a good sort at heart.'

'Hey, I can hear you, you know,' he called from the car.

'Anything you need, just let us know,' Amita squeezed Delice's hand.

Delice walked slowly over to her car, head bowed. She climbed in and drove away, Alby watching her go. When she was clear of the car park, he sauntered around to beside Amita, Jason leaning out of the driver's window.

'Strange one that,' he said. 'Something not right there.'

'You think?' asked Jason sarcastically.

'She's heartbroken,' said Amita. 'And she's not thinking straight, she said that herself. But I'm inclined to agree with you, Frank. There's something not quite adding up with all of this. Who doesn't tell anyone about a vanished partner for weeks – unless you think they've traded you in for a younger model? And who starts bandying around accusations of murder by text message?'

'So, what do we do?' Jason asked.

'Nothing, until she says she wants our help,' said Amita. 'We can't go about poking our noses into other people's business uninvited. You're always telling me that, Jason.'

'And you've listened to that advice how many times now?'

'Give me strength,' Alby groaned.

He climbed into the back of the car and slammed the door. Amita lingered a moment longer, thinking. She was always thinking. And this was going to take all the thinking she could muster if she was going to get to the bottom of Fran Weaver's disappearance. But first there was the pressing problem of Frank Alby.

'Come on, get a move on, Amita!' he shouted from inside the car. 'It's long past my bedtime and I've got my mindfulness class in the morning.'

Amita rolled her eyes. How times had changed.

Chapter 11

COFFEINUM

Amita could practically feel the bags under her eyes. She wasn't sure of the exact medical explanation for this, or even if it was a real thing, but she could definitely feel them. She was always like this when she didn't get any sleep. She also knew that the fogginess wouldn't go until close to bedtime the following day. So, she was stuck feeling like a half-shut knife until further notice.

By the time they had dropped off Alby and returned home, it was close to three in the morning. Jason had gone straight to bed, but Amita was in no mood for sleeping. How she regretted that now. Instead, she had gone back on her word to Jason and spent the wee small hours looking up all she could on Fran Weaver and Grahame Sutcliffe.

Now, this morning, the trusty old chalkboard that she used to help her think things through was wheeled in from the kitchen. Its case-cracking had been incredibly limited lately. So much so that it was being used as an additional clothes horse to dry socks, pants and her best sparkly shell suits. When she'd cleared off all the unmentionables and folded them neatly into a pile on the kitchen table, Amita began to scribble down names, places and the other details she'd managed to glean from the internet overnight.

She had scoured social media and news reports, but there was precious little out there. That was always a red flag in her book. In the modern world, everyone is, rightly or wrongly, overexposed and easily found. If someone with as much curiosity and tenacity as her could find little trace of two men in the prime of their lives, there was something amiss.

What she had been able to unearth was their company name – Clymtech. Delice Weaver had painted the firm as some exciting startup, but again there was little to show for it online beyond a holding page website. Amita had found it registered with Companies House, with Fran Weaver and Grahame Sutcliffe both listed as directors. Beyond that, there was next to nothing. No big announcement, no fancy social media, no industry press talking about the firm, nothing.

Amita's headache had grown so bad that she had to retire to bed. She had crept back upstairs and tried to go to sleep, but to no avail. Before she could let sleep claim her, the children were running wild outside her door, wanting in to sing her a song. She duly obliged even though she was feeling like death warmed up.

Now here she was, listening to Georgie Littlejohn drone on and on about something at the weekly W.I. coffee and catch-up. An occasional nod and smile in her general direction was enough for Amita to at least appear interested. Georgie was the kind of person who needed a target rather than an active participant when it came to conversation.

'And so, I said to the bus driver, it's very kind of you to think I'm not a pensioner, but I get my bus fares for free as I've got a pass,' said Georgie. 'Isn't that right, Amita?'

The sound of her own name set alarm bells ringing in Amita's head. She sat up a little straighter and looked at Georgie holding court.

'What's that?' she asked.

'The bus driver I was telling you about the other day there,' said Georgie, now beaming with pride. 'He thought I wasn't old enough for a bus pass and he tried to charge me for a return to Tebay.'

The newly refurbished village hall was bustling, as it always was on a Tuesday morning. The Yoga-for-Seniors crowd was just clearing out in time for the hardcore quilters, bags and bags of material, needles and thimbles bumping off their legs as they shuffled in through the main doors. Georgie couldn't have picked a worse time to corner Amita. Then again, that was her thing. She felt like even the bust of Hal Mulberry, the village hall's dear, departed benefactor, was looking to her for a response. If only she could remember what Georgie had been talking about.

'Yes, quite,' felt like a safe enough response, if slightly vague.

'Well, thank you for the support, as always, Amita,' she said with a scoff. 'I was completely embarrassed, of course, I don't mind telling you ladies that. It caused quite the scene on the bus. To think that he thought I wasn't a pensioner, let me tell you, it gives you that little boost you need. Don't worry, I won't let it go straight to my head. I mean, he said I didn't look a day over sixty.' She tittered a little. 'Right, well, I think that probably concludes our business this morning, ladies,' Georgie said with a sigh, since no one seemed to be racing to ask for her secret to eternal youth. 'Unless anyone has any other pressing matters that can't wait until next week?'

Coats were already being pulled on and lattes drained.

'Lovely. Well, have a nice week and no doubt I shall see many of you around town,' said Georgie.

Amita didn't finish her tea. She wanted to get out of the hall, back home to stand in front of her chalkboard, trying to piece together what had happened to Fran Weaver. She quickly checked her phone. There was nothing more from his wife, Delice. No message to say she'd made it home safely or that she wanted help. That was puzzling in its own right.

'Amita, could I grab you for a moment, please?' asked Georgie.

'Yes, of course,' she said.

There was an ominous tone in Georgie's voice, like she had caught Amita passing notes in class or smoking behind the bike sheds. She slowly sat down again as Georgie loomed large on the other side of the table.

'Amita,' she began.

'Yes, Georgie,' she replied.

'Can I speak candidly?'

'I don't see why not,' she said. 'In fact, I thought we always spoke to each other candidly.'

'Yes, of course.' That caught Georgie off guard. Amita smiled serenely.

Georgie began to fuss a little. She moved empty cups and plates around the table, lining them up neatly. The more she fussed, the more Amita started to suspect that something might actually be wrong.

'Georgie?' she asked. 'Is everything alright?'

Georgie looked about the room. The place was still busy with a lot of through-traffic. Some of the W.I. women were lingering close to the doors of the hall, while the quilting club had already begun. Smooth jazz played out from a radio set somebody had brought with them.

'It's a little awkward, Amita,' said Georgie quietly. 'If I tell you, you must promise me not to tell another soul.'

'Sounds serious,' she said. 'You absolutely have my full discretion, Georgie. You know that.'

'Yes, I do.'

She pulled out a chair around the table. Sitting down uncomfortably close to Amita, she gave the hall another sweep. Satisfied there were no eavesdroppers or spies, she confided in Amita.

'I have some . . . suspicions,' she said.

She sat back a little and looked at Amita for a reaction. Amita wasn't quite sure what she should say or do, so she just stared back.'

'Suspicions?' she asked, when it became clear that Georgie wasn't going to continue speaking.

She nodded. She looked around the hall again and then leaned in, closer this time. 'Yes,' she whispered. 'I think – and you can't quote me on this, remember – I think . . . And I'm not sure at all, of course. You understand that, Amita?'

'Yes, yes,' she said, wishing Georgie would get to the point.

'But I think that somebody may be pilfering money from the bingo club.'

Georgie sat up straight again. Once more, Amita wasn't quite sure what she was supposed to do.

'Stealing?' she asked. 'From the bingo club?'

'Yes,' said Georgie.

'But I . . . That is to say . . . What are you talking about, Georgie. What money?'

Now it was Georgie's turn to roll her eyes. She tugged on Amita's arm.

'The funds,' she said. 'The petty cash that we keep, for the tea and the biscuits and keeping the lights on every Wednesday night. Money, Amita. The club's money.'

'I didn't think we had any money to speak of,' she said.

'It's not a lot. Pretty paltry usually, actually,' sniffed Georgie. 'We operate on a non-profit basis by and large, but sometimes, just sometimes, we get a good few pounds that we don't have to spend yet. What with our little excursions to big games, the Christmas turkey lunch, a hefty donation to Father Ford and the church for putting us up, normally the money that comes in from the members goes straight back out again.'

'That's what I always assumed,' said Amita. 'In all my years going, I've never been privy to the finances. I thought that was always your remit, Georgie.'

She couldn't resist a little dig. Although the mere mention of a trip to a big game brought back the horrid memories of losing her phone. She shifted a little.

'It has been, Amita. That's why I'm telling you that I think there's something fishy going on.'

Amita had a bad feeling about this.

'Okay,' she said. 'I've got two questions to begin with. The first one is who? And the second is, why are you telling me?'

Georgie hesitated momentarily, which most certainly wasn't like her. In their long association, Amita couldn't think of any time when Georgie was anything but one hundred per cent confident in her own abilities. Even the abilities she didn't have.

'It's like this. I went to the bank the other day there to pay off some bills,' she said. 'You know what it's like on the high street, there are queues coming out of the doors of the banks and there are never any staff on the desks anymore. And I'll be jiggered if I'm using those computer machine things in the wall. And the less said about this online banking malarkey the better, if you ask me.'

'It's not great, is it?' Amita appeased her.

'So, I stand in the queue for about forty minutes and finally get to a counter,' she went on. 'And it takes me about another ten minutes to explain that I'm just the custodian of the bingo club account and that I need to make a payment to get our new gamebooks in before the end of the month, otherwise we'll be playing with nothing. Anyway, the young man just doesn't understand a word I'm saying. It was a dreadful mess.'

'Sounds like it.'

'We eventually get down to business and he tells me that there isn't enough cash in the account to pay the bill.'

'Okay,' said Amita. 'And I take it you weren't expecting that?'

'Certainly not!' Georgie sounded deeply offended. 'Even after the luxuries of our trip to Manchester a few weeks ago, we should still have had plenty in there to cover the costs of gamebooks. They're not *that* expensive, Amita. But we couldn't cover it.'

'How much was left in the account?'

'Pennies,' she said. 'Literal pennies. And I don't know where the money has gone.'

Amita considered this. Georgie had always kept a close guard of the club's purse strings. Of the endless board elections and nominations, she had always seemed perfectly happy being in charge of the money. And nobody had dared, or bothered, to try and wrestle that away from her.

'Georgie, I hope you don't mind me asking this,' she said at length. 'But I suppose I should ask. Are you *sure* that the funds should have been there.'

'What do you mean?'

Amita was trying her best to be diplomatic. 'It's just, well, you've been looking after the money for the club for as long as I can remember,' she said. 'If anything goes in and out, I imagine it goes through you. If there isn't anything left, do you think it might be, you know, a slight miscalculation on your part.'

'A mistake? By me?'

Georgie's decorum had vanished. Amita suspected something like this might happen, but she had to ask anyway.

'Certainly not!' Georgie protested, her voice echoing off the vaulted roof of the village hall. 'I have kept a strict and studious watch over the finances of the club. I can account for everything going back years, Amita. Years! If there is no money in there, it's been taken, without my knowledge. And that's theft in my book. Father Ford pays the money in, then I oversee all the payments out. It's a watertight system. A man of the cloth and a woman of my esteemed standing. No one else should be anywhere near the funds. It's an outrage, a scandal, a . . .'

'Okay, okay. Calm down, please,' said Amita, spotting a few looks from the others. 'I was just asking.'

'Yes, I know you were,' Georgie seemed to settle. 'I couldn't believe it. Honestly, I couldn't. I was shocked, shocked to my very core. Not to mention mortified. The young man behind the desk looked at me like I was dirt on his shoe. The cheek of him. The cheek of *it*, Amita. I shan't live it down.'

'You've answered the first question,' she said. 'Now onto the second. Why are you telling me this, Georgie?'

Georgie adjusted the cuffs of her Italian mohair sweater. She recomposed herself and leaned back closer to Amita.

'I'm going to take a page out of your book and catch this thief red-handed,' she said.

'Pardon me?'

'You heard me,' said Georgie, tapping her nose. 'You're not the only one around here who can catch criminals. I'm going to find out what's happened to this money, who took it, and have them arrested.'

'Georgie . . .'

'I figure if you and that son-in-law of yours can do it, then why can't I?'

'Georgie, please, if I could . . .'

'I mean, it's not like it's a murder or anything. It's just some money that's been taken from our account without permission. I'm certain I can get to the bottom of it. If you can do this investigation lark, I'm sure I can, too. Don't you think so?'

Amita could, quite literally, feel her blood pressure rising over the recommended limits. She knew, all too well, that Georgie Littlejohn could test the patience of a saint. She always knew just how to press the right buttons and in the correct order. Knowing all of this, however, didn't make it any easier to endure. She calmed herself down a little before responding.

'I certainly think you can do this, Georgie,' she said. 'But I should warn you, these kinds of things are rarely straightforward.'

'Oh please, Amita,' Georgie snorted. 'I think I should be able to catch a petty thief, don't you? It's hardly breaking into Fort Knox.'

'True,' she said. 'However, in my experience, you tend to find that the criminals amongst us are rarely as sloppy, or indeed incompetent, as you might first expect. Theft is theft, you're right. But it takes a different mentality, a different mindset, to break the law.'

'Well, thank you for your unwavering support,' Georgie stood up sharply. 'Here I am, trying to do a little bit of good in the world, and all you can do is take the high-handed approach.'

'What?'

'You heard me alright.' She lifted her nose high into the air. 'I thought you would back me up on this, Amita. I thought you would have my back. Our club's future hangs by a thread, thanks to some no-good pickpocket, and all you can do is sit there and tell me I can't be a detective, like you.'

'Georgie, that's not what I'm saying.'

'Oh no. I'm not listening to anymore of your vitriol.' She held up her hands. 'I confided in you for your help, not to be ridiculed. I'll conduct my own investigations and report directly to the police, thank you very much. You won't hear another word on this matter from me. Not one word.'

She pretended to zip her mouth shut. She even went to the bother of locking the phantom zip and throwing away the key. Amita was exhausted. Georgie lingered, pretending to be searching for something in her handbag, ready to make even more of a scene. Amita didn't bite.

'I'm sorry you feel that way, Georgie. Really, I am,' she said. 'If there's anything I can do, please just ask.'

Georgie gave a little grunt and swivelled on her kitten heels. She stormed out, making sure everyone could see just how upset, angry and offended she was. Jason did well not to be steamrollered by her as he came sauntering in through the front doors of the village hall.

'Blimey,' he said as he reached Amita's table. 'Looks like the bee in her bonnet has a bee in its bonnet. What's wrong with Georgie?'

All Amita could do was rest her face in her hands. She leaned down on the table and enjoyed the all-too brief moment of darkness. She could easily have fallen asleep right there, despite the rabble of the quilting club and Jason standing over her.

'That bad, eh?' he asked.

'You don't know the half of it,' she said, voice muffled. 'And I don't have the strength to explain.'

'Good,' he said, pinching a half-eaten biscuit from a saucer. 'You said I was to pick you up at half-past. So here I am. Your chariot awaits.'

Amita sat back up. She looked disapprovingly at his biscuit choice and gathered up her things.

'Ready to head back to university?' he asked with forced chirpiness.

'No, not really,' she replied wearily. 'But needs must.'

'Must they?' he asked. 'Delice hasn't actually asked for our help?'

'Jason, there's a man missing. Maybe two. You and I both know that the police have no time to pick up on missing person cases unless there are suspicious circumstances, which so far, apart from a distressed wife and a wrong number, we have none.'

They walked out of the village hall, past the bust of Hal Mulberry looking dignified and regal. The clouds had gathered overhead and were blocking out the sun. Amita swore she felt a droplet of rain hit her on the forehead. Sometimes in Penrith, it never rained but it poured.

Chapter 12

HEPTACODIUM MICONIOIDES

The campus of Eddington College was not what many people would call an architectural marvel. Jason thought 'dull' was more to the point. For a place dominated by the hard, unrelenting greyness of 1960s' Brutalist architecture, dull was about as generous a description that could be mustered. It had probably once been the cutting edge of modernity, but it had not aged well. Everywhere you looked, the whole world seemed gloomy and decrepit. Jason had never held fond memories of this place. It felt like it sapped his lifeforce every time he set foot on its grounds.

By comparison, the students all seemed perfectly normal, perhaps even vibrant. Whatever he made of them, they made him feel old. The academic year was winding down and there seemed to be a nervous excitement about the place. Despite the concrete and granite. Jason admired their spirit.

'It's very, well, grey here,' said Amita, seemingly picking up on his thoughts.

'It is,' he replied. 'It's how I imagine Aberdeen to be. You know, the Granite City.'

'You've never been to Aberdeen?' she asked.

'Never,' he said.

'Oh, Jason.'

'What?'

'You never fail to disappoint me.'

'Thank you, Amita, that's just the boost I needed today.'

He shook his head as they walked up the street. Sensing that she might have touched a nerve, his mother-in-law tried to lighten the mood.

'You seem very familiar with this place though,' she said. 'I thought you went to university in Manchester?'

'I did,' said Jason. 'Eddington College, however, is a lot closer than Manchester for expert commentary when you need some academic know-how to back up your reporting when you're writing up fancy stories.'

'Fancy stories?'

'You know, stats, numbers, hard research to back up public outrage. We used to do them all the time in the local paper. Anything getting built, any change to local scenery, even the sniff of the possibility that some age-old tradition that nobody even knew about was going to be changed, I'd be sent up here to dig out an old professor and get his thoughts on it. Find a handy historian or environmental scientist and your article looks more like hard news rather than rent-a-gob opinions. Easy.'

'I see.'

'It's hardly the most prestigious institution, but it's handy,' he said. 'One of those sixties colleges that sprung up and offered a genuine alternative to higher education for everyone who didn't want to become a doctor or a lawyer. And it's still going today, look at it. For all of its oppressive buildings, these kids are still getting good stuff poured into their heads.'

Right on cue, they passed a large gathering of students. Colourful balloons were flapping in the wind, streamers hanging from a long row of tables. Students in fancy dress and brightly coloured T-shirts were singing, dancing and shouting into megaphones. Jason had no clue what it was about, but he enjoyed the vibe. Amita covered her ears as they made their way through the throng.

Around the corner was much quieter. A square opened up in front of them. Four stout, bleak, identical buildings guarded each side of the quadrangle. Jason looked around and tried to get his bearings.

'I thought you knew where we were going,' said Amita.

'It's been about six or seven years since I was last here. Give me a break, would you?' he said.

Still not quite sure, he pointed at the building across the square. They slipped through the glass doors and found a directory next to the lifts.

'There we are,' said Jason, more relieved than confident. 'Engineering. Told you we were in the right place.'

'Hmm,' said Amita, distinctly unconvinced. 'And you're sure this is Fran Weaver's department.'

'That's what it says online,' said Jason. 'I looked it up this morning after you left. He's part of the School of Engineering, listed on their academics' page, email address, phone number, you name it. Speaking of phone numbers, did Delice get in touch with you again?'

'No,' said Amita. 'I still haven't heard a word from her.'

'So, we're here unofficially, then.'

'Jason, you know by now that we're *always* here, there or somewhere else unofficially.

Amita felt a tug of guilt somewhere deep inside of her. She didn't like going behind people's backs. And certainly not without their permission. The night before and morning now had been spent debating what was the right thing to do. If two men were missing, two men were missing. They may be in danger, if not already come to harm. Finding them was what mattered.

'What is it you always say?' she asked Jason. 'It's easier to seek forgiveness than it is to seek permission.'

'Touché,' he replied with a smile.

They took the elevator to the seventh floor of the building. Old, tired, frosted glass windows lined the lobby, faded posters stuck to doors bleached and aged by the sun. The smell reminded Jason of school. Even the overly polished floor felt the same and he was transported back to days of missing third-period geography to play football behind the science block.

One of the doors was marked as 'Office', so Jason led the way. He knocked, waited a moment then stepped inside. It was empty.

'Nobody about,' he said.

'Is that something we should be concerned about?' asked Amita.

'I don't know. I just assumed they keep regular office hours. And it's too early for lunch.'

'What do you suggest we do? Wait? I've got other appointments, Jason, even if you don't.'

He ignored the barb. The office had been transported from the early 1990s by Jason's guess. Only the photocopier and computer on the small desk in front of them offered any sign that they hadn't travelled back in time. Across from them was a wall of pigeonholes, stretched from one side of the office to the other. Jason rounded the desk and started looking.

'What are you doing?' asked Amita.

'I'm looking for our friend, Fran Weaver,' he said.

'Well, he's hardly going to be stuffed into a pigeonhole, is he?'

There seemed to be no discernible order to the system. Jason scanned all the names, hoping to find what he was looking for. 'Aha,' he said. 'It's always the last one you find.'

Fran Weaver's pigeonhole sat empty, his name scribbled on a little bit of paper taped to the bottom ledge.

'Strange,' said Jason.

'What is?' asked Amita, joining him.

'When did Delice say her husband vanished? A couple of weeks ago, wasn't it?'

'That's right,' said Amita. 'She said she's not heard from him in at least a fortnight.'

'So why is his pigeonhole empty,' said Jason. 'When everyone else has something in theirs.'

He stepped back and looked at the wall of nooks. Nodding, Amita took them all in, too. There was something in at least every other pigeonhole. Some were stuffed to their limit with envelopes, files, boxes and packages. All except Fran Weaver's.

'You think he's been collecting his mail?' she asked.

'Or somebody has been doing it for him,' said Jason. 'I don't know. I just find it a little odd that his is the only one that's not got something in it when everyone else is clearly still getting mail.'

'Unless he's gone completely electronic,' she said. 'Like me. I get barely anything through the letterbox these days.'

'Come off it, Amita,' he said. 'I'm forever collecting brochures for caravan parks in Devon and the latest active lady catalogues from our front step.'

'Actual mail, Jason, not that kind of stuff. Bills, letters, invoices, I have them emailed to me. He might be the same.'

'I'm not so sure,' he said.

Jason stepped forward and reached into the nearest pigeonhole with something in it. He pulled out a yellow envelope and examined it. 'There. See?' he said. 'This has the postmark of the university on it. It's internal. There's a couple more, too.'

She spotted them dotted about the wall.

'Clearly this isn't just brochures and bills. Somebody has been lifting his mail in his absence. Or he's been doing it himself. Now, why do you think someone would go to that effort?'

Amita wasn't sure. She took the yellow envelope and stared down at the Eddington College logo stamped in the top corner. Jason was proud of himself. He felt like his little grey cells were firing on all cylinders. The joy, as always, was cut drastically short.

'Excuse me!' came a shrill voice from behind them. 'Just what the hell do you think you're doing with my mail?'

Jason and Amita spun around quickly. A very tall, rakishly thin woman decked head-to-toe in tweed was standing staring at them. Her half-moon glasses were tipped downwards, and she was glaring with sharp, hawk-like eyes over the frames.

'Err . . .' said Jason.

'Err . . .' said Amita.

The tweed woman remained expectant. She had the air of a schoolmistress about her, oozing authority from the top of her head all the way down to the soles of her oddly anachronistic running shoes. She put her hands on her hips, barring any escape.

'Well?' she said, her accent thick Lancastrian.

'Your mail?' Jason managed.

'That's what I said, wasn't it?' said the woman. 'You're holding my envelope. I watched you take it down from my cubby.'

'Ah, this?' Jason looked down at the envelope in Amita's hands. 'It's yours . . . Professor Julia Hargreaves.'

He read the name upside down, a trick from his old journalism days. Amita hadn't said a word since the academic had announced herself.

'Yes, sorry about that,' said Jason. 'I think we might have the wrong place.'

'Wrong place?' said the professor. 'This is the engineering department of the college. It's not exactly the London Underground system, is it? How can you possibly have the wrong place when you've had to climb seven storeys, open a door marked "office" and then pilfer my post.'

She was towering over them both in seconds. She snatched the envelope from Amita's hands and stared down at them over her spectacles.

'Well, I'm glad that's all sorted,' said Jason. 'Come on, Amita, time we were leaving, I think.'

'Oh no, no, no,' she said. 'You're not going anywhere until I call security. And I warn you, I was a judo champion when I was a teenager. Could have gone to the Commonwealth Games, too. I won't accept any funny business.'

Being threatened by a woman over six feet tall and entombed in tweed was a new one for both Jason and Amita. But it was a sign of how strange their lives had turned in recent years.

'Professor Hargreaves,' said Amita. 'If you'd let us explain.'

'Explain? Don't make me laugh,' said the academic. 'What could you possibly explain? You're thieves, here to snoop around my research. Have you been put up to this? Did that swine Collins down at UCL put you up to this? He's always been jealous of me, always lorded it over me that he's down in the big smoke and I'm up here in the sticks. The man couldn't explain Kirchhoff's circuit laws if he had a thousand years and a textbook open in front of him.'

Amita was agog. Jason was just as confused. They looked at each other and then at the looming professor.

'We're not here from UCL, believe us,' said Amita. 'My son-in-law and I are looking for someone.'

'Looking for someone? Here?' Hargreaves' nose wrinkled. 'Who could you possibly be looking for here? This is an engineering department.'

'Yes, so you've told us,' said Jason.

'Don't get snippy with me,' she waggled a long, pointed finger at him. 'You're in no position to be flippant.'

'Please, professor, we don't mean any harm,' said Amita. 'We're looking for Fran Weaver.'

The academic's face immediately shifted. Her face softened and she looked back and forth at them in turn.

'Doctor Weaver?' she asked. 'You're looking for him?'

'That's right,' said Jason. 'We're not here to pinch your mail. We're looking for Weaver. Have you seen him?'

Hargreaves's shoulders slumped. She backed away from them a little and flopped into the chair behind the desk. Her face went pale, eyes a little glassy. She looked like a woman given a death sentence with no chance of reprieve.

'Doctor Weaver,' she said again, voice barely louder than a whisper. 'What a terrible loss.'

'Loss?' Amita felt a jolt of panic run up and down her spine.

'What do you mean, loss?' asked Jason. 'What's happened to him? Do you know where he is?'

Hargreaves lifted a quivering hand to her mouth. She shook her head and composed herself.

'Sorry, no,' she said. 'No, I don't know where he is. But I wish I did.'

Amita detected something off. The woman who had announced herself with absolute authority was now a fragment of that figure.

'Professor Hargreaves,' she said softly. 'Is there something you'd like to tell us?'

The academic took three deep breaths. They did little to make her feel better, or to help. She spoke again, this time her voice cracking.

'Doctor Weaver . . . Fran, was, is, a very close friend,' she said. 'You might even say that we were, are, more than friends.'

Jason couldn't quite keep his shock to himself. He let out a loud, clumsy whistle and rubbed the back of his head.

'Man,' he said. 'I was *not* expecting that.'

'Jason, please,' tutted Amita. 'Show a little decorum.'

'Sorry.'

Amita kneeled down so that she was at eye level with the professor. She took Hargreaves' hand and held it firmly.

'I know this is going to be difficult for you,' she said, 'but we're trying to find Fran Weaver. And anything, everything, you know could be the difference between us finding him safe and not finding him at all. Does that make sense?'

'Yes,' said Hargreaves. 'Yes, of course. Please, come with me.'

She stood up and led them out of the office. Amita and Jason lingered a little behind her as Hargreaves marched down the hallway, heading for her own rooms.

'A mistress, eh?' whispered Jason.

'Indeed,' said Amita.

'Who knew the world of academia could be so juicy.'

'Behave.'

Professor Hargreaves stood to one side and ushered them into her office. She looked up and down the empty corridor of the engineering department and made sure there was nobody else about. Then she closed the door behind her and locked it shut.

Chapter 13

ALLIUM SCHOENOPRASUM

'You have to understand something simple and straightforward before I tell you anything,' said Hargreaves, steepling her fingers as she sat behind her huge desk. 'Fran and I, Doctor Weaver, we were in love. There was, or is, nothing tawdry about our connection.'

Amita and Jason sat on the other side of the desk. The room was dark and dusty. An imposing wall stacked high with books, folders and files towered above even the lofty figure of Professor Hargreaves. Amita imagined that being summoned to this room usually meant a dressing down or some fiendishly complex theorem to solve. But right now, the professor didn't look in any state to lay down the law. She looked like a woman bereft, much like Delice Weaver the night before.

'I've heard that old chestnut before, typically before they claim "the wife didn't understand them",' said Jason. 'Usually from people who know what they're doing is going to cause problems.'

'I can assure you that we knew *exactly* what we were doing,' Hargreaves fired back. 'Fran and I, we're kindred spirits. I don't expect either of you to understand, I assume you're not part of the academic world.'

'We're not,' Amita answered, cutting off Jason before he could say something rude. 'Enlighten us, if you wouldn't mind.'

Hargreaves nodded. She reached down into a drawer and pulled out a bottle of whisky, a rather fine malt. She produced a small glass and poured herself a hefty measure. Downing it in one gulp, Amita and Jason could only watch on as she tidied the bottle and glass away without offering them a sip.

'Here at Eddington, and indeed institutions all around the world, we rely on the closeness of our colleagues,' said Hargreaves. 'We have each other's backs, especially in this cutthroat world we call higher education.'

'Cutthroat?' Jason snorted. 'Forgive me, professor, but dusty lecture halls and particle physics don't immediately jump out at me as being particularly dangerous. Let alone cutthroat, as you put it.'

Some of Hargreaves' imperious steel returned.

'I can assure you Mr . . .'

'Brazel,' he said.

'Mr Brazel, what you don't know about academia could fill an infinite universe ten times over.'

Jason quietly accepted that put-down. It was one of the better ones he had heard.

'And particle physics is not my forte,' she added. 'I'm an engineer.'

'The same as Fran Weaver?' asked Amita.

'No,' said Hargreaves. 'Fran's specialty is technology, information technology, programming, software, that kind of thing. I am a civil engineer by trade, if you will. I've lectured here at Eddington for eighteen years, the last seven with Fran here in the department.'

'And you've grown . . . close to him in that time?' asked Jason.

'Yes,' she said firmly. 'As I was saying, higher education, university, academia, it's a cutthroat business. Teachers, professors, researchers, we're all trying desperately to make our marks. And many of us, unfortunately, will stoop to tactics that would make politicians blush.'

'This Collins person you mentioned earlier,' said Amita. 'Is he one of those professors?'

'Yes, unfortunately.' Her mouth curled into a snarl. 'The man is a pompous buffoon who knows how to chat himself into power more than he's ever known about his subject. He once accused me of being a plagiarist. I told him he was probably one of those little snobs at school who just learned how to pass exams rather than do the graft to actually *learn* the subject. Fran couldn't stand him either.'

'And why was that?'

Hargreaves rubbed her eyebrow with a long and pointy finger. She leaned back in her chair.

'There was an incident, some years ago, I forget when, at a conference in Portsmouth. The two of them got into an argument that spilled over.'

'Physical?' asked Jason.

'I'd hardly call it a top-level bout, Mr Brazel,' she said. 'These were two men in their mid-forties who'd spent their lives in a classroom. Not quite a Bruce Lee film.'

Jason nodded. He could imagine. Mostly because he was such a terrible fighter himself.

'What sparked the argument?' asked Amita.

'Me,' said Hargreaves. 'Fran was always the gentleman. We had grown very friendly in a very short time after he first arrived here. He always supported me in my work, my efforts, my aspirations. We all did in this department, but with Fran, it always felt like he went above and beyond for me. He knew all too well I didn't like Collins. And some silly thing was said at the dinner for the conference. The next thing I know, chairs and glasses are flying and they're brawling like something out of a western. It was a scandal, of course, two seasoned, experienced, plauded academics behaving like schoolboys. But something happened that night, down by the sea, that we couldn't hold back our urges anymore. Our affair was born overlooking the English Channel.'

'Sounds romantic,' Jason scoffed.

'It was, I'll have you know,' she hissed. 'We academics aren't natural born romantics, Mr Brazel. And to have somebody defend my honour like that was perhaps, no, it *was* the most romantic moment to ever happen to me. I told you, we were in love.'

Jason rightly kept his mouth shut. He knew already that he was in for a lecture when he got back to the car. Amita pressed on for the moment.

'Delice, Fran's wife, she didn't know about the affair?' she asked.

'No,' said Hargreaves. 'We were discreet. Fran loved Delice too. Although she could never understand the levels of commitment his work and his studies demanded of him.'

'And you could?'

'Of course!' she said. 'We were colleagues. We had similar backgrounds. We both know what it takes to survive in this world and how to get on. Delice Weaver, Fran would be the first to insist, was a good woman, but one who has never set foot on academic pastures. She's a middle manager and, forgive me, an office drone.'

'That's not a very nice thing to say about the wife of the man you're having an affair with, professor,' said Amita.

Hargreaves bowed her head a little.

'No, you're right,' she said. 'It's not. Fran wouldn't hold with anyone saying a bad word against her. Ours was a grand passion, a meeting of minds, but he was too honourable not to be tortured by not being honest with Delice, even if she couldn't offer him what I could.'

'When we spoke earlier, you said that it was a terrible loss,' said Jason. 'Do you think something has happened to Fran?'

Hargreaves remained stoic. 'I'm a woman of science,' she said. 'But what I had with Fran, it was something that science can't explain. Companionship, love, these can't be written down in textbooks or drawn on chalkboards. And when you know something is wrong, something is gone, you just know.'

She let out a long, deflated sigh.

'He wouldn't leave without telling me. I know that in my bones. You must think I'm mad,' she said.

'No, we don't,' said Amita. 'It's not our place to think anything, professor. We're simply trying to find Fran Weaver, that's all.'

'When did you last see him?' asked Jason.

'Around a month ago,' said Hargreaves. 'We were working late and had dinner at my flat just around the corner. He left around midnight, and I haven't seen or heard from him since.'

'Is that unusual behaviour for him?' asked Amita.

'We were having an affair for years,' she said. 'When one partner has a wife and a pretence to put up, you learn very quickly to expect huge swathes of silence. An occupational hazard, if you will.'

'But he's not been to work?' asked Jason.

'No,' said Hargreaves. Sitting up straight, the professor appeared to be working something out in her head. Then she spoke to them both.

'You asked me how I knew something had happened to him,' she said. 'Fran Weaver was dedicated not just to me but to his work, this department, and that business he had started with his partner. What's his name?'

'Grahame Sutcliffe,' said Jason.

'Yes.' Hargreaves clicked her fingers. 'The fact he hasn't been back in this building for just as long as I've missed him is strange. He would *never* do that to his students or his subject. While his ethics around his marriage could be questioned, you could never doubt Fran's dedication to his work. It was, ultimately, his life.'

'And you haven't picked up his mail for him?' asked Amita.

'Pardon?'

She thumbed back out the door. 'His pigeonhole in the office, it's empty,' she said. 'If he's not been here for a month, who has been gathering his things?'

Hargreaves looked bewildered. 'I have no idea,' she said. 'Certainly not me. I wouldn't do something like that.'

Amita had hoped that Hargreaves was the one behind the missing mail. Things would have been a lot less complicated that way. As it was, she had no reason to mistrust her.

'We won't take up any more of your time, Professor,' said Amita, standing up.

Jason did likewise. He didn't want to be left alone with Hargreaves, even for a second. They made for the door.

'You won't tell anyone about what we've discussed here, will you?' asked the academic.

Amita gave Jason a quick glance. 'That depends, I'm afraid,' she said.

'Depends on what?'

'Depends on whether we can find Fran Weaver,' said Jason. 'The police aren't involved, as far as we know, but they will have to be at some point, especially if you think something has happened to him.'

'For what it's worth, his wife does too,' said Amita.

'And you'll tell Delice,' said Hargreaves. 'About Fran and I?'

Amita didn't answer her. She didn't need to. Hargreaves clasped her hands together and nodded solemnly.

'I see,' she said. 'Then she'll know where to find me when she's ready. I'll be expecting her.'

Amita and Jason took their leave. They were down in the elevator and out into the quadrangle before they spoke.

'The sordid lives of university professors, I never thought I'd see the day,' said Jason, as they made their way back to the car.

'They're human beings, just like the rest of us,' said Amita. 'They take their trousers off at night before they go to bed.'

'Too soon, Amita. Too soon,' he winced.

They walked past the noisy students and back down the street towards the car. Jason whistled, spinning his keys.

'You seem particularly jolly,' she said. 'Given the circumstances.'

'Do I? Maybe I am. That Hargreaves woman, it didn't take long for her to crumble, did it? She was very high and mighty until we uncovered her dirty little secret. It makes me wonder what kind of lothario our

Fran really was. If he can keep two women on the go, there could be more. Dark horses and all that. For all we know he's done a moonlight flit to Acapulco with woman number three!'

'Everyone has their secrets, Jason,' said Amita.

'I don't,' he said. 'And you certainly don't.'

'The heart wants what the heart wants,' she said, not quite meeting his gaze.

He slowed a little as she continued on down the pavement. 'What's that supposed to mean?'

Amita didn't answer him. They rounded the corner and immediately came to a halt when they spotted their car up ahead.

'What the bloody hell!' Jason screamed. 'My car!'

The motor was covered in large blotches of shaving foam and clouds of powder paint. Blue, green, yellow, red, purple, all the colours that matched the balloons and T-shirts of the students back up the road. The windscreen was covered, as was the bonnet and the roof. And flyers were plastered onto the wing mirrors and back window.

'Bloody students!' he shouted. 'I'll kill them!'

Amita, while not condoning the mild vandalism, couldn't help but laugh a little. Jason reached the car and started to wipe off the paint from the windscreen. It smeared and left great smudges and streaks across the glass. She was about to help him when her phone buzzed in the pocket of her cardigan.

'Hello?' she answered without checking the number.

'Amita, it's Delice Weaver here.'

Her blood ran cold, and her mouth turned suddenly dry. The conversation with Professor Hargreaves flashed through her mind.

'Hello Delice,' she said. 'Is everything alright?'

'Yes, well, no. You know what I mean. Would you be able to come to my house in Kendal. I . . . I think I do need your help with this whole situation.'

'Yes, yes, of course,' said Amita. 'When would you like us there?'

'As soon as possible, if that's okay,' she said, her voice quivering. 'I . . . I just don't want to be alone.'

'Of course,' said Amita. 'Text me the address and we'll be right there.'

'Okay.'

Delice hung up. Amita felt a sudden dread creep over her. She'd never had to reveal an affair before. This was not going to be pleasant.

Chapter 14

SOLANUM PSEUDOCAPSICUM

'We're sorry to be the ones to have to tell you this, Delice, really we are.'

Amita and Jason were perched awkwardly on tall stools at the breakfast bar in Delice Weaver's kitchen. The house was huge. From the massive rooms to the high ceilings, it had the kind of grand Victorian proportions that make you think of some giant doll's house. Even the furnishings seemed oddly big. From the sofas and tables to the fridge across from them that looked straight out of a science-fiction film, the home was overwhelming.

They should have expected nothing less. The Weaver home was in a leafy suburb of Kendal, with a beautifully manicured garden and surrounded by rich Cumbrian countryside, yet just convenient enough for town. All the houses on the street seemed larger than life, quite literally.

At the centre of it all was Delice. She looked so small and shrunken amongst the lavish setting of her kitchen. Her shoulders were rolled, her head bowed, everything about her screamed broken and defeated. Amita felt absolutely awful about the news she'd just revealed. She didn't want to break this woman's heart. She didn't want to break *anyone's* heart. Affairs and relationships gone wrong could rip families in half.

Amita could only sit there and apologise as Delice tried desperately to compose herself.

'You've got nothing to apologise for,' she said at length, looking at them with bloodshot eyes. 'If Fran wanted to play away from home, then that's his fault, not yours. You're only delivering the bad news.'

'We had to, Delice. We couldn't *not* tell you, especially if it might lead to finding Fran.'

'I understand,' she said, and Amita believed her. 'Do you think this Hargreaves woman is involved?'

The truth was, Amita didn't know. They'd barely had time to digest everything that had unfolded in the engineering department of Eddington College. And Jason was still fuming over what the students had done to his car. He had spent most of the journey mumbling to himself, with occasional outbursts of profanity. Even now he was perched beside Amita, staring into the distance, most likely trying to work out where the nearest carwash was.

'I can't be sure,' she said. 'There are still too many variables, I'm afraid. Professor Hargreaves seemed genuinely concerned. I know that's probably not what you want to hear, but it's the truth. She claimed to have no idea about Fran's whereabouts over the last month. And she didn't know who was collecting his mail.'

'His mail?' asked Delice. 'What mail?'

'At the university. The lecturers and professors in the department all have little cubbies where their letters and mail are posted. Everyone's we saw had something in it, except Fran's.'

'That's very strange,' said Delice.

'We had sort of hoped you'd shed light on it by telling us you'd been collecting the mail.'

'Not me,' she said. 'I barely ever set foot on campus, let alone in the department. That was Fran's domain. He liked to keep his work life and home life separate. I can see why now. I've got my gardening and my baking, he's got his data and his students – I never thought to question the arrangement. What a fool I was.'

A flash of anger made her cheeks flush. Amita could hardly blame her. She'd spent weeks searching for her husband, believing he'd come to harm. Now she had found out he'd been having an affair with a colleague for years. Amita felt her chest tighten at the thought and how she had been the one to deliver the bad news.

'Have you gone to the police?' she asked, trying to change the subject a little.

'No, not yet. I wanted to speak with you both first,' said Delice. 'For what it's worth, I think you're right, I know you are. The police have to know if two men are missing. It's important.'

'Is there anyone else who might already have reported Grahame Sutcliffe's disappearance?' asked Amita.

Delice laughed at that. 'Chance would be a fine thing,' she snorted. 'The only people who'd miss that flash git would be the bookies and the nightclub owners.'

'Old rocker is he?' asked Jason, finally joining the conversation.

'The oldest rocker in town,' said Delice. 'He's drank, fought and been thrown out of every pub from here to the Humber. If he can rub somebody up the wrong way, he'll do it. And if he can't, he'll invent something instead. Sutcliffe is bad news. I don't know why Fran always let him stay in our lives, let alone go into business with him.'

'Sutcliffe doesn't have any family?' asked Amita.

Delice moved over to the giant fridge. She pressed some buttons on the outside and the whole thing whirred and bleeped. It produced a little stream of espresso into a tiny cup, and she sipped from it gingerly. Amita began to wonder if anyone was ever going to offer her and Jason a drink.

'I think his old mother is still alive,' she said. 'Isobel her name is. A fierce woman, very aggressive, especially if she has a drink in her. I can't be sure if she's still pottering about Kendal. He probably tried to sell her, too, at some point, but there was no market for her. She used to live in the town centre, a little flat above the butcher's shop.'

'Take a note of that, Jason,' said Amita. 'Maybe we should pay her a visit to see if she knows where her son might be.'

Delice leaned on the huge island in the middle of the kitchen. It was her turn to stare off into space now.

'You hear about all of this kind of thing, don't you, on social media and in the news. But you never think that it will happen to you.'

'Delice, Fran and this Sutcliffe character will be found, we promise you,' said Amita.

'No, I mean the affair,' she sniffed. 'You see it all the time, it's everywhere. Magazine covers, celebrity scandals, broken homes and broken hearts. You just never think that it will be you. And then boom, out of nowhere, it's your turn for your life to collapse, and you're left sitting there with the ruins in your lap like a pile of concrete blocks. Funny old world, isn't it?'

Amita's insides were churning. If she had been in Delice's shoes, she would have wanted to know. But still she felt terrible guilt.

'Delice . . . I'm truly, truly sorry,' she said.

'It's not your fault, I told you that.' She seemed to snap out of her daydream and smiled weakly at her. 'It wasn't you who decided to ruin our marriage. I barely even know you, Amita.'

'You've got no idea who might have been taking your husband's mail?' asked Jason.

'No, no idea at all,' said Delice. 'I can't think what anybody would want with something like that. He was an academic, a scientist. Who the hell wants to read what a scientist gets through the post?'

'I suspect that whoever *has* been taking the post probably has something to do with your husband's disappearance,' said Amita. 'Covering their tracks perhaps. Or maybe they want information.'

'Information on what?'

Delice's frustrations boiled over. She walked around the huge island in the kitchen, her fists clenched into balls.

'This is what I keep coming back to,' she said. 'Over and over and over again, for the past month. I keep asking why? Why would Fran vanish? Why would anybody want to harm him? Why is this happening to me? I can't get any answers, no matter how much I think about it. And it's driving me insane.'

'I know it's difficult, Delice,' said Amita. 'If we're to try and find Fran, we need to know if he had any enemies.'

'Enemies? He was a university lecturer!' she yelped.

'That's not as innocuous as you think,' said Jason.

Delice's face went slack. 'And what's *that* supposed to mean?' she asked.

Jason blinked. While he had slipped out of his sullen mood over the state of the car, it seemed he hadn't quite fully woken up from the daydream. Delice Weaver calling him out appeared to do the trick.

'I . . . err . . . well, I was just saying that the world of higher education might be a bit more cutthroat than you think,' he said. 'At least, that's what I've heard.'

'Cutthroat?' Delice looked sceptical.

Jason wasn't about to go into the details of the conversation he'd had with Professor Hargreaves. That would have put him further in the bad books. Thankfully, Amita stepped in to save the day. As usual.

'What Jason is rather clumsily trying to say is that everyone has enemies, Delice. Even the most innocuous, quiet, selfless soul. We can't all please everyone and somebody is likely to have had their nose put out of joint at something, somewhere along the line. Is there a chance that Fran could have trodden on any toes? Especially with this business venture of his.'

Delice seemed a little more placated now. Jason silently thanked his mother-in-law for her tact.

'The only person who would hurt Fran is that rat, Grahame Sutcliffe,' she said. 'If you want to help me, you'll find him first and haul him down to a police station.'

It was clear that she was growing more and more upset the longer the conversation went on. Amita had learned a few things since accidentally becoming an amateur investigator. The most important was knowing to call it quits when you aren't winning. This was one of those scenarios.

'I think we had best be going, Delice,' she said, standing up from her perch. 'The day is wearing on and Jason and I have lots of things we need to be getting on with. Let us know if you make that call to the police – I would advise it. And we'll try and find this Sutcliffe character.'

Delice made no protest. Jason silently agreed, relieved to be leaving. She saw them out to the front door. The multi-coloured car was parked in the wide driveway outside the house. Delice gasped a little when she saw it.

'Yeah, sorry about that,' said Jason. 'Some students thought it would be hilarious to vandalise my motor.'

Delice looked confused. She turned to Amita for some explanation, but there was none beyond what Jason had already said. All she could do was shrug.

'He's not normally like this,' she said. 'Normally he's much worse. So, you'll have to excuse the state of our transport, Delice. I'm sure you understand.'

She bid them farewell and Jason and Amita headed for the car. Jason cursed as his hand squelched on the paint coating the door handle, still wet from the prank. When they were safely inside, Amita waved back at Delice.

'Something's fishy,' she said.

'That's the paint, Amita. Those bloody students have probably used emulsion to make my car look like a unicorn's fart.'

'No, I mean with Mrs Weaver.'

Jason leaned over to look at Delice staring down at them from the front door. She looked more like she was seeing them off rather than waving them off.

'You think she's hiding something?' he asked, starting the engine.

'Absolutely. She knows something that she's not telling us.'

'Nothing new there, then, is there?'

'She keeps mentioning this Grahame Sutcliffe, like he's some master villain. But the man is missing, just like her husband. It doesn't add up to me. Surely, she should be more concerned, they're business partners.'

'Maybe they've run off together,' he said, pulling the car out of the driveway. 'Maybe that was the plan all along.'

'And the affair with Professor Hargreaves?'

'That's just her side of the story,' said Jason. 'How do we know she wasn't part of it.'

'Then there's the police, too. Why hasn't she reported them missing yet? That would be the first thing I would do if you vanished.'

'Aww, you sweetheart,' he laughed.

'Jason, please,' she tutted. She pulled out her phone and began tapping away.

'Who are you messaging?' he asked.

'I'm trying to find Sutcliffe's mother, if she's still alive or not.'

'I don't think you can just google something like that.'

'Jason.'

She gave him a distinctly unimpressed look.

'What? What's that look for?'

'You know *exactly* what that look is for, Jason,' she said. 'I would like to think you knew better than to assume I was just googling "Is Isobel Sutcliffe still alive". What kind of amateur do you take me for?'

'Don't tempt me,' he said.

Amita's phone vibrated in her hand. She smiled.

'Turn the car around!' she shouted.

Jason almost jumped out of his skin. The wheel wobbled and he hit the brakes. 'What? Why?' A chorus of horns tooting behind them.

'I've found her,' said Amita. 'I've found Isobel Sutcliffe.'

Chapter 15
BIDENS ALBA

The sun was shining down on Kendal. The beautiful, crisp blue skies of the spring were showing off the market town in all its historic glory. The River Kent, that snaked its way through the heart of the place, was glistening and shimmering in the sunlight. People had smiles on their faces as they went about their lunchtime business. The last remnants of winter felt truly banished and everyone seemed that little bit more positive about life.

Everyone except Jason Brazel. The honking of horns, the laughing and pointing at traffic lights, all of the attention his multi-coloured car was attracting was beginning to wear on him. His already sour mood was growing even more bitter by the second.

'I'll have my revenge, mark my words,' he said. 'Just you wait and see, Amita. I'll hunt down every one of those pesky, spotty-faced students who did this, and I'll have my vengeance.'

'Oh, stop being so dramatic,' she said. 'It's only a bit of paint and they were having some fun. That's not a crime.'

'Vandalism isn't a crime? Are you kidding me?'

'The car isn't ruined, you can still drive it. I'm sure once you get your sponge and bucket out, the paint will come right off. Just wait and see.'

Right on cue, a group of schoolkids all started shouting and hollering at them as they waited for the lights to turn green. Jason fired them a sneer but that just made it worse. They blew raspberries and upped their mocking.

'Brats,' he said, pulling off.

Amita directed them to a car park and they left the motor in a quiet, shaded corner, so as not to attract any further unwanted attention. A short walk around the corner brought them to the front door of the butcher's shop Delice had mentioned. Tall, creaking scaffolding reached up the side of the four-storey building, the historic sandstone front apparently being cleaned. Amita shaded her eyes and stared all the way up to the box windows that lined the roof.

'What do you think the odds are that Mrs Sutcliffe lives on the very top floor?' she asked.

'Knowing how our luck is going, I'd say quite high. Or low, I never know how odds work. I'm not a gambler.' Jason shrugged.

'I'd wager you're right,' she said.

A few doors down from the butcher's, an opening broke up the row of shops. Amita and Jason headed through and were brought out at a small courtyard away from the main street. There were a couple of parked cars and back doors to the businesses. One of the doors had an intercom panel beside it and they went over. The bottom name read Sutcliffe and Amita looked smugly at her son-in-law.

'Yes, yes, very good,' he said. 'The powers of the bingo club network never cease to amaze me. Go on, press the buzzer.'

Amita duly obliged. There was no answer. She tried again.

'Nobody in,' said Jason.

Amita checked her watch. It was close to three. 'Too late for lunch. Too early for dinner,' she said.

'Maybe by your standards.'

'And you have different standards, I suppose?'

'I'm saying that everybody has a different pattern to their day,' he said. 'If I was on a nightshift, I wouldn't get up until early afternoon. My breakfast could be my lunch, my lunch would be my dinner, that kind of thing.'

'I don't think Isobel Sutcliffe is doing night shifts, Jason.'

'No, I'm not saying that, Amita. What I'm saying is . . .'

'Who is it? What do you want?'

A harsh, metallic voice snapped them out of their argument. They both quickly realised that somebody had answered the door buzzer.

'Hello, Mrs Sutcliffe. My name is Amita Khatri,' she said, pressing the button. 'I wondered if I could come up and chat with you about your son.'

'You're selling what?' came the reply.

'No, Mrs Sutcliffe, I'm not selling anything. I wondered if I could come up to your flat and have a quick chat about Grahame.'

'Who?'

'Your son, Grahame!' Amita shouted.

'Who?'

Jason rolled his eyes. He should have given Mrs Sutcliffe the benefit of the doubt, maybe her intercom wasn't working, or she was hard of hearing. But he just knew that this exchange between them would go on forever unless he intervened.

'Mrs Sutcliffe, Jason Brazel. I'm from the *Kendal Times*,' he said, barging Amita out of the way. 'I wondered if I could chat to you about all the scaffolding and the work the council is doing to your building.'

'The council! The bloody council! I'll tell you what I think about the bloody, half-witted council alright. I . . .'

The static on the intercom conveniently intervened as Isobel Sutcliffe shouted and swore down the line. Amita winced with every graphic, vulgar word that made it through the hissing and crackling reception. When the woman finally stopped for a breath, the door buzzed and unlocked.

'Thank you, Mrs Sutcliffe. We'll be right up.'

Jason winked as he opened the door and let Amita in first. They began to climb the stairs to the top floor.

'How did you know that would work?' she asked. 'Not that I'm condoning lying to an old woman.'

'Call it instinct,' he said, tapping his temple. 'If I had a quid for every disgruntled call or complaint we used to get called in to us about scaffolding, roadworks or potholes, we'd be climbing stairs in Miami Beach or Bel Air right about now. As it stands, we're in Kendal about to deal with a very angry lady who is probably worried sick about her missing son.'

Amita had to give it to Jason. When he wanted to, he could still pull a few surprises out of his bag of tricks. She made a mental note to help him clean the car when they got home.

The top floor of the building was cramped. The roof sloped inwards and Jason had to duck when he climbed the last of the stairs. The fire door on the landing was open. They slowly went inside, Jason taking the lead.

'Mrs Sutcliffe,' he shouted. 'It's Jason Brazel, we were just chatting downstairs. Are you there?'

They walked cautiously down the hallway. Jason was about to call out for Mrs Sutcliffe again when a door was yanked open. Amita didn't see the old woman quickly enough, but she spotted the brush. The brush-head came whirling through the air like a boomerang and battered Jason in the back of the head. The surprise more than the impact was enough to send him tumbling forward.

'Bloody hell!' he shouted, rolling on the carpet, clattering into an ancient telephone table, the handset flying.

'Jason!' Amita yelped.

The owner of the brush darted into the hallway. Mrs Sutcliffe was small but solid, her gaze locked on Amita as she brandished her weapon of choice.

'Who are you?' she said, punctuating every word with a jab of the brush handle. 'Who are you really? What do you want?'

Amita backed off, her hands raised. 'Steady on, Mrs Sutcliffe,' she said. 'We don't want any trouble.'

'Who are you and what are you doing in my home?' she shouted. 'Get out, the pair of you! Get out!'

'We're from the newspaper, Mrs Sutcliffe,' said Jason, slowly getting to his feet.

He rounded the old lady. She jabbed at him with her brush, too. He eased his way to beside Amita and they both tried to explain.

'Remember, I wanted to talk to you about the scaffolding and work outside,' he said.

'I don't think that's going to fly, somehow,' said Amita.

'I'll call the police!' Mrs Sutcliffe threatened. 'Coming into the home of an elderly lady like this. Pretending to be something you're not. Scammers, that's what you are. Scammers! You should be ashamed. I'm not frightened of you. I'll defend myself. I was in the territorials, you know!'

'Should we be scared?' whispered Jason.

'Not now,' said Amita.

They backed all the way to the door. Something tinkled at Amita's feet. She looked down and saw an empty whisky bottle on the floor. She remembered then what Delice had said about Mrs Sutcliffe and drinking. Suddenly it was beginning to make a bit more sense.

'Mrs Sutcliffe, please,' she started. 'We don't mean to cause you any harm. We just want some information, that's all.'

'Quiet you!' she rasped. 'A woman of your age, robbing people's houses. You should know better.'

Jason sniggered under his breath. Amita ignored him.

'Mrs Sutcliffe, please put the brush down. We just want to talk to you about your son.'

The old woman changed in an instant. Her grip on the brush loosened enough that Jason thought he might stand a chance. He reached forward and took it from her with ease. She stood there, looking at them both, her eyes tearing up.

'Grahame,' she said. 'Grahame. My special boy. He'll be the end of me, you know. Sick with worry I've been, ever since he was born.'

Jason stepped back, still holding the brush. Amita eased forward, her hands still high in the air.

'Mrs Sutcliffe, Isobel, we gather your son hasn't been in touch with his business partner, so we're trying to find out where he might be,' she said. 'Jason and I, we've been talking to Delice Weaver. We understand her husband, Fran, was Grahame's business partner, and he's vanished too. I'm sure there's nothing to worry about, but we really do need to find Fran. Grahame might be able to help. Perhaps they've gone on a work trip together. We wanted to know if you knew anything about where they might have gone.'

Mrs Sutcliffe stood still for a moment, then turned away quickly. She hurried further into the flat. Amita and Jason followed at a safe distance, wary that she could swing a brush with the best of them.

She scurried about her kitchen, opening cupboard doors and shutting them again quickly. Making her way around the place, she finally found what she was looking for – a half-drunk bottle of Scotch. She unscrewed the lid and drank a hefty belt that made Jason's stomach turn just looking at it. Mrs Sutcliffe wiped her mouth on her sleeve and then used the bottle as a pointer. At least this time Amita was relieved none was offered.

'Are you one of his girlfriends, then?' she cackled.

'Me?' Amita coughed. 'Girlfriends?'

Jason laughed loudly. He was enjoying this. Amita was affronted.

'No, Mrs Sutcliffe, I'm not,' she said. 'I think I'm probably a little too old for your son.'

'And then some,' said Jason.

She gave him a dirty look.

'He's got lots of girlfriends, my Grahame.' There was a pride in her voice. 'Ever since he was at school, all the girls liked my Grahame. He looks like his dad. He was a looker, too, back in his day, until the drink and the gambling got a hold of him. Don't cry for him though, dear. He's better off in the ground. We all got some peace when that old so-and-so kicked the bucket.'

Jason was doing his best not to laugh. Amita didn't find any of it at all funny.

'Do you know where your son is?' she asked, trying to stay on topic.

'No idea,' Mrs Sutcliffe shrugged her shoulders.

'And you're not worried?'

'I'm always worried about him, dear,' she said. 'Like I said, I've been worried sick ever since I fell pregnant. It's the deal you make when you become a mother. You don't stop being anxious about them just because they grow up, do you? And when you're a looker, like my Grahame, it's even tougher. He's a charmer, always has been, but I'll admit he doesn't always know how to stay out of trouble with the ladies. I've always tried to do my best by my Grahame. It wasn't easy, of course, not when your husband was as bone idle as mine. He was the only man in this country to remain unemployed across three decades. Bless the Job Centre staff, they tried everything, but he always found an excuse. All the while I was out scrubbing latrines and baking bread just to keep this roof over our heads.'

'I hope she washed her hands in between,' said Jason under his breath.

'I probably didn't give Grahame enough attention when he was a nipper – that's why he's not stopped looking for it since. He's had more girlfriends than hot dinners, I tell you.'

Mrs Sutcliffe took another almighty swig from the whisky bottle. With a satisfied sigh, she clapped her hands and hurried past them both and out of the kitchen. She disappeared into one of the other rooms of the little flat. Jason and Amita just stared at each other.

'This is all very strange,' she said.

'You're telling me,' he agreed. 'I've just been assaulted by a geriatric whirling dervish!' He rubbed the back of his head.

'Found it!' Mrs Sutcliffe shouted.

She returned to the kitchen carrying a biscuit tin, the sticker on the lid faded and torn. She placed it down on a worktop beside the fridge with a thump and pulled the top off. Inside was a large collection of photographs. Mrs Sutcliffe happily started leafing through them, smiling to herself.

'Precious memories,' she said, scattering them about the surface.

Amita could feel the situation getting away from them a little. She walked over to be beside Mrs Sutcliffe and gently took her arm.

'Mrs Sutcliffe, we really do hope Grahame might be able to help us find Fran Weaver,' she said softly. 'Do you know where he is?'

The old lady was playfully leafing through the old pictures, laughing every now and then at one that pleased her. Amita pressed on.

'Professor Weaver. Does that name ring any bells?'

'Afraid not. But if he's with Grahame, he'll turn up. My boy always does,' she said. 'He's usually out with his fancy-women. He loves the ladies, and they love him. I told you that, didn't I?'

'You did,' she said.

'And it's been all the more since he came into all that money,' she said. 'Ah, Brighton beach, 1987. We had such a lovely time then.'

She showed Amita the photo in her hand. It was of Isobel Sutcliffe and her husband and a young Grahame. They were all enjoying ice cream with the beach and sea behind them.

'What money would that be, Mrs Sutcliffe?' asked Amita.

'Oh, I don't know,' she said, looking sadly at the photo. 'He was talking about some deal he'd struck with a load of Americans. Or Canadians, I can't remember which. They've bought up his company. Gave him a million pounds. Can you believe that? My little Grahame, who grew up in this flat, getting a million pounds. Not that I've seen any of it. It's funny how the world turns, isn't it?'

Amita nodded. 'Can you tell me when you last heard from your son, Mrs Sutcliffe?'

'Oh, he's a free spirit, my boy. Like I said, often off gallivanting. But he loves his mum. He always writes home or calls or textual messages or whatever they're called.' Mrs Sutcliffe looked around for her drink, picking up an old tumbler, disappointed to find it empty.

'Can you remember the exact date of when you last spoke?' Jason pressed.

Mrs Sutcliffe's mood changed. She slammed the photo down on the kitchen worktop.

'I know what you're trying to do. This is a test, isn't it? You want to prove I'm dotty and should be in a home. Or you'll be trying to tell me to cut down on my little tipples. Well, I'm not having it. You can clear off. I'm tired,' she spat. 'I'm going back to bed!'

Before Amita or Jason could stop her, she hurried out of the kitchen. She was gone in a flash, the bedroom door slamming shut, the whole flat rattling. Jason blew out his cheeks.

'Lovely old lady,' he said. 'Got a good swing on her, too.'

He rubbed the back of his head again. Amita took a last look at the pictures scattered about in front of her. A much more recent photo of Grahame Sutcliffe and his mother at a party caught her eye. She lifted it and showed it to Jason.

'Good-looking fella,' he said. 'If you're into that smarmy, greasy look.'

'A ladies' man,' said Amita. 'Coming into money and then vanishing off the face of the earth. This is all heading in the one direction, Jason. And I think Delice Weaver will like the way it's going.'

He agreed. Amita put the picture back amongst the others. They headed for the door but stopped when they heard knocking.

'More visitors?' whispered Jason.

'Seems a bit strange,' Amita whispered back. 'Mrs Sutcliffe doesn't strike me as the kind of woman who does a lot of entertaining.'

'How did they get through the downstairs door?' he asked.

That question made Amita's blood chill. There was another knock, this time a little harder.

'What do we do?' she asked.

'What can we do?' he said. 'We're not Mrs Sutcliffe and we're probably breaking a whole load of trespassing rules just being here.'

'So, what?'

'So, I think we just open the door, excuse ourselves and go.'

'What if it's Sutcliffe?'

'Then we've reduced our workload by fifty per cent. I'm alright with that.'

'Jason, honestly,' she shook her head.

'Come on.'

A third knock met them as they reached the front door. Jason took the handle and opened it quickly. They were about to leave when Frank Alby met them on the other side.

'Brazel!' he shouted.

'Alby!' Jason shouted back.

'What the hell are you doing here?'

'We could ask you the same question, Frank,' said Amita, the shock making her limbs tingle.

Alby's moustache bristled. He tried to look over their shoulders.

'Grahame Sutcliffe's mother, she lives here, yeah?' he asked.

'That's right,' said Amita.

'She's just gone back to bed,' said Jason.

'Bed? It's the middle of the day?'

'I'm surprised she was up at all,' said Jason sarcastically.

'What are you doing here?' asked Amita. 'Are you following us?'

'Don't be so thick,' he said. 'Follow you two? Give me some credit, would you, Amita? I used to be a detective for goodness sake.'

'Such a good detective you're following up on our leads,' said Jason. 'That's about the measure of it, Frank?'

Alby didn't answer. He glowered at them and then held up his hands. 'Alright, alright, fair cop,' he said. 'Maybe, just maybe, the inner peace and tranquillity of retirement isn't all it's cracked up to be. And maybe, just maybe, getting my teeth stuck into a good missing persons case was just the kick up the jacksie that I needed.'

'No missing person case is "good". Quite the opposite,' said Amita sternly.

'Yeah, of course. Sorry,' he said. 'So, I thought I'd do a bit of digging and, well, here I am. Grahame Sutcliffe's mother's flat. The fact that you two are already here makes me think I was right.'

'About what?' asked Jason.

'That there's something dodgy going on with these two business partners.'

Amita nodded grimly. 'I think we should all just calm down,' she said. 'And get a cup of tea before heading home. I have a splitting headache, and you need to be brought up to speed.'

It was the most welcome thing she'd said all day.

Chapter 16

SACCHAROMYCES CEREVISIAE

Amita had never cared for pubs. She wasn't a big drinker. There were usually long periods of time between her libations, taken only on very special occasions. A cappuccino with slice of cheesecake was more than enough excitement for her.

The recent, booze-fuelled trip to Manchester wasn't helping. While she had made little to no effort to remember more of the 'lost weekend', she definitely didn't feel that enough time had passed between visits to the pub. Alby, however, in his usual manner, had insisted. And here they were, in some dark and dingy place north of Kendal and still miles from home.

'It isn't bad in here,' Jason said, a thick moustache of foam on his top lip. 'Did you say this was an old police pub, Frank?'

'Brazel, what have I told you about calling me by my Christian name,' said Alby, his eyes closed and a look of weariness on his haggard face. 'If you call me Frank one more time, I'll . . .'

'Yes, yes, yes. You'll feed me to the dogs or have me strung up by the unmentionables. I've heard them all,' he said.

'Just call me Mr Alby in the future.'

'Whatever,' Jason said under his breath.

The pub smelled vaguely of damp. Or wet dog fur. Amita was sitting on a stool by their table. She held her handbag on her lap with both hands. She didn't trust the floor wouldn't be so sticky that she'd be unable to lift it again when they went.

There was no music, and the barman looked like he'd been on the receiving end of one too many thrashings. His face was all out of shape, his flat nose the centrepiece of a poorly put back together collage. He had glared at Amita as soon as they'd walked in, as if the presence of a woman was something to call the police about. Thankfully, Alby had seen to dealing with him and none of the other barflies, mostly elderly men like the former detective, had ignored her.

Now they were holed up in a corner, close to a grate. Amita was counting down the seconds until they could get back outside into the fresh air. This was doing nothing for her headache.

'You haven't touched your tea,' said Alby, swirling what was left of his pint of bitter.

'No, it looks like drain water. I'm not drinking that.'

The water in her mug was an unpalatable shade of grey. She was certain she had heard the barman almost choke when Alby had ordered it. This place, Amita suspected, was not used to the female touch. The dust gathering on the mantelpiece above the fireplace enough of a sign.

'So, what have you found out?' asked Jason.

'Hang on a minute, I'm supposed to be the one asking the questions,' said Alby, prodding his own chest. 'I'm the retired detective inspector, aren't I?'

'You might be a retired inspector, Alby, but we were the ones who found Isobel Sutcliffe first. Come on then, out with it.'

Alby drained the last of his pint. He leaned on the little round table, its legs creaking as he did so. A pound or two more and Amita was sure the whole thing would have given way.

'Firstly, you tell me how you got on with Sutcliffe's mother,' he said. 'I was under the impression that he was somewhat of a cad. A real god's-gift-to-women type.'

'Yes, we heard that, too,' said Amita. 'Even from his mother, who seemed to think there was nothing unusual about him being out of touch for a while.'

'So, the timelines match up, then?' asked Alby. 'You know, the times, the points of disappearance. That Weaver woman, she says she hasn't seen or heard from her husband in, what, a month? Same goes for Grahame Sutcliffe.'

'Which still doesn't explain how I got Sutcliffe's number,' said Amita. 'Or why Mrs Sutcliffe hasn't tried calling it. Still, a month seems to be the same amount of time that both men have been missing,' she said. 'Did you find anything else out about Mrs Sutcliffe?'

Alby straightened, the table groaning with relief as he sat back up. He looked about the pub and tapped the side of his nose.

'I've still got some friends on the inside,' he said. 'Somebody ran a next of kin for me, gave me the address. Do you know that Sutcliffe still hasn't been reported missing. Same for Fran Weaver. That's a bit odd, if you ask me.'

'I agree,' said Amita. 'We went to see Delice earlier. She said she was going to report her husband as missing. But why would she wait so long?'

'Maybe she knew about the affair,' said Jason.

'Affair?' Alby yelped. 'What affair?'

'Keep your voice down, would you?' Jason hushed him.

Nobody in the pub seemed to care at all. Alby leaned in again.

'What affair?' he whispered.

'Fran Weaver was having an affair with one of the other professors at the university where he worked,' said Jason. 'Had been for years. Amita here had to break the news to Delice about her.'

'Yes, unfortunately,' she said. 'I still don't feel very good about it.'

'Was she angry?' asked Alby.

'She wasn't happy, if that's what you mean,' said Jason. 'Although there was something about her when we spoke to her. I don't know, maybe I'm being paranoid. She called us round but then couldn't wait to get rid of us, after we shared the news of the affair.'

'You think she knew then?'

'Maybe,' said Amita. 'But it does put her husband in rather a different light. And the professor he was in a relationship with seems devastated.'

'The professor?'

'Professor Hargreaves,' said Jason. 'She's a bit of a dragon. A distraught dragon, but a dragon nonetheless.'

Alby took this all in. He sat silently for a moment, weighing it all up. 'Do you think this merger has something to do with it all?' he asked them.

It was Jason and Amita's turn to be flummoxed.

'What merger?' he asked.

'Their company,' said Alby, reaching into the pocket of his coat. 'Clymtech. It all seems done and dusted. I got the boys at the station to give me a little background check when they were looking for next of kin.'

He pulled out a set of crumpled, dog-eared papers. Handing them over, Amita quickly scanned them.

'These are legal contracts,' she said. 'How did you get a hold of these?'

'Don't ask silly questions, Amita,' said Alby. 'I'm the police.'

She decided to take his advice.

'I've only had a quick glance at them on the bus down here. But it all looks legitimate. Fran Weaver and Grahame Sutcliffe are listed as company directors. And a merger took place about three weeks ago.'

'It says that Clymtech was valued at over a million quid,' Jason said, craning his head to read the documents. 'Of course. Didn't Isobel Sutcliffe say that her son had been splashing the cash, living it up?'

'She did,' said Amita, furrowing her brow. 'She also said that's why she wasn't surprised he hadn't been in touch with her. That the women liked her little Grahame.'

'I told you this was juicy,' said Alby. 'These two blokes come into a bit of money. One's a party animal and the other one is playing away from home. This has got one of two things written all over it.'

He tapped the papers on the table. Jason and Amita sat expectantly.

'Fraud,' he said.

'Or what else?' asked Jason.

'Midlife crisis,' said Alby. 'We're more likely to find these geezers in Panama than Penrith at this rate. They've cashed in, ditched their wives and mothers and I bet they're sipping Piña Coladas in some beach bar without a care in the world. You'd be surprised how many people just walk out of their lives when they come into money.'

'You've forgotten a third option,' said Amita. 'Murder.' She felt a sudden chill as a gust blew down the chimney and out through the empty grate. It spewed coal dust out across the floor, although the barman and other denizens didn't seem to care. Or notice, for that matter. She clutched her handbag a little bit tighter.

'People have been killed for much less than a million pounds. If we think that Weaver and Sutcliffe are dead, who would stand the most to gain from their untimely demises?' she asked. 'Delice? Professor Hargreaves? Somebody else?'

'All sorts of people might have been eyeing up that kind of windfall,' said Alby. 'Although the scorned wife or the desperate lover are very plausible. In the majority of murder investigations I worked on, the victim was known to the killer. And we usually rounded them up pretty soon after we established motive. See, most murders are spur of the moment, they happen a couple of minutes after the victim and the killer have met each other. There are fewer people sitting around planning death and destruction than you think – most are either crimes of passion, opportunistic or miscalculations. Which is comforting in some ways. Or more terrifying, if you imagine it means any one of us could turn into a killer given the right circumstances . . .'

He pointed up towards the bar. The barman was drying glasses and looking scornfully about the place. An old man with a hunched back and dirty trousers and shoes was coughing as he stared aimlessly into his pint glass.

'Say our barman pal decides to off the old boy, right here and now,' said Alby. 'It could be over anything, an argument, lover's tiff, not paying his tab, you name it. But he's not planned it out, our bloodthirsty barkeep. Our murderer hasn't thought about all the CCTV outside the pub, up and down the high street, all over town. The old boy will have passed through countless checkpoints and be on endless security streams. Then there's his phone. If it's a new-fangled thing, he'll be traced and tracked from dawn til dusk. Same for the killer. That's how we catch them on the force. We're methodical in the face of our culprit's whims and passions.'

'But it wasn't always like that, surely,' said Jason. 'I remember covering cases when I was a cub reporter, and we didn't have phones back then. We barely had five channels on the telly.'

'Hello!' Alby wrapped his knuckles on the table. 'Can you hear me all the way back in the twentieth century! Get with the times, Brazel. I'm talking about a modern murder investigation.'

The point was well made. Jason didn't retaliate.

'That's all well and good, Frank,' said Amita. 'But what if our killer, or indeed killers, *did* have premeditation and took all of this into account. What if they were planning the whole thing?'

'There's the rub,' Alby smiled. 'Those are the tricky ones. The puzzles, the dark minds and silent schemers. And that's when you need a good detective.'

Jason was going to say something, but Amita hushed him down before he could.

'Where does that leave us, then?' she asked.

Alby inhaled the foul air through his nose, making it whistle.

'We've got two missing men with money to burn,' he said. 'A wife who's just found out her husband is cheating on her. A university professor distraught that her lover has vanished. And the mother of a womaniser who doesn't seem to care.'

'Right where we started,' said Jason. 'You could have just said it leaves us right where we started, Alby.'

'You're the journalist, I thought I'd put it all in terms you can understand – why use three words when you can use thirty?' he smirked.

Amita ignored the verbal sparring between them. It didn't matter. What *did* matter was that Jason was right. There was next to nothing to go on, no instinct, no gut feeling she should follow a pathway that might shed some light on what was going on. She hated these moments in cases, the sense that nothing she could do might help. It was like being trapped in a locked box that was sinking to the bottom of the ocean. There was no escape and until they found the key to this crime, it was hopeless.

'There must be something more we can do, even if they're not being reported as missing,' she said. 'There must be some detail or little tidbit that we've overlooked along the way. And you can lean on your old colleagues, can't you, Frank – CCTV and whatnot? People don't just vanish into thin air these days. It's impossible. Isn't it?'

Jason shrugged. Alby slid out from behind the table, collecting his empty glass. 'If there's a will, there's a way,' he said. 'Again, you'd be surprised how often people just go for a walk and never return home.'

'He's right,' said Jason. 'It's a sad affair usually. We used to get them all the time in the paper. Missing person reports. If somebody really wants to disappear, they'll find a way. And there's nothing anyone can do about it. The families were the ones I always felt for. That sense of not knowing what's happened to their loved one. Dreadful.'

'Like Delice Weaver,' said Amita. 'Or Professor Hargreaves.'

'Grim,' Alby agreed.

He ambled his way around the table and started for the bar. He hadn't gone very far when he stopped. Clicking his fingers, he turned around to the others.

'Wait a minute,' he said. 'Where did Sutcliffe stay?'

'She's just around the corner,' said Jason.

'No, not the mum, the son,' he snapped. 'Grahame.'

Jason and Amita looked at each other. Neither of them knew.

'You've not got his address and turned his place over?' asked Alby. 'Are you joking? I thought you two were a couple of top-flight investigators hot on the trail of another mystery.'

'Yes, well . . .' Jason had nothing.

'That is to say we've been, well . . . busy,' Amita offered.

Alby had a wry smile on his face as he walked up to the bar. 'What would you two do without me, eh?' he called back over his shoulder.

Amita conceded that he was right. Jason was a little less happy about the fact.

'He makes a good point,' she said to him. 'We were so pleased about finding Mrs Sutcliffe's address, we haven't even got round to Sutcliffe's home.'

'I'm telling you now, Amita, if we turn up to his gaff and he's been laid up in bed all this time with flu, or a floozy, that's it, I'm through,' said Jason.

'I think, if that's the case, Jason, we're *both* through.'

Chapter 17

RICHARDIA GRANDIFLORA

Grahame Sutcliffe's home was not what any of them had been expecting. Mostly because they couldn't see it beyond what they could glimpse through the gate at end of the driveway. Crumbling walls blocked most of the view and while they could peer between the rusted struts of the cast-iron gates, paint peeling off the poles, beyond that were overgrown shrubs, bushes and well-established oak trees. The house itself was fully shrouded. Jason did his best to see something more through the firmly locked gates, but it was useless.

'Are you sure we're at the right address?' he asked. 'It doesn't exactly look like the pad of a millionaire tech entrepreneur.'

'It's where the boys at the station sent us,' said Alby. 'If you want to blame your mother-in-law's sense of direction, you go right ahead, mate.'

'That's not what I'm saying,' said Jason firmly. 'I'm just a bit confused, that's all. I was expecting a penthouse apartment in some flashy newbuild. Not the wreck of the Addams Family's Cumbrian holiday home.'

Amita laughed a little at that. She walked up to the gates and took a look for herself. A long pathway seemed to stretch on forever between more overgrown climbers and brambles. While it was still bright, as the afternoon wore on, everything beyond the walls and gates appeared dark and gloomy.

'Eerie, isn't it,' she said to the others.

'Not the most welcoming of places I've ever seen,' said Jason. 'Are you absolutely *sure* this is the right place?'

'For the last time, Brazel, yes. This is the address that Grahame Sutcliffe is registered to on our databases. I can't help it if he wants to lock himself away in the woods like Howard Hughes, can I?'

'Regardless of whether it's the right address or not, we won't be getting much beyond this, anyway,' said Amita. 'These gates might be old, but they're locked.'

She tried them. The huge gates clanged but stayed firm.

'That's that, then,' said Jason. 'Back to the drawing board.'

Amita looked at Alby. She was surprised to see he was giving her the same glance back. Jason picked up on it.

'What are you two doing?' he asked. 'You're not thinking what I think you're thinking. Because if you're thinking what I think you're thinking and you think I'm going to be onboard, you can think something else. Because it's a firm no.'

'Oh, come on, Brazel! Don't be such a wet blanket,' said Alby, pulling off his coat. 'Is he always like this?'

'Mostly,' said Amita. 'But he does have his uses from time to time.'

'I'm right here,' he said.

Amita and Alby walked a little way down the main road outside the gates and wall. They found a small clearing in the brush and he backed himself against the wall. Cupping his hands, he smiled at her.

'I'll bet this is the first time you've hopped a wall in a long time, am I right, Amita?' he said.

'You'd be very surprised how often it comes up in my life, Detective Inspector,' she said.

She put a muddy trainer in his hands. For a man of his age, weight, diet and general demeanour, Alby was remarkably strong. She was hoisted up to the top of the crumbling wall before she knew it. Only her quick thinking and reflexes were enough to stop her flying headfirst right over. She settled on the top, a leg dangling over each side of the wall. 'That was fun,' she said, looking down at Alby.

Jason had made his way to join them. He didn't look anywhere near as enthusiastic.

'Come on, I'll give you a hand,' she said to him.

'Shouldn't it be, you know, me who's helping you two get up there?' he asked.

'What's that supposed to mean?'

'Well, I'm the youngest here by a considerable margin. Twenty something years. I feel that I should be doing the heavy lifting and all of that. Not the other way around.'

'Brazel, if I thought for one second you were capable of doing *anything* properly, do you think I wouldn't let you?' asked Alby.

'That's a loaded question,' he said.

'Well shut up and get up this wall like a good lad. Come on, I'll give you a leg up.'

Jason did what he was told. Amita helped him and he scrambled as best he could.

'I wasn't made for climbing,' he said, out of breath. 'I'm not a climber. I'm a sitter. At most, a leisurely walker. Climbing is *not* in my repertoire.'

They reached down and each took one of Alby's hands. The former detective clawed and scrambled his way up the wall. Dropping down onto the other side, Amita caught her breath.

'Takes me back to my old scrumping days,' said Alby, dusting himself off. 'Down near Witherslack. A big group of us used to sneak down there at dusk, climb the wall and go take the apples in the orchards down there. The farmers used to go berserk. Can't say I blame them. We were little toerags.'

'And now look at you, you're a big toerag,' said Jason.

Alby didn't retaliate. He pulled on his coat and nodded towards where the path disappeared into trees. The three of them walked slowly and carefully among the undergrowth. The whole place was neglected and overgrown, nothing trimmed, pruned or cared for. Much like the gates and wall at the edge of the estate, everything here seemed like it had been forgotten.

They made their way through the thicket until suddenly the trees receded. A large, flat, open space lay ahead and at its centre was a sizeable old house. Much like the rest of the property, it had seen better days, but its former grandeur was still obvious. Thick wooden boards covered all of the windows. A partial attempt at scaffolding had been put up along one side, green netting flapping in the wind like some doomed galleon lost at sea. Warning signs and hazard markers were sprinkled about the perimeter of the house. The front door was barred with a pair of heavy metal sheets, bolted straight onto the stonework.

Beyond the decay, Amita could see the beauty in the place. It was clearly in need of serious repair, but the strength and character of the mansion house was still there. Like so many other places just like it around Cumbria, this one had been left to the elements for far too long. But it could be grand once again, if given a chance.

'She's a fixer-upper alright,' whistled Jason.

'Looks like Sutcliffe has been getting work done.' Alby pointed across the flat, open yard at the front of the mansion.

A digger and what looked like a portable toilet were clustered together on the edge of the woodland.

'That explains the warning signs,' said Amita. 'He must be renovating the house.'

'Doesn't look like much renovation is getting done today,' said Jason. 'It's not even four and everyone has clocked off for the day.'

'If they were ever here in the first place,' she said. 'Let's go explore.'

The three companions made their way towards the front door. Sutcliffe's mansion rose up above them. Amita reckoned it was at least two hundred years old. And much like her, age was just a number to these kinds of places. Good bones counted for a lot.

The metal sheets on the front door were bolted solid. Alby tried a little to open them, but it was no use.

'We're not getting in this way,' he said. 'Hannibal and his elephants couldn't break that down.'

'Let's try around the back,' said Amita.

They all marched around the perimeter of the building. Amita felt a chill as they passed into the back courtyard of the building.

'Bad memories,' said Jason to her, quietly.

'Yes, I'm afraid so,' she agreed. The memory was of what, or rather who, they'd found behind another once-grand, old Cumbrian house.

Things were much darker and cooler around here. The windows at the rear of the property were also boarded up. All except one. At the far end of the building, a wooden board was lying on the gravel. As they approached, Alby kneeled down and inspected it.

'It's been prised open,' he said, pointing to the splintered and broken edges of the board. 'Somebody has been getting handy with their crowbar.'

The freed window beside them was open. Amita suddenly felt very uncomfortable. There was something foreboding about the darkness beyond.

'Abandon all hope, you who enter here,' said Jason, sensing her mood.
'Quite,' she said.
'Go on then, Brazel. In you get, there's a good lad,' said Alby.
'Why me?' he blurted.
'Because you were having a right good go at your mother-in-law and I for being too old climbing that wall back there. Here's your chance to be the hero.'

Jason couldn't argue with the logic. He tried to ease himself into the window as best he could. He failed, falling down into the darkness. Amita's heart leapt into her mouth.

'I'm fine,' he shouted back. 'There's an awful lot of broken glass in here though. Just mind your step.'

Alby helped Amita inside and then joined them. They each turned on the torches on their phones and shone the light about the room.

'Definitely what they call "ripe for renovation",' said Amita, who had watched enough property shows to fancy she'd make a decent go of doing up houses, if only someone could lend her a few million to get going.

'Can you both smell something?' Jason sniffed. 'Oil or grease or something? Fried fat, maybe?'

'Your imagination is playing tricks on you, son,' said Alby. 'First rule of policing, never, ever lose your head when you're at a crime scene. Don't imagine you can smell, hear or see something. That's how mistakes are made.'

'Crime scene?' asked Amita fretfully. 'We don't know any crime has taken place.'

'Missing man, abandoned house, it's not looking good, is it?' asked Alby.

'As much as it pains me, he's right, Amita,' said Jason. 'I think we should perhaps prepare for the worst.'

'The worst.' No matter how many times she heard that phrase, Amita could never quite deal with what it meant. She had pondered, many times, whether she was still cut out for this kind of thing. Dead bodies, murder, villainy. What always got her through, what was always there waiting for her at the end of these lengthy debates, was the truth. The truth of what had happened to a victim, to an innocent bystander, to anyone who found themselves unfortunate enough to be wrapped up in this kind of thing. Grahame Sutcliffe, Fran Weaver, they were the same. She owed it to them and those they'd left behind, to get to that truth. No matter what that involved for her.

'Careful,' she said, as she pressed on into the gloom. 'We don't want to accidentally uncover a gaping hole in the floor where the workmen haven't started yet.'

Gingerly, she led the others on into the house. The darkness enveloped them. The lights of their phone torches were soon little more than tiny beacons amid the void, barely bright enough to pick out the pair of eyes glinting in the darkness, watching their every move from a safe distance.

Chapter 18

ANACARDIUM OCCIDENTALE

Every step felt like it was making a racket. Amita wasn't one for haunted houses. Whenever Jason and Radha wanted to watch a horror movie at home, she always made some excuse to be out of the room. Check on the kids, do the washing-up, practise her hula-hooping, anything. Halloween in the Brazel household was never a bundle of laughs for her – death felt a little too real to her rather than entertainment.

To be deep inside a derelict old manor house with nothing but her phone torch for illumination was a form of torture she knew she didn't deserve. It didn't help matters that Jason and Alby weren't at all bothered.

'Aren't you two going to pretend to not be enjoying this?' she whispered.

'What do you mean?' asked Jason, his head bobbing in front of her.

'You've both been tittering like a pair of schoolboys with every room we set foot in. Whereas I'm a nervous wreck every time I step on a loose floorboard.'

'This is real police work,' said Alby. 'It's not ghosties and ghoulies out to get us that I'm concerned about.'

Alby had no sooner spoken when something crashed down in front of them. They all let out a shout and trained their torches on the floor ahead. An empty paint tin lay spinning a few yards ahead of them.

'Bloody hell,' said Jason. 'I thought you were a goner, Alby.'

'Watch where you're putting your big feet, Brazel,' said Frank. 'The last thing we need is for you to go about kicking cans all over the place.'

'You're the former copper, Alby. If anyone went blundering in with their jack boots, it was probably you.'

He shone his torch in the retired detective's face. Alby did the same to Jason.

'I didn't touch it.'

'Well, neither did I.'

'Yes, you did. You're at the front.'

'I'm beside you.'

'I'm just . . .'

'Enough, the both of you,' Amita said sternly. 'We don't need this kind of distraction. Any minute now we could come across Grahame Sutcliffe's body and you two are fighting like toddlers on a road trip to Blackpool Illuminations.'

Both men stood solemnly quiet. The bright whiteness of the torchlights each had shone on the other made them look like apparitions amongst the darkness of the mansion. Amita moved swiftly on.

They made their way through the house's main level, passing through rooms of varying states of distress. Some were habitable, with complete walls and roofs. Others had gaping holes in the rafters and half-demolished entranceways. Drills, saws, toolboxes, everything the workers would ordinarily use had been left where they stood. Rolls and rolls of copper wiring and other materials were stacked up in corners.

'Whoever was here last left in a hurry,' said Jason. 'They've not even bothered to take their gear with them.'

'Could be that they downed tools on a Friday expecting to come back after the weekend,' said Alby. 'But they never showed up again.'

'Surely the fact their tools are still here implies they expect to come back,' said Amita. 'I don't think I've ever known an electrician or a plumber to knowingly cast aside their work apparatus.'

'True,' Alby conceded. 'It stinks all the same though.'

'You can smell it, too?' asked Jason. 'I told you, burning fat or oil or something.'

'No, I mean the situation,' said the former cop. 'This Sutcliffe character is coming across as being quite shady. The more we know about him, the less surprised I am that he's done a runner. Maybe he'd promised these people top dollar to do up the house, then he's done a disappearing act when it all got too pricey.'

Amita and Jason were in silent agreement. This whole house, where it was, the state it was in, only added to the mystery. The thought that around any corner they might discover a corpse only made matters worse.

The three continued until they got to a large, airy entranceway. Inspecting it, they realised they'd reached the other side of the front doors. Two lavish staircases reached up to a higher level, like tentacles emerging from the dusty, litter-strewn floor. Amita followed their path with her torch. When she reached the upper landing, she thought she saw something.

'What was that?' she asked the others, the words catching in her throat.

'Up there! In the shadows!' she pointed.

'Where?' asked Jason, flashing his torch to the upper level.

'You two are getting jittery,' said Alby. 'Why I've let you amateurs in here with me I don't know.'

'I saw something move,' said Amita. 'Up on the balcony, just out of reach of my light. I saw it, a shadow, moving quickly.'

'It's all shadows up there,' said Alby angrily. 'Maybe a bird or mouse or two.'

'I saw something, Frank, I know I did.'

Alby shone his torchlight up to the balcony. He followed the banister all the way from one side of the room to the other. There was nothing. Just dust, crumbling plaster on the walls and emptiness.

'There's someone in here with us,' she said. 'I can feel it.'

'Don't be ridiculous,' said Alby. 'We're the only people here.'

'If we're the only ones here, who prised the wooden board off the window and broke in?' whispered Jason.

'Probably some local kids looking to cause a bit of trouble. Or to come and smoke where their parents can't find them. A dozen explanations.'

'If you're so sure, why don't you go up and take a look?'

Alby hesitated. Even in the darkness, Jason and Amita could see him puffing out his chest.

'It's like that, is it?' he said. 'Send in the hired muscle when the *real* work needs to be done. I shouldn't be so surprised.'

He headed for the nearest staircase. Jason and Amita followed at a safe distance. They reached the balcony. There was still nothing there. At either end were open doors leading to more corridors and hallways of the mansion.

'There, see,' said Alby. 'Nothing, like I said. Honestly, you two. I've said this before and I'll say it again, some people are just not cut out for police work and I . . .'

He was stopped by the sound of an almighty crash. Metal clanged against metal before a scream whistled through the whole house. The three companions stood motionless for a second, wondering what was going on.

'What was that?' Alby gasped.

'Most probably just the shadows,' whispered Jason. 'Or a very big mouse . . .'

'Help me!' came an awful, high-pitched cry.

'Come on!' Amita shouted, bolting across the balcony.

Jason and Alby didn't argue. They set off after her. Amita wasn't sure what she was heading into. The darkness somehow seemed more intense up here on the first floor. It didn't matter though, not anymore. The first sign that somebody was in trouble, she knew what she had to do.

The voice kept crying out to them. They followed it as best they could, weaving and winding further and further into the house. At last, they reached a room where a warm orange glow was spilling out into the hallway.

'Good grief!' said Amita, skidding to a halt.

A huge hole in the floor lay just ahead of them. Two hands were clutching desperately onto the ragged edge of the floorboards.

'Help! Is there anyone there?' came the same voice again.

'Quickly!' Amita shouted to the others.

They raced ahead and reached down to grab the hands. Heaving, Amita, Jason and Alby pulled as hard as they could. They all collapsed backwards as a young woman emerged from the hole, sprawled out on the floor in front of them. Amita climbed to her feet with the help of her son-in-law. They were all gasping, from the effort and the shock.

'My dear, are you alright?' she asked.

The woman was on all fours, trying to catch her breath. Jason peered into the hole. It was quite a drop to the floor below – the mystery woman could have really come a cropper. Amita looked around the room. A small lamp and heater were placed in the corner, a camping stove with a frying pan and a few pots scattered about beside them. An old, dirty mattress was nearby with a sleeping bag opened on top of it. There were other food bags and packets, plus a charger and phone plugged into a battery pack. It was clear that this woman was camped out here in this dark and dingy place. Amita felt her heart ache.

'Are you okay?' she reached down to the young woman who was still gasping for breath. 'You could have really hurt yourself. This place isn't safe.'

'Can you . . . Can you call an ambulance please,' she said, through broken breaths.

'An ambulance?' Jason blurted, wiping sweat from his brow. 'You must have had a terrible shock, but you're alright now. What's the matter?'

'I think . . . I think my waters just broke.'

Nobody said anything. Amita could have kicked herself for not spotting it sooner, but the young woman was carrying a large bump and was, quite possibly, in the early stages of labour. The shock dissipated instantly, and her maternal instincts kicked back into gear in a big way.

'Jason!' she commanded. 'Get an ambulance here! And quickly!'

Chapter 19

GYPSOPHILA

No matter how many times Jason visited a hospital, he couldn't stomach The Smell. From his earliest memories of having his tonsils removed as a lad, to the more recent visits under different circumstances, it was always there. He'd spent a lifetime trying to work out what The Smell was, exactly. A mixture of sterile cleaning products and stagnant air, a touch of eau de cafeteria and a dash of plastic fumes. As he sat in the waiting room of the maternity unit, Amita beside him, he suddenly wished for the cooked fat and grease of Grahame Sutcliffe's manor instead.

'This takes me back,' he said, nudging his mother-in-law.

Amita snorted a little. He'd caught her dozing. Jason could hardly blame her, they'd been sat in this waiting room for close to five hours. Any hope of dinner at home, or even sleep in his own bed, were rapidly fading.

He felt a sudden pang of jealousy for Frank Alby. The former detective had protested all the way to the hospital, claiming he was too old for these kinds of emergency runs. When they'd reassured him that they'd stay in the waiting room, let him go back home and get some kip, he'd taken off so quickly, Jason thought his combover might have come loose.

'What takes you back?' she asked, rubbing her eyes.

'This. All of this. Sitting in a waiting room at the hospital with you, biting my nails, waiting on news of a new arrival.'

'Takes you back to Josh and Clara?' she asked.

'Of course,' he said. 'What did you think I was talking about?'

'You'll have to forgive me, Jason,' said Amita, stretching. 'But I was rather busy looking after my daughter who had an excruciating labour. And you were nowhere to be seen in the delivery room.'

'Oh, come on. Be fair,' he said. 'You know what I'm like with blood.'

'Yes, I do, unfortunately,' she said. 'But while you were out here, helping yourself to tea and crisps and whatever else from the vending machines, I was on the frontline with your wife making sure she didn't file for divorce.'

Jason nodded sadly. He'd wanted to be there for Radha, on both occasions, but it had all been too much for him in the end. And while his wife battled hard through both labours, he had been worse than useless, a pale, quivering mess cowering in the corner of the room. In the end, both times, he hadn't been what she needed. That duty had fallen to Amita.

'I suppose you're right,' he said, bowing his head a little. 'It was all for the best in the end. You were at least able to hold her hand and give her encouragement.'

'And everything else,' she jabbed.

'And everything else,' he repeated. 'I was less useful than a chocolate teapot unfortunately. I still can't believe that poor girl is in there on her own.'

They sat in silence for a moment. The rest of the maternity unit was busy, filled with worried faces, overworked staff and the distant, faint coos and cries of newly born babies.

'I guess all of this has brought it back,' he said. 'We've had no reason to be back in this place since the kids were born. It's funny how being in a certain room, after all these years, can suddenly transport you right back there, emotions and all.'

'Very true,' said Amita. 'Worry and strife, it's just part of being a parent.'

'You don't realise that, do you, until you are one,' he said. 'I mean, you always think you know what it's going to be like. But until those little bundles of joy arrive, kicking, screaming and desperate for attention, it's not the same.'

'I remember when Radha was born,' said Amita with a smile. 'I used to think I knew it all. And to this day, I never doubted myself as much as I did when she arrived. It was everything, every cough, every gurgle, you thought to yourself that you'd done something wrong.'

'And that the end of the world was nigh,' Jason smiled too.

'Now look at her, a woman, a successful woman, with children all grown up of her own. Time, Jason, it makes fools of us all in the end. As much as you think you've got a handle on things, quick as a flash, it all changes. I guess that's part of the fun.'

'Something like that,' he agreed.

They fell into a comfortable quiet while the madness of the waiting room unfolded about them. Jason couldn't really remember speaking with Amita about parenting so candidly. Or at all, for that matter. Their relationship was one of strict roles. To hear her talk so freely about something they had in common was a nice break from the norm. It wouldn't last, he thought. He'd put his foot in his mouth, and she'd be back to berating him within moments.

Seconds would have been more accurate. A doctor in full scrubs came walking quickly out of a set of double doors where the young woman they had found had been taken. She looked about the waiting room and stopped when she spotted Jason and Amita.

'Heads up,' said Jason. 'I think we might be on here.'

Amita got to her feet. They greeted the doctor who offered them a warm smile.

'Mum and baby are doing great,' she said. 'We've just had a successful delivery.'

'And what is it?' asked Amita.

'A little boy,' said the doctor. 'He's being looked after as we speak. Mum was a little shaken, as you'd expect given the circumstances. But I'm confident they'll both be fine. Congratulations, Daddy.'

She took Jason's hand and shook it. He felt his face flush.

'Oh no. No, no. I'm not the father,' he said.

'Pardon me?' asked the medic.

'No, I'm not Daddy. I mean, I *am* a dad, just not to this little sprog.'

'I'm confused,' said the doctor, puffing out her cheeks. 'You're not Dad and Granny?'

'No, I'm afraid not,' said Amita. 'To be perfectly honest with you, we don't know that young woman in there. We were just in the right place at the right time to make sure she got here safely.'

'And you waited for her?'

'That's right,' said Amita.

'She was in labour for over four hours.'

'We know,' said Jason. 'I'm considerably worse off for all the money I've pumped into those vending machines down the corridor there.'

The doctor rubbed her forehead. Jason couldn't blame her for the confusion. Explaining who they were and why they were in the strangest of situations had become something of an occupational hazard. In the old days, he would simply flash his press card, and nobody would think any more of it. Either doors would be opened or they'd be slammed in his face. Now, without the luxury of a 'real job' he had to do a lot more explaining.

'It's a long story,' he said. 'And I'm sure you don't have the time to hear it all. So, we'll just be on our way now that we know the girl is okay. Isn't that right, Amita.'

He tugged at his mother-in-law's arm. She didn't budge. He was going to try harder, but the doctor stepped in.

'Look, I don't know what's going on here,' she said. 'I see all sorts come through those doors. My concerns are for Mum and baby. Whoever you guys are, you did the right thing and stopped a tricky situation from becoming very messy. She wants to speak to you, both of you.'

'She does?' Amita couldn't hide the joy in her voice.

'Yes,' said the doctor. 'As you can appreciate, it's normally just friends and family, but I'm not about to go back to a young woman who's just gone through that kind of labour alone and tell her no. Just don't make a song and dance about it that the press might get wind of, okay?'

'Actually, I'm . . .'

Amita elbowed Jason in the ribs before he could finish his sentence.

'We'd be delighted,' she said.

The doctor nodded. She showed them through the huge double doors and started along a lengthy corridor. Through here was the action zone, Jason thought. He'd only been in here after everything had unfolded yet he remembered it all like it was yesterday. The screams, the tears, the laughter, the joy, all contained within one ward. Lives started, lives changed forever, behind the bland wooden doors of the labour suites.

'Remarkable,' he said quietly.

'What's that?' asked Amita.

'Nothing,' he said, but silently promised to give Radha and the kids a tighter hug than usual when he finally got home.

The medic stopped at a door close to the end of the corridor. She knocked on it once and then stepped inside. The young woman they had rescued from Grahame Sutcliffe's mansion was sitting up in bed. She cradled her newborn son in her arms, swaddled in a bright white blanket with a blue woollen hat on his tiny head. Jason and Amita beamed as they shuffled into the room behind the doctor, their eyes locked on the baby.

'I'll leave you all to it,' she said. 'If you need anything Enni, just call, okay?'

'Thank you,' said the young woman.

The doctor gave a little nod and left the room, closing the door gently behind her so as not to wake the baby. Jason and Amita just stood there, their hearts bursting, watching as the child slept in his mother's arms.

'Thank you, both of you, for saving our lives,' said Enni. 'I don't know what I would have done if you hadn't been there to rescue me.'

'Oh, nonsense. We didn't do anything,' said Amita.

'Just in the right place at the right time. Or the wrong place at the right time. Or is that the right place at the wrong time, I'm not so sure.'

'Jason, pull yourself together,' she said to him.

'Sorry,' he apologised. 'It's newborn babies, they always make me act and talk like a blithering idiot, I'm afraid.'

'What's your excuse the rest of the time?' asked Amita quietly.

He ignored her, leaning over to get a better look at the infant. Enni smiled at him.

'Would you like to hold him?' she asked.

Jason blinked. 'Are you sure?' he asked back. 'I mean, you don't even know who we are.'

'You saved his life before he was born, and then you waited to see if we were okay,' said Enni. 'That's all I need to know about you both right now.'

Jason felt his throat tightening at that, the sting of tears behind his eyes and nose. He looked at Amita who was much the same. She nodded and he reached down and took the baby. It may have been years since he was in this position, but the knowledge was still there. Like riding a bike, he never forgot the joy and the special pleasure of holding a newborn. 'He's a little cracker, isn't he,' he said, showing him to Amita. 'Have you thought of a name?'

'No,' said Enni, resting her head on her pillow. 'Grahame and I had thought about naming him after *his* dad. But I'm not so sure. I'm not even sure Grahame *wants* the baby. Can you imagine?'

The mention of Grahame Sutcliffe brought everything hurtling back to reality for both Jason and Amita. The bubble of the maternity unit, the baby, the memories of their own family were gone in a flash.

'Jason is a very good name,' he said, trying to recapture some of the magic. 'I'd recommend that. It's seen me okay over the years.'

'And I'm Amita,' she added. 'We're very pleased to properly meet you, Enni. And your little one.'

'It's been quite a day, hasn't it?' she asked with a sad smile. 'I just wish Grahame had been here to see all of this. But he's probably out there with some tart. One of his tarts.'

'Are you and Grahame together?' asked Amita.

'That's a polite way of putting it,' Enni snorted. 'We met about a year ago and, as you can see, one thing led to another. My mum and dad weren't happy I was seeing somebody older than me when I told them. In fact, my dad went nuts. Grahame's only a couple of years younger than him. He made all these accusations. It really hurt, hurt both of us, or that's what Grahame said anyway. You can imagine what my dad said when I told him I was pregnant. Dropping out of uni was bad enough for him. But this, it was awful.'

'Will you tell him about the baby?' asked Amita.

'I suppose I should,' said Enni. 'He's a grandfather, he should act like it. Although I'd like to tell Grahame first. He'll know what to do, he'll look after us both. To hell with my old man.'

Amita's stomach clenched tight. She darted Jason a quick look as he rocked the baby, walking around the end of the bed and over to the big window of the suite.

'When did you last hear from Grahame?' she asked.

'It's been weeks,' said Enni. 'I haven't seen him, haven't had a call, a text, nothing. I'm afraid that the prospect of impending fatherhood has frightened him off. I know he's been away for business, he does that regularly, but normally he's always at the end of the phone for me, especially in the last few months while I was pregnant. I don't even know where my phone is to call him now.'

She weakly tried to sit up, but Amita eased her back down.

'Don't worry about that just now,' she said. 'Just think about getting your energy back. Like you said, you've had quite a day.'

'I don't know what I would have done if you hadn't pulled me out of that hole,' said Enni.

'What were you doing in that place anyway?' asked Jason. 'It's a death trap.'

'It's Grahame's place,' she said. 'He's doing it up. We're going to live there, as a family. It'll be gorgeous when it's finished. I had nowhere else to go. My lease was up in town, and I haven't really got any friends round here I could crash with. I'd not heard from Grahame in weeks, so that was the only place I could go to be close to him. I thought I'd just go there and wait. It's going to be my home after all. Our home. When all the work is finished.'

'So, you broke in?' asked Amita.

'I had to,' she said. 'You should have seen me, eight months pregnant, clambering in through a broken window. Took me back to my days backpacking around India. It wasn't all that bad. It could get quite cosy at night with the blankets and a few candles.'

'Didn't the workies spot you?' asked Jason.

'They've not been there for months,' she said. 'They walked out when Grahame stopped answering their calls. And stopped paying their bills. I don't blame them. If he's not answering my calls and I'm the mother of his child, what chance do the sparkies and joiners have, right?'

Jason nodded. He looked down at the little baby in his arms. He could see the similarities with the photos he'd seen of Sutcliffe, even this early on. The same nose, the same brow.

'This is going to sound very impolite, Enni,' said Amita. 'But you don't have any ideas exactly where Grahame might be? Or who he might be with?'

'I wish I did,' she said. 'If I knew where that cheating rat was, I'd gut him like a fish. And even that would be too good for him.'

'He's not good boyfriend material, then?' asked Jason.

'Grahame? The man can't walk past a mirror without admiring himself for twenty minutes. Sure, he acted delighted he was going to be a father when I told him, but that quickly evaporated, like all of his promises. As if it wasn't bad enough, this business deal, this company he's sold, it just went straight to his head. He bought that wreck of a mansion and then couldn't pay the bills. Now he's left me, a pregnant woman, pretty much homeless. "Don't worry sweetheart," that's what he always said. "We'll be fine, all three of us, in that big house. We'll be like royalty." And I believed it. That's the worst part.'

Amita shook her head. Every turn of this sordid tale got worse and worse. But a clear picture of Grahame Sutcliffe was forming in her mind. And he was hardly the upstanding member of the community that she imagined he'd like to be seen as.

'Is there anything we can do to help, Enni?' she asked.

'You've already done enough for us both,' she said. 'I can't thank you enough for being there. And waiting too, you didn't have to do that. Most people would have dumped me at the front desk and gone, legged it as fast as they could.'

'What about your parents?' asked Jason. 'Will you contact them and let them know?'

'I will,' she nodded. 'My mum will want to see her grandson, even if my dad might not. She'll come and see me when she can get here.'

'What about Grahame's mum?'

'Grahame's mum?' asked Enni as Jason handed her back her son.

'Yes, Mrs Sutcliffe,' said Amita.

'I don't understand?' Enni adjusted the baby. 'What about her?'

'She'll want to see the baby too, surely?'

'I don't think so, somehow,' she said. 'She's been dead for about twenty years.'

Amita felt her forehead crinkle. Jason was doing the same.

'Grahame doesn't have any family,' said Enni. 'His mum died when he was just out of uni. It's just been him all this time. I know that because he gave me the old pony about being delighted that the baby would be part of a new generation of Sutcliffes. The family he's wanted for so long and all that. That's why we talked about his dad. But his mum has been dead for years.'

Enni looked at them both. A dawning realisation made her shake her head in disbelief.

'That was all lies too, am I right?' she said. 'Honestly, that man. He couldn't help but lie, even when it was about nothing. A real piece of work.'

'I'm sorry,' said Amita. 'Truly I am.'

'It's not your fault,' said Enni. 'You shouldn't apologise for him. Nobody should. He should take responsibility for his actions. He's a father now for god's sake. He should grow up and stop all this running around sleeping with strangers and drinking until all hours. Cash or no cash, he's a father now. If I ever see him again, I'll strangle him. I really will.'

The baby began to cry. Enni soothed him back to sleep, cradling him close to her. Jason felt awful. He didn't want to leave, but he knew he had to. In the very short amount of time he had known her, Enni seemed like a capable, sensible young woman. A survivor. Wronged by Sutcliffe, sure, but she had character, a spine, an inner strength that not only was admirable, it was clear it was necessary.

'We should be going,' said Amita. 'Can we get you anything? Can we help you with your parents? Are they local?'

'They were, but they live in Florida now, a nice retirement in the sunshine,' she said. 'I'll call them. They'll be here in a few days, I'm sure. Who knows, maybe my dad will bother his backside to come over, too.'

She smiled weakly. Amita squeezed her hand and they both retreated out the door to the sound of the baby gently snoring. They started back down the corridor towards the waiting room.

'What a world,' said Jason, sadly. 'She's a remarkable young woman. Caught up with that dirtbag Sutcliffe, and now facing everything on her own.'

'She won't be on her own for long,' said Amita. 'I'm sure even her father will come around to the notion of being a grandparent when he sees that little baby. How couldn't he?'

'It's still not right,' he said. 'Guys like Sutcliffe, they don't know they're living. They just breeze through life leaving devastation and people hurt in their wake. Hot shots and the oldest rockers in town. They never think about anybody else other than themselves. And it's all left to people like Enni in there to deal with the consequences.'

'Funny,' said Amita.

'What's funny?' he asked.

'You, Jason Brazel, the great sceptic,' she said. 'Developing a conscience, are we?'

'I'm just saying, Amita, that's all,' he said. 'Being a dad is a privilege, not a right. This Grahame Sutcliffe has known he's going to be a father for months and, you heard her, he's been running around all over town with who knows what kind of crowd. It really makes me sick, sick to my back teeth when people don't appreciate what's right under their nose.'

He stopped suddenly. Amita stopped too, a little surprised.

'You know what,' he said. 'I'm not going to put up with it.'

'Put up with what?' she asked.

He spun around quickly and started back up the corridor towards Enni's room.

'Jason?' Amita called after him. 'What are you doing?'

He was fired-up, the blood in his veins boiling with a determined flame. He stomped up the corridor. He couldn't remember the last time he'd felt this way. But some things had to be done. There was a proper way of behaving, even if Grahame Sutcliffe wanted to believe otherwise.

Jason knocked once on the door before opening it. Amita was at his back, bewildered.

'Enni!' he said, his voice far too loud for the labour suite.

'Jason?' she looked up at him.

'I know this is going to sound utterly strange. And feel free to say no. But . . .' he trailed off.

She looked at him expectantly. Amita did the same.

'Would you like to come and stay with us?' he asked. 'I mean, until your parents arrive. We don't have a whole lot of space. But it's warm and it's safe and it's the right thing to do. I bet my wife has still got baby stuff in the loft, and my kids have got heaps of toys they'd be happy to pass on.'

Enni's eyes filled with tears. And for the first time since they met, she flashed them a smile.

'Yes,' she said, her voice cracking. 'I would love that.'

'Good,' said Jason, taking a deep breath. 'That's settled then.'

He turned to Amita who was also crying.

'Best make up the sofa bed then, eh?' he said to her. 'And dig out the cot. We've got a new arrival to tell Radha about.'

Chapter 20

SOLANUM LYCOPERSICUM

Whoever said that a week was a long time in politics had clearly never spent any time at the Penrith Bingo Club. By the time Amita took her seat, she felt like she was finally catching a breath. Could it only have been seven days ago when she was last here, when all they had to worry about was a few tipsy shenanigans on their minibus trip to the big smoke?

Events had certainly taken a turn for the stranger in recent days. While she might not quite have longed for the worry and brain strain of working out where two missing men had gone, she would never have guessed she'd be playing nursemaid to a newborn baby boy. Yet here she was, rummaging through her handbag searching for her blotters and finding burp cloths and dummies.

'Blimey, Amita,' said Sandy, peering over her shoulder. 'Are you teething or something? Shall I get you some Bonjela?'

Amita was affronted. Instinctively she closed her bag over as he wheeled Ethel around to her usual place at the end of the table.

'They're . . . not mine,' she said feebly.

'I thought as much,' said Sandy, chuckling. 'I know you should never comment on a woman's age, but I thought, even with your fresh-faced good looks, you were a bit too old for a dummy.'

The hall was still relatively quiet. Amita was grateful. She knew she could confide in Sandy. Anything between them would never go any further – unlike most of the loose lips at the bingo club, Sandy was a man who prided himself on keeping his counsel. She got up from her chair and hurried around to him as he took off his big overcoat.

'Could I speak with you, privately, Sandy? It won't take very long,' she said.

'Of course,' he looked about the hall. 'Over there, shall we get a cuppa? Is everything alright?'

'Yes,' she said.

They walked slowly towards the giant urns and plates of biscuits laid out for half time. Amita was strangely paranoid. Sandy filled two mugs and started on a third for Ethel.

'Are you alright, Amita?' he asked again. 'You seem on edge, a bit jittery. Has somebody threatened you? If they have, I'll go and have a word with them and sort them right out.'

'No, no, nothing like that, Sandy. Nothing at all like that,' she said. 'But thank you for that reassuring threat.'

'I used to bounce doors in Soho. I know my way about a bit of persuasive conversation.'

'Don't I know it. But it won't be needed this time. No, it's something a little bit more delicate and personal.'

'Personal?' his moustache twitched. 'I don't like the sound of that.'

'There's no quick way of telling you why, Sandy, but we've got a newborn baby in the house.'

Sandy almost choked as he gulped at his tea. He began to cough and had to set down his mug and catch his breath.

'A baby?' he spluttered. 'Has Jason been up to no good?!'

'Keep your voice down,' she hushed him. 'This is why I wanted to tell you privately. You know what the gossips are like in here. They make a nest of vipers look like a box of chocolates at Valentine's Day. And no, it's not Jason's.'

'Bloody Nora, Amita. What have you got yourself mixed up in now?' he asked.

'Don't worry, it's nothing sinister. Not yet anyway. The mother is living with us too.'

'The mother, too?' he said. 'What are you lot doing? Taking in the waifs and strays? Is Jason starting a workhouse or something?'

'Sandy, please,' she said. 'I thought I could trust you with all of this.'

He dried his moustache on the sleeve of his shirt. He looked at her with sad eyes.

'I'm sorry, that was bang out of order,' he said. 'Of course you can trust me.'

She patted him on the arm. 'Thank you,' she said. 'And I should apologise too. It's a bit of surprise to drop into conversation over the custard creams.'

'It certainly is,' he said. 'And while I'm not one to cast doubts over your generous spirit, as your friend I can't help but ask how well you know these unexpected guests? How the hell did you find yourself playing nursemaid again to, who I assume, are strangers.'

Amita explained the whole case to Sandy. With every twist and turn of what had happened, his face grew more and more grave. By the end his brow was so low he looked like a time-travelling Neanderthal. All he was missing was a club and an animal skin.

'Blimey,' he breathed. 'That all sounds awful. What a bounder this Sutcliffe fellow sounds.'

'It is awful,' she said. 'But now we have a young woman with a newborn baby to worry about. They're no problem at all, of course they aren't. And I think Radha is quite enjoying having a little bairn back in the house. At least, she is now that the shock has worn off. I can't say I was expecting this sudden chivalry from Jason. You know what he's like. It's been quite heartening to see him take to Enni and the little boy though. Even at two in the morning when the house is in uproar.'

'I'll bet,' said Sandy. 'So why are you telling me all this? I'm a bit out of practice at burping and pram walks.'

'No, I'm not drafting you in for daycare,' she said. 'Although it does keep you young at heart having a nipper to hold. No, I rather thought you might keep your ear to the ground about these missing men. I don't think either of them are likely to turn up at Crown Green Bowls or your Rotary Club lunch, but it never hurts to ask. What about the Garden Club? You used to have an allotment, didn't you? Spread the word, would you, Sandy, in your usual tactful way.'

'I will do my best,' he said. 'For you, Amita, and your tiny houseguest. Although I don't know if I'm welcome down at the Garden Club. There's been a terrible rift between the flower gang and the fruit and veg faction. Roses versus runner beans – it's not a battle I want to fight. But if it'll help you and a wee baby, I'll run the gauntlet.'

Amita watched as Georgie Littlejohn, Barbara McLemore and Pauline Saxon all arrived at the hall. They waved over as they took their regular seats. Amita's heart beat that little bit faster. She was quite certain

Georgie had supersonic hearing at the best of times. Even more so when there was juicy gossip to be shared.

'But as much as anything, I'm confiding in you, Sandy, as I'm feeling fit to burst,' she said. 'I've got all these weird and wonderful theories running around my head and I can't think straight. From Fran Weaver's affair to this elusive deal that their company has been involved in, it all just doesn't add up. And when I get like that with a case, sometimes I need to talk it through.'

'Throw a baby into the mix and your brain must be like scrambled eggs.'

That made Amita laugh. She took his hand. It felt so natural, so perfectly normal that she hadn't even thought about it. She just expected it to be there, and it was. It *always* was. For a little moment, she felt less nervous, less anxious, that everything was going to be alright. Then she remembered where she was. She let go of Sandy's hand much quicker than she wanted. He just smiled at her.

'If there's anything I can do, Amita, anything at all, you only have to ask,' he said. 'Although I don't have much practice changing nappies and the like. I'm always happy to give it a go. Now we had better get back,' said Sandy. 'Otherwise, we'll be accused of fraternising over the fondant fancies, and you know that's how rumours start.'

'And we don't want that,' she said. 'They'll have us eloped and wed before the first house.'

Sandy chuckled warmly. They fetched their tea, Sandy carrying Ethel's, and returned to the table.

'Good evening, you two,' said Georgie, sitting proud like the Queen of the Castle in her usual spot. 'What were you both giggling about over there.'

'Me? Giggle?' Sandy sniffed. 'I don't think I've ever giggled about anything in my life, Georgie. And even if I did, I wouldn't chatter about it, would I?' Sandy moved over to Ethel's end of the table leaving Amita stranded with Georgie.

'Some people just don't have the detective gene like we do,' she sneered, turning her attention to Amita. 'And where have you been all week, anyway? I was expecting to see you at the community council meeting on Monday night. You missed a rather thrilling debate on whether the pedestrian zone at the farmers' market on Sundays should be extended fifteen feet down the high street.'

'I got a little tied up, I'm afraid,' said Amita, sipping her tea.

'Tied up?' Georgie yelped. 'This was about our civic infrastructure, Amita, not some lurid investigation of yours. I was expecting your valued input into the debate.'

'Like I said, Georgie, I was tied up with other business.'

She had to keep her cool. Georgie Littlejohn was like a Great White sniffing blood in the water when it came to anything out of the ordinary. The merest suggestion that everything was not hunky-dory and she'd be on you in seconds.

'Speaking of investigations, I've had a little bit of a breakthrough with my own,' she said.

It took Amita a few seconds to work out what she was talking about. 'Investigation?' she asked.

'Yes, my investigation. You know . . . The money?'

She rubbed her fingers together.

'Ah, yes, of course,' said Amita. 'The plundered pocket money.'

'I'd hardly call it pocket money. It's hundreds of pounds, if my calculations are right,' she said.

Amita tried to look interested. 'Go on then, what's this big breakthrough?'

A delighted Georgie huddled a little closer to her. It was clear that she could barely contain her excitement. Amita tried to remain openminded.

'Well, you know Margaret Cullen?' she whispered.

'You know I do,' said Amita.

'So, it seems she's been having a bit of work done to her house. You know it, on the edge of that big new estate on the east side of town.'

'I've never been, but I know where she lives,' said Amita.

'Anyway, I heard through very reliable sources, and I mean watertight sources, Amita, not the usual gossip merchants, that she's had the workmen in for the last six weeks straight. There's a skip outside her house and everything. Day and night they're round there, hauling out bits of wood, walls, even carpet. I've heard, again from impeccable sources, that she's getting a new bathroom suite fitted. They're expensive, Amita, you and I both know that. A couple of thousand at least. Now, I'm not one who likes to talk about others.'

Amita waited for the punchline. There wasn't one.

'But where do you suppose someone like Margaret Cullen is getting the money for a brand-new bathroom suite at her age?'

'She's younger than both of us,' said Amita.

'Only by a few months. It hardly matters, does it? I mean, if she's forking out a lump sum and getting the workmen in, in this economic climate, it makes you think that she's come into a little money, doesn't it?'

Georgie was now happy for Amita to speak. She pursed her lips and sat back expectantly, waiting to be praised to the hilt. Amita scratched her head.

'Does Margaret even have access to the bingo club funds?' she asked.

'I'm sure she could weasel her way into getting a look from Father Ford,' Georgie fired back. 'I think *anyone* could, if they put their mind to it. The man is a wet blanket through and through, a knitted balaclava.'

She caught herself before she said anything more. She looked about the hall for the embattled pastor, but he hadn't come in from greeting club members at the front of the hall.

'And you've got no other evidence to prove it's Margaret, other than she's getting a new, possibly expensive, bathroom suite installed?' asked Amita.

'What further evidence do you need?' Georgie raised her voice a little. 'I mean, it's staring you right in the face, Amita. The money goes missing and then Margaret Cullen is spending cash like it's going out of fashion. I would have thought even an amateur like *you* would have been able to piece it all together.'

Amita smiled at that. The arrogance of Georgie Littlejohn could be baffling at times. The woman's ego was so huge that it would take Everest just to crush it.

'Well, you're right that it's a suspect and motive I wouldn't have been likely to spot,' she said.

'Of course I'm right,' sneered Georgie. 'Honestly, you and Jason, you seem to make such a hash of things when you're doing these little investigations of yours. You should rope me into one of them sometime, I'll catch the culprit in a few days. I've done it this time, haven't I?'

She leaned back. She was smug, smugger than usual, beaming a delighted smile at Amita, her pearls glistening in the light of the church hall, her mohair sweater and matching neck scarf tied with military precision. Amita was just relieved she'd resisted the urge to team it all with a Deerstalker hat now she was convinced of her new calling.

'Well, it's certainly a novel theory,' said Amita, awkwardly. 'I just can't believe that Margaret would stoop to something like this. Especially after her fall.'

Georgie's face dropped like it had been dragged down by an anvil.

'Fall? What fall?' she asked.

'Margaret's fall,' said Amita. 'Must have been about two months ago now. Maybe longer. Didn't you hear?'

'No, no, I didn't hear anything,' said Georgie. 'What happened to her?'

'Ice,' said Amita, sucking air through her teeth. 'She had a nasty trip walking home one night from here. You know how icy the pavements can get outside, especially on the bitterly cold nights. The council, it's always the council.'

'Yes, yes, the bloody council. What happened to Margaret?'

Amita had her – a fish on the line.

'From what I understand, she went about three feet in the air and landed with a thump,' she said. 'Cracked something in her coccyx. The poor thing could barely walk. You must have noticed that she wasn't playing the numbers for a couple of months. And what I heard was that she was really struggling at home, you know her house, on the edge of that big new estate on the east side of town.'

Amita was enjoying this. Georgie's face was growing paler by the second.

'Anyway, I had heard, from watertight sources, probably the same sources, that she was getting one of those walk-in showers fitted. She was never that steady on her feet at the best of times. In fact, didn't you always say it was because she was weighed down by all the bonus bingo lines she won?'

'Yes,' Georgie croaked. 'Something like that.'

'I think she won on the night of her accident, too. Forty-seven pounds. Still, what use is that if you're in as much pain as she's been these last few months. Isn't that right?'

'Yes, yes, I suppose it is,' said Georgie.

Amita finished her tea. The hall was getting busy now, their table almost full. Father Ford closed the main doors and went to take up his usual position at the numbers machine.

'Still, if you think she's pilfered the cash, you should let the police know,' said Amita, fetching her dabber. 'It's probably all just a coincidence that she fell, almost broke her back, needs a walk-in shower, had a settlement from the council and is being cared for by her family. Wouldn't you agree?'

Georgie looked distraught. She was drained of colour and seemed suddenly very old. She mouthed something and opened up her bingo book.

'Yes,' she eventually managed. 'A real shame.'

Amita felt quite good about herself. Investigations, it seemed, weren't quite as easy as Georgie Littlejohn thought.

Chapter 21
THEOBROMA CACAO

Jason really needed to scratch his nose. He'd tried to fight the urge, resist it with all of his might, but it was becoming unbearable. Once the idea was in his head, it was all he was able to think about. The seconds ticked past like minutes, then hours, then days. All he could do was sit, in silence, and hope that the itch would go away.

'Please stop itching,' he whispered to himself. 'For the love of all that's holy, please just stop itching.'

Ordinarily, he would have just scratched the itch. That would be the logical thing to do. And he considered himself to be at least *somewhat* logical. However, with a newborn baby sound asleep in your arms, all logic tended to go straight out of the window.

Radha was nowhere to be seen. Neither were his own children. He'd been sitting contentedly after the baby had finally drifted off. He was breathing lightly, a little lump in Jason's arms as they sat on the couch, burrowed into the corner, cushions and blankets strewn about them.

The little sprog had only been with them a night or two, but already things had been tough. His poor mother was sleep starved and sore. And he didn't seem at all interested in sleeping through the night. The whole house was in an uproar with this one, single bundle of joy. Now Jason was lumbered with an impossible choice – move and scratch or stand firm and suffer. He was pretty sure there were rules against this sort of thing in the Geneva Convention.

'Radha,' he said, as loud as he dared.

He kept one eye on the little boy in his arms. There was no response from his wife.

'Radha. Help,' he said again.

Still nothing. To make matters worse, he'd never known the house to be so quiet, or empty. The kids were somewhere upstairs, getting ready for bed. Enni was sound asleep in his bedroom and Amita was at bingo. Maybe Radha had finally run away and left him. He could hardly blame her.

She had been wonderful, as always, when he'd delivered the news about Enni and the baby. Over the decades of their relationship, he had tested her patience more than the other way around. From endless work projects to the investigations and freelance stories of the last few years, Radha Brazel had always stood by her man. Sure, she'd tear strips off him when he overstepped the mark on a case or dropped the ball at home, but she also loved him with a passion that he could never repay – he could only try to through a life of devotion. Even when he announced a newborn baby and his mother were coming to stay, she had remained buoyant and positive. More so than he deserved, or she had to.

Now he needed her again. This time for the innocuous. Jason had a theory that the real glue of marriage was not the flowers and gifts but the humdrum, the shared daily life, in all its challenges, punctuated if you were lucky by equal parts joy and grief. When he was desperate for his wife to scratch his nose, that's when he knew he'd made it as a husband.

'Radha,' he tried once more.

The baby stirred in his arms. He was round-faced and adorable, as most babies are. Swaddled in a blanket Radha had found packed away in the cupboard under the stairs, Jason could smell his own kids in the warm soft wool. He had always wanted to be a dad. And when he thought of how different this little boy's entry into the world had been to his own kids', it made him sad and furious all in one breath. If he ever caught up with Grahame Sutcliffe, he vowed to give the lothario a piece of his mind. And a swift boot up the backside for good measure.

'Did you call on me?'

Radha's head poked around the living room door. Jason could have wept.

'Can you scratch my nose, please,' he whispered. 'I'm somewhat incapacitated by this beautiful young fellow.'

Radha clicked her tongue. She was carrying a bottle of milk, shaking it up to mix in the formula. She reached down and tickled the end of Jason's nose.

'Thank you,' he said.

She sat down beside him. They just stayed there for a moment, looking at the little baby. She leaned her chin on his shoulder and smiled.

'Remember when our two were this size?' she asked.

'No,' said Jason. 'I don't. I'm lucky if I remember what we had for breakfast two days ago let alone all those years ago. Plus, we were pretty sleep-deprived and terrified. Not a good combo.'

'Even the second time around with Clara,' she agreed.

'I think it was *worse* with Clara. You knew what was coming. At least with Josh we were ignorant enough to be arrogant and think we could handle it all.'

'We got there in the end though,' she said.

'We did. And we picked up a seventy-year-old tearaway to look after along the way too.'

'Don't let her hear you say that,' said Radha. 'Remember the caravan trip to Skegness when you accused her of being just as bad as the kids.'

'Remember it? I'm still paying for therapy.'

'Behave,' she said.

She shook the bottle until she was happy with the milk. She checked her watch then nudged Jason.

'Time for a feed?' she said.

'Really?' he asked. 'But he's just gone down. Seems a pity to wake him.'

'That's why I've made up a bottle,' she said. 'I don't want to wake up that poor girl. She hasn't slept a wink in days. Not to mention everything else that's going on.'

'I know,' Jason shook his head. 'It just makes me so angry.'

'Which part?'

'All of it,' he said, nodding to the old chalkboard on the far side of the room. 'This Grahame Sutcliffe character, whoever he really is. Vanishing, getting mixed up in who knows what, all when he knew, he actually *knew* that he had a baby on the way.'

'At least Enni can see through him,' said Radha, reaching over to take the baby. 'Some men and women just turn a blind eye to philandering and bad behaviour. It catches up with them in the end. It's all in a day's work for a lawyer, I've seen everything from cheating partners to disappearing acts.'

Jason handed the little boy over. He rolled his shoulders and felt the tingling in his arms and hands. Radha gently popped the bottle into the baby's mouth, and he began to drink, making gurgling sounds with every swallow.

Jason stood up and stretched. He wandered over to the chalkboard. Amita had updated it with as much information as they had. Circles, lines and zigzags all darted between names, places and things. He couldn't make much from it. She had a system. He wasn't privy. He knew everything there anyway.

'Do you think that's all this is?' he asked Radha. 'That Sutcliffe has done a runner because he knew he had a kid on the way?'

'I've known people to run off for less important reasons,' she said. 'And you've told me he's hardly an upstanding member of the community.'

'He most certainly isn't,' said Jason. 'He makes your mother look like Saint Peter.'

'That's okay, you can tell her that.'

'Good grief, are you kidding?' he laughed. 'We'd never hear the end of it.'

He cracked his fingers as he looked at the chalkboard again. Everything they knew was up there. And yet it didn't make any more sense. There were too many gaps between the key parts.

'It's like there's a curtain hanging over us, Radha,' he said. 'Like we're not getting to look behind it. Something or someone is holding back.'

'You think it's Delice Weaver?' she asked.

'I don't know,' he said. 'I haven't looked to see if she's reported Fran and Sutcliffe missing yet. But even then, it's taken her a month. She was so quick to assume that Sutcliffe had done something to Fran. It just didn't seem right.'

'Maybe she knew Fran was having an affair all this time,' said Radha. 'Maybe it was just an act when you confronted her about it.'

'See, that's what I mean.' He clicked his fingers. 'I've seen people lie. I was a journalist, most people did it, especially if they were in power. She didn't come across as anything other than genuine when we told her that Fran was playing away. You can't fake that kind of reaction, surely.'

'No, I would agree,' she said.

'And that's what I mean by hiding behind a curtain,' he said. 'I could believe that she knew more than she was letting on if she had been lying to us about the affair. But I don't think she was. She was devastated, Radha, absolutely gutted. It's something else she's keeping from us.'

'And what about this extra woman?' she asked. 'You think she might have something to do with it all?'

'Who knows,' he shrugged. 'If I've learned anything from these cases, motive for bad behaviour usually comes down to love or money and both of those are mixed up here. Professor Hargreaves loved Fran Weaver, that much is obvious. For a woman of science, she couldn't hold back her upset when she was talking about him. But I can't see her doing anything that would hurt him. Or Delice Weaver for that matter.'

'Really?' Radha asked.

'Yeah,' he said. 'Some people go a bit crazy when they have affairs, but the Prof wasn't painting Delice as some terrible harpy. She was one of the most reasonable other women I've met, come to think of it.'

'And just how many scarlet women have you met, Mr Brazel?'

Jason smiled at his wife.

'You know what I mean,' he said. 'People in those kinds of secret affairs can do stupid things, as if the affair isn't stupid enough already. Do I think that Professor Hargreaves wanted to be with Fran all of the time? Yes, absolutely I do. Do I think she would cause any undue harm to his wife, absolutely not. She seems like a good egg, someone who couldn't choose who she fell in love with.'

'You old softie,' she said.

'And this brings us all the way back to the elusive Grahame Sutcliffe,' he said. 'The man who dragged us into all this in the first place – with his phone number. He must have planned his flit if he cancelled his number.'

He stared long and hard at the chalkboard, especially the area with Sutcliffe's number written on it, hoping something new would pop out at him. But no inspiration came. He was tired and hungry, a deadly combination for Jason Brazel. Radha finished feeding the baby and lifted him onto her shoulder for winding. He began to cry. They both tried to hush him down, but it was no use.

The living room door opened and Enni appeared. She still looked tired, bleary-eyed, but she was smiling.

'You should have woken me,' she said. 'I could have fed him.'

'Don't be daft,' said Radha. 'You need your rest. Labour isn't a walk in the park, despite what some men think.'

'Oi,' said Jason. 'You're my hero, you know that.'

Enni laughed. She took her son and rocked him gently, wandering around the room. Slowly he began to settle.

'You're a natural,' said Jason.

'I hope so,' she replied. 'Not much use to him if I'm not.'

'You'll be fine. Can I get you something to eat?' asked Radha.

'Oh, yes please. A cheese toastie and a cuppa would be great,' said Jason.

'Not you!' she tutted. 'I meant Enni.'

'I'm okay, thanks,' she laughed.

Radha excused herself. Jason sat back down on the sofa and rubbed his head. He was exhausted. His head was spinning with the lack of sleep and the details of this case. For the first time in his life, he was jealous of Amita having the distraction of bingo.

'What's all this then?' asked Enni, wandering over to the board.

'Just something Amita and I are working on,' he said. 'We're trying to find your elusive partner. I think Amita filled you in on why we were in the mansion when we found you. We don't make a habit of breaking and entering normally.'

'Well, I'm glad you did that day,' she scoffed. 'And good luck with your search but I've learned that if Grahame doesn't want to be found, he won't be. He has a knack for pulling a Houdini at the drop of a hat.'

'Yeah, you're telling me. You don't have any idea where he might have gone? I appreciate you've probably already checked.'

'No clue,' she said. 'He's probably got little boltholes and fancy women from here to the English Channel. And then some abroad too, I bet.'

'Quite a character,' he said sarcastically.

Enni snorted. She stopped rocking the baby and leaned in a little closer to the myriad of names and details sketched across the chalkboard.

'Hang on a minute,' she said. 'What's this doing here?'

Jason yawned. He got to his feet and tried to rub the sleep from his eyes. 'What's what doing where?' he asked numbly.

'This,' she tapped a name on the board.

Jason blinked and focussed. 'Eddington College?' he asked. 'That's where Fran Weaver, Grahame Sutcliffe's business partner worked.'

'Business partner?' asked Enni. 'Doctor Weaver? No, you've got that wrong.'

'Pardon?' asked Jason.

'Doctor Weaver was my tutor,' she said. 'Before I dropped out of uni, he was my tutor. And why is Professor Hargreaves' name up there, too? What's she got to do with all of this? She retired from the faculty like eighteen months ago.'

'What?'

'Yeah, she left just after I dropped out. She had a big farewell lecture with drinks after. We were all invited. I didn't go. I thought it was a bit too fresh, a bit too raw for me to show my face around those parts. She's not a professor there anymore.'

'Retired? She's not that old.'

'No, she isn't,' said Enni. 'But she left anyway, said her time was up and she was glad to be going. What's her connection?'

Jason stared at Fran Weaver's and Julie Hargreaves' names on the board. He could feel the curtain obscuring the answer to this puzzle twitching. Either that or he was fainting. Regardless, he had to sit down.

'I don't know, Enni,' he said. 'But I'm going to find out.'

Chapter 22

ACTINIDIA CHINENSIS

'Are you absolutely sure Enni said that Fran Weaver and Grahame Sutcliffe weren't business partners?'

Amita was panicking. Jason could always tell when she was riled. She asked the same questions over and over again, usually of him.

'For the last time, Amita, yes, that's what she told me last night,' he said.

'I'm just wanting to be absolutely sure that we have our facts right before we go storming into this place. You know I don't like to be left with egg on my face. It's so unbecoming of a woman of my years and respected authority.'

'Facts, schmacts,' said Alby, who had joined them for this excursion. 'Somebody is lying to us and you both know how I feel about lies.'

'The Sheriff of Penrith rides again,' he said under his breath. 'And this time she's brought along Tonto.'

The huge Eddington College building where the engineering department was housed rose up in front of them. Jason and Amita didn't hang around this time. They knew where they were going and marched straight in without dallying, Alby following closely behind them. They took the lift and got out at the seventh floor. Once again, everything was quiet. Not a soul around. The doors of the landing were all closed, including the office.

They marched over and knocked on the frosted glass window. There was a pause before a man's voice called them in.

'Can I help you?' he asked.

He was young, dressed in a tatty jumper with patches sewn on the sleeves. His glasses were thick and square and looked far too old for someone as young as he was. When he saw Jason, Amita and Alby, he sat up a little straighter, like he'd been caught slacking off.

'Are you in charge here?' asked the former cop, deciding the direct approach was the best one.

'Err . . . Yes, I guess you could say that,' said the man. 'I mean, I'm looking after the office this afternoon.'

'You work here?' asked Amita.

'Well, that is to say, I'm a doctorate student,' he said. 'I don't exactly *work* work, but I help out sometimes, just to keep the wolves from the door.'

'Close enough,' said Alby, closing the office door. 'When did Professor Hargreaves retire?'

The student was confused by the question. The former detective inspector went for the jugular, relieved he didn't have to take the softly-softly approach. 'Julia Hargreaves, she was a professor here,' he said. 'Out with it man, we don't have all day!'

He slammed a fist on the desk. Amita was surprised by his sudden outburst of aggression. He flashed her a quick wink as the student gulped for air.

'Err . . . Professor Hargreaves? Civil Engineering?' he mumbled.

'That's what I said,' snapped Alby. 'She used to teach here, had tenure, all of that academic cobblers. She's gone now, right?'

'Yes, yes, she has,' said the student.

'When?'

'I don't know, I can't remember.'

'Come on, son, pull the other one,' said Alby. 'You're expecting me to believe a bloke of your age can't remember when there was a party with free booze. Don't mess me around here, I don't have the time.'

'I can't remember, honestly,' said the student, his face shining with sweat. 'I just study here and help out in the office now and then. I've got more important things to worry about than when the professors left.'

'But if a professor left, there'd be a job opening, right?' asked Jason, thinking on his feet. 'And I know what you grad students are like – the first whiff of a job, you're all over it like flies around a cowpat.'

'Jason, please,' said Amita, squinting her face. 'That's disgusting.'

'Yeah, take it easy, Brazel,' said Alby, relishing the rare chance to take the moral high ground.

'But you . . .'

He was cut off.

'Those the pigeonholes?' asked Alby.

'That's them,' said Amita.

He rounded the desk and began searching and sifting. The student made a feeble attempt at stopping him. A hefty, well-practised policeman's glare was enough to sit him back down in his chair with a squeak.

'There's mail here for her,' he said, pulling out two envelopes and a flyer. 'If Hargreaves is retired, why is she still getting mail delivered here?'

'I . . . I'm not sure,' said the student. 'It could be anything.'

'Think hard, son,' said Alby. 'I'm losing my patience with you.'

Jason knew all too well how short Frank Alby's patience could be. Watching it from afar and not being the intended target was actually quite something. He had a newfound and strange admiration for the retired detective's Jurassic methods.

'I don't have the first idea what might be in those letters,' said the student. 'But if it's like anything else here at Eddington, there will be some database somewhere that needs updating. I'm still getting emails about the Y2K bug.'

'You've been here that long?' Jason yelped.

'I matriculated in September 2019,' said the student. 'Been here ever since.'

'You should have a word with your lecturers, son,' said Alby, flicking through the mail. 'If you've been here for over two decades and still not passed your exams, something is amiss.'

The student just gulped. Amita had sympathy for him. He looked like a lost little boy in a supermarket searching desperately for his parents.

'What about Fran Weaver's snug?' she asked.

Alby traced the names. There were two envelopes and a flyer in Fran's pigeonhole. Alby snatched them and handed them over to Amita.

'Same stuff,' she said. 'Two letters and a flyer for a student protest later this week.'

'I'll make sure I won't bring the car that day,' said Jason bitterly. 'Lest I want another rainbow paint job.'

'The last time we were here, Doctor Weaver had no mail. Do you know anything about that?' she asked the student.

'I don't work here all the time,' he said. 'Just the odd day here and there when the department is a bit short-handed. Everything has been in a bit of a state of flux recently. With Professor Hargreaves leaving and then Doctor Weaver vanishing, we're two experienced lecturers down. Exams are around the corner, the department is running on fumes.'

'And you don't know who would have been collecting his mail?'

'No clue at all,' he shrugged. 'To be honest, I didn't even notice he was still getting mail. I'm only here to answer the phones and lock up in the afternoons.'

'Jobsworth,' said Alby.

The student tried to look ashamed, but it was beyond his acting abilities. He just blinked and looked between the three of them.

'Now what?' asked Jason.

Before the others could answer, there was a knock at the office door. A tall figure was blurry on the other side of the frosted glass. The student's eyes went so wide they almost fell out of his head. He looked alarmed, searching the others for what he should do.

'Bloody hell,' whispered Jason. 'What do we do?'

'In here, quick.' Alby opened a door beside the wall of pigeonholes. Amita and Jason hurried in. Before he joined them, he dug a finger into the chest of the student.

'Not a word,' he said. 'And act normal, got that?'

The student nodded numbly. Alby slithered behind the door and kept it open just a crack. Inside was a dark and cramped stationery cupboard that reeked of stale air and old textbooks. Jason and Amita were tightly cramped into the back, Alby's backside pushing them further and further in.

'Mind your elbows,' Amita whispered.

'You're standing on my foot,' Jason fired back.

'Shut your gobs,' Alby hissed. 'I'm trying to see who's out there.'

'Why did you force us in here?' she asked. 'We haven't done anything wrong.'

'We're asking questions, that's sometimes all you need to have done for people to get the wrong impressions. Just trust me on this. We don't want to be dragged into anything.'

'What a surprise,' said Jason, face pressed against a huge stack of printer paper. 'DI Alby knows better than everyone else.'

'Shhhhh.'

They fell silent. The muffled voice of the student drifted in through the crack in the cupboard door.

'Come in,' he said.

There was a pause then footsteps clicked into the office. The student started with pleasantries, although there was panic in his voice. Amita could hear it, even pressed all the way back into the stationery cupboard.

'Oh, it's you,' he said. 'I wasn't expecting to see you.'

'Yes, sorry for not calling ahead,' came a reply.

'Who is it? Can you see?' she asked Alby.

'I can't see a thing,' said the former DI. 'Stop wriggling back there.'

'I've got cramp in my foot,' Jason moaned.

'Shut up.'

More footsteps. A shadow passed the crack of the cupboard door. There was the sound of some rifling before the strange voice spoke up.

'My mail,' they said. 'What's it doing here on the desk?'

'*My* mail,' whispered Amita, a sudden realisation dawning on her.

'Oh . . . err . . .' the student's panic levels were reaching a new high.

'He's going to sing like a canary,' said Alby through gritted teeth.

'Jason, I think it's . . .'

'My foot!'

The cupboard door gave way, swinging open and smashing into the pigeonholes with a loud bang. Alby spilled out first, Amita and Jason landing on him with two heavy thumps as letters, flyers, packages and more rained down on them from the cubbies.

'You've done my back!' Alby screamed in agony.

'My foot's cramped up!' Jason replied.

All Amita could do was look frantically about the office, searching for the stranger. Then her eyes settled on her, standing over them, a look of shock on her face.

'Good grief!' said Professor Hargreaves, clutching her mail. 'What's going on?'

'Professor!' Amita shouted. 'We'd like to have a word with . . .'

'Grab her!' Alby shouted at the top of his voice.

That was enough for the academic. She turned on her heels and bolted out of the office as fast as her incongruous running shoes would take her.

'Bloody hell fire!' Alby groaned.

'Why did you shout that?' asked Jason, untangling himself from the others. 'Couldn't you have just said hello?'

'Get after her!' the former DI yelled, scrambling for the door.

He and Jason gave chase. Hargreaves was fast, much faster than either of them had expected. She was clearly a runner. Jason should have known. The shoes were a dead giveaway. But there was also typical bad luck at play here.

'Will I ever get to chase down a couch potato like me?' he gasped, dashing down the corridor behind Alby.

'Shut up and run,' snapped the former cop.

Hargreaves shouldered open the fire-escape door and disappeared inside. Jason and Alby were close behind. The ex-detective went first. Jason was right behind him. He skidded and slammed into the safety banister on the other side of the door.

'Bloomin' hell,' he said, staring down the draught shaft that led to the bottom floor. 'I could have taken a tumble.'

'Brazel! Move!' Alby cried back at him, already starting down the steps.

The two men hopped and jumped down the stairs. While their leaps were ungainly, Hargreaves' was elegant and balletic. She was already two clear floors below them and picking up speed.

'Who is this woman?' Alby puffed. 'Sally Gunnell?'

'Please, Alby, don't make me laugh,' said Jason. 'I've got a stitch.'

'Move! She's almost at the bottom.'

Hargreaves continued her descent. She was skipping three steps at a time, vaulting over the banister. When her feet hit the concrete of the bottom floor, Jason and Alby were just arriving at level four. She paused as she opened the fire-escape door and looked up at them. There was a hint of a smile on her face that Jason caught between gasps of air, sweat beading on his top lip.

'Oi!' Alby shouted at her. 'Stop right there. I'm the police! I'll nick you!'

Hargreaves ignored him. She pushed the door open and slipped out, letting it clang shut behind her.

'Damn it!' Alby sneered. 'Get moving, Brazel. Hurry up!'

They reached the bottom, utterly exhausted. Jason felt like his lungs were going to burst out of his chest. He pawed at Alby as they pushed through the fire exit door and out into the main lobby of the building. He was about to collapse on the ground when Alby reared up in front of him. Jason bashed his nose on the former detective's shoulder. He let out a little yelp as his eyes watered.

'I'll be jiggered,' said Alby.

Jason staggered about a little, holding his face. He wiped the tears from his eyes and gawked. Amita was standing at the front door, her hand firmly gripping Professor Hargreaves by the scruff of the tweed-clad neck, her face crimson with anger.

'You two took your time,' she said. 'Amazing how fast these modern elevators are. I'm surprised you didn't think of it first.'

Jason leaned against the wall then slumped onto his backside.

'Just once,' he said out loud between breaths. 'I'd like to take the easy route. Just once. That's all I ask for.'

Chapter 23

JUNIPERUS

'Bloody students,' Alby moaned. 'They don't even know how to drink properly these days. Ten quid this round cost me. I thought this was supposed to be a bloody student union!'

'Ten quid for two pints and a gin and tonic is a steal these days,' said Jason, taking his beer from the tray. 'You'd be lucky to get a single drink for that in some of the bars up town.'

'And another thing,' said the disgruntled former detective. 'How come we're the only ones drinking here? I thought this was a university. Don't these bloody kids have any fun anymore.'

'It's a common misconception that you have to drink alcohol to enjoy yourself,' said Professor Hargreaves. 'In fact, it's quite old-fashioned thinking.'

'So old fashioned you won't want that G&T then, will you, professor?' Alby snapped.

Hargreaves was quiet after that. She sipped at her drink as they huddled around the small table close to the entrance of the student union bar. Amita was fascinated by this place. A stark departure from the pub Alby had taken them into in Kendal – it was almost pleasant here. Airy, light pouring in through the huge windows that lined the far wall, even the din of the fruit machines and video games seemed welcoming. They hadn't even batted an eyelid when she'd ordered a cup of tea. She had never studied at university, but she reckoned if she had, this kind of place would have been right up her street. The fact that none of the students about them were drinking only made her happier.

'You two could learn something from these kids,' she said. 'It's barely gone noon and you're already on the pints.'

'Hey, I've done my exercise for today,' said Alby. 'Chasing after this one filled my cardio quota for the week, if not month.'

'What he said,' agreed Jason, wiping froth from his top lip.

'And you're not having a go at Einstein here, even though she's drinking,' added Alby.

'Einstein was a physicist, I'm an engineer,' said Hargreaves stuffily.

'A dog born in a barn and all that,' he fired back.

Hargreaves glared at him. Alby felt satisfied he'd won the argument and gulped down half of his pint. As expected, it wasn't to his liking.

'Next time put some beer in the glass, would you?' he shouted over to the bar.

Nobody answered him. Hargreaves was the first to speak after the little outburst.

'I'm sorry I ran, that was stupid of me,' she said, bowing her head. 'I don't know what came over me, I've never done something like that before.'

'It doesn't exactly paint a pretty picture, professor,' said Jason. 'Much like my feet when I get home, I expect. I can feel the blisters already.'

'Jason, please. Nobody wants to hear about your feet,' said Amita.

He brooded over his pint, stretching out his legs and wincing. Hargreaves looked into her own glass. She was spinning it around slowly between her hands.

'I miss him,' she started. 'I miss him more than words could ever describe.'

'Oh, come on, love. Don't give us all that old pony,' said Alby between sips. 'If you think you're going to sit there and spoon feed us some old tosh about the love of your life being missing and you not knowing what to do, you've got another thing coming.'

'Frank,' said Amita, trying to calm him down.

'No, I'm serious,' he said. 'I've got much better things to be getting on with, like watching paint dry or the grass grow. You did a runner as soon as we caught you lifting your mail. We know you don't work there anymore, professor. So cut the nonsense and tell us what the hell you've done with Fran Weaver.'

He stared, expectant, at the academic across the table. While Amita wasn't a great supporter of the method, she couldn't deny that he was right in his meaning. Jason was just as quiet, resisting his usual urge to dive in with a follow-up question. They all looked at Hargreaves.

'Alright, alright. I admit it,' she said. 'I've been taking Fran's mail these past few weeks. I have . . . an arrangement.'

'An arrangement?' asked Amita. 'That doesn't sound at all comforting, professor, if you don't mind me saying.'

'It sounds downright dodgy to me,' said Jason. 'I think we should call the police straight away.'

'No, wait, please!' Hargreaves begged them.

'Too late sweetheart,' said Alby, reaching into the pocket of his ill-fitting blazer. 'I just happen to have the chief inspector on speed dial. I think I'll give him a call right now and ask him to send some of the boys in blue down here right away.'

'No! No, please. I'm begging you, don't get the police involved. Please!'

There was a desperation to her. The stern, well-mannered professor was gone. In her place was a vulnerable human being. The tweed armour was broken.

'Please, I'll tell you whatever you want to know,' she said. 'Just don't involve the police.'

Alby let a little smirk tug at his top lip. He looked to Amita and Jason for direction. They both nodded and he put his phone away.

'This better be good,' he said. 'Because I'm not a patient man, professor.'

'I can confirm that he's not,' said Jason. 'Infuriatingly so.'

Hargreaves didn't seem to acknowledge them. She was staring into the distance, her eyes turning a little glassy. Her bottom lip trembled, and Amita decided that a break from the testosterone-fuelled approach was probably a good thing.

'I wonder, Jason, would you be able to get me something to eat?' she asked.

'What? Now?' he said.

'Yes, I quite fancy one of those slices of pizza I see some of the students with.'

Jason craned his neck around. He spotted what she was talking about.

'Pizza? You?' he asked again. 'Are you feeling alright?'

'Forget the bloody pizza!' Alby barked. 'We want answers.'

Amita didn't want to have to spell it out. She flashed Jason a quick look, hoping he would understand. Thankfully he did as Hargreaves did her best to fight back the tears.

'Pizza, okay,' he said. 'I'll see to that right away. Alby, shall we have a drink at the bar. I think I owe you.'

'Eh?' asked the former cop.

'Bar. Drink. Pizza. You and me. Let's go.'

'Thank you, Frank,' said Amita.

Alby didn't know what to say, so he stood up and followed Jason deeper into the union bar. When they were safely out of earshot, Amita turned to Hargreaves.

'I'm sorry about them,' she said. 'They get a little bit too excited when they think we're close to a breakthrough. Jason means well, he used to be a journalist. And Frank, well, he's from a different century I'm afraid.'

'I understand, thank you,' said Hargreaves. 'It's all a bit too much, this. These past few weeks, they've been like something out of a nightmare. It's not how I thought retirement from academic life was going to be like.'

'You're a little young to retire, aren't you?' asked Amita.

'I've not stopped working if that's what you mean,' she said. 'Just hung up my mortar board, so to speak. Fran offered me a job at his company.'

'Clymtech?' she checked.

'Yes,' said Hargreaves. 'I was heading up the research department. Proper clever stuff, Fran was a pioneer in his field. I was just there to add a little academic prowess to the team, really. Give them credit and a little blurb when investors came knocking.'

'You'll have to forgive me professor,' said Amita. 'But I'm still confused as to this company and where Fran fitted in. You see, we've heard from different people that Fran was either an equal partner or running it all on his own, or even that it was already sold off. You can appreciate that it can't be all of those things, right?'

'I don't understand,' said Hargreaves. 'Clymtech was Fran's brainchild. And only his. He wouldn't partner with anyone, he didn't trust anyone to do as good a job as him.'

'Except you.'

'Yes, except me.'

Hargreaves paused for breath. She drank the remains of her gin and tonic, shivering as the last gulp went down.

'It's all such a mess, Amita,' she said. 'The whole thing. The affair, Fran's disappearance. I've spent the last month questioning everything I've ever known about him, about what he told me, whether he loved me or not. I just . . . I just can't work out what went wrong.'

'That makes two of us,' said Amita. 'You've been collecting Fran's mail, you say?'

Hargreaves nodded.

'Why?'

'I don't know really,' she said. 'But it helped me cope with him disappearing. To think that I had some small part of him, that I could give it all to him when he finally resurfaced, that it was maybe a good reason to contact him, you know, if he'd decided the affair was over. I don't know. It was stupid of me. I didn't plan it. I'd gone looking for him at the department a few weeks ago and that grad student, the same one in the office today, he'd told me I was still getting mail of my own. Then and there I thought I could just take Fran's too, pass it on to him. Like I said, I don't know what I was thinking. I knew immediately when I looked at it that there would be no clues to where he was – all the mail was just circulars, flyers and invitations to give a talk or donate to something. I've not opened more than a letter or two.'

'I think it technically counts as theft, you know,' said Amita.

'I'm sure it does,' Hargreaves agreed. 'But I needed to do it, I needed to have something of his, Amita. Just to hold. Something fresh, something new. I just *needed* to be close to him. So, every few days I'd go to the department under the pretence of collecting my own things. It all works so slowly there, nobody noticed. That's when I met you for the first time. I panicked when you said you were searching for Fran Weaver. I couldn't lie, not there on the spot like that. I had to tell you. And I'm telling you now, I don't know where he is, and I haven't done anything to him.'

Amita let all this sink in.

'Frank is convinced you might have killed him,' she said. 'And I can't say it's not crossed my mind, too.'

'Killed him? Fran? I loved him! I love him! I couldn't hurt him, not at all, I swear,' she said, her voice getting louder. 'Fran Weaver is the most brilliant, funny, handsome, kind, giving and genuine man I've ever met in my life. I couldn't hurt a hair on his head, let alone murder him.'

'I didn't say you did, professor. I said you could have done,' said Amita. 'With all the lies you've spun to us and countless others, you can understand my suspicions, I'm sure.'

Hargreaves was going to protest, but she stopped herself. There was nothing to protest about. Amita was right. And she knew it.

'I'm sorry,' she said, her shoulders sinking. 'I've made a complete pig's ear of all this, haven't I?'

'You have to be honest with me, that's a start,' she said. 'Tell me everything you know about Fran Weaver and Grahame Sutcliffe.'

Hargreaves drank the melted ice water from her glass. She nodded. 'Okay,' she said. 'But I warn you, it's not pretty.'

Jason and Alby returned to the table with a fresh round of drinks. Amita ignored her pizza, giving the academic her full attention.

'I'm not sure how they met exactly,' she said. 'One day, a while back now, it felt like Grahame Sutcliffe appeared out of the blue. Fran and I had been enjoying lunch together in his office at work when we got a knock on the door. It was Sutcliffe. He introduced himself, said he was a local businessman who was investing in startups.'

'I thought he was an old pal of Fran's, from what Delice said. And you say he already knew about Clymtech?' asked Amita.

'Yes,' said Hargreaves.

'Let me stop you right there,' said Alby. 'Maybe I'm just too old fashioned a copper but would somebody mind explaining to me what the hell this Clymtech business is, exactly.'

'Security, Mr Alby,' said Hargreaves. 'Fran Weaver is one of this country's most preeminent technology engineers. There's nothing on the face of the planet he can't program. Clymtech, in short, is a new security system built and based on biological material.'

'You mean like fingerprints and retinal scans,' said Jason.

'Exactly that,' said Hargreaves.

He looked about the table, waiting for some praise for his technological know-how. None was forthcoming.

'Only that technology is dated. There have been fingerprint scanners and retinal readers for decades. What Fran was working on, had developed rather, was a way of digging straight into the DNA, the organic material that makes up all of us. We all have a unique genetic code that can't be replicated. It's nature's own security system or PIN, if you will. Fran believed that if you could harness that individuality, you could make security systems that could never be breached.'

'And make a good few quid in the process, too, I imagine,' said Jason.

'Absolutely,' said Hargreaves. 'But that was never Fran's motivation. He was an engineer, a scientist. He wanted to simply see if he could do it. That's where Sutcliffe came in. He was the businessman, the ideas man, the brand management, if you will.'

'How did he know about Clymtech in the first place?' asked Amita.

'I've no idea. We hadn't done any PR at that point.'

'You didn't ask?'

'We're scientists, Amita,' she said flatly. 'Some of the ways of the world are a little lost on us. We were in it for the science, for the advancement of technology and the human race. Can you imagine a way of harnessing the very fabric of what makes us human? It's the stuff of science fiction and Fran had it in his grasp.'

Hargreaves was smiling now. There was a glow about her, even as she sat among them. She was proud, fiercely proud of her lover.

'He made excellent strides in the last few years,' she said. 'Especially since Grahame Sutcliffe had secured funding for us. The business potential was growing, growing enough that Fran's time was increasingly stretched. He was lecturing too, of course. I tried to help as much as I could, but it was getting to him, you could tell.'

'How?' asked Alby.

'He wasn't so kind anymore, if that makes sense,' she said sadly. 'To me he was fine, but he told me of fights between him and Sutcliffe, him and Delice, him and his students. That was never Fran. He had time for everyone. But I think the demands of juggling so much were taking their toll.'

'And the takeover?' asked Amita.

Hargreaves thought carefully. 'I don't suppose that helped,' she said. 'It was some American firm, I don't even have their name, Sutcliffe handled it all. Said it all had to be hush-hush and on a need-to-know basis until the deal was inked. He said that they were wealthy beyond our imaginations, and they wanted the security technology for private enterprise. He claimed they had government contracts lined up and everything. All Fran had to do was sign everything over to them and he'd be rich. Clymtech would continue the research, and he would recruit me as his senior researcher. That's why I quit this place.'

She looked about the bar.

'Only it didn't pan out that way,' she said. 'We never saw any money. Not a penny. I haven't been paid in months now. Sutcliffe kept promising that the cash would come in shortly and that everything would be alright. Then Fran vanished. I haven't seen or heard from either of them in a month, like I told you before. It's all so strange. I'm worried sick.'

She rubbed her forehead. Amita looked at the others. It seemed like a take-the-money-and-run scenario.

'I just wish I knew where he was,' said the professor. 'A message to say that he's alright, that's all I want. If he doesn't want to see me again, I'll be heartbroken. We were in love. But I'll recover. But why he'd leave his research, that I don't understand.'

'You'd really be okay with that? If he was leaving you but carrying on his work?' asked Jason.

'Fran Weaver is a visionary,' she said firmly. 'You don't get to choose who you fall in love with. And you certainly can't help it if they are about to change the world. We all bear the weight so they can make a brighter tomorrow.'

There was a finality to her words, an unshakable faith. Amita admired her, she admired her conviction. But they weren't any closer to finding the missing men.

'I should go,' said the professor. 'I can't leave Clymtech empty. Perry will be wondering where I am.'

'There's an office and staff?' asked Alby.

'Staff is stretching it a bit,' she said. 'It's a one man and his dog type operation.'

'But there are others,' said Jason.

'Yes,' she said. 'Apart from myself, we have an office admin, Perry. He's very nice. A former student of Fran's. He looks after the building. Although that makes it sound rather grandiose. We're effectively a modular building in the middle of an industrial estate in Wigton.'

'Ah, sunny Wigton,' said Jason. 'Maybe we should pay this Perry a visit.'

'You're a bit late. He only works a half day on Thursdays,' she said, checking her watch. 'And he'll be gone by now. You'll have to catch him tomorrow. Without any direct contact with this mystery American company, and no money or lead researcher, there's very little we can do. But it seems poor form to abandon it. I keep imagining Fran's going to walk back in, tell me he's been on some top-secret posting with the US firm. I can't just give up on him. I should be there now.'

She stood up. The others did too. Hargreaves lingered for a moment before reaching for Amita's arm.

'Find him, Amita,' she said. 'Find him and make sure he's safe. He's important to me, he means the world. I don't know what I'd do if he's . . .'

She caught her breath.

'We'll try,' said Amita. 'Thank you, for all of this.'

Hargreaves gave them a sad smile and slowly left them behind in the student union bar. When she was gone, Alby whistled.

'She did it,' he said.

'What?' asked Amita.

'She's our killer.'

'We don't even know Weaver and Sutcliffe are dead yet, Alby. Cool your jets.'

'I'm telling you both, right now, she's our man. Or woman. Bet you a fiver. She's come out of this deal with no career, no new job, no marriage proposal from her lover. She's lost everything – that can drive someone to dark deeds. Jilted mistresses are lethal, I tell you.'

Amita turned away from him in disgust. She knew she had invited him onto this case, but there were times when she could happily punch him on the nose. She wasn't so convinced of Professor Hargreaves' guilt.

'We need to speak with this Perry character at the Clymtech offices,' she said. 'Maybe he knows something she doesn't. A young tech whizzkid. What if he's a hacker? Sold state secrets? Corporate espionage?'

'You're barking up the wrong tree, Amita,' said Alby. 'I'm telling you. What's this office admin going to know?'

'You've clearly never spent enough time in an office,' said Jason. 'In my experience, the office administrators are usually *completely* in the know when it comes to everyone's business. Nothing gets past them. Affairs of the heart, how to unjam the photocopier, who's nicked someone else's lunch from the staff fridge. All human life is there.'

He threw his arm around Alby who immediately shrugged him off.

'Don't touch me,' he snarled.

'Detective inspector,' said Amita.

Jason and Alby looked at her.

'Detective inspector,' she said again. 'That's what you used to be.'

'Yes, what about it?' asked Alby.

'The police. Jason, the police. What about the police?'

'What about the police?' he asked.

'Why aren't they involved in all of this, still?' she asked. 'Delice said she was going to report her husband missing but nothing. Isobel Sutcliffe doesn't think there's anything wrong with her son vanishing. And Professor Hargreaves is the secret lover. None of them have made any report to the police for over a month now. Why not?'

Jason shrugged. 'I've no idea,' he said. 'Are you suggesting some kind of joint enterprise plot? Penrith's answer to the weird sisters conspire to take down these guys?'

'I don't know, Jason,' she said. 'But one or all of them hold the answer to this. If they're not telling us the truth or calling in the boys in blue, we need to rinse their contacts. We *must* find this Perry chap first thing tomorrow and get some *real* answers.'

Chapter 24

ARTOCARPUS ALTILIS

By the time Jason and Amita had dropped Alby off at his house and returned home, they were both feeling weary. They limped into the hallway, just glad of the silence. The relief was short-lived. Silence in this house was usually a bad sign. Especially with a newborn baby under the roof.

'Where is everyone?' asked Amita.

'I'm not sure,' whispered Jason. 'I don't want to shout, the baby might be asleep.'

'Good thinking,' she said.

They crept slowly and carefully along the hallway. The kitchen door was open, but there was nobody inside. Next, they tried the living room.

'Bless,' said Jason.

Sprawled out on the floor were his children, fast asleep under a pair of blankets. On the far sofa was Enni, also sound asleep. Radha was closest to them, legs draped over the arms of the big chair by the window. She looked exhausted but happy, a warm glow about her as she slept too. And in the middle of them all, the baby snoring gently in his Moses basket. The television was still on, some colourful children's show dancing across the screen. The early evening sunshine was pouring in through the window, casting everything with a comfortable golden light. Jason turned to Amita.

'I don't think there's any room for us,' he said.

'No,' she agreed. 'Maybe we should take in some of the evening air instead. Clear our heads.'

Jason nodded in agreement. They crept back out of the living room. The comfortable evening breeze met them outside. Amita was at pains to make sure she didn't disturb her sleeping family and the baby. She closed the door as quietly as she could and waited for a moment, listening for any life.

'Evening, Amita. Evening, Jason.'

The voice almost made her jump out her skin. She spun around quickly and saw their neighbour, Patrick Bidmead, leaning on the fence between their front gardens. He was smiling at them, smoke curling from his yellow teeth as he puffed on his pipe.

'Good evening, Patrick,' said Jason. 'Starting the annual mowing regime?'

'You can't let the grass grow, can you? Literally or metaphorically,' he said, needlessly chirpy. 'Although you usually seem to prefer the "rewilding" look, don't you? Gave me quite a start to see you with the mower the other day. We'll have to get you down the allotments, if you're that keen. You know the Garden Club is open to all – anything but astroturf we say. I don't want you to think I'm slacking, anyway, so the first thing I did when I came home was pour some petrol in the mower. She's just warming up nicely around the back. Can't wait to roll my sleeves up and get stuck in.'

He was wearing his customary shirt and tie. Jason didn't really have a problem with Patrick Bidmead. He was a good neighbour, by and large, although a little overbearing. He had the tendency to look down his nose at Jason, despite only being a few years older than him, but Jason could cope with a few jibes about his lack of green fingers because he was no bother really. But Amita couldn't stand the man. She hated snobs – always said Patrick was the kind of man who chose to wash his car on the street just to show it off.

'Off out for a jaunt, are we?' he asked them.

'Just a stroll,' said Amita, keeping it polite.

'Ah yes, I don't blame you. A lot of people in your house these days, eh?'

His eyebrows hopped up and down like two jittery caterpillars.

'Pardon me?' she asked, knowing exactly what he was getting at.

'I noticed that you've got a young lady staying with you?' he said, taking his pipe out. 'Relative of yours? Cousin? Niece?'

'Yes,' said Amita. 'That.'

'That? That what?'

'Just that. Come along Jason.' She took her son-in-law's arm and guided him down the path towards the pavement.

Patrick didn't have a chance to quiz them further. Amita made sure they walked in the opposite direction, keeping well away from his front wall.

'Bloody Patrick Bidmead,' she cursed, once they were far enough down the road. 'The news we've got Enni and the baby staying with us will be all over town before bedtime.'

'So what?' said Jason. 'I'm rather proud that we're helping her, even if it is only for a few more days until her parents arrive. I'm so glad her dad came round to the fact he's a grandad.'

'It's alright for you, you don't have the pensioner rumour network to navigate,' she said. 'And you're right, I *am* proud of what we're doing too. I'd just rather not have to field questions about it all and explain what we're doing to Georgie and the other gossips. I bet Bidmead is on the phone to her right now. She's got spies everywhere you know.'

'Let them gossip,' said Jason.

They walked a little further down the road. The street was quiet, all the cars from the rush hour safely returned home. Some kids were out playing football, laughing with every kick and every dive. The trainline was up ahead and they climbed the old cast-iron bridge that took them out towards the allotments.

'I like this walk,' he said to Amita, thumping down the stairs of the bridge. 'Radha and I used to come out every afternoon or evening in the summer when we first moved into the house. Before the kids.'

'And before me,' said Amita.

'Yes, when we were happy.'

She tutted loudly. Jason laughed.

'Just kidding,' he said. 'You know you drive me nuts, really.'

'Changed days,' she said.

'Ain't that the truth,' he whistled. 'Back then I didn't have any grey hairs, was about three stone lighter and had a full-time job doing what I loved. Now look at me. The only thing glowing about Jason Brazel is his liver after being dragged to the pub by Frank Alby.'

'He's a bit much, isn't he,' she said. 'Maybe it wasn't such a good idea roping him into this case.'

'He's been helpful, at times. And he's kept his insults on the more educated, finessed end of the scale. I doubt it will last though. You know what he's like.'

Amita did, indeed, know what Frank Alby was like. She had valued his experience on this investigation. But she knew he'd be as frustrated as them that they didn't have any firmer leads.

They walked around the perimeter of the allotments, some with tumbledown sheds, others with regimentally neat beds of freshly dug soil ready for spring planting. There were a few dog walkers out enjoying the evening sunshine. A train rumbled past in the distance, sounding its horn like a mournful warning. Amita's gaze landed on a patch of flowers and dayglo-green grass. Sandy had said there was a rift between the flower and veg growers and she thought now that people, even as mild-mannered as the Garden Club members, would always find something to fight over.

She spotted Brunger's shed, firmly locked up. She quietly wondered what he had inside right now. Was it a load of tinned bananas or tartan paint? She smiled at the thought.

'What's so funny?' asked Jason.

'Nothing,' she said. 'I was just thinking about Malcolm Brunger.'

'I'm very sorry to hear that,' he sighed.

'He's not so bad, really.'

'I'm not convinced,' said Jason. 'Although I will give him one thing, he knows how to sell. I mean, who else would be able to convince bonafide gardeners like the ones here to use some of that artificial grass stuff. In an allotment of all places.'

'What?'

Jason pointed over the wall at the allotments. A patch of ground opposite Brunger's shed had been dug up. A large roll of sickly green plastic grass had been laid around an herbaceous border. Amita continued to smile. She shook her head.

'Honestly,' she said. 'What is he like?'

'Don't tempt me to answer that, Amita,' said Jason. 'He'll have conned somebody into putting that stuff down. Probably as a place to plant the magic beans he threw in for free.'

They walked back up the footpath towards home. As they reached the playing fields, they saw the kids playing football had paused. They were bouncing their ball and started laughing, pointing at Jason's car, or more accurately, the multi-coloured paint job the students had given it.

'Yes, yes, very funny,' he said, shooing them away.

Patrick Bidmead was pushing his lawnmower back and forth across the pristine grass of his front lawn. When he saw Amita and Jason walking up their path, he conveniently decided to begin trimming the near side of his garden. Amita didn't want another invitation to go and start growing giant marrows. She hurried into the house and left Jason to lock up.

The first thing they heard when they stepped into the hall was laughter. The whole house that had been so quiet, so peaceful a matter of thirty minutes earlier, was now alive. The children were running around and the baby was crying. The sound of pots and pans clanging came drifting out the kitchen door. And somewhere in the distance, the television had been cranked to full volume, a rousing rendition of 'Incy Wincy Spider' greeting them. Jason kicked off his shoes.

'Well, that was fun,' he said. 'Now back to work.'

'Indeed,' said Amita.

They both headed deeper into the house to greet the others. The mystery of Fran Weaver and Grahame Sutcliffe would have to wait, until the morning at least. And that was okay. This was family time, for everyone involved. A welcome distraction that would keep them occupied until bedtime.

Chapter 25

DISANTHUS CERCIDIFOLIUS

For a company that was on the verge of a major takeover, Clymtech's headquarters, the hub of its operations, looked distinctly downtrodden. Industrial estates were among Jason's most hated places. He always found them so alien, so full of mysterious sounding companies that sold or made or distributed things he didn't understand, and such a strange soulless atmosphere. He'd always thought in the past that the empty units that usually sat between the bustling ones would be a good place to hide a body. But right now, that wasn't a comforting thought.

Clymtech may have been at the forefront of exciting science and dramatic change, but every revolution had to start somewhere. That somewhere was a drab-looking portable building with rust creeping over the walls and a leaking gutter. Derelict land and an obligatory chain link fence framed the building. The only sign that Jason and Amita had found the correct address was a small plaque on the front door.

'Whoever said science was full of exotic locations and beautiful people?' he asked.

'Beggars can't be choosers,' she reminded him.

Two cars were parked beside the building. One was modest and muddy. The other was gleaming in the morning sunshine – a luxury model with a vanity plate and aggressive looking wheel trims.

'Sutcliffe's?' she suggested.

'Possibly,' said Jason. 'Although knowing our luck, I highly doubt that we'll open this door and find Grahame sitting with his feet on the desk ready to welcome us.'

'Unfortunately, I think you're right.'

Jason knocked once. The portable building looked like it had completely given up. Even in the brightness of the spring morning, the whole thing seemed to sag and groan, tired from a life facing the elements.

There was no answer. Jason tried again. Still nothing.

'Should we try the door?' asked Amita.

'Bit rude, is it not? Just barging in there. We don't even know if there's anyone inside.'

'Whose are the cars then? And the lights are on, look.'

She pointed at a window down the far end of the building. A harsh glow was seeping out from behind the protective grill covering the glass.

'Can you hear anything?' she asked.

'Amita, I'm standing right here,' said Jason. 'If you can't hear anything then I certainly can't.'

'What I mean is, put your ear to the door. Maybe this Perry character has music playing and hasn't heard you knock. We're not expected.'

Jason pressed his head against the door of the office. At first, he struggled to hear anything. Apart from the indignity of his actions, it all seemed pretty pointless. Then he heard something muffled coming from the other side.

'Hold on,' he said. 'I think I can hear something.'

Amita stepped up closer to him. It was very faint, but distinctly there. Then the muffled sounds grew louder. It was apparent then that there was some sort of argument going on inside the cabin. Back and forth, shouting growing louder, Jason couldn't make out any details of the row.

'There are two people in there,' he said. 'At least I think there are. Somebody's not happy. I think they're fighting but I can't seem to get a handle on . . .'

An explosion of pain ripped through the side of Jason's face. He tumbled backwards and landed flat on his backside with a heavy thump. Before he could even begin to think about what had happened, a woman was standing over him.

'What . . . what happened?' he asked her numbly.

Amita was suddenly by his side. She helped him up to his feet as the shock and surprise wore off. He shook his head, rubbing the side that had been hit. He could see the door of the cabin was open and figured he'd just been whacked in the face by it.

'Can I help you?' asked the woman.

She was sour faced, with an air of meanness that floated around her like some aura. Short, square-shouldered and dressed in an expensive, shimmering faux fur coat, which looked two sizes too big for her, the woman's hair was peroxide blonde and cut short. Sharp eyes leered at Jason and Amita from beneath a wrinkled brow – the result of too many sunbeds.

'Err, we're here to see Perry,' said Amita, still holding on to Jason.

'Perry?' snorted the woman. 'That little pipsqueak is in there. Although he's beyond useless, like a glass hammer. Whatever you want from him, you'll be lucky if he knows how to spell it.'

With that, the mean-looking woman walked off. Jason and Amita watched her climb into the luxury car and speed off, dangerously close to knocking them down. She tore off through the industrial estate and vanished out of the main gates.

'Charming,' said Jason, still a little groggy. 'She didn't even say sorry.'

A young man appeared at the door. He looked bewildered, shaken, like he'd just seen a ghost.

'Has she gone?' he asked Jason and Amita, his accent from somewhere in the Highlands.

'Yes, I think so,' said Amita.

'Not before she gave me a concussion,' said Jason.

The young man didn't even notice the large, reddening mark growing on Jason's face, let alone proffer any help. He just slumped against the door and mopped his brow on the sleeve of his shirt.

'Thank goodness,' he said. 'I thought she was going to string me up or something.'

'I'm sure she could have, if she'd had a mind to,' said Jason. 'I'm surprised that door isn't off its hinges. Or that I've still got all my teeth.'

'Perry, is it?' asked Amita.

The young man's relief began to retreat. He stared down at them both, as if only now just seeing them.

'Who's asking?' he asked with trepidation.

'My name's Amita and this is my son-in-law, Jason. Professor Hargreaves said we might find you here. You're the office administrator for Clymtech, yes?'

Perry remained steadfast in the doorway. Amita resolved that if she came clean about why they were there, that they knew exactly who he was, they may stand a better chance of getting some answers.

'We're not here to cause any trouble,' she said, offering her hand. 'We're searching for your bosses, Doctor Weaver and Grahame Sutcliffe.'

It took a moment for Perry to weigh up his next move. Amita didn't know who the awful woman they'd just met was, but she clearly had enough of an impact on the young man to make him a jittery wreck.

'You'd better come in,' he said, standing to the side of the door.

'Thank you,' said Amita.

They followed him into the cabin. The inside of the Clymtech headquarters was almost as drab and soulless as the exterior. Four desks, two at either end of the cabin, were set up, each with a computer. The two furthest away were piled high with papers, unopened mail and other folders and files. The wall behind them was taken up by huge processor stacks, cables running from each of them like the arteries and veins of some giant robotic lifeform. The lights blinked on and off seemingly at random and their fans and motors filled the cabin with a disconcerting hum.

Perry sat down at a desk at the opposite end of the cabin. His was neat and tidy, filled with pictures of friends and family and a selection of desk toys and fidgets that suggested Hargreaves was right – this was the desk of a man trying to look busy, and failing. Across from him the desk was completely empty, stripped of even the most basic of supplies. Amita drank it all in, filing the details away in her mind, letting her eyes linger on anything odd, anything unexpected, any aspect that might help their investigation.

'Before you ask, I haven't seen them for over a month,' said Perry, fetching some water from a cooler. 'And I've got no idea where they might be.'

Jason made a loud groan. He was rubbing his face. Perry offered him water and he took it.

'That's our bubble burst at the first hurdle,' he said sceptically.

'What?' asked Perry.

'We didn't suppose you had seen them,' said Amita. 'We just wanted to know if you had any information that might help us.'

'Information? Me? I'm just the office lackey!' he said.

'Come on, mate. Throw us a bone here, would you?' said Jason.

He pulled out the chair from beneath the empty desk and slumped into it. He was still cradling the side of his head, wincing in pain. Amita was beginning to worry.

'What we're saying is, Perry, you being in the unique position you're in here at Clymtech, you have a certain all-encompassing observation of the ins and outs of the company.'

'Look, I know what you're trying to say, missus. Really, I do,' said Perry. 'I used to temp at a big mobile phone network, and we always got all the juicy gossip with what was going on with the higher-ups. I get it. But it's not like that here. I mean, look at the place.'

He waved at the office.

'Professor Hargreaves comes in here at nine in the morning, sits down at her desk, looks shattered and pale and doesn't say anything until she leaves again at five. Doctor Weaver is hardly the life and soul when he bothers to show up at all, which hasn't been for weeks. And as for Mr Sutcliffe, well, I don't think he's used to office life at all.'

'What do you mean by that?' she asked.

Perry nodded at the empty desk.

'I've worked here since they opened this place. Do you know how many times I've seen Mr Sutcliffe use that desk? Twice. Once when we first opened up and another time at a Christmas party for the four of us. He's a ghost. If I hadn't met him those times, I'm not sure I'd believe he existed.'

'How can that be possible?' asked Jason. 'The guy runs the business.'

'I'm not paid to ask those kinds of questions,' said Perry. 'Not that I've been paid at all recently.'

'You haven't had your wages?' asked Amita.

'Not a penny for at least two months.'

'Then why are you still here?' asked Jason.

Perry's eyebrows arched. He smiled forlornly and sat down at his desk. Picking up one of the photos, he showed it to Jason and Amita. It was a large family, two parents at the back and six kids of varying ages in the foreground. A large, sweeping countryside rolled off into the distance behind them.

'That's my family. We're from a place called Tongue, in Sutherland,' he said. 'Ever heard of it?'

'Can't say I have.'

'My dad is a farmer. My grandparents were farmers, their grandparents before that. Up every morning, all year round, in the wind, rain and snow to tend to the animals and livestock. My brother and sisters still do it. I left to go to college, and I've worked indoors ever since.

But it's still here, inside me, that work ethic.' He prodded his chest. 'Not turning up for work because there's a cashflow problem, that's not my style. And my mum and dad would kill me if they ever found out.'

Amita wanted to give Perry a hug. It was like he'd read her manifesto on parenting and memorised every page. Jason was less admirable.

'I think you and I *both* need our heads examined,' he said. 'Having a strong work ethic is one thing, Perry. Being bloody stupid is another.'

'Stupid it may be,' the young man fired back. 'But I wouldn't be able to look at myself in the mirror if I didn't show up for work anyway. And that's something I've got to live with every day. Call me old fashioned or stupid or whatever you want, but it's who I am. And I'm glad I've still been here at nine every morning, waiting for the others. And I'd be lying if I wasn't also waiting around to see if this magic money tree Grahame mentioned when the American deal was signed was going to start bearing fruit.'

'I think you're a very sensible young man,' said Amita. 'And Sutcliffe and Doctor Weaver are very lucky to have you.'

'Thank you,' he smiled. 'Although I question myself something awful when people like that woman come around here making threats. Weaver said it would be like being in at the early days of Apple or Amazon, but so far all I've got to show for it is an extension on my overdraft, wild threats from that woman . . .'

The nobility and dignity Perry had shown just a moment before was quickly replaced with fear. He fumbled with his hands.

'You know her, then?' asked Amita. 'She wasn't some big shot American coming here to celebrate the deal.'

'Lord, no,' said Perry. 'No, she's something altogether more horrible.'

'If the way she leaves buildings is anything to go by, I think I prefer Americans,' groaned Jason.

'Who is she, Perry?' asked Amita.

The young man tried to gather himself. He filled his plastic cup with more water and sank it in one gulp.

'Her name is Christina McGann,' he said.

Jason immediately sat up in the chair. Amita looked at him.

'Christina McGann?' he asked. '*The* Christina McGann?'

'You know her?' asked Amita.

'You don't?'

'Clearly I don't, otherwise I wouldn't be asking, would I?'

Despite the redness in Jason's face from the door thump, it had distinctly lost colour.

'Christina McGann is one of Cumbria's most notorious lady mobsters, Amita. Her nickname used to be 'Migraine' McGann for the headaches she used to give cops back in the day. I should have recognised her. We used to do stories on her all the time. Although back then she looked a little bit different – she had the biggest perm this side of Hadrian's Wall. Racketeering, fraud, bribery, you name it, McGann was into it right the way up to her ears. She managed to keep getting other people in her organisation sent down instead of her, but it all caught up with her in the end. I thought she was still in jail.'

'Clearly not,' said Amita.

'I can't remember the details,' said Jason. 'It must have been about a decade ago, she was finally sent down for a stretch. It was big news at the time, made the national papers and television, too I remember. The problem with Migraine McGann was that you could never tell what she was up for at any given point, there were just so many cases all on at once. We used to joke in the newsroom that she did it all deliberately, just to give the police the run-around. The different departments wouldn't know where to begin.'

'Is she dangerous?' asked Amita.

'I don't think she was ever accused of murder or anything like that, if that's what you're asking' said Jason, thinking hard. 'But I wouldn't like to get on the wrong side of her, if that's what you mean.'

'You were on the wrong side of a door from her and look how that turned out,' she said.

'There you go, proof of the pudding. I can't believe that was Migraine McGann. She was the stuff of legend at the paper when I first started. I never worked on any of the cases, but some of the older hacks made careers out of solely following her various exploits. And that was just what we could report on.'

'What was she doing here, then?' asked Amita.

They both turned to Perry. Jason's familiarity with the mobster hadn't helped the situation. The young man was looking more frightened by the second.

'She wanted to know where Mr Sutcliffe was,' he said timidly. 'I told her I didn't know. She said I was lying and that she'd be back every day until I told her where I could find him.'

'Blimey,' whistled Jason.

'What does that mean?' asked Perry.

'If Migraine says she's going to do something, she'll do it. She's like a bulldog. She doesn't have a reputation for giving up easily.'

'Jason, you're not helping,' said Amita.

'Oh lord,' said Perry, clapping a hand to his mouth. 'She's going to kill me, isn't she? I'm going to end up wearing a concrete overcoat and supporting a flyover, aren't I?'

'Calm down, Perry,' said Amita. 'Just calm down. Nothing like that is going to happen to you. We don't have many flyovers round here for a start.'

Perry blanched. 'Then I'll be sleeping with the fishes in Windermere!'

'Now, now,' said Amita. 'I was joking. It's a bad habit I seem to have acquired from my son-in-law. She'll not harm you, I'm prepared to bet.'

'How do you know? Didn't you hear what he just said? She's a gangster!'

'She is,' she said. 'But that means there's a certain logic to her actions, in a strange sort of way. Now think, very carefully, why would somebody like this Christina McGann woman want to know where Grahame Sutcliffe is so badly that she would threaten you?'

Perry tried to control his breathing. He was panicking, but Amita was doing her best to keep him calm. 'I can only think it has to do with money,' he said at last.

'Money?' she asked.

'Yes,' said Perry. 'Clymtech is haemorrhaging cash on a monthly basis. See those computers over there, they cost a small fortune just to keep the power and lights on. I don't know what they do, but they're integral to Doctor Weaver and Professor Hargreaves' research. Without them, they can't do any work. And they cost tens of thousands just to buy. Plus, there's everything else – rent, insurance – the business is floundering before it's even started. Mr Sutcliffe knew this, I have a raft of emails from him telling me to cut back on costs, not order any more office supplies, keep the lights off for as long as possible, that kind of thing. Anything to scrimp and save until the US dollars landed. We don't even have a cleaner, I have to use the loo at a local cafe, everything to keep the cash flow under control.'

'But the big takeover will solve it all?' asked Jason.

'Allegedly, but there's been no money up front,' said Perry. 'The last time Mr Sutcliffe spoke to me, he told me to sit tight, that the Americans were going to send the first installment of their buyout over within a few days. But nothing happened, he vanished, and no money has gone into the company accounts. Let alone my pocket.'

'And you think McGann might have something to do with this?' she asked.

'I don't know how well you know him, but Mr Sutcliffe can be quite . . . creative when it comes to keeping the ship afloat. He's done business with some dodgy people before. It wouldn't surprise me if he owed this McGann woman money. And now she wants it back.'

'That makes sense,' said Jason. 'McGann was never short of a few quid. She always had the best lawyers, the best gear, the best of everything. You saw her car, Amita. Not bad for a woman who's been in the clink for a decade, eh?'

Amita nodded in agreement.

'Thank you, Perry,' she said. 'You've been very helpful. Might I suggest that, against your better judgement and character, you stay at home until this whole thing is resolved. There's no point in you risking your own neck with these people, if you don't have to.'

Perry looked a little more relieved at that news. He looked down ruefully at the picture of his family. Amita could almost see the gears of his mind and imagination whirring around inside his head.

'Thank you,' he said, croaking. 'I might just do that.'

'Come along, Jason,' she said, heading for the door of the cabin.

They stepped out into the fresh air. Amita was trying to piece together parts of the puzzle in her mind. She needed her absolute concentration to work out what they were going to do next.

'You better not be thinking what I think you're thinking,' said Jason, looking at his bruised face reflected in the office window.

'You absolutely know that I *am* thinking what you think I'm thinking, Jason. That's why we're such a good team.'

'I thought as much,' he said. 'You also don't need me to tell you how bloody stupid and dangerous it's going to be. That is, if we can even get access to Migraine McGann. She doesn't exactly help out with the bingo club or the W.I., you know.'

'I do know that, thank you,' she said, walking towards the car. 'Thankfully, with my contacts, there's somebody I have in mind who might be able to set up an introduction.'

Jason stopped. Amita reached the car and opened the door, flecks of yellow, blue and red paint coming away in her hand.

'Who?' he asked, confused.

She simply smiled back at him and tapped the side of her nose.

'Trust me.'

Chapter 26

SOLANUM BURBANKII

'You've got to be pulling my leg, Mrs K,' said Brunger, sucking in air through his teeth. 'Migraine McGann? Are you serious?'

Her proposal had shocked the wheeler dealer so much that he'd stood up from his seat in his shed. The pile of egg timers he had been peeling 'faulty' stickers from scattered about the ground in front of them. Jason did his best not to stand on one. He suspected he'd be charged full price if he broke anything.

'We wouldn't ask unless it was life or death,' said Amita. 'I understand that this McGann woman has something of a reputation.'

'Reputation? That's putting it lightly,' said Brunger. 'Reputations were invented for women like Migraine McGann. In fact, she revels in having one. The meaner, the more dangerous, the better, that's what I understand.'

'You know her then?' asked Jason, always the sceptic.

'I know *everybody*, Jason. Come on, what kind of businessman do you take me for? I'm only as good as my clientele.'

Jason snorted. He'd never been inside Brunger's allotment holdup before. And he couldn't quite believe so much junk could be crammed into such a small place. But that was him all over. Fast, loose and just that little bit iffy.

'We're not here to judge, Mr Brunger,' said Amita.

'Malcolm, please, Mrs K,' he said.

'Yes, Malcolm. We're not here to ask questions about *how* you know McGann. Just if you could somehow put a word in the right ear that we'd very much like to speak with her about Grahame Sutcliffe. After all, you're the one who brought him into our lives. You sold my mother-in-law his old SIM card.'

Brunger puffed out his cheeks. Amita had never seen him so rattled. He was always friendly and approachable. His manner, his happy-go-lucky charm was what endeared him to the members of the Penrith Bingo Club. He was always happy to help, offer a hand, get them what they wanted at rock-bottom prices. To see him so edgy was making her feel a little uncomfortable.

'Maybe this wasn't such a good idea,' she said. 'I'm sorry for wasting your time. Come along, Jason.'

'No, wait. Hang on a minute,' He said.

Brunger eased past them to the door of the shed. He looked about the allotment not once but twice. Ushering them both into the little hut, he pulled the door closed and made sure it was shut tight. Jason and Amita shuffled up to let him back in, their backs pressed against boxes, bottles of vodka, spare parts for motorbikes and at least one crate of bananas.

'What the hell is it with us and tight spaces?' Jason asked.

'Sorry about the squeeze, folks,' said Brunger, manoeuvring his way around them. 'But I'd rather we kept all of this just between ourselves.'

'Here we go,' droned Jason.

'Is there a problem there, mate?'

Jason hadn't been expecting a direct retort. He shook his head, folding his arms across his chest so as not to break anything. 'Nope,' he said.

'Alright then,' said Brunger.

Amita tutted loudly.

'This all stays strictly confidential, if that's alright, Mrs K.'

'Absolutely,' said Amita. 'We're hardly going to go gabbing about personal information. Are we Jason?'

'No,' he said flatly.

'It's not that I'm worried as such,' said Brunger, taking his seat. 'It's just, well, in my line of work, reputation and image is everything. Does that make sense?'

'It does,' said Amita.

'Look, I'm not trying to pretend that I'm an angel or anything. I mean, the contents of this shed alone could probably put me in a spot of hot water with John Law, if you catch my drift.' He looked about his wares. 'I get my stock from very respectable vendors, but not always with the right paperwork, you see. And the phones are a case in point. Lots of people bring me ones I can sell. I just check they're blank, pop a new SIM in and off you go. All above board. But the one you chose, Mrs K, I confess I don't seem to have a record of who it came from. And it had a SIM already in, which is not my usual way. But I knew you were very keen on that model, so I didn't want to quibble.'

'It's all over my head, that stuff,' Amita said. 'Jason sorted out getting my old number back and all my things. Are you telling me now that I've been using a stolen phone? I'll be run out of town! Imagine the scandal.' Amita looked horrified.

Brunger shook his hood. 'Now, now, Mrs K. I would never stay "stolen". That's such a strong word.'

'And accurate too, knowing you,' chimed in Jason.

'It's just been separated from its provenance,' Brunger went on. 'Most households in Britain have got old phones lurking in their junk drawers. I like to do my bit for the planet – creative recycling, I call it.'

Jason's eyebrows shot up. 'Right, now we've established that you're not going to jail for handling stolen goods, Amita, can we get back to why we came. Christina McGann.'

Brunger whistled. 'Migraine McGann, she's a different kettle of fish. She's on a whole other level to anything I'd get involved with. And as such, I try to avoid her like the plague.'

'But you'll have *some* contact with her, surely,' said Jason. 'Doing what you do, Brunger, you can't help but run in the same circles from time to time.'

Brunger sucked more air through his teeth. He scratched the back of his head, like he was wrestling with something. 'I'm not saying no,' he said. 'But I think you should both know that when you get tangled up with somebody like the Migraine, it's not as easy as just walking away. She's a spider, she's spun her web and if you get tangled up in it, she'll eat you all up in one gulp. I promise. You can't go in there playing Butch and Sundance with her, it won't work. Plenty have tried and they've *all* failed.'

'We wouldn't be asking if we didn't already know the risk,' said Amita. 'Without going into too much detail, that new phone number you sold me, it's led us into something of a missing persons investigation. And we think that Ms McGann may be able to help us in some way.'

Brunger let out a long sigh. 'You have to promise me that you know what you're doing, Mrs K,' he said. 'I don't think I could live with the thought that I'd put you into harm's way without you knowing the full consequences. McGann is bad news. She's vicious. She's ruthless. If she takes a disliking to you, you'll know about it in a hurry. I knew a bloke once who used to ship Beanie Babies in from the continent. He missed a shipment in Dusseldorf once, a shipment that McGann had very conveniently paid to have fall off the back of the bloke's lorry when he was passing through Carlisle. He vanished, too.'

'Did he ever turn up again?' asked Jason, his mouth dry.

'Oh yeah, a couple of weeks later. His wife was going spare, calling up Interpol, the lot. Turned out he'd been in intensive care for a while, roughed up something good, jaw broken so he couldn't speak. That was the end of his little stuffed-toy racket, I can tell you.'

'Bloody hell,' said Jason. 'Amita, are you absolutely sure we want to go down this road?'

'What other choice do we have?' she asked him. 'If Grahame Sutcliffe owes McGann money, then she'll know where he is, or what's happened to him more recently.'

'And what if you don't like what she has to say?' asked Brunger. 'What then?'

Amita hadn't thought that far ahead. She was putting up some sort of mental block, fearing what the options would be.

'We'll just have to cross that bridge when we come to it, won't we,' she said succinctly.

Jason threw up his hands in exasperation. In the process he knocked over a small jar of mechanical teeth. They started to chatter and clack away on a shelf. Brunger drew him a dirty look.

'Sorry,' he said.

'Where might we find Ms McGann, Malcolm?' she asked.

'If you're absolutely sure this is what you want to do, then I suppose there's no stopping you,' he said. 'You're only going to go ahead and find her anyway, even if I don't help you, right?'

'That's about the measure of it, yes,' she said.

'I thought as much.'

Brunger stood up from his little chair. He looked about his stock and settled on a large stack of unmarked boxes close to the back of the shed. Rifling around in the top one, he reached in and pulled out what appeared to be a glass skull.

'Here,' he said, handing it over.

'That is the ugliest thing I've ever seen in my life,' said Jason.

'Good job it's not for you then, isn't it, mate,' said Brunger.

Amita took the skull. Clear liquid was sloshing around inside. At the top of the skull was a neck with a cork firmly stuck in it, a blue ribbon tied around the glass. Dutch writing was printed onto the fabric in gold lettering.

'Gin,' he said. 'From a brewery in Arnhem. They make it in bathtubs or something, I don't know. There are a few customers who like it, so I try and get it in as often as I can. But it's hard to come by on the open market. And the customs lads will charge you a fortune for it if you go online.'

'Why are you giving it to us?' asked Jason.

'I happen to know that Migraine McGann absolutely loves the stuff, can't get enough. Thankfully, she doesn't ask me to get it in for her anymore, she'll have something going in the Netherlands she can pick it up herself. If the pair of you are dead set on having a word, then I suggest you take that as an ice breaker. A sort of gesture of goodwill. With any luck, she won't have one of her heavies knock out your front teeth. Not when you first arrive, anyway.'

Amita held up the skull to the light from the dusty, filthy window of Brunger's shed. There was something savage about the bottle, but she couldn't take her eyes from it. The weight made it feel expensive, like something she would never forget if she ever dropped it.

'How much do we owe you, Malcolm?' she asked.

'Your safe return to the bingo club on Wednesday night will be more than enough payment, believe me,' he said.

'No, we can't . . .'

'Please,' he held up his hands. 'If you're planning on asking for a favour from Migraine McGann, the last thing you need is worrying about how expensive that bottle is. Just be careful, that's all I'm asking for in return.'

'Where do we find her?' asked Jason.

Brunger took a deep breath. His charm and wit had all but disappeared. He looked worried.

'If there's anything McGann loves more than money and gin, it's horses.'

'Equestrianism?' asked Amita.

'No, betting, gambling, racing horses,' said Brunger. 'There's a meeting on Saturday at the racecourse in Carlisle. It'll be top hat and tails stuff, a proper showing. McGann never misses these kinds of things. She'll be in the director's box or the VIP section, whatever it is they have up there.'

'Right,' said Amita, turning to go. 'Thank you very much for all of this. It means a great deal to us, to us both, isn't that right, Jason?'

'Yeah, it's a real lifesaver,' he said sarcastically.

Amita was getting ready to leave. She stopped as she reached for the door.

'How exactly do we get in to meet with her if it's a VIP section?' she asked.

'If you mention her name at the front desk when you arrive, you won't have any problems,' said Brunger. 'Nobody goes looking for Migraine McGann voluntarily. If you look the part and have that glass skull full of gin with you, you'll get in no problem.'

'I don't like the sound of that,' said Jason.

'I don't blame you,' said Brunger. 'And if we could keep all of this between the three of us, I'd be duly obliged.'

No sooner had he made his request when the door rattled on its hinges. The three of them froze, scared to move. Brunger ambled his away around them.

'Yeah?' he shouted through the door.

'Malcolm, it's Dotty. I'm here to collect the . . . thing.'

Brunger ambled off to see his next client. Amita and Jason excused themselves, sliding past Brunger and Dotty and out into the allotment. Amita stopped to look at the green shoots of the veg and delicate flowers promising spring was coming. Brunger noticed them leaving and waved. 'I know he's never done a straight deal in his life,' said Amita. 'But you can't deny he's a useful sort.'

'So useful, he might very well get us killed,' said Jason.

Chapter 27

PAEONIA

There had been a time when Friday nights were quiet, laid-back affairs in the Brazel household. With clothes strewn across the upstairs landing and stairs, this was *not* one of those occasions.

'I can't find my cummerbund!' Jason shouted to nobody in particular. 'How the hell do you lose a cummerbund? It's the least used thing in the universe!'

'It's in the box of odds and ends at the top of the cupboard!' Radha shouted up the stairs.

'What?' Jason asked. 'We have a box of odds and ends?'

He should never have doubted his wife. It was a fatal flaw that, time and again, he succumbed to. Sure enough, in the cupboard, on the top shelf, there was a box. And inside were indeed odds and ends. Strings of pearls, an old charging cable and, most importantly, Jason's cummerbund. He fished it out and immediately set about fastening it around his waist.

'Surely not,' he said, wandering around to the full-length mirror they had behind the door. 'How the hell can a cummerbund shrink?'

He sucked in his gut and, miraculously, he was able to fasten it closed. He stood looking at himself trussed up in his old tuxedo and dress shirt. His trousers were creased, probably beyond redress. And he was pretty sure there was the ghost of a stain on the front of his shirt. Curry sauce was the most likely suspect. The last time he'd worn this outfit was for some local press awards about a decade before. A boozy affair, everyone had drowned their sorrows and resorted to takeaways at the end of the night. The vaguest of lectures from Radha about looking after his 'good shirt' came trickling back. He was paying for it now.

Amita stuck her head around the door. She looked him up and down as he held out his hands.

'What do you think?' he asked. 'Will I cut the mustard in a room full of yobs, hoods and gangsters?'

Amita furrowed her brow. She stared down at his feet. Jason wriggled his toes, a hole in each of the bright yellow and red striped socks he'd been wearing all day.

'I won't be wearing these socks, Amita. Give me some credit at least,' he said.

'I think the socks are the very least of our worries, Jason,' she said. 'But it'll have to do, we don't have any time to fix it and nowhere will rent you some tweeds. We need to be in Carlisle tomorrow morning.'

He looked down at his feet and then again to the mirror. He looked like a man who'd been stuffed into somebody else's clothes. He decided to unfasten the cummerbund and breathed a little sigh of relief.

'Come and help me with this stupid frock, would you?' she asked, disappearing behind the door.

He followed her into the hallway. The sound of Enni's baby crying drifted up the stairs. The poor lad had been upset all day. Now, after dinner, there was no consoling him.

Amita stood on the landing. She was dressed in a long, flowing dress that sparkled when she moved. The bottoms of her tracksuit trousers were poking out from under the frock. And she was struggling to zip up the back.

'Just pull it up, would you?' she asked Jason.

'You know, you're meant to take your other clothes off before you change into a new outfit,' he said, helping her. 'I'm surprised you don't have your cardigan on under this.'

He fixed the zipper. Amita twirled around.

'What do you think? Will it do?' she asked. 'I've gone through my entire wardrobe and barely anything fits anymore.'

'I know the feeling.'

'Granny looks like a film star.'

Clara and Josh were watching them both through the gaps in the banister. Amita smiled and did another twirl.

'Shall Cinderella go to the ball?' she asked her grandchildren.

They both nodded, flashing wide, toothy smiles. Radha appeared behind them, ushering them up the stairs.

'Come on you two, time for a bath,' she said.

She stopped when she saw Amita and Jason.

'Blimey,' she said, trying to hide a smile of her own. 'Don't you two look the pair. It's a tough gig this detective work, isn't it?'

'Oh, stop it, Radha,' Amita tutted. 'We're working hard.'

'Oh yeah, of course, I forgot,' she said. 'A jolly up to Carlisle Downs on a Saturday, really a proper grind.'

Jason and Amita had kept the details scant. They had only figured Radha would worry. Or worse still, not let them go at all. It probably wouldn't do for the husband of a lawyer to be seen fraternising with the local underworld kingpin. Everything had been kept subtle and brief when they'd explained the upcoming trip. No mention of Migraine McGann or her ilk.

'Do you think this looks okay?' Amita asked her.

'You look gorgeous, Mum, even with the tracksuit bottoms,' she said. 'I don't think I've ever seen that dress before.'

'I don't suppose you would have, I wore it at our wedding reception.'

Both Jason and Radha stared at her, agog.

'Seriously?' asked Jason. 'That must make it vintage – or do I mean antique?'

'Jason,' Radha slapped him.

'Yes, this is from our wedding reception,' she said. 'I'm as surprised as you both are that it still fits. I think it's probably going to stretch at the seams, but I've had it all these years.'

'And you never wore it again?' she asked.

'No,' said Amita. 'I never really had occasion to. I was raising a family, looking after my husband, making sure the house was clean, tidy and respectable. I had my activities, of course. But you don't ever really want to dig something like this out of the cupboard unless it's absolutely necessary.'

'And this is absolutely necessary?' asked Radha, sceptically. 'You're going to the racecourse with a load of gamblers and drunks. What happens if it gets covered in booze or you tear it?'

Amita flattened down some of the wrinkles in her special frock. She thought about that question, had thought long and hard about it long before her daughter had asked. Was she doing the right thing, walking into Migraine McGann's lair like this? Was it dangerous, foolishly so, more dangerous than anything she had ever done before? And all for what? To find a man she'd never even met.

Recent years had brought up questions like this more often than Amita Khatri had ever thought would be possible. And every time she rounded and circled on the same answer. The right thing was the right thing. It always would be. She was a woman of principle and strong beliefs. Doing the right thing wasn't always easy. But it had to be done. If that meant making sacrifices, then so be it.

'Yes,' she said, forcing a sad smile. 'It is, darling. It's only a dress after all. What it means, the memories, they all live in my head anyway. It's not like I have to look at it to be reminded of your father, or our wedding day. I think about him every day already and the dress has been tucked away in the closet somewhere, gathering dust. It's the right thing to do.'

Radha walked over and gave her mother a big hug. Jason, feeling a little awkward, did the same. No sooner had his arms gone around both of them when Amita jerked free.

'What are you doing?' she asked.

'I thought we were . . . I thought this was, you know, a special family moment.'

'It was until you butted in,' she said. 'Now let's get out of these bloomin' clothes and go help that poor girl downstairs with her screaming baby.'

Radha went to help her own kids in the bathroom. Jason retreated to his bedroom and Amita lingered a little longer on the landing, alone. She watched the sequins sparkle as she moved the dress fabric back and forth under the light. Memories of her first dance, the smiling faces, the well-wishes, came flooding back into her mind.

She closed her eyes and was immediately transported there, back through the decades to her wedding day. How happy she had been back then, no responsibilities. Late nights, long lie-ins, dancing and romancing. Then the children had come along and, soon after, widowhood, so there had been little cause for sequinned sparkles for years. While she was alone, and had been for a long time now, she knew that she would never be on her own. A new family had grown up about her, with new additions replacing the old. Amita wouldn't trade that family for anything. The dress, and it was only a dress, was just a reminder of days long gone by.

She opened her eyes and the world came slowly back into view. The baby was still crying, Enni trying desperately to calm him down, to wind him, to do anything to make him happy. All of those memories were still to be made for her. And the baby? He was just at the beginning of his adventure. The very least she could do was try to find that little boy's father.

Amita headed down the stairs. She found Enni cradling the child in her arms, walking about the kitchen, trying to console him. She hushed him down, a lullaby playing on her phone. When she saw Amita arrive in her dress, she gave a tired smile.

'Sorry,' she said. 'I didn't mean to disturb you guys. I know you're busy.'

'You're not disturbing us, don't be daft,' said Amita. 'You're our guest and that little baby is days old. He doesn't know any different. And even if he did, it wouldn't matter. We want you to feel at home here.'

'You're all too kind,' said Emmi. 'I don't know what I would have done without you.'

The baby was crying, his face bright red. Nothing his mother was doing would calm him down. Amita reached over and took him from Enni. She collapsed into a chair by the kitchen table.

'Here's a little trick I learned with my children,' she said, the boy still crying. 'And it worked a treat for my grandkids too.'

'As it stands, I'll try anything,' said Enni.

Amita reached for her phone. She opened the music app and started typing. The opening accordion of *The Lights of Old Aberdeen* began to play. Enni looked confused.

'The Alexander Brothers,' she said. 'You're far too young to know who they are. But trust me, in about a minute, this little laddie is going to be sound asleep.'

Amita began to gently rock the baby in time with the music. Waltzing around the kitchen, she sang along with the beat.

'"When I was a lad, a tiny wee lad, my mother said to me. Come see the Northern Lights my boy, they're bright as they can be. She called them the heavenly dancers."'

She moved with a gentle grace, all the while looking down at the little boy in her arms. It could have been Radha, or Josh or Clara. The emotions would never change or dull over time. Slowly, he started to quieten down, his eyes heavy as he rubbed at his cheeks. The song went on and Amita continued to waltz with him until, a minute later, he was fast asleep. She nodded to Enni to turn the music down.

'Works every time,' she said with a wink.

Enni gave her a quiet clap of approval. Amita handed the little boy back to his mother and felt a lump forming in her throat. She had to find Grahame Sutcliffe. He had to know what he was missing out on.

Chapter 28

RANUNCULUS REPENS

The beautiful Cumbrian weather didn't last. As was typical of Jason and Amita's luck, the bright blue skies of spring that had welcomed them all week now felt like a distant memory. Wall-to-wall grey clouds and just a smattering of rain was making for an uncomfortable entrance into Carlisle Downs.

Not that the crowd seemed to care. A long, snaking line stretched into the car park from the main entrance of the huge building that overlooked the racecourse. Spirits were high as the brightly coloured hats and dresses stood starkly against grey and black suits and tails. Happy faces, bubbling conversation, the prospect of a day at the races beckoned, despite the gloomy skies. Amita and Jason huddled close to the back of the line, keeping as low a profile as they could.

'Do you think we should have invited Alby?' she asked.

'No, absolutely not,' said Jason, keeping their umbrella steady. 'Migraine McGann knows every police officer from here to the Democratic Republic of the Congo. Not to mention their past, their families everything. He'd stand out like a sore thumb.'

'He does that at the best of times,' she added.

'Unfortunately.'

A distant cheer went up from the head of the throng. Gentle ripples of gossip filtered all the way to Jason and Amita that the main doors had been opened. The day could begin. Slowly, the line began to move. The main building rose up like a huge monument to the sport of horse racing. Older, more historic parts had been altered and augmented by steel and glass. Every inch of the building looked expensive and debonair. Amita was feeling desperately out of her comfort zone. And it wasn't just her heels rubbing against the strap of her stilettos that were causing her grief. This whole scenario suddenly felt very real.

'I'm a little worried,' said Jason, almost reading her mind.

'Why?' she asked.

'Apart from the obvious, you mean?' he said. 'I'm a little worried that McGann recognises me, too.'

'And why would she do that? I thought you said you never covered any of her stories or cases.'

'Yeah, I didn't,' he said. 'But this woman is one of the most dangerous, well put-together, slickest operators in the country. She's got rackets up and down the land that extend well beyond Cumbria, believe me. She's been the head of an underworld network for forty years or more. You don't last that long in the mobster game unless you're thorough and you do your homework.'

'You're just nervous, I don't blame you,' she said. 'We'll be alright if we keep our heads.'

'I don't doubt McGann knew all my old colleagues at the paper – the editor, the crime team. Who's to say she didn't expand that research to the rest of the newsroom? She doesn't strike me as somebody who would forget a face.'

'We'll just have to wait and see then, won't we?' she asked.

'Not very reassuring, Amita,' he replied.

The throng slowly crept closer and closer to the main entrance. A high hedge ringed around the outskirts of the race ground. Two huge busts of stallions guarded the main gates and turnstiles. The line was filtered through each of the entryways once guests had shown their ticket or pass. Beyond was a large open forecourt before the main building of the venue reached high into the sky above everything else.

As they approached the turnstiles, Amita checked she still had the glass skull full of gin. It had been weighing down her handbag since they left the house. She thought she could hear it laughing at them on the journey up to Carlisle. It was only her imagination. She hoped.

Before they could properly prepare, the queue seemed to disappear in front of them. Suddenly they were at the turnstiles and a team of smartly dressed security staff in bright yellow jackets beckoned them forward.

'Let's just keep our heads,' she said to Jason. 'Nothing daft, nothing odd, just straight to the point. And remember to be polite.'

'Easier said than done,' he tugged on the collar of his good shirt, his bow tie feeling distinctly like a noose.

'Tickets please, folks,' said a huge security guard.

'Good morning,' said Amita. 'Lovely day for it.'

The guard was blank. He stared down at them, waiting for a pass.

'We were wondering if you could help us,' she said. 'My son-in-law and I are hoping to be part of today's festivities. But we don't have tickets.'

She could see the pulse in the guard's temples.

'Actually, as a matter of fact, we were hoping we could get access to the VIP section, too.'

Amita's request elicited a smile from the guard, his wide face stretching.

'You're joking, right?' he said. 'You're telling me you don't have tickets, but you want to get into the VIP section? Oi, Gino, are you listening to this?'

He beckoned over another slab of a security guard. Gino sauntered over, taking out an earpiece to listen to his colleague.

'These two jokers want in for free,' said the first guard. 'Not only that but they want let into the VIP box.'

Gino eyed Amita and Jason up and down. A ludicrous grin had formed on Jason's face. He could feel it, knew how ridiculous he must look, but there was nothing he could do about it.

'Are you one of those YouTubers?' asked Gino.

'Pardon me?' asked Amita.

'You know, these internet pranksters, the ones that film their jokes and their antics in secret and then post it online. Are you one of them? Are you trying to make us look like a pair of wombats or something?'

He stepped forward. Jason instinctively tugged at Amita's arm.

'No, we're not. Very sorry, shouldn't have come. Let's go, Amita,' he said.

She didn't budge. She remained calm, craning her neck to meet Gino's eyes.

'I can assure you, sir, we aren't jokers or pranksters,' she said. 'I'm a respected member of a number of committees and groups in Penrith, such as the W.I., the Bingo Club Committee and the Musgrave Monument Conservation Society.'

Amita's resume held no sway with Gino.

'If you're not pranksters then what's your game?' he asked. 'Today's meeting has been sold out for months. The VIP section even longer.

We don't just let any old Tom, Dick or Henrietta in, you know. This is a respectable establishment.'

'I'm sure it is,' said Amita. 'That'll be why Ms Christina McGann is in attendance today, is it? A known criminal and mobster with an extensive underworld network under her control?'

'Oh no,' said Jason, covering his eyes. 'You've done it now, Amita.'

For the first time in their conversation, Gino and his colleague were speechless. The well-groomed guards simply stood there, like a pair of frozen, neon giants turned to stone. Amita waited for them to catch up.

'Am I right?' she asked.

Gino was the first to blink. He searched for something, anything, that could constitute a response.

'How . . . Why . . . Where did you . . . How do you know that?' he finally managed.

Amita unclipped her handbag. She pulled it open to reveal the glass skull. The two guards peered inside.

'A gift for Ms McGann,' she said. 'Her favourite tipple.'

'From the Netherlands,' added Jason.

'We'd very much like to give it to her in person,' Amita added. 'As a gesture of goodwill on our part to her. We know how highly she regards manners, especially good ones. It would be a dreadful shame if word got to her that we weren't allowed in to meet her to deliver this little present ourselves.'

Gino didn't hesitate. He tapped the monitor in his ear, said something into a mic on his lapel and immediately ushered Jason and Amita to follow him. They bypassed the main gates and were marched all the way up to the sprawling entranceway of the racecourse building. Another guard, this time dressed in an expensive suit, black shirt and tie was waiting for them. Tattoos crept up from below the collar of his shirt and he gave Amita and Jason a confused look when they arrived.

'These two are guests of Ms McGann,' said Gino. 'Please let her know we allowed them straight access.'

The guard in black grunted an acknowledgement. He stood to one side and opened a glass door that led into the main building. Inside were another couple of heavies, dressed in similar suits and outfits. They pressed for a lift and then ushered Jason and Amita into it when it arrived with a ping.

The doors slid closed. They both let out long breaths.

'Bloody hell,' said Jason. 'What have we got ourselves into this time?'

'This must be how the other half lives,' she said. 'Being passed from pillar to post by extras from a James Bond henchman convention.'

'I've got news for you, Amita. I'm no Sean Connery and you're *not* Honor Blackman.'

'If I knew what any of that meant I'd probably not approve,' she said. 'As it stands, let's just keep focussed, stay sharp and hope that there's a quicker way out of here than how we came in. Just in case we have to make a sharp exit.'

The lift slowed down. The light above the door flashed the number ten and there was a soft, rounded bleep. A voice told them to stand back from the door as it whooshed open. Then, suddenly, there was nothing between them and the lair of Migraine McGann. They took one last deep breath and stepped out.

Chapter 29

ALLIUM CEPA

Amita had never been somewhere that seemed so obnoxiously expensive and exclusive. From the overly polished floor to the gaudy upholstery and furniture, the VIP lounge of the racecourse was clearly aimed at both the very rich and the very tasteless.

A sprawling bar took up most of the far wall to their left. Staff members were in crisp white shirts and red velvet waistcoats, none of them were smiling as they delivered trays of drinks to the guests dotted about at sofas and tables across the rest of the lounge. The opposite wall was all glass, sliding doors that led to a balcony overlooking the racecourse itself. In one corner, a string trio were playing something distinguished. Nobody was listening, too obsessed with the sound of their own voices and guffawing at crude jokes.

In the centre of all this, like a bulbous spider, was Migraine McGann. The same woman Amita and Jason had met outside the Clymtech headquarters was perched on a chaise longue, holding court to a throng of people. Several security staff moved slowly around the area, making sure nobody unwanted got close to her. Staff were delivering trays of food and tall flutes of champagne to McGann and her inner circle in a show of opulence and excess. To complete the look, she was eating grapes from a bunch, one at a time as guests were vying for her attention.

'Queen of the Nile,' said Jason under his breath. 'Do you think this is all for show or is she really this egotistical.'

'A little of both, I suspect,' said Amita.

A broad-shouldered security officer in the now customary black suit, shirt and tie came marching towards them as soon as they stepped out of the lift. He held up a huge hand that was bigger than Jason's face and they stopped.

'Stay sharp,' Amita whispered to Jason as he approached.

'I understand you're here to see Ms McGann,' said the security guard.

'That's right,' said Amita.

'Hold on a moment please,' he said.

He snapped his fingers. Two other guards came promptly over, a man and a woman. The one in charge stepped to the side.

'You won't mind a search of your persons then,' he said sternly.

Jason and Amita didn't have a chance to answer, let alone protest. They were frisked quickly and given the all-clear. The guard in charge dismissed his lackeys and beckoned them forward.

Amita felt her hands getting sweaty. Her sparkling frock seemed to be glowing in the lounge, the grey light seeping in through the far-off windows making every step shimmer. She thought her heart was beating so loudly that the whole room could hear it. The glass skull in her handbag had never felt so heavy.

The guard cleared his throat as they came to a stop just short of McGann's area.

'These two are here to see you, ma'am,' he said.

McGann was in the middle of chewing when the guard spoke. She held up a single finger that immediately quietened him down. Over and over, she chewed the grape. When she was finally finished, she beckoned them forward.

The guard stood to the side. Amita and Jason slowly stepped forward, presented at last to the boss.

'Hello, Ms McGann. Please let me introduce . . .'

Amita was cut off by the same finger that had commanded the guard to be quiet. She did as she was told, a strong, burning anger welling up in her stomach.

'I understand you have a gift for me,' said McGann, not looking at them, instead reaching for a glass of champagne. 'What is it, then?

'Yes, as I was saying,' said Amita. 'We're here with something for you, some gin. Your favourite, we understand.'

She reached into her handbag with nervous hands. Scooping out the glass skull, she felt certain she was going to drop it. Clinging on for dear life, she presented it to McGann who still hadn't looked her way.

'From the Netherlands,' she said.

'Arnhem,' added Jason. 'Very expensive.'

McGann sipped at her champagne. She watched the bubbles rising up the edge of the glass. She was heavily made-up, her peroxide blonde hair styled as much as its short length could take. She wore necklaces and bangles, rings on every finger. The jewellery looked expensive, and Amita didn't doubt that it was. But there was a brashness to it all, the make-up, the hair, the clothes, everything seemed tainted by the streak of malevolence that could not help but shine through. Designer dresses and expensive accessories might as well have been prison scrubs.

'Now tell me something,' said McGann, sitting up and finally looking at them both. 'How can two people I'd never met a week ago suddenly appear in my life *twice* in a matter of days.'

There was a coldness to her tone. Her face was impossible to read. Amita thought about playing dumb, pretending like the brief meeting at Clymtech had never happened, but she knew that McGann was far too clever for that. It wasn't worth the consequences if she was found out. To her surprise, and completely off script, Jason answered before she could.

'We're looking for information on the whereabouts of an associate of yours, Ms McGann,' he said. 'Grahame Sutcliffe.'

Amita couldn't be sure, but the mention of Sutcliffe's name seemed to spark the attention of some of the other guests. Nobody was brave enough to come forward. However, there was a distinct tension creeping through the room.

McGann smiled at Jason, much like a cat would to a mouse cornered with no chance of escape.

'How's your jaw?' she asked him.

'Sore,' he replied. 'Somebody bashed it with a door a couple of days ago.'

'You shouldn't be trying to listen to other people's conversations then, should you. Naughty boy,' she tutted. 'That's why you were sniffing around that dump then? Looking for Sutcliffe?'

'We're helping to locate him and Doctor Fran Weaver,' said Amita. 'His wife is concerned that some harm has come to them.'

'Harm?' McGann laughed, showing off her immaculate false veneers. 'Chance would be a fine thing.'

She clicked her fingers. The chief guard stepped forward. McGann nodded at the glass skull of gin and he immediately snatched it from Amita. It was hurried away from the reserved area.

'You want information, then?' McGann asked. 'You'd better take a seat.'

Staff hurried to find two comfortable chairs. They were parked behind Amita and Jason before either could blink. They sat down and were immediately offered drinks.

'No, thank you,' said Amita. 'Still a little early for me.'

Jason made a low grumble and raised his eyebrows. Amita immediately corrected herself.

'Champagne, lovely,' she took a flute, as did her son-in-law.

McGann was offered a fresh flute too, which she took. She drained half of it in a single gulp and sloshed it around her mouth. Swallowing, she lounged back in her own seat.

'What's in it for you two, then?' she asked. 'You can't be police. You're too old and the Boy Wonder here doesn't look like he could investigate his way out of a paper bag.'

'Boy Wonder?' Jason repeated.

'Quiet, sonny,' McGann hushed him down. 'The adults are talking.'

Amita felt her grip on the champagne flute tightening. She had to make sure she didn't snap it in half by accident.

'It's a rather long story,' she said, remaining calm. 'In short, we're trying to find both men. Or at the very least find out what's happened to them.'

'Interesting,' said McGann. 'And you're doing this off your own backs. You're not getting paid?'

'We're not,' she said.

'Why the hell would you do something like that?' the mobster laughed. 'I don't want to blow smoke up my own backside but bluffing your way into my little sanctum to find two strangers you've never met before, all for free, that doesn't sound like a very smart thing to do.'

Amita hadn't thought about any of that. She certainly hadn't expected to be questioned on her motives.

'Our reasons are our own, Ms McGann,' she said flatly. 'I'm sure a woman of your experience and savvy can appreciate that when the bug bites you, you just have to see it all the way through to the end.'

'I like you,' McGann laughed. 'I like you a lot. What's your name?'

'Amita Khatri,' she said proudly.

'Amita Khatri. And who's your toyboy here?'

'Jason, he's my son-in-law,' she said.

'I see.' McGann cocked an eyebrow in his direction. 'Let me fill you two in on a little secret. See all of this, the wealth, the power, the money, it's meaningless. It's just for show, there's nothing to it. Over there, by the balcony, there are police chiefs, judges, lawyers, the owners of this place, everyone. They all work for me, answer to me. And at the drop of a hat, I can drop *them*. But it works both ways. Everyone has a price, and everyone is looking for something. As long as I provide my services and they do the same for me, everyone is happy. Equilibrium, keeping the status quo. Rock the boat one way more than the other and things start to get complicated, not to mention messy. As soon as that arrangement is broken, you're little more than rotting flowers at the side of a grave. Do you understand me?'

There was an intensity to McGann that made her seem ten times larger than she had been before. She was still sprawling on her chaise lounge, but she could have been standing in front of an army, ready to lead them into battle. That cool, calculated stoicism was unshakable. Amita didn't know if she should be terrified or in awe.

'And did Grahame Sutcliffe rock the boat, so to speak?' she asked.

'Sutcliffe? Don't be daft,' said McGann. 'That moron wouldn't know how to row if his life depended on it.'

'You seemed pretty eager to find him the other day,' said Jason.

'Ah, ah, ah,' McGann waggled a finger at him. 'What did I just say, darling. Keep your mouth firmly shut, there's a good boy.'

Jason didn't argue. McGann smiled at Amita.

'You need to keep his leash tighter, Amita. Your boy doesn't know when it's his turn to speak and when he should let a lady do the talking. That can be a dangerous mistake in my company. Plenty have made it in the past, believe me.'

'I believe you,' said Amita, her throat closing with anger. 'What was your relationship with Mr Sutcliffe? Did he work for you?'

'He did,' said McGann, reaching for her grapes. 'On and off, here and there. Doing odd jobs whenever I needed a spare set of legs. He wasn't exactly blessed with great entrepreneurial nous, let's put it like that, but he was silver-tongued.'

'He was an investor, though?' Amita asked. 'He was part owner of Clymtech and they've just been bought out.'

'True and not true,' McGann conceded. 'Sutcliffe was better at investing other people's money than making his own. And he loved a deal. He sensed an opportunity with Clymtech. You know what the Yanks are like – they love anything us Brits put under their noses, especially if it's got the whiff of academia. Show them a castle and an old bit of cloth and they think it's the Bayeux Tapestry. More than that, they'll think they can buy it up for a song. Sutcliffe came to me looking for money, so I gave it to him.'

'How much?' she asked.

'Fifty grand.'

McGann said the sum like it meant nothing to her. Judging by the opulent surroundings, Amita could believe that was true.

'And you gave it to him?'

'Of course I did,' she said.

'What for? Were you confident of getting it back?'

'Absolutely not,' she said.

'So why did you give him the money?'

McGann laughed loudly at that. She pretended to wipe away a tear from her immaculate eyeshadow.

'Oh, Amita. I could bottle you up and sell you on the internet,' she said. 'Lending money to deadbeats like Sutcliffe is how I *make* money. The interest rates are sky high and there's never any way out of it. Either the investment itself comes good, or the interest on the loan does, I can't lose.'

'What happens if he doesn't pay it back?' she asked.

'I couldn't possibly say,' said McGann with a wicked grin. 'I don't deal with that part of my business, unfortunately. That's left up to my security staff, the boys in the black suits. Although, I should warn you, like I warned Sutcliffe, they do have hot tempers on them. Ex-military and special forces mostly. Cost me an absolute fortune but they're the very best and they know what buttons to press when it comes to street rats like Grahame Sutcliffe.'

Amita looked about the room. The guards had all seemed ferociously intimidating before. Now they were downright sinister.

'I know what you're thinking though,' said McGann. 'I like you, Amita, I really do. There aren't enough women of our age out there living their own lives, free of fear, resentment and pressure from the rest of society. I like your guts and I like your will. That's why I'm going to throw you a bone for your little investigation. Free of charge.'

'That's very kind of you,' said Amita.

'I didn't have Sutcliffe roughed up,' said McGann. 'I've only ever met the bloke a couple of times, and he was a weasel. He liked to think he talked a good game and he wasn't bad looking, that's why I went looking for him myself instead of sending the boys. I like the company of handsome men, even the unconventional ones.'

She cocked an eyebrow in Jason's direction. He immediately blushed, the colour finally returning to his face.

'But I haven't had the chance to question when I'll be getting my money back,' she went on. 'Simply because I don't know where he is. So, if you find him before I do, please tell him that I'd like a quiet word. Otherwise, I'll make sure every lowlife, every mercenary, every tanked-up loser who wants a quick five hundred quid for a scalp knows what he looks like and that I've got cash on the hip. It's nothing personal, just business you see. I can't go about letting standards slip.'

McGann held Amita's gaze for a second longer than was necessary. Amita nodded.

'I understand,' she said. 'This fifty thousand pounds, did he mention what it was for?'

'Sorry your time's up, deary,' McGann clapped her hands.

Three security guards stepped forward, signalling that the meeting was well and truly over. Amita and Jason rose to their feet and were getting ready to leave.

'He said it was to do with securing a buyout,' said McGann. 'Didn't say who by, Americans was all he said.'

'The mystery American tech moguls again. I'm starting to think they don't exist and it was all a ruse to line Sutcliffe's pockets,' said Amita.

'That's a possibility,' said McGann. 'I didn't ask. Quite frankly, I didn't care. I still don't. As long as I get my stake back in the end. With interest. If you see him, send him my way. You won't forget now, will you?'

She held out her left hand. It dangled in the air as she shifted her gaze to Jason.

'Well, sweet cheeks?' she said to him. 'Aren't you going to give me a goodbye kiss?'

Jason winced. He looked about at the guards, all stony-faced and unshifting. McGann waited impatiently. He stopped forward, took her hand and kissed it quickly before retreating to Amita's side.

'Good boy,' she said. 'You've got a useful one there, Amita. Still a little rough around the edges but that can be fixed.'

'Thank you, Ms McGann,' Amita gave a little bow.

The mobster dismissed them with a wave. The guards moved them quickly back towards the lift. The doors slid open and they were about to step inside when McGann called out to them. The whole VIP lounge came to an immediate silence.

'Make sure I never see either of you two ever again,' she said. 'Do I make myself understood? I was feeling generous today, but as a rule, I don't like questions.'

Amita and Jason weren't given a chance to reply. The guards bundled them into the lift and the doors closed. As it started to descend to the lower floors, Amita slumped against the wall. Jason did the same.

'Charming lady,' he said. 'I wonder if we should send her a Christmas card.'

Amita didn't answer him. She just wanted to go home. This had been a trying morning, if indeed it was still morning. Time had lost all meaning as soon as they set foot in the building. They were escorted from the grounds and left to their own devices in the car park. A row of neon-clad security workers watched their every move as they climbed into the car and set off back towards Penrith. Amita needed a shower and a scrub. She felt dirty, polluted. McGann was not to be trifled with. But at last things were starting to take shape in her mind.

Chapter 30

LACTUCA SATIVA

The Penrith Bingo Club had a lot of faults. Mostly, a lack of tea towards the end of every meeting. The mad scramble to get one final cup and some crumbs of biscuits usually descended into unfiltered chaos. But while the members never usually saw eye-to-eye on anything, one thing could always be relied upon. They loved babies.

Enni hadn't seen her newborn son since she first set foot in the church hall. Amita had persuaded her to pop in for half an hour. At the first sign of the little tyke, the old men and women had been clustered around him. From cooing to cuddling, the baby was slowly making his way around every one of the tables set up for the game. The usual strict timekeepers seemed to lose all track of when the bingo should begin. And the urns were still full, biscuits untouched. Everyone wanted to hold the new arrival, gifts of money being handed over like it was going out of fashion. Amita could normally find fault with almost every other member of the club, but tonight she was happy just to watch them all melt at the sight of the little boy.

Sandy, in particular, took a real shine to Enni and her son. He had the baby resting on his huge shoulder as he sat down at the table across from Amita. After a while, Enni did her best to fend off the rest of the regulars, answering questions politely and patiently but clearly hoping for some peace and a sit down.

'He's a little cracker, ain't he?' said Sandy.

'He is,' agreed Amita. 'A beautiful, bouncing, baby boy. The apple of all our eyes.'

'I'll bet,' he said. 'I never had children of my own. I always wanted one or two or a dozen, but it just never happened. I've always loved babies. Probably because I used to be one.'

Amita laughed. The last few days and weeks had been tough. Never before had she felt like every route, every hunch, every clue had led to so many dead ends. Nothing was working. She felt like she was hitting her head against a brick wall. Frustration didn't cover the half of it.

Yet here she was, watching Sandy playing with a baby who was less than a fortnight old. And somehow, right then, nothing else mattered. She was safe, the baby and his mother were safe, and she was surrounded by people that she knew she could trust. Even Georgie Littlejohn, for all of her faults.

'Has she decided on a name for him?' asked Sandy.

'Not yet,' said Amita. 'She's waiting for her parents to come over from America. The circumstances have been absolutely dreadful and yet she's carried on, ploughed on, in fact, regardless. She's a trooper, as they say.'

Enni was still fielding all kinds of advice, questions and general attention. She caught Amita's eye and shrugged, smiling.

'I think she's going to be an excellent mother,' she said to Sandy.

'A baby!' shouted Ethel, more in surprise than anything else. She'd been gently snoozing, much like the newborn, at the end of the table. Sandy eased the little boy down from his shoulder and cradled him, showing him off to the oldest member of the club.

'Isn't he just adorable,' he said.

Ethel rubbed the sleep from her eyes. She cracked a broad, friendly smile as she looked at the child. 'Can I hold him?' she asked.

Sandy hesitated. He looked over to Amita who was just as cautious. It wasn't that they didn't trust Ethel. She was just very frail.

'Please,' she said. 'I'd like to hold the baby.'

'Are you sure?' asked Sandy. 'He's only a few days old.'

'Sandy Prentice, what do you take me for? A dithering old fool?' Ethel levelled at him. 'I'm not going to drop him, am I? I'm in a bloody wheelchair!'

Amita couldn't fault her for her conviction. Sandy considered the proposition and then nervously moved over to hand Ethel the baby. She took him, with expert ease. Her face beamed as she stared down at him, gently rocking him from side to side. Sandy was hovering about her chair, ready to pounce should anything go awry.

Amita had known Ethel for years. The oldest member of the club had something of a reputation. She danced to her own tune, whether by accident or design. But Amita knew that she wasn't half as doddery or forgetful as she made out. She was a proud woman with a fierce intellect that, yes, may have been eroded a little through her nine decades, but there were more flashes of her sharp mind than many folk realised. Watching her now, with the little baby, there seemed to be a new lease of life about her. She whispered to the baby and caressed his forehead with her finger. The boy was quiet, staring up at her, blithely unaware of the near century between them.

The rest of the club had noticed, too. Everyone had gathered around the table. Enni moved around and sat down beside Amita. Nobody spoke. They all just sat there and watched as Ethel sang a lullaby to the newborn in her arms. Slowly, his eyes began to get heavy. He tried to fight the sleep, but he was too warm, too comfortable, too happy. Everyone held their breath as, finally, he drifted off.

'Sleep well, little angel,' Ethel whispered.

She kissed him gently on the forehead and looked up to see everyone staring at her.

'Can I help you?' she asked the group.

In that little instant, she was back to being the same old cantankerous Ethel who everyone knew. A few groans went around the crowd as it began to disperse, huffs from those who hadn't had a chance to hold the baby. Amita, however, knew what she had just seen was something very special, something she'd never expected before from crochety Ethel. She had been instantly at ease with the baby. Amita realised then that she knew nothing about who Ethel was beyond the walls of the bingo club. Nobody did. Unlike so many of them, she never spoke about her past, any family, or brought any visitors along to bingo nights. To them she was the constant in the corner, the one who shouted odd things from time to time and was, Amita felt bad to admit, a little embarrassing. Nobody could remember the last time she'd ever won anything. But she was always there, a reassuring presence.

After a little while, Sandy gently took the baby from Ethel. He brought him around the table to Enni who gladly welcomed him back. She sat for a moment, making sure he hadn't woken up.

'Thank you for this, Amita,' she said. 'It was really very kind of you to get me out of the house. And everyone here has been so lovely.'

'They're a good bunch,' she said. 'Mostly. And they do mean well. We don't get many young visitors, especially not ones as utterly cute as your little bairn.'

'He's certainly left an impression, hasn't he?'

'He has. Usually everyone gets excited when Jason turns up. That shows you how utterly starved we are of new talent.'

Enni laughed. Amita helped her with her bag as they walked to the door. Radha was waiting in the car just outside. She climbed out and opened the back doors, one of the kids' old baby seats coming in handy. She and Enni strapped the little boy in and got back in, waving as they left Amita. She was about to head back into the hall when a hissing sound distracted her.

Georgie Littlejohn was down the street, crouching behind an overflowing bin.

'Georgie?' Amita asked, trying to stifle a laugh. 'What are you doing?'

'Come here, quickly,' Georgie rasped.

Amita looked about. The street was empty, nobody else about. She skipped down to the bins as Georgie continued to cower down behind one.

'Get down,' she said, grabbing her cardigan.

'Georgie, what on earth are you doing?'

'Shhhh,' she said.

'What's . . .'

'Would you get down, you're going to give us away.'

Georgie tugged at Amita. She kneeled down, feeling her knees and ankles crack. A rancid smell was coming from the bin.

'Georgie, we're hiding behind a bin, for goodness sake,' she said. 'Do you mind telling me what exactly you think you're doing?'

'It's a stakeout,' she said, peering over the top of the receptacle.

'A stakeout? It's still light outside. And you've leant your stick up against the bin in full public view.'

She gestured behind them. Georgie was undeterred. She was staring intensely towards the entrance of the church hall and beyond.

'I know what I'm doing,' she said. 'I've spent every waking moment, morning, noon and night trying to get to the bottom of this missing money. And I've cracked it, Amita. I've finally cracked it.'

Amita wasn't sure if it was just the odd surroundings or not, but Georgie seemed altogether less put together than usual. Her hair wasn't in its usual hairsprayed bouffant, her roots showing. Her sweater was crumpled and not colour coordinated with her scarf like usual.

'Are you alright?' Amita asked her.

'What? Yes, fine, of course I am. What kind of question is that?' came the reply.

She was on edge, tetchy, more so than even for her. Amita decided that she should probably step in before this got out of hand.

'Georgie, would you mind telling me what you're up to with this alleged stakeout?' she asked. 'Only, this doesn't seem like normal behaviour to me. And you're going to miss bingo if you stay out here much longer.'

'That's the point,' she said. 'I'm waiting.'

'For what?'

'For Pauline Saxon,' she said.

'Pauline? What do you want with Pauline?'

'*She* stole the money.'

Amita did her best not to sigh. She could see from Georgie's enthusiasm, her intensity, that this whole investigation of hers meant a lot. Even if it was bearing no fruit.

'Go on,' she said.

'Pauline Saxon,' she said. 'She's the culprit. She has to be. I've gone through the whole list of members, Amita. She's the newest one.'

'She is,' she said. 'That doesn't make her a thief.'

'Doesn't it?' Georgie yelped. 'We've had no problems for years and years. And then suddenly she shows up and the money dries up. I'm on to her though, I'm telling you.'

'Is that your theory, then? That she's the last one in the door so she must be a thief.'

'Isn't it obvious?' asked Georgie.

'No, it's not,' said Amita. 'In fact, it's pretty rude. If I said something like that and Jason was around, he'd probably drag me over the coals for being so absurd. You need evidence, Georgie, hard evidence that proves your point. And if it doesn't exist, then maybe, just maybe, you're wrong.'

'Shut up, she's coming.'

Georgie grabbed Amita's arm. They peered around the bin as Pauline made her way down the street. She was smiling to herself, lost in a daydream as she frequently was. No sooner had she set foot on the bottom step of the church hall, than Georgie was up like a whippet.

'Got you!' she cried, running up the street.

'Oh lord,' said Amita, a few paces behind.

Hi, Georgie. Hi, Amita. I'm glad you're both here. I thought I was going to be late and—'

'Don't try to worm your way out of this one, Saxon,' said Georgie, interrupting her.

Pauline blinked. Amita was too late, Georgie was already in full rant mode.

'What did you do with the money, then?' she asked her. 'Come on, out with it. I'm making a citizen's arrest. Amita, call the police, tell them we've caught the bingo club funds thief. Might want to ring Jason and let him know about the story. The papers will want in on this.'

'Thief?' asked Pauline.

'Something wrong with your hearing, just like your morals, eh?'

She grabbed Pauline's arm. The other woman didn't know what to do. She just looked at Amita, hoping for some help.

'Alright, that's enough now, Georgie. Let her go,' she said.

'She's the thief! I caught her!' Georgie was starting to go a little manic. 'Call the police. Get them down here right away! Hurry up, Amita, before she turns violent.'

'Violent?' asked Pauline. 'I'm a lifelong conscientious objector.'

'Just a front,' snapped Georgie. 'You thieves and criminals are all the same. Shame on you for preying on the old-age pensioners of the bingo club. They can't defend themselves like some of us younger women. You should be locked up and the key thrown away.'

She began tugging on Pauline's arm. Amita decided that enough was enough and broke them apart.

'You better go inside, Pauline,' she said. 'I'll deal with this. I'm very sorry.'

'What are you doing? You're letting her go!' Georgie shouted.

'That's enough!' Amita shouted.

Pauline retreated up the stairs. She hurried inside the hall, the big, heavy doors slamming closed behind her. Amita waited until the coast was clear and then let Georgie go.

'That wasn't right, Georgie. You shouldn't have done that,' she said.

'But she's the thief!'

'And what proof do you have? What evidence, other than your own imagination. The first thing you do in *any* investigation is gather that proof. It stops you from going about making false accusations at anyone and everyone who are, usually, quite innocent. You scared the absolute living daylights out of poor Pauline there. And you know how wavy gravy she can be.'

Georgie looked about the street frantically for a moment. Then something clicked in her mind. The intense stare, the bedraggled, haggard persona of somebody who was being driven mad by their own imagination appeared to lift. She held a hand to her mouth.

'Oh god,' she said. 'What have I done? Amita, what have I done?'

'You haven't done anything,' she said, taking her by the shoulders. 'Not yet. And it's perhaps best if we keep it that way. No calls to the police to send in a crack squad to arrest pensioners on a whim.'

Georgie nodded. She slumped down onto the steps of the church hall. Amita sat down beside her. The two women rested for a moment, enjoying the silence.

'I should apologise,' said Georgie. 'At length.'

'You should. Pauline is lovely, she'll understand.'

'No, I mean to you,' she said.

Amita was surprised. She looked at her friend.

'What for?' she asked.

'This investigation malarkey, it's harder than it looks,' she said. 'I thought it was easy. Easier than easy, in fact. All of the cases you and Jason have been involved with, I used to think that I could do that, with my eyes shut and a hand tied behind my back. But it's not easy, it's not easy at all. Any old fool can come up with a suspect or who they *think* is the crook. Finding out who it *really* is, that's a skill, a gift. And I don't think I have it, Amita. You're Penrith's answer to Poirot. I don't think I'm cut out for a life of crime fighting. I mean, just look at me.'

She showed off her creased sweater and tugged at her hair. 'I look like I've not seen a bath for a week. And I smell just as bad, too.'

'It does pong a bit round here,' said Amita, smiling. 'But that'll be all the bins you were hiding behind. How long were you there for?'

'Since six this evening,' sighed Georgie. 'I saw everyone go in, even that little baby. I thought if I cornered Pauline she would confess and make my life a bit easier. What an old fool I am.'

Amita nodded, then stopped. She nudged Georgie in the ribs and decided to offer an olive branch.

'Apology accepted,' she said. 'Come on, let's go in and play the numbers. That always cheers you up.'

'Oh, I can't go in there, not like this,' said Georgie, getting up. 'I have a reputation to uphold, Amita. I can't go in there looking like this. People will talk.'

Amita stood up, too. She made sure Georgie was okay then sent her on her way, back down the street, heading for her car.

'Penrith's Poirot,' she said to herself. 'Not bad, that, not bad.'

Chapter 31

NEPETA CATARIA

'I don't like this,' said Jason. 'Why does he have to be so mysterious all of the time? I swear he does it just to make me nervous.'

'And it's working, isn't it?' asked Amita.

'Of course it's working. It's Alby, he knows exactly how to get under my skin.'

'I thought you were both getting on splendidly, actually,' she sniffed. 'Better than I thought you would.'

Jason gave her a sidelong glance.

'What happened to the whole "I wish we'd never involved him" patter?' he asked. 'That didn't last long, did it?'

'I'm merely remarking how you two haven't strangled each other by now, that's all. I'm allowed to make my observations, you can't stop me, Jason.'

'Oh, I wouldn't *dare*,' he said.

The pair were sitting at a bus stop on the high street. Alby had messaged them late the night before, insisting he meet with them in a public place. When Amita had tried to coax more details from him, he'd fallen silent. She wasn't alarmed, not really. She blamed the meeting with a notorious gangster and the general strangeness of the case for making her a little more hardened to surprise than usual.

'It's been a strange couple of weeks, hasn't it?' she asked her son-in-law.

Jason shielded his eyes from the sun. He'd been sitting watching the traffic and the lunchtime commuters whizz past them. He'd secretly been quite enjoying the wait, just people watching.

'It has,' he said. 'Although, I suppose strange is a relative term.'

'What do you mean?' asked Amita.

'I was a journalist for most of my adult life. Strange goings on were sort of bread and butter for me, Amita. Giant marrows and cute dog competitions aside, you never really knew what was going to come across your desk on a given day. We saw the very best – and the very worst – of human nature.'

'You really should be writing some stories, Jason,' she tutted. 'I haven't seen you type a word for weeks now.'

'I've been busy trying to find two missing men, Amita,' he said. 'Throw me a bone why don't you?'

He was bouncing his knees up and down. They sat for a moment longer and he checked his watch.

'Where is Alby, anyway?' he asked. 'I don't like knowing that he's out there somewhere and I can't see him coming. I swear the man is light as a feather on those flat feet of his.'

'Are you fantasising about me again, Brazel?'

Jason almost jumped out of his skin. Frank Alby had appeared beside them, quite silently, sitting down on the bus stop bench like another punter.

'Bloody hell, Alby,' said Jason, patting his chest. 'How do you do that?'

'Do what?'

'Manage to sneak up on me. It's every time.'

'You try keeping your mouth closed from time to time,' said the former detective. 'That way you won't ever be caught out.'

'I see you've come in disguise,' said Amita.

She nodded at Alby's dark sunglasses and straw fedora. He smiled at her.

'Worked, didn't it?' he said.

'Surprisingly so,' she said. 'Not many other folks in Penrith are sporting an outfit somewhere between a hitman and the Man from Del Monte. Now what is it that you wanted to speak to us so urgently about? You were quite oblique in your message last night.'

Alby held a finger to his lips. He stood up and looked up and down the street. Then, with a flick of his head, he left the bus stop.

'We had better follow him,' she said, standing up. 'Who knows what he's up to.'

They hurried to catch up with the former policeman. He weaved his way through the lunchtime crowd, walking further and further down the busy high street. Jason and Amita followed as close as they could, but Alby was deceptively quick. He was like a silver fish, streaking through the shoppers, overtaking the dog-walking dawdlers at pace. The others followed clumsily behind him until it appeared Alby had come to a stop outside a shop.

He leaned against the wall, staring out at the street ahead. Jason and Amita joined him.

'What's going on, Frank?' she asked.

'Take a look at that,' he said, nodding back to the shop window. 'Tell me if anything stands out to you. I'll wait.'

It took Amita a moment to work out what exactly she was looking at. Alby had come to a halt outside a local estate agent. The usual spread of properties were listed in the window, small pictures and big prices with a brief description were displayed from floor to ceiling.

'I don't follow,' she said. 'It's an estate agent. And a pricey one at that. So what?'

'Take your time,' said Alby. 'I'm in no hurry.'

Amita looked to Jason for some help. He had his nose pressed against the glass.

'Here, Amita, look at that house, it's around the corner from us,' he said. 'Look how much they're asking for it! Maybe we should think about selling up.'

'Oi!' Alby barked. 'Focus, Brazel. This isn't *Escape to the Country*. I've brought you here for a reason. Get looking.'

Amita was ignoring both of them, as she had grown accustomed to doing. She systematically scanned the properties in the shop window. There were a lot to choose from. It seemed that everyone in Cumbria was on the move. Bungalows, terraced houses, apartments, flats, even a disused church somewhere near Crackenthorpe was listed, at an eye-watering price, too.

She was about to give up. Everything was blurring and merging into one.

'It might help if we knew what we were looking for,' she said to Alby.

The former detective had tipped the brim of his fedora upwards. He'd turned his face towards the sun, the grey hairs in his moustache sparkling among the ginger ones.

'Keep looking, you'll find it,' he said.

'Give over, Alby,' said Jason. 'If this is some sort of game you're playing, just knock it off. We don't have the energy. Fine, you're the smartest person on the street, congratulations. What do you want, a medal?'

Jason was stopped by a tugging on his arm. Amita was bent over, staring at one listing card in particular, right at the base of one row.

'What?' he asked.

'Is that what I think it is?' she asked him.

Jason craned his neck. The glare on the window was too bright. He shaded his eyes and peered through the glass. A listing, tucked almost out of sight, showed a house. A large house, one they knew, was looking back at him. The front drive was shown off, the immaculate gardens and the gleaming kitchen, with its huge island and tall stools.

'No,' he said. 'Surely not.'

'It is,' said Amita. 'It's Fran and Delice Weaver's house. It's up for sale.'

Jason felt his eyebrows pinching together. He stood back up and looked at Alby.

'What . . . What does this mean?' he asked.

'Took you both long enough,' said the ex-cop. 'I was starting to think I was going to have to roll out the paint by numbers.'

'How the hell did you find this out?' Jason pointed down at the listing.

'My wife,' he said. 'Honestly, if there's a house that's for sale in Cumbria and she doesn't know about it, I'd be flabbergasted. She's always wanted a property portfolio but with prices the way they are, it's only a dream. It doesn't stop her looking though. She has emails about anything new between here and the border, I hear her getting alerts and messages at all hours about some new drum that's up for sale. She showed me that place last night. The address seemed to ring a bell. Then I remembered, my pals at the station, they'd sent me through all the gaffs of the Weavers and Sutcliffe. Low and behold, it all matched up. Been on the market for about a fortnight. Which, by my calculations, is around the time that we met Delice Weaver for the first time.'

'Coincidence?' asked Amita, already knowing the answer.

'I don't believe in 'em, Amita, you know that. Rarely, very rarely, do coincidences happen in my line of work. Do you know why that is?'

'No, but I'm sure you'll tell us,' said Jason.

'Simple, my dear Brazel. Coincidences don't happen when somebody is working the situation from the back. Delice Weaver, you said she was devastated her husband was having an affair, inconsolable that he'd vanished. And yet she hasn't called the police, hasn't reported him missing and, it would seem, is about ready to up-sticks and move, all within the space of a few weeks of losing her other half. Sound iffy? You bet it is.'

Amita stared at the listing. It was unmistakable, the Weaver house was staring back at her. The same address, the same property, the same garden, everything. She pulled out her phone and began sifting through the messages.

'What are you doing?' Jason asked.

'Checking the last time I had anything from Delice,' she said. 'Nothing, not for weeks now. I've sent her messages to make sure she's okay but no reply. It's like she's vanished off the face of the earth.'

'We've heard that one before,' said Alby. 'It's looking more like we've been led a merry dance. Delice has most likely gone off to join her beloved, who's been setting up their new life in the sun with their ill-gotten gains. The problem is, which fellow has she run off with and who really is our missing man?'

Amita shoved her phone back into her pocket. She was angry, upset, a little frightened.

'I'm going in there,' she said.

'Wait, what?' asked Jason.

Amita barged the door of the estate agent open. Inside was stuffy and overbearingly warm. A middle-aged man was sitting at the desk closest to the door, a chocolate doughnut midway to his mouth. When he saw Amita, he put down his snack.

'Hello madame, how can I help you?' he asked.

'That listing you have in the window, the big house outside Kendal, who put it up for sale?' she asked.

The estate agent looked around numbly.

'Which . . . Which property is this?' he asked.

Amita pushed past him and pulled the little card out of its slot in the window display. She flattened it on the man's desk as Jason and Alby came tentatively into the office.

'This one,' she said, pointing furiously. 'Who put this up for sale?'

'I'm . . . I'm not sure I'm allowed to say and . . .'

'Just tell us!' Amita demanded.

'Amita, cool your jets, would you love?' said Alby. 'You're terrifying this poor man.'

'We have to know,' she fired back at him. 'We have to know if it was Delice Weaver or somebody else who stands to benefit.'

'Amita, he can't tell us,' said Jason, trying to ease her away from the desk. 'Client confidentiality and all of that.'

'He's right, madame,' gulped the estate agent. 'I'm afraid I can't disclose the details of the seller. Unless you were going to be buying the house.'

'Okay, fine, how much do you want for it?' she asked.

'Amita!' Jason thought he was going to drop dead with shock.

'I'm serious, I'll give you what you want,' she said. 'Name your price.'

The estate agent looked baffled. He laughed a little and then stood up, crumbs from his doughnut dropping off his shirt and tie. 'I think there might be some sort of misunderstanding here,' he said. 'Is this a joke or something?'

'I'm not joking, tell me your price and I'll give you the money right now. If that's what it takes to find out who listed the Weavers' house, then so be it.'

'Amita, I really think you have to calm down,' said Jason. 'Do we really look like the kind of clients who have a spare half-million lying around?'

Amita could hear her son-in-law speaking, but she didn't take heed of what he was saying. All she could think of, all she could see in her mind's eye, was Delice Weaver, laughing at her, laughing at them. Alby decided it was time to step in.

'Right, I think we've all had enough excitement for one day, don't you?' he said, easing her away from the desk. 'Sorry to have interrupted your lunch, sir. It won't happen again.'

Alby guided her out of the door, Jason following right behind them. A bus roared past, blowing dry dust and grit up and around Amita's face. She blinked and coughed a little. It seemed to wake her up from her fury. She pushed the hair back from her forehead and turned to face the others.

'Sorry,' she said.

'Don't be silly,' said Alby. 'I probably shouldn't have set you up like that. What can I say, I was excited that I'd found a lead – that I hadn't lost my knack. And all that investigation has given me an appetite. I don't know about you, but I'm starving,' said the former detective. 'What say you treat me to lunch for being an excellent detective, eh, Brazel?'

Jason muttered something under his breath, and they started off down the street. Amita lingered a little longer. The estate agent replaced the Weaver house listing card back in the window display. He gave her a funny look before retreating to his desk.

Amita was determined not to let it lie. No contact from Delice Weaver for weeks, her husband gone, his business partner vanishing too. Debt, gangsters and pioneering science. It all added up to one almighty mess. And she was in the thick of it all.

Amita pulled her phone from her pocket. First, she hit the internet and brought up the listing for Delice's house. Then she scrolled through her expansive contacts list, overjoyed that they'd finally managed to transfer from the cloud or whichever spatial realm they'd been on. She came to a stop at Detective Inspector Sally Arendonk's name. She thought about what she and Jason had discussed, about being wary of alerting the police without proof a crime had been committed. But what other choice did she have? Their investigation had started out with one missing person and rather than solving it, they'd only ended up with more people vanished off the proverbial.

Making sure Jason and Alby were far enough away, she rang the number. DI Arendonk answered immediately.

'Amita Khatri,' she said cheerily. 'To what do I owe the pleasure? You haven't found another dead body, have you? I've got enough of those as it is, unfortunately. In the shops for Christmas and all that.'

'No, I haven't,' said Amita slowly. 'I'd like to report at least one missing person, please.'

'At least one?' asked the DI. 'You haven't finally had enough of Jason, have you?'

'No,' she said again, this time more sombre. 'But you'll probably want to sit down while I tell you the details.'

Chapter 32

DATURA STRAMONIUM

The police appeal was ramping up. It felt like every news report on television and online featured the hunt for Delice and Fran Weaver and Grahame Sutcliffe. Calling DI Arendonk had proven to be the right thing. She hadn't dismissed Amita or accused her of wasting police time. It had only been a day or so and already there had been reports of sightings. But nothing had led to any real leads. And at least now they could spread the net wider with the police involved – they could check their bank accounts, request phone logs, check with the airports. And all this extra firepower had only led to more questions. DI Arendonk, as usual, had warned Jason and Amita that she wouldn't be able to share details on an active investigation any earlier than they released them to the rest of the press or public – but the fact that neither the Weavers nor Sutcliffe had been immediately located made Amita sure there was more to come.

Enni had agreed to be part of the appeal. She had spoken at a hastily called press conference, asking the public for their help in finding the father of her son. DI Arendonk had sat stony-faced beside her, nodding politely as Enni did her best to put across her angst and worry. Amita and Jason had congratulated her on her bravery, and now they were playing the waiting game. Amita regretted not coming forward sooner. The whole of the Cumbria Police Constabulary was out looking for Delice, Fran and Sutcliffe. They had already covered more ground and used more resources in a day than her own investigation had managed in weeks. And that made her feel rotten.

She sat in her big chair by the television and sulked as she looked at her investigation chalkboard. Jason was sprawled on the sofa behind her.

He knew there was something wrong. But finding the right words had been difficult.

'It wasn't our fault, you know,' he said.

'What wasn't our fault?' Amita asked, broken from her daydream and bad thoughts.

'That we couldn't find our guys,' he said.

'I know that,' she sighed. 'I just think we could have gotten the police involved earlier than we did. I mean, we *should* have.'

She pointed to the screen, the early evening news showing another reel of the story. Pictures of Delice and Fran Weaver smiling, another of Grahame Sutcliffe were punctuated with footage outside the Weaver house.

'What's the point of all this?' she asked.

'My point is, whatever has been going on with the Weavers and Sutcliffe and everyone else involved in this sorry affair, we didn't have the whole picture. So, we couldn't act in the best interest. I mean, you saw how this whole thing started. Delice Weaver thought Sutcliffe had murdered her husband and she was ready to confront him about it. We should have seen the signs earlier that she was up to no good.'

'That's true,' she nodded. 'Maybe I was too hasty to trust her. Maybe I just wanted to put that lost weekend in Manchester behind me that I was desperate to do some good.'

'The lost weekend,' said Jason, laughing. 'Remember that?'

'No, that's the problem,' she said. 'We don't know Delice was involved though. I mean, she'd disappeared too. Anything could have happened to her. McGann could have gotten to her, or who knows what. I just don't like loose ends.'

'I know you don't,' he said.

The baby started crying, his wails carrying down the stairs. Jason and Amita looked to the ceiling as they heard Enni's footsteps going to care for her child.

'You know who the real victim is in all of this,' said Jason. 'That little baby. Sutcliffe, whatever he was into, has left Enni alone with their child, his son. That's unforgivable.'

'Enni will be fine,' said Amita. 'She's a clever young woman with a sensible head on her shoulders. She'll look after her son as best as anyone can, with Sutcliffe or without him.'

'I'll miss them when they're gone,' he said sadly. 'It's been nice having them here. It's made me think of when Josh and Clara were that size. How time flies, eh?'

'Try being a grandmother,' she said.

They relaxed into an easy silence. The front door clicked open and Radha came in, her hands full of files, folders and her laptop bag. She slumped down on the couch beside Jason and kicked off her shoes.

'What a day,' she said. 'I mean, every day is what a day. But today was particularly brutal.'

'Bad one, love?' he asked.

'Just hectic. Where's the baby?' she asked.

'He's upstairs, with his mother,' said Amita. 'I think she's feeding him just now.'

'Okay,' Radha yawned.

Jason changed the channel. The appeal for the missing people was on the other side. Radha tutted loudly.

'Just awful what's happened to them,' she said. 'You were right to go the police. It's a strange one though,' Radha took her jacket off and ran a hand through her hair. 'Reminds me of that identity thing from a few years ago.'

'What identity thing?' he asked, watching the news story.

'You remember. That conference I was at in Birmingham, about five or six years ago.'

'Radha, I can't remember what I had for breakfast,' he said flatly.

'I was down in Birmingham for the Midlands Law Expo,' she said. 'It's the usual old rope, networking, aching feet, bags of swag. But there were talks and they had this detective from Calgary in Canada at it. He was talking about a case he'd just completed, where a husband had effectively erased the identity of his wife who died years before.'

'How can you erase a dead person's identity?' asked Amita.

'With remarkable ease if this copper was to be believed,' she said. 'Once he'd disposed of the body, he effectively set about deleting her from history. Slowly but surely, she ceased to exist. No credit cards, no insurance, no bank accounts, nothing. And nobody noticed either, which was the eerie part. Her family just assumed she'd gone missing, and her body was never found.'

'How was he caught?' asked Amita.

'This was the really eerie part,' said Radha, sitting forward. 'The guy had been prolonging it for so long, his wife reached pension age. So, he ended up committing fraud by claiming the money for her. When the pensions department, or whatever it is over there, cottoned on, he ended up confessing the whole thing. He'd duped almost every service, everybody for years and years. And he was undone by his own greed. It just goes to show you that you never know how easy it is to be forgotten,' Radha added. 'You just always assume that somebody will come looking for you, if you disappear. But it didn't happen to that poor woman and her husband banked on it. We're so used to digital communications these days that it's much easier to take over someone's identity, much easier to put off any friends or family that do check in with a text or an email to say you've gone away. Pretty scary when you think about it.'

'It is,' said Jason. 'And on that cheery note, I'm going to collect the kids.'

He pushed himself up from the sofa and headed for the door. Amita kept her eyes on the television, watching the end of the report on the missing trio. Another shot of the house was shown as the reporter spoke about the search efforts ongoing.

With Radha's words echoing in her head, something, somewhere clicked. She sat forward as the screen changed, flicking back to the news studio. 'Radha, pass me that remote for a second,' she said.

Her daughter did as she was asked. Amita paused the screen. Fumbling with the buttons, her hands shaking, she flicked it back a few frames to the shot of the Weavers' home. She paused it and leaned closer to the screen, squinting at the shot.

'You alright, Mum?' asked Radha.

Jason came back into the room, searching for his keys. 'What's wrong with her?' he asked his wife. 'Her glass eyes fallen out again?'

'I don't know,' said Radha, handing him the keys.

Amita was silent. She looked hard at the screen. She didn't know what she was looking for. Only that something was off, something wasn't right. Up and down, left to right, she analysed every inch of the picture. Her memories of the house flashed in her mind as she desperately tried to recall every minute detail of her visit to Delice Weaver. 'I can't put my finger on it,' she said to the others. 'But there's something not right here . . .'

She trailed off. Amita Khatri could count on one hand how many times her blood had frozen so cold it felt like her heart was going to stop. She had survived coming face to face with victims, and even their killers, but there was a particular kind of ice that ran through her veins when she felt the pieces of the puzzle coming together, when she got glimpses not just into the actions of evildoers, but into their motivations. Most of those occasions had happened in the last few years. No matter how many times it did happen, she never got used to it. Some might call it a penny dropping, others an epiphany. It didn't really matter, the outcome was always the same.

'We have to get down to Kendal,' she said, leaping up from her chair. 'We have to go, right now, Jason. It's urgent.'

Amita hurried out of the living room, the door clattering behind her. She was halfway down the path before she remembered she didn't have her trainers on. 'Hurry up, Jason!' she shouted back into the house.

'What about the kids?' he asked. 'I'm meant to pick them up from swimming. I can't just leave them there doing lengths.'

'I'll get the bloody kids,' said Radha, standing up too. 'I know that look in my mother's eyes. It's when she's got an idea in her head and it won't go until she does something about it.'

'Yikes,' said Jason.

'Yikes indeed.'

Jason leaned in and kissed his wife gently on the cheek. He followed his mother-in-law out of the house and down towards the car. There, he thought, goes a quiet evening.

Chapter 33

DIANTHUS CARYOPHYLLUS

'Do you want to run that past me one more time, just to make sure I understand?' he said.

'Watch the road,' said Amita. 'I want to get there in one piece.'

'I *am* watching the road, Amita. You just concentrate on telling me what the hell is going on here.'

'Language,' she chastised him. 'It's perfectly simple.'

'If it was perfectly simple, I wouldn't be asking.'

Amita was concentrating. Jason was going at the speed limit, she knew that, but she was willing the car forward just that little bit faster. The journey to Kendal wasn't that far, but every minute was agonisingly slow. She always felt like this when the puzzle pieces fell together. It was like her head was going to pop open if she didn't see it all through to the end.

'Delice Weaver, she's at the centre of all this. I'm certain now,' she said.

'That's the part I don't understand,' said Jason. 'Where have you got that from so suddenly? And might I remind you that she's also a missing person.'

'It was what Radha said, back in the house, about that man in Canada. It just got me thinking, that's all. Then the news report about the Weavers. The house, there was something about the house. It's been bothering me this last day or so since we saw it in the estate agent's window.'

'Don't remind me,' he rolled his eyes.

'Those video shots of the house, it didn't look right, it didn't look the same,' she said. 'There was something different and I just couldn't work out what was missing. I couldn't see it. Do you know how frustrating that's been?'

'Probably as frustrating as this conversation,' he said. 'What's your point?'

'My point is, I was looking at it all wrong,' said Amita. 'It wasn't that there was something missing. It's that there was something *new*.'

'I'll be honest, I'm still none the wiser.'

The leafy suburbs of Kendal engulfed them. Jason pressed the car down the road that led to the Weavers' home. They drove past similarly lavish and beautiful houses, some tucked behind giant hedges, others gated off.

A bright 'For Sale' sign was standing in the front garden of the Weavers' house. Jason pulled up outside and they got out. Amita stared at the sign. She felt like it was mocking her, just standing there, bright, garish and brash.

'No police about,' said Jason.

'It's not a crime scene,' she said.

'I know. But I thought there would be *somebody* about, the press, a camera crew, something. The place is as quiet as a grave.'

Amita walked up the path that led to the front door.

'What exactly is it we're looking for?' he asked her, following.

'Here, get the listing for the house up on my phone.'

She handed the device to Jason. He took it and began scrolling. Amita looked around trying to get her bearings. The front path led around the side of the house to the garden at the back. She followed it and walked onto the lawn. The Weavers' home stood in front of them, as grand as it looked in the pictures in the estate agent. She tried best to picture what she had seen on the television earlier.

'Have you got it there?' she asked Jason.

'Hang on . . . Yes, here we go.'

He handed back the phone. The listing for the house was on the screen. She tapped the picture that gave them the same view they were looking at. She felt a tingle as finally she could see the key to the whole case.

'Now, tell me what you see,' she said to Jason.

'Oh, bloody hell. Not you, too, Amita,' he said. 'I've had enough of the cryptic teasing from Alby, thank you very much.'

'Just look at the picture and then the house,' she said. 'Tell me what's wrong.'

Jason peered at the picture. Then he looked up at the house. Nothing seemed particularly different. But there was something.

'I see what you mean,' he said. 'There's something off.'

'Keep looking.'

Jason focussed. He felt like he was sitting his driving exam or back at his desk in school, burrowing away with a maths problem. Back and forth he checked both the picture and the real house. Then he spotted it.

'Hold on,' he said. 'That flower bed over there.'

He pointed towards the back of the house. A small patch of the lawn had been dug up, the mud and dirt freshly unearthed, a stunning display of flowers taking pride of place. When he checked the picture on the estate agent's website, the flower bed wasn't there.

'That's odd,' he said. 'Those pictures online can't be that old.'

'They aren't,' said Amita. 'Remember what Alby said. The listing went up about the same time we first met Delice Weaver. That means those pictures are two, maybe three weeks old at the most.'

'So, what? She told us she loved her gardening, what if she planted this bed to deal with the loss.'

'No,' said Amita, gravely. 'That's not what I'm thinking at all.'

Jason's hands suddenly went cold as the dawning realisation of what his mother-in-law was implying. He looked back over at the flowerbeds and swallowed, his throat dry and arid.

'Bloody hell,' he said. 'What do we do?'

'I think we should probably investigate.'

'Is that really very wise?' said Jason. 'I mean, if what we think is under that flower bed, do we really want to be the ones who find it? Or them?'

Amita had been asking herself that question the whole trip down to Kendal and beyond. 'Maybe you're right,' Amita said. 'Let's just take a closer look to see if we should call DI Arendonk.

'Hopefully there's nothing,' said Jason. 'And we can go home. I haven't had my dinner yet and there's an interesting documentary on later about how St Paul's Cathedral was built and . . .'

He stopped suddenly. Amita held her breath.

'What's wrong?' she asked.

Jason's face was a ghostly white. His arms were sunk deep into the hellebores, right up to his elbows. He was breathing heavily, shoulders bobbing up and down.

'I think . . . I think I might have found something,' he said. 'Something cold, metal maybe. It's stuck on something.'

'Right,' said Amita, her whole body now gripped with fear.

'You'd better stand back,' he said. 'I don't want whatever this is to cause you harm.'

'I'm not leaving you alone,' she said. 'Whatever it is, we'll look at it together. Alright?'

She gripped him on the shoulder. Jason looked at her hand and then up to her.

'Okay then,' he said. 'You ready?'

'Ready as I'll ever be,' said Amita.

Jason took a deep breath. He steeled himself for a lingering, agonising moment, then he pulled his arms free from the soil. There, in his hands, was a wristwatch. Caked in mud, an earthworm was wriggling and dangling from the strap. He cleaned the face and the back and showed his mother-in-law the inscription.

Amita could never have prepared herself for what had been buried in the flower bed. No matter how much she had tried to steel herself, nothing could prepare her for the shock. Not even the knowledge that she had been right.

'To my darling Fran,' she read aloud. 'The love of my life, the light of my days and my nights. Yours forever, Delice.'

Amita took the wristwatch and stared down at the flowerbed. 'I think we need to get DI Arendonk down here right away,' she said. 'I think we might have found Fran Weaver.'

Chapter 34

MYRISTICA FRAGRANS

As soon as the police arrived, Jason and Amita were moved to the front of the house. There was a strange calm about how the whole thing unfolded. Despite Amita's recent experience with this kind of scene, she still always felt uneasy. Mostly, she thought, it was to do with the grim circumstances. Usually if she had called in the cavalry, there was something or someone in need of dire attention from the authorities. But there was another reason for her unease: self-doubt.

Until everything was cleared up, she always worried that she'd made a dreadful mistake. While Jason always warned her about dangerous accusations and ruining reputations, she liked to think she'd grown as an investigator over the years. Her track record was something to be proud of. This business with Georgie Littlejohn and the pig's ear she'd made of sleuthing out the bingo club money was some comfort to Amita. She knew her way around an investigation alright, especially a murder one.

But that payoff only came when everything was confirmed. As she and Jason were ushered out of the garden and away from the real police work, she had that nagging fear as always that this whole thing had been a ghastly mistake. While she was never gleeful when evidence was found, there was also relief that she hadn't sent the Cumbrian constabulary on a wild goose chase.

'What's wrong?' asked Jason.

He could sense her malaise. He always could. They stood by their battered old car as more and more police arrived at the Weavers' place.

'Nothing,' she said.

'Why is it when you say nothing, Amita, there's *always* something?' he asked.

'It's really nothing.'

'Your face says it's not just nothing. Come on, out with it, spill your guts.'

'Jason,' she tutted. 'It's just, well, I really don't like this part.'

'Which part?'

'This part,' she nodded at the arriving police.

Another squad car pulled up and more officers in hi-vis jackets climbed out. They nodded at Amita and Jason as they followed their colleagues around the back of the house.

'When we don't know if we're correct or there's something awful about to happen,' she said. 'It's the worst part.'

'You mean worse than confronting murderers or listening to Frank Alby in your ear day after day?'

Amita nodded. Jason took a deep breath.

'I hadn't really thought about it like that before,' he said. 'I guess you're right. It's like staring at the envelope that holds your exam results. You're desperate to know but you also don't *ever* want to know, do you?'

'I'm a little old to remember that, Jason,' she said. 'Don't you feel the same, when we do this kind of thing?'

'Not really,' he said. 'But that's the reporter in me. You learn when you're on the newsbeat to bury your emotions over this kind of stuff. I've told you horror stories before and this is looking like it'll be another one for the casebook. Thick skin is what it's called at large, but we journos think of it as one of the tools of the trade. But you've got a good heart, Amita, that's all this shows.'

He reached over and took her hand. He gave it a gentle squeeze and Amita felt a lump in her throat the size of a watermelon.

'And if you tell Radha or *anyone* else that I said that, I'll have you evicted from the house,' he said.

Amita smiled. A third police car pulled up outside the house. By now the police presence was alerting the neighbours. Curtains were twitching furiously as everyone tried to subtly find out what had happened at the Weaver household.

'One way of coping, I've found, is distraction,' he said. 'Thinking about something completely different to the ghoulishness that's unfolding in front of you. I remember counting the roof tiles during a police press conference once as some litany of awfulness was read out by a chief constable.'

'Sounds like a good idea,' she said. 'You go first.'

'I knew you'd say that.'

Jason inhaled some of the evening air through his nose. He started to think. His mind was racing, but he managed to sift through most of the noise and settle on something he knew would work, if a little bleak.

'Even in the face of ugliness, we can always choose to find beauty,' he said.

'What?' Amita wrinkled her nose.

'I mean right here, it's a beautiful garden, tended with love, I'd bet. I mean, did you see those bobby dazzlers in the flowerbed back there?' he asked. 'They were lovely. I wonder what they are, I think they'd look really nice in that patch below the living room window in our front garden. Or better yet, the patch beside Bidmead's fence. He'd go spare if we really showed him up next summer and . . .'

Jason's voice faded away. It felt like an explosion had just gone off in Amita's head. The flowers, right where they suspected there was a body. She slowly pushed herself off the car. Jason stopped talking.

'Hellebores,' she said.

'What's that?' he asked.

'Hellebores,' she said again, staring wildly at the Weavers' house. 'Hellebores, in the back garden, on that patch around there. The flowers you're talking about, they're hellebores. Just like . . .'

She trailed off. Jason felt his chest tightening.

'Amita, are you alright? You've got that look in your eyes again.'

'We have to hurry,' she said, pulling the passenger door open. 'Quickly Jason, get in.'

He didn't question her. He was in the car, the engine started and rolling down the road within a matter of seconds. She directed him past the police cars as they sped away from the Weavers' house.

'What's the matter?' he asked her.

'Hellebores, in the back garden,' she said. 'I saw them when we arrived and they triggered something, up here.'

She tapped her temple. Jason pushed the car onwards as she directed them back in the direction of Penrith.

'I didn't think anything more about it really. I should have. I was bloody foolish!' she said.

'What? You're not making sense, Amita,' he said. 'And when you don't make sense, I start to get nervous!'

She had so much spinning around in her imagination it was difficult to put into words. But she tried, for the sake of everything that had gone on.

'The allotments,' she said. 'We need to get back to the allotments.'

'That's it? That's all I'm getting?'

Amita didn't answer him. She just stared at the road ahead of them. Jason knew that look, that stare into the distance that meant she was in her zone. Whether it was a murder investigation or the bingo on a Wednesday night, she was gone, out of his reach. All he could do was drive.

They reached the allotment in what must have been record time. Jason was certain he broke the speed limit at least a dozen times in the short jaunt back to Penrith. He was as surprised as he was proud that his battered old car could still manage those top speeds.

The allotments were dark. A faint glow from the streetlights beyond the fences made everything look sinister. Jason searched the rickety boundary until they found a missing panel and squeezed in.

'Over here,' said Amita.

She pointed towards Brunger's shed.

'Brunger?' said Jason. 'This has got something to do with that toerag?'

Amita hurried over to the shed. The light was dismal here, too far away from the pools cast by streetlights. She pulled out her phone and switched on the torch. Jason did the same. Amita scanned the ground ahead of them, weaving back and forth with the circle of light over the cabbage patches

She stopped suddenly. There, bathed in the harsh glare of the phone torch, was a long patch of artificial grass, ringed by hellebores.

'There,' she said.

'What?' asked Jason.

'Fake turf,' said Amita. 'I saw it before, when we came for a walk, do you remember?'

Jason was silent.

'I didn't think anything of it at the time, although it seemed to be pretty strange,' she said. 'A great big lump of plastic grass here, amongst all the carefully cultivated veg and herbs. And it was something that Sandy said before, about the Garden Club here, how they're fiercely protective of everything that goes in the ground. It's all got to be just right and, most importantly natural. I wondered, then, how somebody in that club would ever think to put down a strip of this Astroturf stuff, especially amongst their flowers. Patrick Bidmead even said as much, how this stuff is the absolute cardinal sin for gardeners. It's not right that it's here. Not right at all.'

She fell silent. Jason worked everything out in his head.

'You mean . . .' he trailed off.

Amita shone her torch in his face. He was ghostly white, not just from the glow.

'Yes,' she said. 'If there's artificial grass here then I think, *think*, there may be something underneath. And I don't mean an early crop of spuds.'

'Good grief,' Jason gulped. 'This just gets worse and worse.'

Amita turned away from the patch of artificial turf and started back towards the road. Jason remained behind, standing guard over the hellebores and their secret. A small arched gate led to the street, beside it a noticeboard. Amita stopped and leaned against the old, flaking wood. She composed herself, drinking in as much of the night air as she could. When her head stopped spinning, she unlocked her phone and dialled DI Arendonk.

'Hello, Sally,' she said. 'It's Amita.'

'Amita, I'm a little busy at the moment,' said the detective.

'Yes, I know, and I'm sorry to be adding to the pile, it's just . . .'

She trailed off as something caught her eye. The noticeboard beside the main gates of the allotment was dotted with notices and flyers. There was an advert for the Garden Club's annual end of summer show and a memo about keeping patches neat and tidy. Brunger's business card was there, about a dozen of them pinned to the board.

But it was something else that made Amita's head pulse. A faded sheet of paper was stuck to the top right corner. It was browned with the weather, but a list of names was recorded under the banner 'Penrith Garden Club Plots of the Year Winners'. Amita's legs turned to jelly when she scanned the names, coming to a stop at the very bottom. It was then that her worst fears were confirmed.

'Amita? Amita? Are you there?' asked Arendonk, still on the line.

'Yes, sorry, I was . . . I was distracted by something,' she said.

'Distracted?'

'Yes, sorry Sally. It's just, well, I think you're going to have to get a second team down here to the allotments in Penrith as soon as possible,' she said. 'I think there may be something worth digging up here.'

'The allotments?' Sally asked. 'Have you lost your marbles? This is no time for a spot of gardening, Amita.'

'No,' said Amita. 'I'm afraid it's far more serious. I think there might be something, or someone, in the ground in one of the plots. Or, more precisely, Delice Weaver's plot.'

She ended the call and stood staring at the noticeboard.

Jason bounded over. 'Forget about 'Best Misshapen Potato' or whatever you're reading, Amita. I'm more worried that someone might be out there in the gloom watching us right now. Someone who's already offed Fran Weaver and might not like the fact we've potentially stumbled across another body. There are plenty of people with grounds to bear a grudge against Fran – Delice, Hargreaves, Sutcliffe – all of them could have wanted him out of the picture. And what if we've put ourselves on their list by digging about in the veg plots and flowerbeds.'

Amita ran her finger down the list of names. 'Look. Best snowdrops: Mrs D Weaver. I think we're looking at Delice's allotment here. Stop worrying about the culprit for a moment, Jason. I feel our duty is to the dead as much as the living. The question is, if there is a body beneath the flowers, which one of our missing trio is it?'

Chapter 35

RICINUS COMMUNIS

Amita tried not to look at the Weavers' house. By now, the whole street was illuminated by blue lights. The drive back to Kendal had been done mostly in silence. Both Amita and Jason seemed to like it that way. And with the unfolding major police incident that awaited them, keeping their heads down was for the best.

It hadn't taken DI Arendonk very long to scramble her team. Most were still in the area from the initial search of the property and garden. After the events of tonight and Amita's calls, the search for Fran Weaver had, sadly, now been called off.

Jason hadn't said a word since arriving. He was leaning on the car beside Amita, his head bowed, too. They had been standing there since they'd arrived back. Officers were creating a cordon on the street and the house had been sealed off. Forensic teams in white jumpsuits and masks had very quickly made their way around the back of the house with their equipment.

'Did you let Radha know we would be home late?' she asked him, as much to break the silence as to hear the answer.

'I did,' he said.

'Have you mentioned all of this? What we found.'

'I said we'd be held up with a police matter,' he said. 'I think she'll be able to read between the lines. Plus, nothing has been officially confirmed yet. I imagine whoever they have found back there will need to go through formal identification and all that stuff. Not to mention what's happening at the allotments.'

'All of this,' she waved at the police, at the crime scene. 'Why can't people just get along? Every time we stand here, I always just want to scream at the top of my voice, "Be kind to one another!" Or if you can't be kind, be quiet; find a healthy way to work off your rage – I mean look at my powerwalking, or that kickboxing for pensioners course I did. We're meant to be a modern society – therapy, talking cures and all that – but sometimes I fear we're all still savages underneath it all.'

Jason nodded sombrely. He couldn't disagree with his mother-in-law. He could tell that this case in particular had hit her harder than usual.

'I know,' was all he could offer her. 'We spend all this time trying to puzzle out what's happened, but I don't think we'll ever truly be able to get into the heads of people who do these kinds of things. Much smarter folk than us have tried and arguably failed. Saying that, I don't think I'd much want to be able to think like a killer, to be perfectly honest.'

Amita smiled at her son-in-law. She took his arm and squeezed it.

DI Arendonk came wandering over to them through the flashing lights and police barricades. She had two steaming cups with her and handed them over when she reached them.

'What is it with you two and a huge police presence?' she asked them. 'Wherever you go I end up having to call a code red and scramble the seventh cavalry.'

'We ask a lot of questions other people don't,' he said, sipping the hot tea. 'And that, for some strange reason, angers a lot of people.'

'Yeah, I can imagine,' she said. 'How about you, Amita. How are you holding up?'

Amita wanted to cry. The anger, the frustration from earlier had gone. But in its place, she felt hollow. All the questions from before were still swirling around inside her head. And while they'd made a grim breakthrough, she still needed answers.

'Not great, detective,' she said. 'But it hardly matters how I feel. I assume you've found remains back there.'

'We have,' said Arendonk. 'That's off the record, Brazel.'

'Don't worry,' he said. 'My brain is like scrambled eggs. I couldn't string two sentences together if my life depended on it.'

'There's a joke in there but I'm not about to make it,' said the detective. 'But yes, I'm afraid so. No cause of death yet, that'll be for the lab boys to take a look at once it's clear we can move the remains.'

'Yes,' said Amita. 'It *is* Fran Weaver though, I take it.'

'Again, off the record, I think so. We're fairly confident it's him. And then there's whatever we turn up in Penrith, at the allotments. It's looking like more human remains. I got a call from my sergeant on the scene. We're spread thin tonight, but we'll get there. You really do like to give us a challenge, don't you?'

'I wish we didn't,' said Amita.

'Yeah, I hear you,' she sucked in the night air. 'Burial is meant to be a one-time only affair. I don't envy my team doing the digging.'

Amita felt queasy. The tea was swirling in her cup, but she had no appetite to drink it. It wasn't just the thought of two bodies, alone in the dark quiet of the soil, it was the shockwaves that would undoubtedly ripple out and impact the living – those left behind.

'I'll need statements from you both, when you're fit and ready,' Arendonk added. 'No rush though. And if it helps, I can arrange one of our therapists to come and chat to you when convenient. This kind of thing can take its toll up here.'

She tapped her forehead. Amita was grateful for the gesture.

'Thank you, Sally,' she said. 'I think we'd both just like to get home, if that's okay. We can pop down to the station in Penrith first thing in the morning, if that works for you.'

'Sure,' she said.

There was a minor commotion from somewhere behind them. A flurry of police officers was clearing a path around from the back of the house. Tape was lifted up as a forensics team pushed a trolley towards the street. An ambulance was waiting for them and the remains were gently lifted inside. Once the doors were closed, the ambulance drove off, heading down the street with its sirens on.

'Sorry you had to see that,' said Arendonk. 'If you don't feel like driving, I can get one of the team to drop you off.'

'It'll be fine,' said Jason. 'I'll stick some heavy metal on and annoy Amita, that should do the trick.'

Sally laughed a little. Amita didn't.

'Okay. Well, I'll keep you both posted when anything develops tonight, if it's Delice under the plot in Penrith, or whether it's Sutcliffe in the allotments. You said there were next of kin that need to be informed.'

'Yes,' said Amita, climbing into the car, relieved to be able to sit down. 'Enni. She was Sutcliffe's girlfriend, if you could call their relationship anything like that. She's the mother of his child. Then there's his own mother, too. She's here in town. I can get you the address.'

'We can handle that,' said the detective. 'Let's just hope it's not another person unnamed.

A chilling thought struck Amita. She didn't think she could handle a third body in one night. She composed herself.

'Right,' said Arendonk, rubbing her forehead. 'We'll have to see what we're dealing with first before they can be formally identified. But I'll see you tomorrow morning at the station. I don't think any of us will be getting much sleep tonight.'

'Thank you, Sally, for everything,' said Amita.

'No problem.'

Amita closed the car door. The cabin of the car was quiet after the buzz of walkie-talkies and hum of chatter. It was just what Amita needed. Jason fastened his seatbelt and rested his hands on the steering wheel.

'You've got that faraway look, Amita,' he said. 'You don't think they're going to find Delice tonight, do you?'

Amita felt Jason's voice clang around her head like a church bell ringing for Sunday service. It wasn't quite a wake-up, she'd never felt more awake in her life, but suddenly she realised she'd been missing a bigger picture.

'No, I don't,' she snapped her fingers. 'She was never going to tell the police because she already *knew* where her husband was.'

'You think she found out about the affair and decided to get a bit physical?'

'Possibly. I don't know and we won't know until the forensics reports come back, I suppose. But if that is the case, where does Grahame Sutcliffe figure in all of this?' she asked. 'Did he know about the murder? Did he witness it? Did he help even?'

'That's a lot of questions, Amita,' he said. 'And we don't even know if Delice is guilty. We don't even know if she's alive. Not reporting Fran is strange, but she's not the only one. Enni hadn't called in Sutcliffe's disappearance. Who else has been keeping schtum?'

Amita furrowed her brow.

'Sutcliffe's mother,' she said.

'Isobel. If we suspect we know why Delice didn't call the police, why didn't Mrs Sutcliffe? You heard her, he was the apple of her eye.'

'Apple schnapps, maybe,' said Jason.

'I don't believe for a second that she wasn't worried about him, didn't care that he'd gone missing. What was it she said to us? She knew he'd be somewhere, out with some woman, like his father.'

'She painted quite a picture,' said Jason. 'Although I'd just been beaten about the head with a brush, so I might not have taken it all in.'

'If Grahame was missing for as long as he was, surely she would have been worried, she would have called the police and started the search, but she didn't. Now why do you suppose she would do that?'

'I have no idea,' said Jason. 'Fear that if he was found he'd also be accountable for the child he'd fathered, or the loan he'd taken from McGann?'

'Even if that was the case, I think she'd still be in touch with him – even if he was in hiding. What if she *was* being told that everything was alright,' asked Amita. 'What if somebody was there, regularly visiting her, making sure she didn't ask questions or make sure she didn't do anything rash like call in the police search dogs. Now, who do you suppose would be able to do something like that?'

'McGann?' he asked. 'I mean, she seems perfectly capable of finding these kinds of things out, addresses, family connections, anything that might give her one up on her drones or clients, or whatever you want to call them.'

'Knowing about Isobel would certainly give her leverage on Sutcliffe, if she ever needed to use it,' said Amita. 'She's a nasty piece of work.'

'What about Professor Hargreaves?'

Amita nodded.

'I mean, she's always put herself across as being this dedicated academic. But you saw how she ran and gave us the complete runaround. The amount of times we've been lied to in this case, I wouldn't put something like this past her. Not if she put her mind to it.'

'Do you think she could kill?' asked Amita.

'Given the night we've been having, Amita, I believe *anyone* could kill. We've got bodies pushing up the daisies, quite literally, everywhere we look. Who's to say that the esteemed professor didn't lash out in a fit of temper and things spiralled from there?'

'It's like what Alby told us. We think we're all good law-abiding citizens until the moment we cross that line. Whether it's calculated killings or accidental homicide, death is closer than you think.'

'Don't I know it!' Jason replied. 'Look at Isobel attacking me with that brush. You wouldn't have her down as a psychopath from first glance, but I could have been a goner. I've got a skull like an eggshell, I swear.'

'That's it.' Amita looked wide-eyed as she pulled her seatbelt across and clicked it shut. 'Step on it, Jason,' she said. 'I have a feeling I know where Delice Weaver might be hiding. And I don't think it's six feet under.'

Chapter 36

PIERIS JAPONICA

The back court off the main street was quiet. The sun was almost gone and only the faintest rays of amber were touching the rooftops high above them. Jason and Amita looked about the courtyard. The parking bays were empty and there was nobody about. A cat was rifling through some bin bags in the far corner. The old banana skins and apple cores weren't to its taste.

Amita went for the buzzer that led to the flats, but Jason stopped her.

'What if someone's up there with Isobel,' he whispered. 'Whether it's Delice, Hargreaves or McGann's goons, I think they'll be smart enough not to let us in.'

'Good point,' said Amita. 'How do we get up there, then?'

Jason looked about for some inspiration. The flats above them were mostly dark, save for Isobel Sutcliffe's home and another one just below her. He began counting in his head.

'What are you doing?' she asked.

'Hang on, I'm trying to work something out.'

When he was done, he pressed one of the buttons on the intercom. There was a brief moment before the other end of the line crackled into life.

'What is it?' came a hard, metallic voice.

'Ah, yes. Good evening, sir. Thank you for answering,' said Jason, thinking on his feet. 'I was wondering, do you play the postcode lottery at all?'

'Eh?' asked the man, confused. 'What is this, some sort of joke?'

'No, not a joke, sir. Just a simple question,' Jason smiled at nobody.

'I do. What about it?'

'Then I'm very pleased to say that you've won one of our jackpots.'

'What?' The man couldn't contain the excitement in his voice, even over the ancient intercom. 'Bloody hellfire and biscuits! Are you serious?'

'I am deadly serious, sir. If you could just buzz us in, we'll be right up to give you your cheque.'

'Of course! Of course! Come on in!'

The door buzzed loudly and unlocked. Jason pushed it open and hurried Amita up the stairs.

'Quickly,' he said. 'Before he gets to his front door and realises that we're fraudsters.'

They both climbed the stairs as fast as they could. The door to the man's flat was unlocking as they skipped past, climbing another storey. He was out on the landing shouting back down the stairs by the time they reached Isobel Sutcliffe's front door.

'Where's my cheque?!' echoed up the stairwell behind them.

They reached Isobel's door. Jason looked at Amita and then grabbed the handle. He turned it and, to their surprise, it opened. Jason eased himself in front of Amita, making sure he went in first.

'Stay sharp,' he whispered to his mother-in-law. 'We don't know what's waiting for us in here. If your suspicions are right, our not-so-grieving widow, Delice, could come running at us waving a knife or something and we'll have to fight her off.'

'Or Isobel Sutcliffe with her trusty brush.'

'Yes, that too,' he said. 'I've still got a lump from last time. But your theory does explain why she was so quick to attack me.'

Jason eased the door of the flat open. Inside was a mess. More empty drink bottles were scattered about the hallway. A nasty tear had been made in the wallpaper and a mirror was cracked at the far end. The place was silent, and Amita was beginning to get worried. If Delice was a killer, she surely wouldn't think twice about murdering Isobel Sutcliffe once she'd served her purpose. The prospect of finding another dead body made her a little short of breath.

They passed the first rooms, both were empty. The kitchen was directly on their right. It was empty, too. The smell of fried food and stale air made the whole place stink. The faint sound of the television was coming from the living room at the end of the hallway. Jason thumbed in its direction and Amita nodded.

Pushing the door open as gently as they dared, the tinkle of glass bottles made them stop right away. Amita's eyes went wide and Jason held his breath. There was no rebuke, no sign of life from within. They continued in silence, creeping over the mess.

The television was on in the corner. It was an old set, its picture grainy and blurry at the edges. A single armchair was sat facing it and, over the edge of the tatty fabric, they spotted a head of hair. Amita held on to Jason's arm. They rounded the armchair and found Isobel Sutcliffe sitting there, head to one side, mouth wide open. She looked frail, her veiny, spindly hands clutching a near empty bottle of Scotch.

'Is she . . . You know?' Jason nodded at her.

'I . . . I don't know. I think . . .'

Isobel's eyes opened suddenly. It was hard to tell who got more of a shock – the old lady or Jason and Amita. Mrs Sutcliffe immediately screamed, her mouth of crooked and missing teeth opening up. A rasping cry almost sent Jason and Amita out of the window.

'Mrs Sutcliffe, please, it's okay,' Amita tried to calm her down, when her skeleton returned to her skin. 'It's me, Amita. We're just here to make sure you're okay.'

Isobel blinked. She stopped screaming as the sleep and shock cleared. She sat back in the armchair and wiped her face.

'You almost gave me a heart attack, deary,' she said. 'I thought my time had come.'

'You're not the only one,' said Jason, rubbing his chest where his heart used to be.

'I'm sorry,' said Amita. 'We don't have much time. I think you should probably come with us.'

'Go with you? Whatever for?' she asked, unscrewing the cap of her bottle. 'This is my home. I'm not going anywhere. I've got help, I don't need to go into care or wherever it is you're trying to take me.'

'Isobel, you just said you had help. Has somebody been here with you?' asked Amita. 'Has someone been living here these past few weeks? It's okay, you can tell us.'

The old woman took a long swig from her whisky. Amita noticed her hands had started to shake.

'You don't have to be frightened,' she said, kneeling down beside her. 'We're here to help.'

'It's alright, it's okay, I'm okay,' said Isobel. 'She says my Grahame has sent her over to make sure I'm alright while he's away on business. She looks out for me, makes me dinner, that kind of thing. I bet he thought it would be nice to have some company for a change, while he is away. I can get quite lonely here.'

There was an oddly robotic tone to her voice. As if she was reading rehearsed lines.

'Mrs Sutcliffe, are you sure?' Amita ventured, patting her on the shoulder, half fearing she might wallop her, after what she'd done to Jason on their first visit. Isobel Sutcliffe shooed her away, the sleeve of her blouse riding up as she did.

'Mrs Sutcliffe? Isobel? Has this woman hurt you?' asked Amita.

Isobel blinked. She was holding back tears now. Her hand instinctively went to her left arm. Amita gently reached out. Isobel's wrist was like a twig, brittle and frail. She rolled the sleeve back to reveal a series of bruises.

'Those look like finger marks to me,' said Jason.

'Did a woman do this to you?' asked Amita sternly.

Isobel nodded. Then she smiled, trying to hide her upset.

'It was my own daft fault,' she said. 'I was trying to go down to the shops to get something. She told me I didn't have to go out while she was here, she would do all the cooking and look after me. I went to leave and she stopped me. It was just a silly mistake. I'd had too much to drink. It was my fault, honestly it was.'

Amita looked up at Jason. He was angry, she could tell. His eyebrows were pinched and his mouth curled downwards.

'Come on, Isobel. Let's get some things together in a bag for you,' she said. 'You can come stay with us for a little bit until this is all sorted out.'

Isobel bowed her head. She nodded and Amita helped her out of the chair. She was unsteady on her feet and winced in pain as she stood up.

'Isobel! I'm back!'

Delice Weaver's voice echoed down the hallway. Jason, Amita and Isobel froze where they stood.

'One of your neighbours is down in the street shouting and bawling, something about being done out of money. I just ignored him,' she said, the front door slamming shut. 'I've brought you some fish and chips. They didn't have any sausages so you can have fish instead. It all tastes the same anyway.'

She appeared at the door of the living room, peering into a plastic bag. When she looked up, she spotted the three of them immediately. They just stood there for a moment, nobody really knowing what to do or say. Then Delice slowly lowered the bag and stayed firm, barring the only way out. They were trapped.

Chapter 37

ATROPA BELLADONNA

'You've finally worked it out then, I take it,' she said with a bitter laugh.

'You've been abusing an old woman,' said Amita. 'That tells me all I need to know about your character, even without everything else we've discovered in the last 24 hours.'

'Abusing this old drunk? Please, don't make me laugh. She can give it out as good as she takes it, believe me.'

'You should be ashamed of yourself, Delice,' said Jason, stepping forward. 'This poor woman isn't well and you've been knocking her about. Look at her, she can barely stand up.'

'And what the hell would *you* know about anything, eh?' Delice flashed a fierce scowl at them all. 'Who gives you the right to interfere with other people's business?'

'You did,' spat Amita. 'When you said you thought your husband had been kidnapped. But that was all just a load of rubbish, wasn't it Delice? You knew exactly where your husband was all along.'

'I don't know what you're talking about,' she tried to dismiss them, rattling her car keys and putting the bag down. 'My husband is missing and I'm afraid I won't see him again.'

'He's been found,' said Jason. 'We have to leave it to the law to tell you exactly what they've found, but I'll say this much, I don't think I like the brand of fertiliser you've been using to help your garden grow.'

'Rubbish,' she said. 'You're making it all up. I should call the police, this is harassment.'

'The police know,' said Amita. 'We were there. We found Fran's watch under the flowerbed. The bodies are being examined right now, as we speak. But I don't think we're looking at natural causes, are we? No one trips over and buries themselves in a shrubbery, do they? That puts you squarely to blame in our minds, Delice. The fact that we found you here all but confirms that.'

Delice Weaver was unshifting. She pursed her lips and shook her head. 'I have no idea what you're talking about,' she said. 'You're just a pair of interfering do-gooders with vivid imaginations. What are you trying to say here? That I murdered my husband and Grahame Sutcliffe? Is that it?'

'Grahame? My Grahame?'

Isobel wobbled. Her knees buckled under her weight and Amita caught her before she could fall. She eased her back into her armchair.

'What's she saying?' She clawed at Amita's cardigan. 'What's that woman saying about my Grahame? Is he alright?'

'It's okay. Just calm down, Isobel. Everything is going to be okay.' Amita tried to talk her down, but the old lady was having a panic attack. At least she hoped it was a panic attack rather than something more terminal. There had been enough bodies this week.

'Leave her,' said Delice angrily. 'She always pulls that wilting flower act when she doesn't get her own way.'

'What's happened to my Grahame? Where is he?' Isobel was sobbing.

'For goodness sake, let us get this woman some help,' said Jason. 'She's not well.'

'None of you are going anywhere,' said Delice.

She stepped into the living room. There was a menacing presence about her suddenly. Her whole manner had changed. Amita was rubbing Isobel's hands, trying to get some warmth back into them. The old lady was heartbroken, weeping uncontrollably, her breath short.

'Please,' she said. 'Whatever you've got planned for us, Isobel doesn't need to hear it.'

'What's happened to my Grahame?' she kept asking.

Delice thought on what she was being asked. Then she stood to one side. She flicked her head and Amita helped Isobel to her feet. They walked slowly out of the living room and across the small hall to the kitchen where the older lady sat down. Delice was watching, her eyes like a hawk's, making sure nothing brave or heroic was attempted.

Isobel was shaking, tears making her wrinkled cheeks shine. Amita fetched a cardigan that was hanging over the back of a chair at the small kitchen table and draped it over her shoulders. The older woman looked exhausted, devastated. All Amita could do was rub her shoulders and return to the living room.

'This is ridiculous,' said Jason. 'You can't seriously expect to keep us here.'

'I'll do what I like,' she fired back. 'And you can sit down and shut up for starters.'

'Excuse me?'

'You heard what I said.'

'Delice, please,' said Amita, trying to bring some order. 'I really think we should take care of Isobel. She's not well. I'm worried about her.'

'You would be, wouldn't you?' she smirked.

'What's that supposed to mean?'

'I'm saying you can't help but interfere, can you? You're forever poking your nose in other people's business. Answering my texts, snooping around the university with that bloody professor woman. The fact that you found me here, in this dump, speaks volumes.'

'Now just hold on a second here,' said Jason, getting angry. 'We've not done anything wrong. We're also not the people who've been beating up defenceless pensioners and holding them hostage in their own homes.'

Delice was laughing now. Amita was worried about the older woman. She kept looking out the living room and towards the little kitchen. They needed to get her some medical attention, she was slipping into a state of shock. And that couldn't be good for her.

'Delice, please, whatever is going on, you have to understand that Isobel needs help,' she said. 'Let her go and we can talk everything out.'

'And what is it you want me to talk to you about?' she hissed. 'That my husband was cheating on me? That I was cheating on him? What?'

'You were having an affair, too?' asked Jason.

Delice opened the plastic bag. She started picking out chips from the supper. She was thinking, Amita could see that. Her eyes were darting around the room and they were a little glassy, like something deep inside her was hurting.

'Fran was a nice man,' she said. 'He was too bloody nice for his own good. And sometimes, when you're married to somebody like that, you just want them to notice you.'

'He didn't pay attention to you?' asked Amita. 'He was too consumed with his work?'

'Hours and hours he would spend at that lab,' she said bitterly. 'Sometimes I wouldn't see him for days on end. He'd come home late, still be asleep when I left for work in the morning and then he'd be away before I came home. On the occasions we *did* speak, he tried to assure me that it would all be worth it, that this Clymtech project would give us enough to retire on and be together. That was years ago, and I was still waiting. Then he stopped caring. If we saw each other in the house, he'd have nothing to say. And I wouldn't know what to say to him. It was clear that he had found somebody else, somebody he could relate to, speak with, work with.'

'Professor Hargreaves,' said Jason.

'The great Professor Hargreaves,' Delice laughed. 'I don't know what he saw in her. Tall and lanky with fashion sense from another century. But that was Fran all over. He could never see the woods for the trees.'

'And so you decided to have an affair yourself?' asked Amita. 'Who with?'

Delice's eyes fell to a small wooden table in the corner. Some pictures were dotted about the top, old and new. She walked over and picked up one of Grahame Sutcliffe, smiling, bare chested, somewhere hot.

'Sutcliffe?' asked Jason. 'You were sleeping with Sutcliffe.'

'He was a handsome man,' she said, staring at the photo. 'And charming. He had all the patter, all the right words and just when you needed to hear them.'

'You had an affair with your husband's business partner?' Amita asked.

'Don't be so thick.' The anger returned to Delice. 'Fran Weaver could design pioneering security systems that would be the envy of the world, but he didn't know the first thing about business or how to market it. He barely knew how much a pint of milk cost!'

She threw the picture down, the glass and frame cracking on impact.

'Sutcliffe only met Fran *because* of me,' she said. 'That's how this whole Clymtech nonsense came about.'

'How did you meet?' Amita asked.

A large mirror hung on the wall above the fireplace. Delice stood and looked at her reflection. She fixed her hair, flicking stray strands away with her little finger.

'A night out, in town,' she said. 'Just some after-work drinks one night. He was in the bar, we got chatting and it went from there. He was good at all that, loved being out and about, among the action, that's what he liked to call it. We saw each other a couple of times, he came round the house and that's when we got talking.'

Amita heard a sob from across the hallway then a laboured breath in. Isobel was not a well woman. They had to move fast.

'I told Grahame about Fran's work,' Delice continued. 'How he was working on something that nobody had ever seen before. I didn't understand the science, nobody does, that's the whole point. A unique selling point. I could see the pound signs in Grahame's eyes, so we concocted a plan. He would introduce himself to Fran, gain his trust, tell him that he could market and sell the Clymtech business to the Americans or the Saudis, whoever bid the most, and we'd all be filthy rich.'

'Money,' said Amita. 'It's always about money.'

'And what's wrong with that?' Delice laughed. 'Don't tell me you're high and mighty about that, too? Money makes the world go round, Amita. Any fool knows that. Look at that poor old bag in the kitchen – she doesn't have a pot to pee in and is rotting away in this place.'

'So, Sutcliffe did what he said he would,' said Jason. 'They started up the business, but there was no money to turn his academic research into a juicy business proposal to pitch to overseas firms. That's why he needed a loan from that mobster McGann.'

'The research was taking too long,' said Delice. 'Fran was used to thinking about details and discoveries, not flashy business promises. Grahame knew they needed to move fast, get a deal inked. Everything was costing too much and the more it cost, the less the profit would be.'

'And you decided to kill your husband for what? Insurance?'

'No,' said Delice. 'No, it wasn't as neat as that.'

She turned and faced them.

'The Americans finally came up with the money. They paid Grahame, but he was dawdling about giving Fran his share,' said Delice. 'Fran was thrilled his work was going to go global, and he stopped burning the midnight oil at the faculty and started appearing more and more around the house. I thought we'd gotten away with it for a while, Grahame and me. But he started to ask questions. It was like a cloud had been lifted from him, he started noticing little things here and there, extra dry cleaning, used mugs and cups, that kind of thing. It became clear that he was on to us, on to the affair. And if he decided to divorce me, then I wouldn't get a penny of his share, so we had to act quickly.'

'You killed him,' said Jason. 'That's what you call acting quickly.'

'Grahame agreed that it would be best for everybody if Fran was out of the picture,' she said coolly. 'I would inherit his personal wealth, and he would get full control of Clymtech and the shares, all of that. We would even discredit Fran after he was gone, let everyone know that he and that Hargreaves woman had been together all this time. We'd take the money and sail off into the sunset. A new life far away from Penrith. It was perfect.'

'Murder is far from perfect,' said Amita angrily. 'It's the worst thing you could possibly do.'

'We had it all planned out,' Delice ignored her. 'Fran was going to come home for a romantic dinner for two. I had told him I wanted to patch things up, start afresh now that the business was going to be a success. I cooked us dinner – his favourite meal – and then, when he wasn't looking, I caved his head in.'

There was a cold, callousness to her words that Jason and Amita couldn't quite believe. She just stood there, talking to them, like her husband was nothing more than a piece of meat.

'It was remarkably easy, actually,' she said. 'I didn't think it would be, but when push came to shove and he was just sitting there, all my frustration, all my hatred towards him, it just came bubbling to the surface. Years of playing second fiddle to his work, and then to Hargreaves. I hit him across the back of the head with a cast-iron pan and that was that. He fell forward, face first into his cheesecake and he was gone.'

'Good grief,' said Amita. 'That's ghastly.'

'It is, isn't it?' agreed Delice. 'It's awful. Really awful, but it happened and there's nothing we can do about it now.'

'I don't understand,' said Jason. 'What happened to Sutcliffe? He was your lover, you had a plan with him, you were running away like star-crossed lovers?'

Delice strolled casually over to the bag with the fish and chips. She began eating again, twirling a stray chip around as she spoke.

'Turns out that a womanising dirtbag like Grahame Sutcliffe isn't to be trusted,' she said. 'When I called him to tell him I'd done it, I'd killed Fran, he started having cold feet about the whole thing. I told him it was too late. Said he had to meet me at my patch on the allotments. I knew I needed to go and get my tools and some plants if I was to get rid of Fran before morning.'

Amita shuddered at how calmly Delice was telling them all this. She almost sounded excited to be sharing it. Delice looked put out – like a child who'd been told 'No'.

'When we met up, it was fine at first. We dug up some of the hellebores, then agreed we'd go back and bury Fran. But then Grahame started saying he couldn't be seen at mine again, couldn't help me dispose of the body. He was spouting some rubbish about how he had a baby on the way, that he didn't want to spend his life in jail when he had a child to look after. I told him he had to keep his nerve, there was no going back. I could tell he was weaselling out of it all, that his nerve had gone, so I took action with him, too.'

'You killed him,' said Amita.

'I did,' said Delice, finally eating her chip. 'When he wasn't looking, I ran him through with the garden fork. Took me a couple of stabs. I think I must have been tired after Fran. Luckily Grahame fell into the hole he'd just dug. I scraped the soil back, yanked a bit of artificial grass over it and rushed home to tuck Fran into the new flowerbed too. He never appreciated the effort I put into that garden.'

She stood there, silently, thinking about everything that had gone on. Amita felt ill, but she remembered what Brunger had told her about the veg patches being a rarity – a CCTV-free area of Penrith. Jason was unmoving, standing over her to keep her safe. Or at least trying to.

'It's quite funny actually,' said Delice, snorting. 'There I was, little old me, suddenly standing up to these men who thought they could mess up my plans, one my husband, the other my lover, and within the same hour they were both dead as Pharaohs, pushing up hellebores rather than daisies. Life comes at you fast, as they say.'

For a brief moment, the monumental chaos and consequences of what she had done seemed to dawn on Delice Weaver. She seemed lost, for a split second, in her own thoughts, perhaps her own morality. Amita thought she could make a move, do something to get them out of there. But the moment was fleeting and gone in an instant.

'You have to be able to think quickly if you're a double murderer,' she said. 'And it's remarkably freeing. You don't have anything left to lose. You know that if you get caught then it's prison, for a long time. But if you get away with it, well, the sky is the limit.'

'How very Lady Macbeth of you,' said Jason.

'Don't knock it until you've tried it,' she laughed. 'You're trying to tell me there's nobody you've ever thought about bumping off, Jason? What about your mother-in-law, eh? Or that foul-mouthed ex-policeman you were kicking around with when we first met. Shows what he knew, he didn't have a clue.'

'You faked Fran's and Grahame's disappearance, then,' said Amita. 'You made it look like they were enemies, you thought that by painting Grahame as the villain, that he might want to harm his business partner, that would throw the scent off you.'

'I'd grabbed Grahame's burner phone, the one he'd always used for our relationship, and I knew I could wipe it. But then I thought it could actively help me. When I nipped back to the allotments the next day to check the flowerbed looked okay after my midnight gardening, I saw that dodgy Malcolm Brunger chatting to one of the other allotmenteers. He'd left his shed open and it seemed like a gift. I could see his big tub of phones – I just dropped Grahame's in.'

'Then why text? Why bother sending the messages if you thought the phone was just mouldering away in Brunger's shed?'

'I had to make it look like I cared, Amita,' she laughed. 'I couldn't just sit at home and feel sorry for myself, could I? I had to least show some semblance of feeling that I wanted my husband found. If the police had got involved, I was going to show them my sent messages. Graham's burner phone was an old model, I thought no one would take it off Brunger's hands. And in fairness, I wasn't quite expecting Scooby-Doo and Shaggy to answer the messages and go digging around my life the way you two have.'

'We have a nasty habit of catching scumbags like you, Delice,' said Jason.

'So it would seem,' she wiped her hands of the grease. 'Anyway, it's been lovely chatting to you. But I think we'll call it a day, shall we?'

'What are you going to do?' asked Jason. 'There are three of us and only one of you. The odds are stacked.'

'Really?' asked Delice. 'Didn't you hear what I just told you, Jason? I murdered my husband and my lover in cold blood. You think I won't have any problems taking care of you lot? Two pensioners and a lanky fellow like you?'

She stepped out of the living room, heading for the kitchen to check on Isobel. Amita shouted at Jason.

'Go, now! While she's distracted, get help!'
'But . . .'
'Go!' she screamed.

Jason took off. He darted across the living room and slipped out of the door. He was about to make for the front door when Delice came running back out of the kitchen, a marble rolling pin in her hands. She screamed and swung wildly, catching Jason just above the eye. He went tumbling down the hallway, rolling and landing in a heap by the front door.

'Jason!' Amita screamed.

Delice hesitated, her eyes wild and filled with madness. She was panting, gasping for breath, deciding her next move. Then the door opened.

'What the hell is going on up here?' asked the man from downstairs. 'Did the lottery people come to the wrong door or something. I haven't—'

He was cut short by Delice Weaver. She barrelled into him, shouldering him out the way as she bolted out the front door. Amita got to her feet, making sure Isobel Sutcliffe was okay. She surveyed the carnage in the hallway of the flat, catching her breath. Jason was groggy, groaning, a trickle of blood running down his cheek from a cut above his eye. The man from downstairs was bright red and rolling around.

'Make sure they're okay,' Amita said to him. 'And call the police.'
'Eh? What?'
'Just do it!' she threw over her shoulder as she gave chase to Delice.

Chapter 38

MENTHA PULEGIUM

A car honked its horn loudly as it swerved to miss Amita. She had careered down the stairs and out through the courtyard, onto the street before she really knew where she was. The bright lights of the traffic blinded her for a moment and she was disoriented. Looking up and down the main road, she began to panic, fearing she had lost Delice Weaver. Then she spotted her, running down the pavement, heading for the River Kent.

Amita gave chase. The adrenaline was pumping around her in overdrive. She could feel her legs and her arms tingling with fright and shock. She just hoped that the man from downstairs was looking after the others.

Delice was fast. She hurtled down the street, trying to get away. Amita did her best to keep up. The killer barged into a couple walking the other way and it slowed her down. Amita tried to close the gap, apologising as she ran past the others.

The streetlights retreated the closer they got to the river. Things grew dark quickly and Amita strained to keep Delice in sight. She kept pressing on, not really thinking about how all of this could end, that she was risking her life in chasing down this woman. She just had to catch her up, bring her to justice, let the truth be known.

Delice had climbed the small hill of the bridge over the Kent. When she reached the top, to Amita's surprise, she stopped. In the gloom, she turned to look at her, a savage smile giving her something of a feral look against the dark night sky. Amita slowed to a trot. This was dangerous. It could be bait. Delice clearly had no scruples about adding more bodies to her count and Amita didn't fancy her chances in one-to-one combat. Amita decided that talking her down was her only course of action.

'It's over, Delice,' she called to her, getting closer and closer. 'There's no point running. The police have been called, they'll be here any minute. How long do you think you can evade them? You might as well give up.'

'I thought you'd say that,' said Delice. 'See, that's the thing about you, Amita. You're not even halfway as clever as you think you are. You've found me out, sure, but it's all been luck. Just stupid luck. I had it all sorted, I had it all planned. I was going to make the world think that my husband had been murdered by his partner. It was easy, in a strange way. Nobody cares about you when you're the quiet wife, when you're the victim.'

'You're not the victim,' said Amita. 'Fran and Grahame are the victims. As are Professor Hargreaves, Isobel, Enni and that little baby. He'll grow up without a father now, and that's because of you.'

'As if Grahame could ever be a good father,' she spat. 'I've done that baby a favour, making sure Grahame never has anything to do with him.'

'That's not for you to decide!' Amita yelled at her. 'You don't have that right! And even if you did, it's not fair that you get to decide what happens to other people's lives. Can't you see that, Delice? Can't you see what you've done?'

Delice was sneering now. The cocky confidence and self-satisfaction had drifted away, like the waters of the Kent running under their feet. Amita tried to get through to her, a last roll of the dice to make her see reason.

'It's not worth it, Delice,' she said. 'You don't have to do this. You're only hurting yourself in the long run.'

Delice just stood there, looking at Amita.

'You know, I thought I had a chance to be happy,' she said. 'I really did. I thought with Fran out of the way and the money from the Americans, there was a real possibility that things could be okay with Grahame.'

'I don't think Grahame Sutcliffe was the settling down kind,' said Amita. 'Did you know he had a decrepit mansion he was renovating? That's where we found Enni.'

Delice's bottom lipped trembled.

'Men,' she said with a sad laugh. 'You just can't trust them, can you Amita? I was a fool to think that somebody like Grahame Sutcliffe could change. I think I always knew he was a liability. But to have the attention, the wining and the dining, even the awful chat-up lines, it was such a change to Fran.'

'Now they're both dead,' said Amita. 'At your hands.'

'Now they're both dead,' she echoed. 'You're right. I killed them both. And I was going to kill that old lady back there. She knew too much, she knew that Grahame was missing. I was smart enough to grab his wallet along with his phone before I buried him. I knew it was the only way I'd be able to get my hands on the cash. But it was a slow process, and Isobel would have called the police long before I'd transferred enough of the money to escape somewhere nice and hot and forget about all of this.'

'Then I think it's best that you just stop, Delice. Just stop all of this madness and come with me. The police will be here soon.'

Delice leaned against the side of the bridge. She peered over the edge at the rushing water of the Kent. Amita felt her stomach clench. She was still a good few yards away from her. If she decided to jump there was nothing she could do.

'Maybe you're right,' said Delice. 'Maybe this has all been some terrible mistake. Maybe the police will go easy on me if I just hand myself over.'

'I think that would be wise,' said Amita, edging closer to her.

'Then again,' said Delice, staring right at her. 'Maybe I'm not ready to go to jail just yet.'

She threw her legs over the bridge wall. Before Amita could reach her, she'd disappeared over the edge. Amita darted forward and saw the splash in the water. The Kent was moving quickly, the reflections of the streetlights on either bank offering a small amount of illumination.

Amita thought quickly. Racing across the street and following the flow of the river, she looked over the edge and back down to the water. Delice had surfaced and was thrashing about, coughing, spluttering, choking. Amita looked about and spotted a life ring housing station. She hurried over and grabbed the buoyancy aid from the locker.

'This is a terrible idea,' she said to herself.

She climbed onto the wall of the bridge and took a deep breath. Then, without another second's thought, she leaped off. The seconds of the drop came crashing to an end as the icy water engulfed her. Her head somehow managed to bob back above the surface of the water as she was being carried down the river, the life ring still in her hands.

'Delice!' she shouted. 'Delice! Where are you?'

The rushing water made it impossible to hear anything other than her own breath. She let the water take her, the icy bite beginning to numb her whole body. She knew there wasn't much time. She had to act quickly and get out of the river as quickly as possible.

Then something bumped into her. It was Delice, thrashing around trying to stay afloat. Somewhere from the doldrums of her memory, Amita recalled some water safety. The information had never been used, sitting silently in the back of her mind for over fifty years. How she was thankful for it now.

'Here!' she shouted, passing the life ring to Delice.

She gladly took it as Amita wrapped her arms under her. Kicking with all of her might, she began to slowly push against the flow of the river and ease over to the bank. Her thighs burned, her arms were strained, but she kept going, one kick, one push after another until she felt the soggy grass. She pulled them both up and out of the water and rolled onto her back.

'We're alive,' she said over and over again. 'We're alive.'

Delice was beside her, coughing up dirty water, exhausted, too. They both lay there for a moment, trying to catch their breath. Amita's clothes were sticking to her, coating her legs, arms and chest like an icy blanket. She had to keep moving, keep the blood pumping around her body, otherwise she'd be in trouble. She pushed herself onto her elbows and looked at Delice Weaver.

'You shouldn't have done that,' she said. 'That was incredibly dangerous.'

'You could have just left me,' croaked Delice. 'What the hell do you care?'

'Perhaps,' she replied. 'But I don't want blood on my hands. And I wasn't going to let you go. Not after what you've done. Grahame Sutcliffe and your husband, the people who are still alive and cared about them deserve to see justice done. Professor Hargreaves loved Fran. And Grahame has a son that will grow up without his father. Making sure you face the authorities and pay for what you've done won't bring either of them back, but it was the right thing to do.'

The bright flashes of blue lights distracted both women. Police cars came screeching to a halt on the road above the bank. A unit of officers, led by DI Sally Arendonk, made their way down towards the river. Delice was arrested on the spot and the others helped Amita to her feet, wrapping her in a warm blanket.

'You don't need me to tell you how foolish that was,' said Arendonk. 'Didn't you ever learn that going for a swim in a river at night is inadvisable.'

'It rings a bell,' said Amita, trudging up the riverbank. 'Is Jason okay?'

'Always hard to tell with him, I find,' laughed the detective. 'No, in all seriousness, he's had a nasty bump and we're getting him checked over, but he's fine. Full of questions as usual. Not so much the walking wounded as the talking wounded.'

'Sounds like Jason,' she replied. 'I know I shouldn't have jumped in, but I couldn't just let her go, Sally.'

They reached the road. Amita and Sally Arendonk stopped at her car. They watched as Delice was led away to a waiting police car. When she was inside, the door was closed with a final, heavy clunk. With that, she was gone, leaving only a trail of drips where she'd stood.

Chapter 39

LILIUM

Hospital food was normally awful. Any time Jason had been unfortunate enough to be served a meal while as a patient, he'd really not enjoyed it. This time, however, was very different.

'You know that trifle was for me, don't you?' said Amita, sitting up in her bed.

'You weren't eating it,' he replied, running his finger around the plastic container, scooping out every last bit of custard and jelly.

'I didn't really get the chance to, did I?' she sniffed.

The room was luxurious, comfortable and spacious. One of the perks of thwarting a double murder case was the private hospital that Cumbria Police had sent her to. Amita would normally have been desperate to get home, they'd had some bad experiences in hospitals over the course of their investigations, but this place showed her how the other half lived.

She'd been admitted as a precaution, given her age and swimming in sub-zero water. The doctors had found nothing wrong with her and she had been assured that she'd be allowed home the following day. Two nights in the lap of luxury hadn't been on the agenda, but she'd been enjoying it all the same, even if the circumstances behind it were ghastly. That was until Jason had decided to help himself to her pudding.

'How's your face?' she asked him balefully.

He stopped his harvesting of her trifle.

'Fine,' he said. 'Looks worse than it feels. Although I'm on painkillers, which is helping matters.'

'Good.'

'Five stitches though. The hair might not grow back at that end of my eyebrow.'

'Hardly the end of the world.'

'No, but it might make me look a bit more dynamic, dangerous even,' he said.

That made Amita laugh. He feigned hurt.

'What? Don't you think I'll look like a bad boy with a scar on my eyebrow?'

'Jason, you couldn't look dangerous if your life depended on it.'

'Is that such a terrible thing?'

'No, I suppose it isn't.'

'There you go then,' he said, finishing off the pudding.

The door of the room opened and the children came rushing in to give their grandmother a puzzle book newly acquired from the hospital shop. Radha was smiling.

'This place is better than our house,' she said.

'There are more channels on the television, too,' said Jason. 'I might just stay here for the foreseeable.'

'Would suit us all,' quipped Amita.

'Now, now, Mum,' said Radha. 'Right, are we all ready to go home?'

The kids reached over and hugged their grandmother, as did Radha.

'Just take it easy tonight, Mum. We'll be around in the morning when you're discharged,' she said.

'Don't you have work?'

'Forget work, you're more important. We'll come and get you whenever you're given the all-clear.'

'I should be coming home right now, really. There's nothing wrong with me.'

'Oh, I don't know about that,' said Jason. 'Jumping into the River Kent after a murderer, that sounds pretty wrong to me.'

'You would have done the same, if you weren't incapacitated.'

'I'm not so sure,' he said.

'Just relax and enjoy your last night in this cushy private suite,' said Radha. 'The house and these rascals will all be waiting for you when you get home.'

She kissed her mother and started for the door. Jason placed the empty pudding container back on the tray with the rest of Amita's dishes and nodded.

'I'm telling the matron you ate that,' she said, reclining in the bed.

He was heading for the door when a knock came. Frank Alby was lingering in the hallway outside, a bunch of flowers so big he could barely get in the room. Radha and the children eased their way past him and she called back to Jason.

'I'll be down in the car when you're ready,' she said.

Jason nodded. Alby trotted into the suite and handed the flowers over to Amita. She took them, dwarfed by how big, overblown and heavy they were.

'These are for you,' he said, furtively hopping from one foot to the other. 'From the missus and I. Hope you feel better soon.'

'Are you alright, Alby?' asked Jason. 'You look like you've got ants in your pants.'

'Hospitals, Brazel, I hate them,' he said. 'Always bring me out in a rash. Don't like to set foot in them if I can. Horrible places. Even here in this swanky version.'

'Thank you for the very kind gesture, Frank,' said Amita, muffled by the bouquet. 'If you could take them back for a moment, I'll make sure the nurses get me a vase and some water.'

He lifted the flowers, looked around the room, and decided to lay them on the floor. He rocked back and forth on his heels, hands in his pockets, face redder than usual.

'You alright then?' he asked. 'I heard from the boys at the station that you'd gone for a dip.'

'Something like that,' she said.

'It was the wife all along then, eh?' he said. 'Thought as much.'

'Get off it, Alby. You were just as much in the dark as we were,' said Jason.

'Well, I admit I maybe wasn't quite as clued up on this investigation as I have been in the past. But there was always something iffy about her. I just didn't know what. Still, you could have called me when you went to collar her. I could have done with the exercise.'

'Yes, sorry about that,' said Amita. 'It was all rather rushed and hasty.'

'I thought you were retired anyway?' asked Jason.

'The law is the law, Brazel. And despite you thinking it's your own personal playground, us experts know exactly what to do in situations like your mother-in-law found herself in. Not that you were much help, heard you were out cold from a whack to the mush.'

'What gave it away, detective? The black eye or the five stitches in my eyebrow?'

Alby snorted. Turning to Amita, his tone changed a little.

'I'm glad you're alright though, Amita,' he said. 'I mean, I knew you would be.'

'That's very kind of you, Frank. Thank you,' she said.

'And just between us, I wanted to say thank you.'

'Pardon me?' Jason blurted.

'I'm not talking to you, dopey,' the former DI snarled. 'I'm trying to have a conversation with your mother-in-law here, if you don't mind.'

Jason held up his hands.

'Yes, what was I saying? That's right. I wanted to thank you, for everything you've done over the last few weeks. It means a lot.'

'I haven't really done anything, Frank,' she said. 'Apart from take a long time to realise I had a killer texting me.'

'No, you have. Whether you meant it or not, it's been important to me, to get off my backside and do something again. Despite what my mindfulness course says, there are only so many Tibetan gong baths you can take a day. This retirement lark, it hits you hard, doesn't it? One day you're still useful, a functioning member of society and literally the next you're on the scrap heap. Especially to an old war horse like me. The police was my life, man and boy. To have it all taken away in the blink of an eye, that was hard. I don't mind telling you that. So, to be back on a case, chasing down scallies, asking questions and putting the puzzle pieces together, it felt good. It felt like I was worth something again. And it's you I've got to thank for that.'

He took her hand and clasped it in between his.

'Oh, Frank,' she said. 'It has truly been our pleasure to have you help us on this case. We don't know what we'd have done without your valuable input. Do we Jason?'

Jason thought he knew exactly what they'd have done. But he kept it to himself. He'd never seen Frank Alby seem so emotional. The man looked vaguely like a human being.

'Of course,' he said. 'It's been good working with you again, Frank. Really it has.'

Alby was smiling, that strange leer that made his face stretch. He nodded, sniffed and cleared his throat.

'Right, well, I'll be going then,' he said.

'But you only just got here,' she said. 'Won't you stop and have a cuppa?'

'No, no thank you, Amita. Got to get back home, I have a forty-minute body scan meditation I've been putting off and putting off all week. Can't let it slip. I'll bid you both a good night. And urge you to stay out of trouble.'

He was out of the door before either of them could protest.

'Body scan meditation?' Jason wrinkled his nose. 'That sounds almost unseemly in Alby's case.'

'Jason, stop it,' she tutted.

'Well, it does,' he said, heading for the door too. 'Who would want to scan *his* body? And what would they find?'

'It's nice to be nice, and he's been very nice with those flowers,' she said. 'Do me a favour though, before you go home.'

'What's that?' he asked, leaning on the end of her bed.

'Put that bouquet in the bathroom, would you? Those lilies are giving me a headache.'

Jason laughed and did as he was asked.

Chapter 40

HYACINTHUS

The coffin was lowered into the grave at a sombre, slow pace. The weather had taken a turn for the worse over the course of the last week. The rain was falling in light sheets. Mourners huddled beneath umbrellas, others just took the drenching in as good spirits as you could in such circumstances. You couldn't complain about drizzle when you were yards away from someone making their last earthly journey.

Amita and Jason remained firmly at the rear of the small congregation. Less than twenty people had turned out for Grahame Sutcliffe's official send off. Most of the faces, they didn't recognise. Although judging by the number of single women there, dabbing their eyes or lurking behind unwarranted sunglasses, they could guess most of the mourners were all members of the ex-girlfriends of Grahame Sutcliffe club.

Amita had thought about forgoing the service completely. Fran Weaver's body had been transported back down to his remaining family on the south coast. She had sent a sympathy card to the address DI Sally Arendonk had quietly, unofficially provided for her. This funeral, however, was on their doorstep. She would have felt awful if she hadn't made the effort.

Seeing the paltry crowd, she was glad to be there. Even if it all felt very strange, very odd to be at the service of a man she had never met in real life. As bizarre as that notion may have been, Amita still felt a connection to Sutcliffe. She thought of how she'd carried his phone around in her handbag. Kicking this all off. Treading in his footsteps, always a few paces behind, she had somehow got to know him quite well. Having Enni and the baby living at home had also tied her to him. He might have had the morals of an alley cat, but he hadn't deserved to have been cut down in his prime so savagely, so ruthlessly, by Delice Weaver.

Enni was at the front of the mourners, holding Isobel Sutcliffe's arm and steadying the old woman. They were both bereft as they stared down into the grave, the coffin now resting at the bottom. The priest who was conducting the service said his final words and instructed anyone who wished to throw flowers. They both took a single rose, as did a few others. Jason nudged Amita gently.

'Would you like to, you know, offer your condolences with a flower?' he asked.

'No, I don't think so,' she said. 'Doesn't seem at all appropriate, I'm not sure what we'd be mourning really, considering we never met the man – just the mess he left behind. It's probably best that we just hang around here, I think.'

'Suit yourself,' said Jason.

'You aren't at all moved by any of this?'

'I'm moved to get out of the rain,' he flapped the arms of his jacket.

'Show some respect, Jason,' she tutted. 'It's a funeral.'

'Don't I know it,' he said. 'Seems every time we step out of our front door, we're on our way to a funeral, or know about a funeral, or are somehow linked to a bloody funeral. Honestly, Amita, we're like some sort of magnet to this kind of thing.'

'Jason, you'll reach a point in your life where memorials become your social life. My funeral coat gets far more outings than my glad rags do these days, and I could rank the best funeral spreads in Penrith by tea strength and sandwich quality at the drop of a hat, but I never fail to be moved. Mind you, it's one thing saying farewell to someone at the end of their days who's had time to say their goodbyes, it's quite another to be standing graveside when someone's been savagely offed. I suppose when we started our investigations, we should have known it would end like this,' she said. 'We can't help it if we're surrounded by dreadful deeds and awful people.'

'True,' he said. 'Much as I can't resist a story, I wonder if we should look into a few cases that aren't quite so bloodthirsty. What about runaway dogs, or raided hanging baskets? I would just like a chance to perhaps *not* deal with sociopathic killers, murderers and wrong 'uns for a change. Especially if they're bashing me around the face. Those stitches hurt when they went in and even more when they came out.'

He rubbed at the scar on his eyebrow. Amita refrained from admonishing him any further. The service had come to an end and the small collection of mourners were making their way back down the path towards the waiting cars. Enni was taking care of Isobel and nodded to them both as she went by. Amita offered a weak smile, the most she could think of.

The smile faded quickly enough when she spotted who was behind them. Migraine McGann, head to toe in black, an astonishing fascinator made of black feathers, which made it look like a murder of crows had perched on her head, stalked through the graves towards them. A wicked smile flickered across her made-up face.

'Well, well, well,' she said. 'Look who's turned up for the show.'

'Ms McGann, I can assure you that we didn't know you were going to be here,' said Jason quickly. 'If we had, we'd have stayed well clear of . . .'

'Yes, yes, yes. Alright. Calm yourself, sugar lips.' She held up a gloved hand. 'If I want my tush kissed, all I have to do is click my fingers.'

She clicked them anyway. Jason winced, fighting the urge to either bow or scarper.

'Don't look so frightened, sweet cheeks.' McGann laughed, the feathers shaking with her. 'I'm not here to collect my debts. The recently deceased had the foresight to pay off his loan to me by departing this world. Turns out Sutcliffe had left a note with his solicitor – 'in the event of my death,' that kind of thing. He'd left an instruction to pay me immediately on condition that I was not to threaten his family. I suppose I had told him I'd torch that wreck of a renovation he owned if he didn't clear his balance with me, with interest. So it turns out maybe he wasn't a complete swine – he wanted to pay me back and keep his mother and that girlfriend and baby out of harm's way. So, no hard feelings. In fact, I'm just here to mourn a rather good customer. It was a nice service,' she said, now turning her attention to Amita. 'It's all you can hope for when you get to our age, am I right, Amita? A few kind words and someone at the grave's edge to throw a handful of soil on the coffin.'

'It won't matter to us, Ms McGann,' she said. 'We'll be *in* the coffin and it's everyone else who'll be left to pick up the pieces.'

McGann laughed at that – a hoarse, harsh, laugh that echoed across the cemetery and scared a few birds from the trees. When she settled herself, she walked past them both and clapped Amita on the shoulder.

'I like you,' she said. 'I *really* like you, Amita.'

They watched McGann stride down between the headstones and off to a waiting car. Two of her heavies opened the doors and let her in. She didn't look back as the door was closed and the bodyguards climbed in the front. The car took off at an unsafe speed, racing along the road through the cemetery and out of the main gates before anyone else.

'Bloody hell, that woman makes me nervous,' said Jason.

'At least she doesn't like you,' said Amita. 'I have the feeling I've made something of an impression on her and that her admiration might be more dangerous than her derision.'

'Rather that than she speaks to you like a dog, I suppose. I suppose I don't mind too much as long as she keeps calling me names like sugar lips. It's hardly an everyday occurrence for me.'

'I wouldn't hold on to that for too long, Jason,' she said. 'And certainly, don't let Radha hear about it.'

'Both good points,' he agreed.

'Amita? Jason?'

They were interrupted by a voice from behind them. Professor Hargreaves was standing close by. The rain dripped in great, heavy blobs from the edge of her huge golf umbrella. She passed the handle from one arm to the other and offered a hand to both of them.

'This feels just like *This Is Your Life*,' said Jason.

'Jason, a funeral is not the time for that line,' Amita hushed him down and turned to Hargreaves. 'Have you been at the whole service, professor?'

'I arrived late,' said Hargreaves. 'I'm not one for churches generally. But coming today felt like my farewell to Fran, too. I didn't make it to his funeral unfortunately. It just didn't seem . . . appropriate. Butchered by your spouse, then cried over by the other woman, I think his family have suffered enough without me reminding them of what a godawful mess this all is.'

'You really loved him, didn't you?' asked Amita. 'I think his family would have understood.'

'They never understood anything else about him. Nobody did,' she said sadly. 'I don't think me turning up out of the blue and introducing myself as his mistress would have made an already hard situation any easier. I wish I had been there, though. For Fran.'

Amita began a slow walk back towards their car. The rest of the mourners had already gone and only the priest's vehicle remained alongside theirs.

'I wanted to thank you, thank both of you, for what you did,' said Hargreaves. 'The police came to question me, so I had to give statements. Detective Inspector Arendonk told me about Delice and how you had been instrumental in catching her. If you hadn't intervened, I don't know what would have happened. I wouldn't know what became of Fran, or Grahame Sutcliffe, for that matter, and they'd probably still be buried beneath the flowers.'

'We did what we had to do,' said Amita.

'We have a tendency to have to do these kinds of things,' said Jason. 'Though sometimes I wish I still judged cute dog competitions. But hey-ho, here we are.'

'It was greatly appreciated, that's all I'm trying to say,' said Hargreaves. 'To get some sort of closure, even this kind of devastating news, it's something. Something to hold on to.'

They reached the road that weaved through the cemetery. Jason went to unlock the car and noticed the priest defrocking a little way ahead.

'Don't you have a motor?' he asked the professor.

'No, I walked,' she showed off her running shoes. 'I needed the air. And to be honest with you, taking my time to get here made me think of a few things, about what comes next.'

'Will you return to the university?' asked Amita.

'I think so, if they'll have me,' said Hargreaves. 'I don't have a job to go to every morning as it stands. Goodness knows what will become of Clymtech now that the lead scientist is dead.'

'And the research?'

'What's done already, well, that belongs to the new US owners, and none of us could continue it, I'm afraid,' she said sadly.

'Couldn't you try?' asked Jason. 'You were Fran's partner, more than Sutcliffe anyway.'

Hargreaves tilted her umbrella so she could meet Jason's eyes. There was an unbound sadness to her, even as she smiled.

'Nobody could do what Fran Weaver did,' she said. 'He was a visionary, a pioneer, the love of my life. I couldn't replicate his work if I tried for a thousand years. That's what I've tried to tell you both, for all of this time. He wasn't just another run-of-the-mill academic or engineer. He was a genius, he lived for his work and those around him. His death, his *murder* will set the field back a generation. If not more. I couldn't continue that, even if I wanted to, I couldn't bring myself to walk in his shoes. He will be missed by a great deal more people than those who showed up here today to mark Grahame's demise. The world will miss Fran, I promise you that.'

She took a deep breath. Getting it all off her chest seemed to brighten Hargreaves' mood. She shook Amita and Jason's hands once again and headed back up the little road in the opposite direction.

'Do me one favour, if you wouldn't mind,' she called back to them.
'What's that?' asked Amita.
'Remember him, would you? Remember his name. Don't let it be lost to history, another needless and anonymous death. Fran Weaver was more than that. He deserved to be remembered. The new owners will probably take all the credit for his incredible discoveries. I couldn't bear it if I was the only one who knew his true genius.'

She wiped away a tear and turned away from them again, walking tall and purposely along the road. Amita watched her go, a little lump forming in her throat. Jason whistled loudly.

'It's been one of those cases, hasn't it,' he said, opening the door of the car. 'Normally it's a body that means we get involved. This time it's taken all this time before we knew for certain anyone had met a sticky end. And now, just when it looks like justice will be served, we've got history to answer to. It's a tough ask – ensuring the legacy of a man we never met who was a pioneer of something we never understood. It makes me think I need to go back to study. Still, thinking of academia, at least the multi-coloured paint has come off the motor, almost. That's a plus. Bloody students.'

'You know, Jason, I almost think I preferred it better multi-coloured,' said Amita, climbing into the passenger seat. 'When you've just stood, all in black, and waved someone off to the great hereafter, a little colour is very welcome indeed.'

Chapter 41

PASSIFLORA EDULIS

Amita stood at the bottom of the steps of the church hall and checked her watch. Time was ticking on, getting ever closer to kick-off. For the first time in weeks, she felt like she could actually enjoy bingo, without worry, without a head full of theories, suspects and other macabre thoughts. She could simply turn up, sit down, get her dabber and bingo books in order and relax. That was always when her best wins came. Even the prospect of Georgie Littlejohn and the other doyennes of gossip were strangely palatable this evening. That was, if everything ran on time. She did like a prompt start.

She checked her watch again. Only thirty seconds had passed since the last time. Still, that was thirty seconds closer to the beginning of the evening's competition.

'Relax, Amita. Just relax,' she said quietly to herself. 'She'll be here. Just take it easy, would you? You're panicking. You're panicking so much that you're talking to yourself.'

That was enough to stop her. A couple of club members drew her odd looks as they climbed the steps up to the church hall. She just smiled politely and hoped they wouldn't gossip. Chance would be a fine thing.

She looked up towards the doors. Father Ford was standing patiently, greeting everyone as they arrived. He caught Amita staring and waved meekly.

'Evening Amita. Are you joining us?' he asked.

'Yes, I should be there in a minute, Father,' she called back. 'I'm just waiting on someone.'

'Oh, anyone I know?'

'No, I don't think so. She's a new member, or a potential new member of the club.'

As if on cue, Georgie Littlejohn's head poked around the edge of the huge wooden doors.

'New?' she wrinkled her nose.

'Yes, Georgie, a new member,' sighed Amita. 'That's not against the rules, is it? To invite someone who might actually benefit from our company on a Wednesday night.'

'I'm not sure,' said Georgie, making a show of scratching her chin. 'We're very selective about who we admit to the club, Amita. You know that. We don't let any old riff-raff in, do we, father?'

Georgie angled the question at the timid pastor in a way that he had no choice but to agree. He blustered and puffed out his cheeks.

'Well, I mean, that is to say, it's quite a delicate subject and . . .'

'Amita!'

A call from across the street was enough to distract Amita. A welcome distraction at that. She turned to see a woman waving at her from the bus stop opposite. She hurried over to help her and they started up the steps towards the hall.

'So glad you could make it, Isobel,' said Amita. 'I was starting to get worried that you might have missed your bus.'

'Don't get me started on the bloody buses,' she said, taking her time with her newly acquired walking stick. 'You wait all afternoon and then a dozen of them all turn up at once. It sounds like the start of a bad joke, but it's true. I was thinking I might treat myself to one of those top-of-the-range mobility scooters with the money Grahame left me. It might as well buy a bit of happiness after all we've been through. I'm selling that wreck of a house too – Enni and her boy deserve a fresh start. What's that saying? Money can't buy you happiness, it just helps you look for it in more places.'

'Right enough,' laughed Amita. 'I've got a couple of people I'd like to introduce you to before we go in. Seeing as they've rolled out the red carpet with a welcoming committee for you.'

They reached the top step. Father Ford immediately offered his hand.

'Good evening,' he said. 'I'm Father Ford, I run this little game we have every Wednesday night here at the Penrith church hall. It's so lovely to meet you . . .'

'Isobel Sutcliffe,' she said firmly, shaking the vicar's hand so vigorously that his arm was almost pulled free from the socket. 'Lovely to meet you.'

'And this is Georgie Littlejohn,' said Amita, with a little trepidation.

Georgie stood there, arms folded, lips pursed, eyeing Isobel up and down like a piece of fresh meat.

'Littlejohn, that's a name I've not heard in about thirty years,' said Isobel.

'It's a fairly unique name,' snapped Georgie. 'My family has been Cumbrian for about a dozen generations. You might say we're Cumbrian through and through. I'm from a long line of white-collar merchants and entrepreneurs, tailors, master makers, that kind of thing.'

'Yes, yes, that's it,' Isobel clicked her fingers. 'Littlejohn. There was a Littlejohn down in Kendal when I was growing up. He ran a greengrocers that was always full of dubious fruit and veg. The whole town knew you used to have to count your change three or four times, too. My parents used to warn me about him, if me and my brothers and sisters were misbehaving. Don't be bad or Mr Littlejohn will come and snatch you away in the night.'

Georgie's face was turning whiter and whiter by the second.

'Was your family originally from Kendal, Georgie?' asked Amita.

It took her a second to react. And when she did, she made sure the typical Littlejohn veneer was intact.

'What's that? Oh no, no, no. My family is from up Carlisle way, Amita. Still, we shouldn't dawdle here in the doorway, we have a game to play and I'm sure . . . Isobel, was it? . . . I'm sure Isobel wants to meet the rest of the club members.'

Isobel tipped a wink to Amita as she was led inside. To see her back on her feet was good. Amita had felt so awful about what had happened to her that she wasn't sure she'd ever recover. The abuse, the lies, the loss of her son, all in a short space of time, it was a lot for anyone to be able to handle, regardless of their age and fragility. Thankfully there had been support for Isobel and she was in a recovery program and being helped at home. She'd even been seeing her grandson in the past few weeks, something that had clearly given her a new lease of life.

Amita was happy to see her now at the Penrith Bingo Club. It wasn't quite on her doorstep, but it felt important that she tried to look after Isobel as best she could. Amita knew she was lucky to have family, and how easily anyone could find themselves without that safety net. For all their digs and backchat, Amita knew the bingo club was a family of sorts – even though she would rather choke on her custard cream than admit that to Georgie.

'Oh, that reminds me,' said Georgie, stopping as they walked towards the tea urns. 'You'll have to pay your annual membership fee, if you're planning on making this a regular thing. I'll give you the new bank details. We've had some, shall we say, indiscretions of late and I'm taking full control of the purse strings.'

'Indiscretions?'

Father Ford's voice cracked.

'Yes, Father. I was going to tell you, but I confess I've been putting it off. I've let you down. There has been some money gone missing from the club account,' said Georgie. 'I thought I'd conduct a little investigation and get to the bottom of it. We have something of a reputation for fighting crime here, after all, don't we?'

Amita rolled her eyes, flashbacks of poor Pauline Saxon being harangued outside the hall springing to mind.

'I'm not sure I follow you, Georgie,' said the pastor. 'You're saying that we've been robbed?'

'In as many words, yes,' she replied. 'A couple of hundred pounds have vanished and we don't know what's happened. Like I said, I tried to catch the culprit, but they eluded even *me*. It's a great pity that we have to be this way in this day and age, Father, but I think we're going to have to change the system. No more honesty boxes and just popping your subs in the biscuit tin. No, it's going to have to be strictly pay-to-play, signing up a month ahead of time. No room for anyone to go stealing the money tin that way.'

'Ah, right.' Father Ford rubbed the back of his head. 'You see, this is where things get a little bit awkward, Georgie. I really wish you had come to see me first before you started this investigation and audit of yours.'

'I didn't think you needed the worry,' she said succinctly. 'You've got enough on your plate, what with your parish duties, sermons, visiting the sick and our little club. I thought I should take on the burden of finding the culprit myself.'

She smiled, waiting for some praise. Father Ford, however, was sweating more than usual. His eyes darted between Georgie, Amita and Isobel.

'Oh gosh, this really is unbearable,' he said. 'Georgie, I really, *really* wish you had come to speak to me first before you took any action.'

Amita sensed that if the vicar didn't speak up, he was going to burst.

'Is everything alright, Father?' she asked him gently.

He looked at her, eyes wide and watery.

'I'm afraid there's been a dreadful misunderstanding,' he said. 'That money, it's not been stolen, it's sitting in the vicarage. In my pantry, to be precise.'

'*Your pantry?*'

Amita and Georgie both blurted the words out at the same time.

'Yes, I'm afraid so,' Father Ford was fumbling with his hands, his shoulders hunched. 'You see, I've been on rather a health kick recently. Too many finger sandwiches at tea with parishioners, you know, can lead to one putting on a little too much, ahem, timber. I've been saying no to every slice of cake I'm offered, I even turned down Pauline's parkin the other day. But well, after bingo the other week, I saw the biscuit tin and I was . . . weak. It felt heavy and I thought I was getting a full chocolate and cream selection. I was only going to take it home and have one or two with my bedtime brew. But then I felt so guilty about borrowing the biscuits I wouldn't allow myself one. And then when I finally did crack, I opened it up and found it full of cash. I was mortified. I was going to pay it in quietly and hope you'd not realise it was late. Oh, what a biscuit-blind fool I've been.'

'You turned down some of Pauline's special parkin?' Amita was amazed. It was the best loaf this side of the north lakes.

Father Ford had gone bright red. 'I do hope you'll forgive me, Georgie. The club means a great deal to me too. I know I might not come across as the flashiest of hosts, Bruce Forsyth I most certainty am not. But I do enjoy it all so greatly watching everyone have such a wonderful time on Wednesday nights, come rain, sleet or sunshine. It's very special. And I'd hate to do anything to jeopardise it by me being responsible for any financial irregularity. This club is too important to me, to us all, I think.'

Amita was quietly moved by the vicar's words and passion. In all the years she had known him, she'd never seen him get quite so worked up or emotional about anything. Least of all the bingo club. The general consensus was that he hated every minute of drawing and calling the numbers. Yet here he was, Father Ford, impassioned bingo advocate.

'Yes, well, we'll see,' Georgie droned. 'Still, at least the money is there. It means we can start planning our next excursion to one of the big games in Manchester. Eh, Amita?'

At that, Amita decided enough was enough. She politely excused herself and Isobel and took a brisk stroll over to their table. She introduced Isobel to Sandy, Ethel, Pauline, Judy and some of the others who were there, before taking her seat. Isobel sat down beside her and nudged her in the ribs.

'Tell me something, Amita,' she said, whispering conspiratorially. 'Dodgy vicars and overbearing drama queens. Is it always this good?'

Amita smiled back at her.

'Believe me,' she said. 'You don't know the half of it.'

Chapter 42
PRUNUS PENDULA

The hallway of Jason and Amita's house looked more like a baggage carousel than a corridor. Boxes of nappies, wipes, bags of clothes, a car seat and endless tins of formula were littered about at the front door. It made for a dangerous assault course for anyone wanting to come in or out.

'Do you think she has enough of everything?' asked Jason.

'Would you stop panicking, she's going to be fine,' said Radha. 'She's only meeting up with her parents, not going on a trek around the Arctic Circle.'

'I know, I know,' he said, rubbing his sweaty hands on his trousers. 'I'm just aware that it's a harsh world out there and that little baby is only a month old.'

'You're panicking, that's what you're doing. And it's very sweet.'

She clasped her hand against his cheek. Jason felt immediately better. The past few days had felt like one long, stressful build-up to this moment. He had grown quite accustomed to having Enni and the baby around the house. The late nights, the early starts, the lack of sleep and rest had all been a small price to pay for sharing the child's magical first few weeks.

'Enni and the baby will be fine, they'll be with family,' Radha said. 'Besides, you've got your own family who need you too.'

'I know,' he said, taking her hand. 'I'm just feeling a bit emotional, that's all. Holding that little tyke, it brought everything we've been through back. It was hard work at the time, the hardest of work, for all of us. But it was *so* worth it. I wouldn't change the kids for the world. Watching them grow up has truly been the privilege of my life. But no small part of me still wishes they were in baby-gros and needed me in a way they just don't anymore.'

Radha laughed. 'I don't know about that. Look at me and Mum. I know we pretend we moved her in here for her own good, but I'm a grown woman and I need her just as much. The kids will always know that we're their home.'

She rested her head on his chest and hugged him tight. They stood there quietly for a moment, among the chaos of the hallway and enjoyed each other's company, silently remembering everything they'd been through as parents.

'It's Enni's turn now,' she said to him. 'And her and her boy are going to get everything they need and deserve thanks to Isobel making sure Grahame provided for them in death in the way he had failed to in life. That Clymtech money is going to do some good in the world, setting that little family up to be independent. And you wouldn't deny her all the wonderful times we've had as a mum and dad. Would you?'

'I certainly wouldn't,' he said. 'Maybe I'll even get some sleep tonight. Who knows?'

'Don't count your chickens, Brazel,' said Radha.

'Is everyone ready down there?' Amita called from upstairs.

'Yes, Mum, we're all set.'

'Good. Here we come then,' she said.

Amita started down the stairs. She was carrying the baby seat, the little boy gurgling inside. Enni was behind her, all dressed and ready to go. Jason felt his chest tighten and his heart ache a little bit more. The moment he'd been dreading since they got confirmation her parents were back in the UK had finally arrived. He was going to have to say goodbye.

'Here we are,' said Amita, showing off the baby. 'Isn't he a champion?'

'He is,' said Radha.

'Definitely,' Jason squeaked.

They all looked at him oddly. He waved them away and made his way through the obstacle course, choking back tears with a giant lump in his throat. He opened the door just as a car pulled up at the end of the driveway.

'Mum! Dad!' Enni rushed past him, racing down to greet her parents.

They hugged at the front gate. Any animosity seemingly buried as the family was reunited. Jason beckoned them in, and they thanked him for looking after their daughter and grandson. He kept his distance, preferring to load up the car while everyone else was distracted.

'It's better this way,' he said quietly to himself, lugging boxes of nappies and wipes. 'Just keep your head down, get on with the packing and nobody will notice you're a gibbering wreck.'

He packed the boot of the car, all while the others were fussing over the baby inside. He spotted Patrick Bidmead peering out of his front window. When he saw Jason looking at him, he hastily retreated, the curtain pulled closed, despite it being only three in the afternoon. He hadn't been so quick to renew his offer for them to join the Garden Club since it turned out Delice's flowers hid a dark surprise.

'Nosey parker,' he said under his breath, returning to the house.

Much to his dismay, there was nothing left to pack into the car. Somehow the endless supplies and enough rations to feed the five thousand had miraculously gone. Jason was certain he had another good few trips to go before everything was safely stowed. Typical, he thought. When he was happy to be the carthorse forever, it was over before he had barely begun.

'We can't thank you enough,' said Enni's mother, coming up and hugging him by the neck. 'You looked after the two most precious things in the world to us. We can never repay you.'

'That's quite alright,' said Jason. 'Happy to do it.'

'Just send us a bill for everything, we'll happily pay you back,' said her father.

'That really won't be necessary,' he replied. 'Making sure they're all okay and well looked after will be all the payment I need. Blimey, I must be sick or something. A journalist refusing payment, whatever next?'

Everyone laughed at that. Enni's parents bid them all farewell and headed for the car. Then it was her turn. She hugged Radha and Amita and took the baby.

'I'll miss you all,' she said. 'Like my mum says, I can't thank you enough for being so generous and kind. I would have been out on the streets or in that awful mansion if it hadn't been for you all. You saved our lives.'

'We only did the right thing,' said Radha. 'It was our pleasure to be of some help.'

'And don't be a stranger, will you,' said Amita, kissing the baby goodbye. 'We want to know how this little man gets on and grows up to be a world beater. Got that.'

Enni started to cry. She wiped away the tears and hugged them both one more time. Then it was Jason's turn. He was standing by the door like a rubbish Beefeater. It was taking all of his will just to stay upright. He wanted to curl into a ball and cry himself to sleep. But that wouldn't do. Not yet anyway.

'I'll never be able to put into words how much your kindness has meant to me, Jason,' said Enni. 'You took us both in without a second's hesitation. A couple of strangers, saved from the streets. You're a special person, and I shall never forget your good heart.'

'Oh, stop it,' he said, bottom lip trembling. 'You've got enough on your hands with this little superstar without having to worry about a broken-down old hack like me.'

Enni lifted the baby seat. Jason bent down and kissed the little boy tenderly on the forehead.

'One last thing, before I go,' she said, stepping out of the front door. 'I've decided on a name.'

'You have? That's wonderful news,' said Jason.

'What have you gone for?' asked Radha.

Enni's face erupted into the biggest smile she could manage. She looked at Jason, great affection in her eyes.

'Jason,' she said. 'He's called Jason.'

That was enough to push him over the edge. All his defences, breached as they were, gave way like the demolition of a dam. Tears ran down his cheeks as he clasped a hand to his mouth. Enni was crying too. But nobody was sad. Far from it.

'Thank you all so much,' she said.

Enni walked down the path with the baby. They climbed into the back of her parents' rented car and drove off down the street, disappearing into the glare of the afternoon sunshine. Radha clapped Jason on the back and headed back inside the house.

'I don't know about you two, but I'm parched. Time for a cuppa,' she said.

'Yes, me too,' said Amita, dabbing her cheeks with a hankie.

She turned to head down the hall but paused. Jason was standing, slumped against the doorway, staring down the street after the car that was long gone.

'You okay?' she asked him, squeezing his arm gently.

'Jason, eh?' he said, smiling. 'Poor little guy.'

Amita laughed at that. She put her arm around her son-in-law and eased him back into their home. The kettle was already on.

TRIBUTES TO WORLD-CLASS SCIENTIST BURIED IN OWN BACK GARDEN

By Jason Brazel in Penrith

A LOCAL scientist has been hailed as a 'world-class talent' amid a raft of tributes paid following his brutal murder.

The remains of Dr Fran Weaver were discovered in the back garden of an address in Kendal following an extensive police search for both Weaver and his business partner, Grahame Sutcliffe.

The academic, who taught engineering at Eddington College, was at the forefront of research into new security systems that mapped the human genome.

Along with his partner, Dr Weaver conducted extensive studies into new forms of scientific discovery and pioneering techniques from his base in Cumbria.

Tributes have flooded in for the university professor and his business partner following the grim discovery of their remains.

One colleague at Eddington College said: 'Doctor Weaver will be sorely missed. His ability to grasp even the most complex of equations, theories and practices were second to none. He truly was a world-class talent when it came to engineering and science as a whole.

'His untimely death has come as a great shock to everyone at the college and the wider engineering community.'

A statement from the university also paid tribute to Dr Weaver, hailing him as a 'one-of-a-kind, generational talent'.

Delice Weaver was arrested and charged with the murders of both her husband and his business partner, Grahame Sutcliffe, whose remains were found in a local allotment.

Ms Weaver pleaded guilty when appearing in court and will be sentenced at a later date.

A moment of silence will be held in memory of the academic at this year's summer graduation ceremony.

It's rumoured that university bosses are considering dedicating the engineering department to Dr Weaver later this year, after a large anonymous donation in his name.

In a related case, local resident Mr Malcolm Brunger has been issued with a community service order after reports that he was offering 'Allotment Assassin' tours alongside selling souvenir flowers from the site as killer corsages.

Acknowledgements

The book you have just read (or perhaps are about to read, I know, I look at this bit first too) is something I'm immeasurably proud of. The writing of this novel came about during what turned out to be an exceedingly busy 2024. I've found myself hopping across oceans, figuratively and literally, jumping back and forth in time and finding mischief and mayhem everywhere I go. Oh, and there was a major addition to the family in August. In all, it's been a rollercoaster and one that I feel *The Garden Club Murders* will always celebrate. I know you're not supposed to have favourite books, they're a bit like children and pets in that respect. But I can firmly say that this novel is by far one of my absolute dearest.

Thanks as always to the wonderful team at HarperNorth. Genevieve Pegg is the wizard who keeps everything in line when it comes to all things Amita and Jason and beyond. She knows them inside out, me inside out and, of course, the Lake District and Cumbria equally inside out. From typos to terrifying villains, she has the calm, collected and completely brilliant attitude, not to mention sheer bloody talent, that brings everything you've just read to life. Working with her is among the privileges of my career.

Alice Murphy-Pile and Hilary Stein are the venerable Dynamic Duo tasked with making sure my potty ideas are fulfilled. No question is too ridiculous and no email or text left unanswered. Without them, I'd be utterly lost.

A huge thanks also to the Canadian team at HarperCollins - Cindy Ma and Brenann Francis - who look after me time and again on the other side of the Atlantic Ocean. I've been made to feel very, very welcome and part of the fold here and I'll always be grateful for their deftness of touch and boundless energy.

I couldn't continue to do this whole writing lark without the wonders of my agent, Elizabeth Counsell. She's my go-to source for inspiration, advice, madcap ideas and everything in between. In what's been an incredibly busy year, she has been the guardian, champion and all-round good egg that's made everything run smoothly throughout. I am truly grateful.

Writing has afforded me so many opportunities so far and I'm always reminded at this stage of all the wonderful people I've had a chance to meet and get to know throughout the writing of this novel. New and old, I'm grateful for the spirited advice and help of Jonathan Hall, Samantha Bailey, Hannah Hendy, Jo Middleton, David Bishop and Vaseem Khan.

A huge thanks also goes to everyone involved in the publishing industry who champion the work of us authors so tirelessly. Samantha Brownley, Victoria Watson, Simon Bewick, Ben Bruce and Jacky Collins are all simply wonderful.

Finally, my gratitude will always be to my family who, among other things, put up with me - not just when I'm writing but ALL of the time (the fools). From late night to unbearably early starts, they are there, 24/7, always happy to offer love and support without ever asking for anything in return. If I've learned anything from *The Garden Club Murders*, it's that you must always hold close to things you love most.

Harper North

would like to thank the following staff and contributors for their involvement in making this book a reality:

Sarah Allen-Sutter
Fionnuala Barrett
Sarah Burke
Alan Cracknell
Jonathan de Peyer
Anna Derkacz
Tom Dunstan
Kate Elton
Sarah Emsley
Simon Gerratt
Lydia Grainge
Monica Green
Natassa Hadjinicolaou
Emma Hatlen
Jo Ireson
Jean-Marie Kelly
Taslima Khatun

Holly Kyte
Rachel McCarron
Alice Murphy-Pyle
Adam Murray
Genevieve Pegg
Amanda Percival
Laura Evans
Colleen Simpson
Eleanor Slater
Matthew Richardson
Hilary Stein
Emma Sullivan
Emily Thomas
Katrina Troy
Daisy Watt
Ben Wright
Jay Cochrane

For more unmissable reads,
sign up to the HarperNorth newsletter at
www.harpernorth.co.uk

or find us on Twitter at
@HarperNorthUK

IF YOU'VE NOT READ ALL OF JASON AND AMITA'S ADVENTURES, FIND OUT WHERE IT ALL BEGAN WITH THIS FOLLOWING EXTRACT FROM THE OPENING OF *THE BINGO HALL DETECTIVES*...

Chapter 1
KELLY'S EYE

"We're not Starsky and Hutch. Would you *please* slow down!"

Jason gritted his teeth. His mother-in-law was a notorious backseat driver. Too fast, too slow, too close to the curb, watch out for that cyclist, wasn't that the turning there, are we there yet? She had mentioned them all. It should have been a scenic drive through the lakes to the peaceful town of Penrith – not the Cannonball Run.

His grip on the steering wheel tightened. "I'm going at the limit, Amita," he said, trying to keep his voice light.

"I don't care what that thing says, you're going too fast," she fired back. "I'd like to be able to see my grandchildren at least once more, if that's alright with you? Which reminds me, do you drive like a maniac with them in the car and I'm not here? Does your wife know about your lead foot?"

"I know where I'd like to put my lead foot," he muttered.

"What?"

"Nothing," he sighed.

Silence descended in the car. Jason had been spending a lot of time with his mother-in-law recently. And it wasn't through choice. It wasn't that he disliked her – Amita Khatri could be very warm and generous when she chose to be. It was when she chose *not* to be that he had a problem. With everything that had been going on, he had enough problems to worry about.

"Bugger, did I bring my glasses?" she said, reaching for her handbag.

"They're on your head," said Jason, concentrating on the road.

"So they are," she tutted. "Rats, have I brought my pen?"

"Front pocket of your bag."

"Yes, so it is," she said, finding her bingo blotter. "Now I can't remember if I have the money to pay Georgie for that magazine subscription –"

"You've rolled up a tenner and put it in the pocket of your cardigan."

Amita patted her tummy where the pocket was. She cocked an eyebrow at Jason.

"Anyone would think you were spying on me."

He thought about answering her back. He thought about saying how she'd spent the last hour before leaving the house going through a very vocal checklist, as if she was packing for an attempt on Everest rather than an evening with Penrith Bingo Club. He thought about telling her that he'd missed most of the news and all of the weather because of the racket she'd been making. Jason thought about lots of things before deciding it wasn't worth the argument.

"Just looking out for my favourite mother-in-law," he said with a forced chirpiness.

"And if I believe that, I'll believe anything," she snorted, a hint of a smile behind her frown.

Jason smiled. He let his grip on the wheel loosen and reached down to the radio.

"You're not putting that on, are you?" asked Amita. "I can't listen to *anything* before the bingo," she said sharply. "It's one of my superstitions. You know this, Jason. You know that I've got to be absolutely in the zone, completely focussed, ready to pounce when those balls come out of the machine."

"Isn't it all electronic now?" he asked. "Don't they have a big screen with a random number generator doing all the hard work?"

"You don't know what it takes to play the numbers," she said. "No radio."

To make sure he had understood, she slapped his hand. He gritted his teeth.

"Fine," he huffed, adjusting himself. "But I want it put on the record that I think you take this bingo far too seriously. It's not the World Cup, you know. It's a load of old folk gathered in a church hall, gossiping about the neighbours."

"How dare you," Amita gasped. "We do *not* gossip. We're there to win."

"Oh, come off it, Amita," he laughed. "You go in there, every week, and talk about everyone who hasn't turned up for half an hour. You play a bit, then you stop for free tea and a Digestive biscuit before kicking off the second half for a right proper bitching session. The clock strikes nine and you all shuffle back out, ready to gather up as much gossip as you can in the week. Cutthroat competition is not the name of the game."

"It is more competitive than you'll ever know," Amita huffed. "Just last week Margaret Cullin won fifty pounds on a full house."

"I'm sure the *Financial Times* was relieved to get a front page that night."

"And then there was last month, when Madeleine Frobisher went home with the rollover jackpot."

"How much was that then?" asked Jason.

"Seventy-five pounds and forty-six new pence."

Jason rolled his eyes. "The excitement never stops," he said. "Look, I never said you didn't play *any* bingo. Obviously you do. All I *am* saying is that you spend an awful lot of time talking about people behind their backs. Is that or is that not the case?"

Amita considered her words carefully. She chewed them over, thinking about the accusations levelled at her. She always did when Jason was the one pointing the finger. She hated to give him an inch. He always took the mile and then some.

"No comment," she finally said.

That made Jason laugh. "No comment?" he said. "No comment? What's that supposed to mean?"

"It means no comment, that's what it means. You're supposed to be a journalist Jason, you should know what 'no comment' means by now."

"I *am* a journalist," he fired back.

"Oh yes, sorry, I had forgotten," Amita folded her arms. "I'd forgotten that watching daytime television in your pyjamas and the latest from the frontline of vacuuming the stairs were cutting-edge reporting these days. How silly of me."

There was a noticeable chill to the air between them now. While Jason knew he'd probably gone too far with his criticism of the bingo club, he thought she was being more than cruel now.

The Musgrave Monument in Market Square loomed through the darkness. Jason felt its clock face was watching him as they drove beneath its glare, almost egging him on to say something. The nineteenth century tower was the focal point of the town; every road seemed to lead to it in the end. If Penrith had a skyline, the Monument's pyramidal peak and bunting would be the highlight.

"No need to kick a man when he's down," he said, his voice like muted thunder. "I'm out of work, you know."

"I know it all too well, Jason," said Amita in that snippy, condescending manner he hated with a vengeance. "I know that, while my daughter is out breaking her back to keep your family afloat, you're messing around on that computer of yours, playing games and watching football highlights."

"I'm trying to find a new job," he said, teeth clamping together, jaw tight. "I was made redundant, Amita, you know this. I'm trying my hardest to get another reporter gig, but it's a very tough market."

"I've told you a million times, Jason," she sniffed. "You should go freelance and make your own work."

Jason had heard this all before – from Amita, from his family, from everyone who cared to have an opinion. The only thing worse than being out of work was being told how to get another job. It made his blood boil.

He was about to launch into a furious tirade when Amita screamed.

"Look out!" she yelled, slamming her hands onto the dashboard.

Jason panicked. He fumbled with the steering wheel as the headlights flashed across the street. A gathered pack of anoraks, corduroy trousers and sensible walking shoes appeared then vanished into the darkness as he wrestled the car out of the way. He slammed on the brakes and they came to a halt – no harm done.

"Bloody hell," he breathed. "They came out of nowhere."

"You weren't concentrating," said Amita, unclipping her seatbelt. "And you were going too fast, like I said!"

He started to plead his case but she was gone, out of the car door, before he got the chance. He caught his breath, pinching the bridge of his nose.

"The Sheriff of Penrith is off to greet her citizens," he said to himself.

But just then he noticed Amita had left her handbag. She was not a woman usually parted from her weapon of choice, and he thought he'd better deliver it to her before he got accused of rifling through its mysterious contents.

Mustering the energy, he got out of the car, stopping first to make sure he definitely hadn't run over any lagging members of the bingo club. The chilly autumn air made his face tingle and woke him up a little. He felt guilty for being so snippy with Amita – she'd hit a sore spot when it came to work. He had little to show for an afternoon of emails and job-hunting. He'd make it up to her with her bag by way of a peace offering.

The gathered group was making quite a noise outside the church hall. Even in the dim light of the evening he could make out Amita at the centre of the action. Something was clearly up.

He pressed the button to lock the car, and it bleeped with a satisfactory chirp as he walked casually over to the assembled gang of elderly Penrith locals.

"What's going on then?" he asked Amita, but before she could answer, a tall, broad-chested old man spoke to him without looking away from the centre of the crowd where Amita was holding court with another well-dressed septuagenarian, both of them vying for supremacy.

"Madeleine's dead," he said bluntly. "Broke her neck."

"Madeleine who?" asked Jason.

"Frobisher," said the old man.

"Is that her that won the monthly jackpot?" asked Jason.

"Aye," said the old man, his moustache twitching as he sneered at him. "That's her."

"Guess she didn't have time to spend it then, eh?" Jason elbowed the pensioner in the ribs, egging him on for a laugh.

The crowd fell silent. Suddenly every pair of bespectacled or laser-surgically-enhanced eyes was on Jason. He could almost taste the contempt hanging in the air as he tried to back away. But Amita pushed her way out to the edge from the centre of the group, grabbed her bag, and locked eyes with him.

"And you are going to write the story?' she said in a voice that Jason knew would lead to trouble.

Chapter 2
ONE LITTLE DUCK

"Awful. I mean, it's just awful. You don't think something like this would happen to somebody you know, do you? Especially not to someone like Madeleine."

Amita dunked her Digestive into her tea. She pulled it out quickly, checking to make sure the integrity of the biscuit was still intact. After a breathless second to see if it still held up, she took a bite, already preparing for the next dunk.

The church hall was more muted than usual. As a mark of respect to Madeleine, bingo had been cancelled for the night. The organisers, the local vicar and the hall's janitor, however, had let the crowd in to get their tea. Jason suspected they feared a riot would break out if they didn't. He sat at the end of a long, foldable table not far from Amita and her cronies, wishing he hadn't got out of the car.

"I really can't believe it," said Amita, as if she hadn't already expressed her shock.

There was a round of muffled grunts of agreement from the other pensioners.

"And Madeleine, of all people," said the well-dressed OAP from outside. "Awful business."

"Yes, I said that already, Georgie," Amita tutted.

The two pensioners darted dirty looks at each other. The rest of the group could only watch in silence as the titans clashed over their cups of Earl Grey.

"Glad she had such concerned friends," Jason said, puffing out his cheeks.

"Quiet, Jason," said Amita. "You know you're really not supposed to be in here unless you've paid your annual membership. That tea is meant for bingo attendees only."

"I'll gladly return it then if we can go home."

"In a minute," she waved him away. "Does anyone know who found Madeleine? Was it a member of her family?"

"Madeleine Frobisher is dead!" boomed a lady in a wheelchair. The whistle of her hearing aids was almost as piercing as her voice.

"We know, Ethel," tutted Georgie. "That's what we're talking about."

"Somebody found her next to that big bloody house of hers," Ethel added.

"It was the postman, that's what I heard," said Sandy, the broad-chested old man who had snorted at Jason.

"Oh no, not Geoff," said Georgie. "He's a lovely chap. What a terrible thing to find when you're at your work."

"Geoff?" asked Amita. "Don't think I know him. Is he new?"

"No," Georgie said with a half-laugh. "He's been doing that delivery route – the posh bit – for *years*. Amita, where have you been?"

A ripple of muted scoffs from those who sided with Georgie and her immaculate blouse and matching neckerchief. The others remained silent, engrossed in their tea. Until Sandy spoke up. He was a man of few words, and Amita had heard more from him tonight than she normally did in a month. There was always a table of men of a certain age who didn't say much and, she suspected, came more for the biscuits than the bingo. "I've never heard of the fella. I have a lovely lady postie who does our patch," Sandy announced.

"I don't live anywhere near Madeleine," said Amita, grabbing the chance. "We're on the other side of town. We wouldn't be on the same delivery route as the road heading towards the lakes. Although, now I think about it, if he does the big houses, you wouldn't be on that route either, Georgie, not where you live. Would you?"

It was a commendable come-back, even Jason had to admit that. When his mother-in-law wanted to turn on the venom she still could. And she was clearly sparring with one of the best here.

Georgie said nothing, her mouth a thin line across her made-up face. She busied herself with a long gulp of tea before smoothing out imaginary creases in her blouse.

"Broke her neck, by all accounts," said Sandy, with an uncharacteristic wobble in his voice. "That's what the chat in the town is, anyway. Seems she was up a ladder cleaning the windows of that big house of hers and, wallop, off she fell. Real bloody shame."

More muted agreements from the table.

"Did you know her well, Sandy?" asked Amita.

The old man sat up a little straighter. He dusted crumbs from his silver moustache, the middle dark with tobacco stains, and shook his head. "Not any more than the rest of you. You'd see her about the town. You'd always know when Madeleine was about, wouldn't you? She beamed a big smile every time she stepped into a room."

Slightly louder agreements from the group around the table.

"Always helpful, too," Sandy continued. "She always volunteered the old stables up at her place if we needed to store tools or compost from the allotments over winter. Very kind. Think she was part of the Women's Institute, too, if I'm not mistaken."

"She was," Georgie piped up. "And very generous with her time she was too. A lovely woman, full of great ideas. She also made a lovely upside-down cake, usually for one of the summer fetes. You don't get a lot of upside-down cakes anymore, do you?"

This time the chorus of agreements was almost deafening. The conversation, Jason concluded, had finally proved that even if they couldn't agree who knew the most about Madeleine's demise, cake was one topic they could agree on.

"Madeleine Forster is dead!" Ethel yelled again.

"Yes, we *know*, Ethel," said Georgie, getting more than a little irate. "It's all any of us has been talking about for the last twenty minutes. Try to keep up."

"Imagine trying to clean windows at her age," the eldest of the group remarked. "It's no wonder she slipped."

The words seemed to linger in the stale air of the church hall.

"No word of when the funeral will be?" asked Amita, sneaking another biscuit.

"She was only found this morning, Amita," said Georgie. "Give the woman a chance to get cold first, would you?"

"I know, I was just . . . well, it's normally quite quick, isn't it, with these sorts of things? Unless, you know, there's something fishy."

"Fishy?" Georgie leaned forward, her eyes sharpening like a hawk that had spied its dinner. "What do you mean by fishy?"

Amita was midway to taking a bite from her biscuit, but stopped. She sensed the group was looking at her. Even Jason had leaned forward a little.

"Fishy, you know, suspicious," she said.

"Suspicious? What could possibly be suspicious? It was a terrible accident, Amita. Poor Madeleine fell and broke her neck. Absolutely awful. Only mercy is it would have been quick."

"I'm not *saying* it's suspicious," Amita said. "I'm merely pointing out that these sorts of things normally have the police involved, don't they? Don't they, Jason? You'd be familiar with this type of thing, wouldn't you. You know, inquests . . ."

The group shifted to stare at *him* now. He cleared his throat. "Yeah, sometimes," he shrugged. "Depends on the circumstances."

"And does what happened to Madeleine Frobisher sound like it has 'circumstances'?" asked Georgie pointedly.

To his surprise, Jason felt a little under pressure. Georgie, it seemed, could be quite intimidating when she turned her glare on him. He found himself stumbling over his words, his hands sweaty. "Well, it's hard to say without all the relevant information," he said weakly. "I don't have contact with the police anymore."

"He's out of work at the moment," said Amita, in a sort of stage whisper. "Has been for six months now."

"Yes, thanks Amita," he said.

"Madeleine Frobisher is dead!" Ethel shouted.

Jason wasn't sure if he was supposed to acknowledge her or not.

"So you think there might be grounds for an inquest?" Georgie's questions continued.

"I didn't say that," said Jason.

"What *are* you saying then? Out with it, man!"

Jason felt very hot suddenly. He tugged at the collar of his jumper, desperate for air. "I'm saying that if the police think there's a reasonable doubt that it wasn't some horrible accident, which it sounds like it was by the way, then they'll investigate. I don't know, I'm not a copper. I don't know how they think with these things."

None of the faces staring at him looked very convinced.

"If I had to guess, they'll take a look at the area where she was found, outside her house, right? If it all looks like it adds up then I guess that's that, a simple but awful accident."

"But what if it *doesn't* look like that, eh?" Amita goaded him. "Then I would be right, wouldn't I?"

Jason held his breathe to stop himself saying something he'd regret. All of this just to prove a point, to score one over her rival, Georgie. He despaired.

"Yes, Amita," he said with a long sigh. "You would be right."

"There'll be one more star in the heaven tonight! Madeleine is dead!"

"We know, Ethel!" Amita and Georgie and some of the others said in unison.

A bell broke up the conversation. At the door, the vicar stood holding the little bell apologetically. The hall janitor was standing beside him, mop and bucket in his hands, a look of disinterest on his face.

"Good evening, ladies and gentlemen," said the pastor timidly. "Just to let you know that we have to vacate the hall now. It's a pity as I think we all could be doing with a little company after hearing of what happened to Ms Frobisher. I'm sure our thoughts and prayers go out to her family and I'll gladly pass on any messages of goodwill and remembrance to them."

The hall erupted in a cacophony of scraping chair legs and creaking bones. The members of the bingo club slowly filtered out of the hall, wishing their best to the vicar, Mr Jones and one another. Amita and Jason were at the back of the procession.

"That bloody Georgie," said Amita, keeping her voice down. "She's always out to get me. Always looking for a chance to cut me down to size."

"She's quite formidable," agreed Jason. "I wonder who sharpens her claws at night."

"She's a widow."

"Lucky bugger got out early then."

"Jason, please," said Amita disapprovingly. "Although I shouldn't have expected any help from you."

"What does that mean?"

They bade farewell to the vicar and walked down the main road towards the car.

"It means when I ask you to back me up I expect a little more than I don't knows and ifs, buts and maybes," said Amita, blowing into her hands.

"Oh, come on," he said. "You can't expect me to say I think this Madeleine woman was killed. I don't even know who she is . . . was!"

"All I'm saying is that it's open-ended."

"You would say that, you're the Sheriff of Penrith, Amita. Any time there's a sniff of trouble you are all over it like a rash."

They climbed into the car.

"And how do you know it's open-ended?" he asked. "You've got as much information as I have. And I know diddly-squat."

"You never know with these things," she said. "A woman found dead outside her home, suffers a broken neck after a fall. These things don't happen in Penrith."

"Maybe not often," said Jason. "But you don't even know if it was a broken neck that killed her."

"Everyone at the bingo club seemed to think it was."

"Ah yes, the bingo club," he laughed. "A bunch of nosy folk with too much time on their hands. Very reliable sources."

"Sounds rather like you, now you mention it, Jason. And anyway, they can be *very* reliable when it comes to the local community," she said. "They have ears everywhere. We take pride in the civic goings-on of our hometown. Something you should take onboard."

"Come off it. I've just seen some of your so-called reliable pals," said Jason, turning the car around. "There are a few in there as old as the ark. You're trying to tell me they have their marbles intact? I've heard of an unreliable narrator but that takes the biscuit."

"That is a very rude appraisal of the elderly community, Jason. I don't approve of it."

Jason shook his head. He could feel his heartbeat getting faster. Another full-on argument was brewing between the two of them. Maybe he had been a bit quick to dismiss Amita's friends. After all, he wasn't in a position to throw stones. He thought better of stoking the fire and reached for the radio instead.

"Don't put on that radio," sniped Amita.

"Why? You're not playing bingo. No more playing the numbers tonight."

"I know. But something doesn't add up. I need peace to think."

Jason nodded. He drummed his hands on the steering wheel as they continued on the road home.

"None of what happened seems suspicious to you, Jason?" she asked.

He took a deep breath, his nose whistling. "Look, bad things happen to people all the time," he said. "It's just the way of things, I'm afraid. We don't live in a wonderful, magical world where we're all wrapped in cotton wool."

"Yes, I'm aware of that," she said. "But you don't know for certain. You don't know, absolutely, that there isn't a sinister side to Madeleine's death. It's not like you've ever done anything like this before."

"Yes I have," he said solemnly.

"What?"

"Years ago, when I was a cub reporter in Manchester, before I moved up here," he said. "Thrown in at the deep end with a pretty awful murder of a young lad who was only twenty or so."

"You've kept that quiet," she said.

"Don't believe everything you see on TV about journalists, Amita," he said, watching the road. "We don't all like to go shouting about the worst and most horrible stories we've covered. Usually, it's a case of getting in and out as quickly and cleanly as possible and trying to forget that it ever crossed your desk."

"I'll bet," she said. "Mind the road."

"I was sent out on what looked like a run-of-the-mill death, or as run-of-the-mill as something like that can be. I had to do a dreaded door knock, to speak to the family of this young guy. His dad and stepmum answered the door. They let me in, spoke to me for hours about how they were utterly heartbroken, gave me some lovely memories, all of that. I was devastated by their words, of course, but delighted to be able to include such a moving tribute. This was a great story. I headed back to the offices, near Piccadilly, and started typing up my notes. Next thing I know, the whole newsroom is in uproar."

"Why?" asked Amita, hooked.

"Between me leaving their house and getting back to my desk, the stepmum had been arrested *and* charged with the young lad's murder."

"What?" she blurted. "She killed him?"

"Yup," Jason nodded, concentrating on the road ahead. "A matter of hours before I'd been sat there, in the front room, chatting away."

"And she didn't show anything? Any guilt? Any remorse?"

"Absolutely not," he said. "She was as calm, collected and outwardly heartbroken as anyone would be when their stepson had been discovered dead. It all came out at the trial, of course. The lad had found out she was ruining his dad financially, dodgy investments, shopping, holidays, running all over town with other men and all of that, proper juicy stuff. The young man had threatened to expose the whole thing and she bashed him around the head with a lead pipe and dumped his body. But she hadn't been too clever covering her tracks. The police caught her on CCTV.

Apparently she'd run a whole load of red lights on the way to and from the train tracks where she dumped him. So maybe you're right – I really should watch my driving."

"Blimey," said Amita. "I had no idea."

"It was a long time ago," he said. "My point is, you're right, you can never tell who or what is going on. Not just behind closed doors, but even behind someone's eyes. I was sat not two feet from a woman who had murdered someone a matter of hours previous and I couldn't tell. But she was caught, pretty easily in the end, because she hadn't thought it out, hadn't planned ahead. You can't go about murdering people willy-nilly, Amita. Not if you want to get away with it."